MAGE BORN

Something crashed into her stomach and Wren fell back against the wall, gasping for air.

"Fight me," he shouted. When she'd regained her breath she stood upright and waited. Her inaction seemed to taunt him and he lashed out again, catching her on her right cheek. "Fight me."

Wren said nothing and did not fight back. She did not reach for her magic or attempt to ward off any of his blows.

"Fight me, coward," said Brunwal, growing more annoyed by the second. "Fight me," he shouted over and over again. Each time he said it another invisible hand slapped her across the face or punched her in the torso. Blood ran freely from her face and one eye was starting to swell shut. Her chest and ribs ached with every breath and still he continued to beat her.

MAGE BORN

STEPHEN ARYAN

www.orbitbooks.net

ORBIT

First published in Great Britain in 2017 by Orbit

1 3 5 7 9 10 8 6 4 2

A CIP catalogue record for this book
is available from the British Library.

ISBN 978-0-356-50847-4

Typeset in Garamond by M Rules
Printed and bound by CPI Group (UK) Ltd, Croydon CR0 4YY

Papers used by Orbit are from well-managed forests
and other responsible sources.

Orbit
An imprint of
Little, Brown Book Group
Carmelite House
50 Victoria Embankment
London EC4Y 0DZ

An Hachette UK Company
www.hachette.co.uk

www.orbitbooks.net

For the Nugecon Eight

CHAPTER 1

The air in the tavern was thick with the stench of fear. To Habreel it was sweeter than any perfume. He smiled at the locals' unhappiness and sipped his ale, pretending to be just another traveller passing through the town of Glienned.

A few minutes later there was a stir in the crowd as the door opened to admit another visitor. Glancing in the mirror behind the bar Habreel saw a tall woman dressed in black leather armour and matching trousers approach and sit down on the stool next to him. He could admit to himself, if no one else, that she was a striking woman. Her raven-black hair and pale skin were not unusual, but the slight tilt to her green eyes and high cheekbones made it difficult to pinpoint her nationality. Her array of daggers, eight that he could see from an initial count, would draw attention as much as her features.

Akosh smiled at the barman, who turned a little red under the intensity of her stare. "On the house," he muttered, setting down a mug of ale before scuttling away.

Habreel frowned at her and she raised an eyebrow. "Something wrong?"

"You're a little conspicuous," he said, gesturing at her outfit.

Akosh rolled her eyes and waved at the mirror and their

view of the room behind them. "Look again." The surface of the mirror rippled as if made of water and her image changed, from the leather-clad warrior to a severely dressed woman with a plain face surrounded by a tight bonnet. Every feature of the woman's face was forgettable. Only the colour of her eyes remained the same dark green, but set in a doughy face they were not enough to draw attention. "They see only what I want them to," added Akosh.

Habreel grimaced but said nothing. Magic. He took a deep breath and reminded himself she was a necessary evil. For now.

"Why here?" she asked him.

"Because Glienned is the doorway to Zecorria," explained Habreel, keeping his voice low. It was the first large town any travellers came to when they crossed the border into Zecorria from Yerskania. It was a hub of information and people from all over the world were known to stop here for the night. Anything that happened here would quickly spread across all kingdoms in the west. If they were lucky it would cross the mountains into Seveldrom and perhaps beyond in the desert kingdoms. Tensions between the east and west from the war a decade ago had faded and trade now flourished.

"Is that all?" asked Akosh, running a finger through the foam on the top of her ale. She languidly licked her finger and grimaced at the sour taste.

"And because I've been visiting the town on and off for weeks," added Habreel. "Zecorria is still the most hated nation in the west because of its role in the war. The Chosen and the perversion of the faith. The Warlock. The Mad King," he said, ticking things off on his fingers. "Now I will turn that into strength and other countries will race to unite behind them. Who doesn't like a redemption story?" he asked rhetorically.

"I hear a lot of words, but don't see anything exciting," said Akosh, in a bored voice. Habreel knew she was baiting him but didn't let her get a rise out of him.

"Come then. It's almost time," he said, draining the last of his ale.

Several people outside the tavern were all walking in the same direction with purpose. Akosh and Habreel joined the flow of bodies and soon became part of a large group that was heading towards the main square. By the time they arrived it was a little before midday. Perhaps three hundred people had already gathered, with more appearing all the time.

The sky was a hazy blue and the air was cold enough for Habreel to see his breath. People were stamping their feet and shuffling about to stay warm but no one complained or suggested going inside. None of them wanted to miss this.

In the centre of the square was a wooden platform normally used for travelling theatre troupes and seasonal festivals. Today the mood of the crowd surrounding it was sullen, like that of a public hanging, although there'd not been one of those for decades. Today there was no gibbet but the Mayor still wore a sour expression. "Everyone is so broody," said Akosh, grinning at the faces all around her. "It's delicious."

Habreel said nothing and tried to remain inconspicuous. A few people recognised him but not enough to start a conversation. Today he wasn't the only visitor in the crowd. All of the taverns and shops would be empty. It seemed as if most of the town had decided to show up. Habreel buried his smile but was secretly delighted at the size of the crowd.

Half an hour later the square was packed with people and a low rumble of unhappy conversations flowed around Habreel on all sides.

A shiver of excitement ran through him as everyone suddenly

fell silent. Despite there being so many people squeezed in, they managed to create enough space for the masked Seeker to walk unobstructed through the crowd. No one wanted to touch the hooded figure.

The bulky robe, long black gloves and stylised golden mask completely obscured the Seeker's identity. With only a slit for the mouth and holes for the eyes, it was difficult to tell much about the wearer. A line ran down the middle of the mask from forehead to chin and a swirling symbol, that he thought came from the east, was painted on the right cheek. The locals probably found it intimidating and mysterious. Habreel just thought it was ridiculous.

The only indication that the Seeker was a man came from the width of his shoulders and significant height. To Habreel his stiff gait suggested a history in the military. He wondered how such a person had ended up as a servant of the Red Tower, the school of magic in Shael.

Shortly after the war rumours had sprung up that someone was trying to reopen the school. A few years later people across the west reported seeing masked strangers showing up, offering to test children to see if they had a spark of magic.

Seekers used to be common but it had not been that way for over twenty years. No child would voluntarily declare they had magic and many successfully kept it completely hidden. When a community made such a discovery the hard way, often with a magical accident, it would mean exile for the whole family at best, drowning for the child at worst.

Then came the war and with it the Warlock who soured people towards magic even further. Because of him and his twisted apprentices, thousands had died in a pointless war. Nations had been torn apart with civil war breaking out in Morrinow in the north. In the south Shael was reduced to a shattered ruin that was still in disarray. All of it had happened because of the destructive power of magic and the evil it inspired.

It was a curse, not a blessing from the Maker, the Lady of Light or the Blessed Mother. Those who wielded magic thought it put them above everyone else. Mages claimed the power came from the Source, the heart of creation, but he didn't believe it. History was full of tales where people had been tricked by beings from beyond the Veil, offering them power in return for favours.

Habreel could imagine that wielding such power would be intoxicating, but it was an addictive lie that inspired arrogance and destruction. The war had shown people that magic could not be trusted and, until the Seekers had returned, the old ways of dealing with cursed children had been enough.

Exile or death. It was hard and cruel, but it had worked for a long time. Accidents with magic were avoided and people kept safe.

Now there was a royal decree in many countries which permitted Seekers to visit any village, town or city once a month to test children for magic. He believed in the rule of law, but when it stood in opposition of the will of the people, Habreel knew change was needed.

All eyes were drawn to the Seeker as he moved to stand beside the Mayor on the platform. She flinched at being so close but the Seeker didn't seem to notice. He was looking out at the sea of upturned faces. Habreel thought there was a certain arrogance about his stance.

"Bring them forward," said the Mayor, as if speaking about the condemned. Instead of a line of chained figures several sets of parents reluctantly came to the front of the crowd with their children in tow. All of the adults looked sick with worry, while most of the children were crying. Their ages varied considerably.

Habreel guessed the youngest child was eight or nine years old and the eldest perhaps seventeen. Despite their differences all of them were united by their fear, which pleased him. The good people of Glienned were raising their children to understand that magic was a blight.

"Don't be scared," said the Seeker, who remained blissfully unaware of the mood in the town. "This is a time to celebrate."

The parents stepped forward and many had to shove their child onto the edge of the platform. Even though they were well outside arm's reach of the Seeker, none of the children were willing to go any closer. A couple of the smaller ones tried to run but were firmly held in place by their parents. Eight children. Eight chances of being cursed.

"How exciting," whispered Akosh, her eyes twinkling with delight.

"Can you tell?" asked Habreel. "Do any of them have the ability?"

Akosh grinned and gave him a conspiratorial wink. "That would spoil the fun."

The Seeker started at one end of the line with a slight girl of about ten. She was shaking so badly Habreel expected her to collapse. The masked mage raised one gloved hand towards the child and a few seconds later lowered it.

"No," he said, shaking his head for emphasis. The girl fell to her knees in a flood of tears. Her parents cradled her, openly weeping in relief.

This gave the Seeker pause and he stared at them with concern. His mask roamed across the many faces in the town square and Habreel saw a noticeable shift in his posture.

"He knows," he murmured. Akosh showed her teeth in an approximation of a smile.

"Did you see the Seeker arrive?" asked Habreel.

"No, why?"

"I wonder if he has a fast horse standing ready. If this continues he'll need it."

Moving more quickly now the Seeker went down the line, pausing briefly in front of each child. Every declaration that the child had no talent for magic was met with relief and often tears of joy. At last there were only two left, the eldest boy and a girl who was keening like a wounded animal. When the Seeker raised his hand in front of the girl her wailing increased in pitch, getting higher and higher. Habreel expected the dogs in town to start howling along.

"If nothing else, she has a future with a voice like that," noted Akosh. The girl's voice had taken on the pitch of a yowling cat on heat.

The Seeker paused in front of the girl and a horrified silence spread over the crowd. Finally the girl's voice either gave out or had become so high-pitched only dogs could hear her.

The Seeker tried to say something but nothing happened. He had to clear his throat and try again. "She has the ability."

At his words the girl's parents collapsed into a tangled heap as if hamstrung. Their wretched cries seemed to fill the entire square. The girl was sobbing, too, begging her mother to take her home, promising she'd be good from now on. Friends were commiserating with the parents, as if the girl was already dead rather than standing right in front of them.

"This is a good thing," tried the Seeker, but no one was listening to him. "It's a gift."

"You mean a curse," snarled the Mayor.

When the girl realised her tears were having no effect on her parents, she grabbed hold of her mother's hand. The reaction was unexpected and surprising. The woman recoiled as if she'd been bitten by a poisonous snake.

"Get away from me!" she shrieked at the girl, staring in horror at her own flesh and blood.

Beside him Akosh was chuckling while doing her best to smother it, but the smile would not stay off her face. She was starting to get some peculiar looks from those around her in the crowd. Habreel elbowed her in the ribs and she tried to turn her laugh into a nasty cough, but it wasn't fooling anyone.

While all of this was happening the Seeker quickly turned to the boy, raised his hand and swiftly lowered it.

"He doesn't have the ability," he said, much to the relief of everyone around the boy.

The cursed girl had fallen silent. Her face was incredibly pale and she stared at her parents with open-mouthed horror.

"Momma," said the girl, pleading with her eyes.

"Maybe we could all leave," suggested the girl's father. "Start a new life somewhere else."

"I have no daughter," hissed the mother, before collapsing against her husband in tears.

When the Seeker tried to lead the girl away she resisted at first but then moved as if in a trance.

"This isn't right," said the Seeker, trying to appeal to anyone who would listen. Habreel could see a few sympathised with him, but they were in the minority and wisely kept their mouths shut. The Seeker was only visiting the town but they had to live here.

"You should take the girl and leave, while you still can," said the Mayor. A low murmur of conversation was starting to flow through the crowd, and the tone wasn't friendly. All of the anger was directed towards the masked stranger.

"More children will be born with the gift," he declared.

"We'll take care of them by ourselves from now on," said the Mayor.

"You don't know how," said the Seeker.

"We managed it for years before the war, long before your kind started showing up again. We'll be just fine." The Mayor received murmurs of support from the majority of the crowd.

At this the Seeker paused, but not for long. He wasn't facing one angry woman. The crowd had let him into the square, but now he must have wondered if they would let him leave so easily.

"You can't do this."

"I am the Mayor of Glienned. I serve the people's will. You should take that child away and never come back. Tell all of your kind, they're not welcome here any more."

At her declaration every person in the square cheered. The Seeker must have realised that to stay would cost more than his pride. As he approached the first row of people the Seeker cleverly used the girl as a shield in front of his body. Everyone recoiled from her as if she had the plague, creating a clear channel through the press of bodies.

As they passed through the crowd, not far away from where Habreel was standing, he saw the girl suddenly lunge at someone. A moment later there was a terrible screeching sound and people began to move backwards in a panic. Something red sprayed into the air and a familiar coppery smell lodged in the back of his throat.

Akosh's reaction was immediate. She pushed forward and he followed in her wake until they were standing in the front row.

The girl lay on the ground, a knife lodged in her throat while the Seeker was vainly trying to stem the bleeding. No one moved to help him save the girl.

"What happened?" asked Akosh, nudging a woman beside her.

"Girl grabbed Tull's knife from his belt," said the woman. "Stabbed herself rather than be taken away." There was a hint of pride in her voice.

"Help me!" said the Seeker but everyone just watched. It didn't take long. The blood pulsing from the jagged wound in the girl's neck slowed and then stopped. Her eyes glazed over and she let out a final breath.

"Leave her be," said the girl's mother, finally stepping forward and taking responsibility. "She doesn't belong to you."

At this distance Habreel could see the horror in the Seeker's eyes. Everywhere he looked in the crowd he was met with the same blank expression. No one was horrified by what the girl had done to herself. The Seeker gently laid the girl down on the street and quickly marched out of sight. Habreel was willing to bet the Seeker wouldn't stop on the road until he was miles away from Glienned.

Once the Seeker had left, the mood of the whole crowd seemed to lift. People began to disperse, quickly going back to their lives as if nothing had happened. Soon only a few remained in the square, including the dead girl and her weeping parents. Habreel and Akosh followed others back to the tavern.

"Well, that was bracing," said Akosh, finally able to laugh out loud without it drawing too many stares. "But it will take more than this to change things. One town refusing the Red Tower will not have much of an impact, even with it being the doorway to Zecorria."

Her tone was mocking but Habreel ignored it. This time it was his turn to grin.

"Did you think I was doing this on my own?" he asked, shaking his head in disappointment. "You have your followers and I have mine. My people are fanning sparks like this all over the west and, any day now, one of them will catch fire."

"You want one of the tests to turn violent," said Akosh, suddenly interested again.

Habreel shrugged. "I dislike violence, but understand that sometimes it's necessary. People are terrified of magic and after what happened during the war, they should be. One mage changed everything. He helped start a war that served no purpose. People lost loved ones and friends in the slaughter and all of it comes back to one mage. In the long run, eliminating all magic from the world will save countless lives. It's been a blight for too long."

"And what if it means killing more children to achieve your goal?" asked Akosh. "Could you do it?"

"I will do whatever is necessary, no matter the cost." He knew what she wanted him to say, but Habreel wouldn't give her the satisfaction. He sincerely hoped he would never have to get his hands dirty, although a small voice in the back of his mind told him it wasn't possible. But they couldn't begin to rebuild without first scouring away those who were already cursed. If it happened, he would find a way to live with it, but in the end it would be worth it to achieve a lasting peace. If a few had to be cleansed to save tens of thousands, then so be it. "Can I count on your support?" he asked.

Akosh's feral smile made a shiver run down Habreel's spine. "Oh, yes. I've not had this much fun in years."

CHAPTER 2

Danoph was screaming again. Tianne had been dreaming of her village in Zecorria but the sound of his voice brought her fully awake in a second. She rolled out of bed and scrambled sideways on all fours like a crab towards his bunk. She was at his side a few seconds later, but other students were already starting to wake up and complain about the noise.

Tianne tried shaking him by the shoulder but he was deep under. Tonight the dream didn't want to let go. Danoph's golden skin was slick with sweat, his dark hair plastered to his face and he smelled ripe with fear.

The nightmares were getting more intense.

"Shut him up!" someone yelled.

Danoph started howling like a mangled wolf, his voice echoing off the bare stone walls. More students were waking up now and the level of noise in the room began to rise. All around her people were yelling and throwing things which rattled off Tianne's back. She tried to shield him from the worst of it, but a few items hit his chest and head. Not that they had any effect. He remained deeply asleep.

"Danoph!" said Tianne quietly into his ear and then more loudly, but still he didn't respond. Normally physical contact and saying his name was enough. A glance through a gap in the curtains showed a foggy sky with no hint of sunlight. The worst nightmares always seemed to swallow him during the hour of the wolf, the darkest part of the night.

He screamed and thrashed about, tangling the sheets, binding his arms to his sides.

"They're burning!" he shouted. "They're all burning."

Tianne was still shaking him, gently and then harder, when she heard the sound of heavy footsteps approaching.

"Shut him up, or I'll smother him with a pillow," said a harsh voice. She didn't need to turn around to see who it was. Brunwal was two years older than her and one of the largest students at the school. He also had the worst temper in the whole dormitory.

"I'm trying," said Tianne, hating that her voice sounded whiny. She couldn't help it. Sometimes she felt Brunwal staring at her in a way that made her skin crawl. Tianne shook Danoph by both shoulders, but he still kept muttering and then started a wordless keening that set her teeth on edge.

A meaty hand landed on her shoulder and Tianne tried to shake it off. Instead Brunwal's fingers dug into her skin and she couldn't help groaning in pain.

"Get out of the way," he said, yanking her aside. Tianne flew backwards, landing badly and trapping one arm under her body. She rolled over and came to her feet in time to hear a loud smacking sound as Brunwal hit Danoph across the face.

It had no effect. He was still asleep and screaming about a fire. Brunwal pulled Danoph off his pillow and slapped him hard the other way, leaving a red mark on his cheek.

"Leave him alone," said Tianne, grabbing Brunwal's arm before he could slap her friend again. With a snarl Brunwal tried to shake her off but she doggedly held on. A nasty sneer crept across his face and he flicked his other hand towards her. An invisible force slammed into Tianne and she was thrown six feet away, only stopping when her back collided with another set of bunks. Spikes of pain ran up and down her spine, black stars dancing in front of her eyes. Gritting her teeth she forced herself onto hands and knees and then slowly upright. After a few seconds the spots faded but she felt sick and dizzy from the pain.

Brunwal was still slapping Danoph, and now he was offering others a turn. Blood was running from the corner of Danoph's mouth and his bottom lip was split open. If this continued for much longer Brunwal might break something. Most people didn't like Brunwal, but right now everyone was more annoyed at being woken up in the middle of the night once again. Usually she managed to wake up Danoph before he disturbed too many people. It had never been this bad before.

Brunwal was bigger and meaner than her. She didn't have any other friends to call on for help and he wouldn't listen to reason. That left her with only one choice.

It was forbidden to duel with magic, but it didn't stop most students at the Red Tower from trying at least once. Everyone wanted to know who was the strongest among them in each dormitory. Normally age and physical size would create a pecking order, but not at the Red Tower. The size of your muscles meant nothing if you had a strong connection to the Source. Tianne's strength was middling, but, as the teachers tried to impress on all the students, a skilled mage could do much with just a little magic.

Tianne reached for the Source and embraced it, feeling its glory flood every part of her body. The ocean of power was always there on the periphery of her senses, waiting for her to siphon off the smallest amount. As she drew the power into herself the pain in her back vanished and her mind became more alert. Her senses stretched and the shadows in the room faded from black to grey. Featureless lumps in the darkness coalesced into beds and the restless forms of other students. For a little while, at least, Tianne felt brave and unafraid.

"Get away from him!" she roared, slapping Brunwal across his back with a narrow bar of power. He squawked in surprise and dropped Danoph back onto his bed. She'd wanted his full attention and now she had it. As he stood up, towering over her, her bravery drained away like water from a bucket full of holes. She fought down the impulse to flee and pretended she wasn't petrified. Brunwal sneered at her bravado, flexing ham-sized fists as he stalked towards her.

"You shouldn't have done that, you black-eyed bitch," he said, rolling his shoulders.

Tianne swallowed hard and glanced around for some help. All of the other students were looking at her with a mix of resentment and pity. Coming from Zecorria had made her an outsider from her first day at the Red Tower. It didn't matter that her family had not been involved with the war. Or that it was ten years ago and she'd been six years old at the time. All anyone saw was her dark eyes and that was enough to condemn her. There were other students from her homeland, but they had to fend for themselves and would not come to her aid.

Since arriving she'd made a few friends, but none of them were willing to stand beside her at this moment. The only one who would was still caught up in a terrible nightmare.

"I'm going to make you scream," promised Brunwal. She sensed him drawing heavily from the Source and started weaving a dense shield around herself. Each layer was formed from a flexible crosshatch pattern that would cushion her from whatever he was preparing, but there was still a risk that the shock could kill her. In the few seconds she had frantically pulled together multiple layers into a dense shield. Tianne hoped it would be thick enough to stop his attack causing any serious damage.

Just as Brunwal hurled something at her, light blossomed in the room as every lantern and candle was simultaneously lit. She had a second to notice before her attention returned to the glowing green ball of energy hurtling towards her head. Tianne had no idea what it was, but she knew that it would hurt as Brunwal relished causing others pain.

Someone finally came to stand beside her, but it was too little too late. She'd never seen an attack like this before and instinctively knew her shield wouldn't be enough to stop it.

Craning her neck, Tianne looked up and saw beside her the grizzled features of Balfruss, a member of the school's Grey Council and one of the most powerful mages in the world.

Originally from Seveldrom, he was a tall man with greying hair, a salt and pepper beard and dark, brooding eyes. But it wasn't his stare that Tianne noticed whenever he came into a room. It was his presence. His will and connection to the Source was so strong it made her teeth ache to stand next to him for too long. Most senior mages took the title of Battlemage, but as a Sorcerer he possessed a depth of knowledge about the Source that few achieved after a lifetime of study.

Balfruss glanced at the glowing green ball the bully had hurled at her and negligently gestured at it with two fingers, diverting its path towards himself. With one outstretched hand he froze it in mid-air, seemingly with little effort.

The ball hovered above his hand and he inspected it, tilting it one way and then the other before closing his fist. Tianne expected him to grimace in pain but there was no reaction. He'd absorbed the energy or banished it. She had no idea how he'd done it. Absorbing power was something she'd never heard about, not even from the oldest students.

"Crude and amateurish," he muttered, so quietly Tianne didn't think anyone else besides her could have heard him. Across the dormitory Brunwal was staring in horror, his mouth hanging open at being caught attacking another student with something so dangerous.

The heavy drumming of boots announced a new arrival in the dormitory. Tianne's throat tightened as Garvey marched into view.

Something invisible picked Brunwal up by the scruff of his neck and hurled him through the air before pinning him to the wall.

It was rare for one member of the Grey Council to come into the dormitory. Tianne couldn't remember a time before tonight when she'd seen two of them at once.

Garvey scared Tianne like no other person and she was not alone in her feelings. Most of the other teachers did their best to avoid him and only spoke to him when strictly necessary. There seemed to be a permanent cloud hanging over his head. Garvey was always seething with rage and quick to anger. With rugged skin, a bald head and a bright red beard he strode into the room as if going to war.

Garvey's snarl was so loud it echoed off the stone walls and sounded like a mastiff getting ready to attack. He stared at Brunwal with such disdain Tianne saw the boy wither under the glare. Eloise entered the dormitory and went straight to Danoph's bedside. His screaming trailed off at her touch and there was an audible sigh of relief in the room in the quiet that followed.

Eloise was the final member of the Grey Council. If Balfruss was the most mysterious and Garvey the most intimidating, she was the most loved by all. None of them would be here at the school if not for her. For nearly twenty years the Red Tower had been a derelict ruin. A few years ago she had reopened it, bringing together all of the teachers, staff and Seekers.

It was because of her determination that so many children had been spared a grizzly fate at the hands of their community. Trying to control the magic growing inside without supervision was dangerous and potentially deadly. Back home in Zecorria many children were still terrified at the idea of finding out they had magic. Tianne had heard countless stories of children disappearing and entire communities denying all knowledge of their existence. It had improved when the Regent had changed the law, allowing Seekers to visit every month, but the fear of magic and what it could do was still prevalent. It was the Warlock's legacy.

Originally from Seveldrom, Eloise had long, blonde hair, flawless skin and her presence immediately made everyone in the dormitory feel at ease.

It wasn't unusual to see the Grey Council around the school, but standing so close to all three of them was more than a little intimidating. Balfruss and Eloise had only been figures from stories until she'd come to the Red Tower. Meeting them and talking to them had not diminished her awe. Being so close to all three of them at once was physically painful. Tianne saw several other students wincing and rubbing their temples.

"Maybe I'll peel the skin off your body, one strip at a time," Garvey said to Brunwal. It was said in such a conversational way it made Tianne feel more than a little sick. She wondered if he'd done it before.

"Garvey, leave the boy and help me," said Eloise.

Garvey moved closer towards Brunwal until his bristling red beard was almost touching the boy's face. It seemed to Tianne he was willing Brunwal to say or try anything with his magic. But even he didn't dare.

Garvey's class on shields was the one at the school that none of them wanted to attend. It was an important subject but he was known for being relentless and without mercy. Quite often he pushed students beyond their limit and many had collapsed or ended up in the hospital.

Eloise and Balfruss were war heroes who had fought against the Warlock and his apprentices. No one knew anything about Garvey's background or even where he came from.

With a harrumph Garvey turned away and went to Danoph's side but Brunwal remained pinned to the wall, feet dangling off the floor. He didn't complain, and barely seemed to be breathing.

"Are you all right?" Balfruss asked her.

Tianne found she couldn't reply. He was a living legend and she was just a student. There were a hundred stories swirling around Balfruss and she had no idea how many were true. One story claimed that he'd been married to a tribal princess across the Dead Sea but had to flee in fear of his life when she'd died. Another story was that he used to carry an axe, which made no sense at all. Why would one of the most powerful Sorcerers in the world need a weapon?

The one story she knew to be true was the critical role he had played in the war. Balfruss had stood alone on the battlefield facing an entire army, and called out the Warlock. The man responsible for starting the war and manipulating all of the rulers in the western kingdoms. It was because of the Warlock that she and every other person from Zecorria were now scapegoats.

Balfruss had done what no other mage during the war had been able to do. He had destroyed the Warlock single-handed, effectively ending the conflict and changing the course of the world.

Remembering all of that made it hard to talk. Instead of speaking Tianne just nodded and remembered to release the Source. The pain flared in her back and she would have fallen if Balfruss hadn't caught her by the arm. He helped her to the nearest bunk where they sat down together.

"Are you hurt?"

When he stared at Tianne she felt her stomach tighten and forced herself to concentrate on not saying something stupid. "My back," she managed, pointing for clarity and then inwardly cursing her stupidity for stating the obvious.

Balfruss rested a hand lightly on her shoulder and she felt a warm glow flood her entire body. It was as if she had sunk into a warm bath as all of her muscles relaxed and tension eased from her shoulders. A contented sigh escaped her lips and her eyelids began to droop.

"Hmm, nothing is broken. Just relax."

Tianne woke to find herself covered with a warm blanket. She was lying on a comfy bed and nothing else seemed to matter. Sleep pulled at her but just as she drifted off she heard someone come into the room. Balfruss sat down on the edge of her bed, offering her a rare smile. The grey in his hair meant he was old enough to be her father but, even so, she thought he was a handsome man. Tianne almost said it out loud but her rumbling stomach saved her from horrible embarrassment.

"Sleep for now. When you wake up, I'll make sure there's some food."

Tianne smiled and felt herself drifting down but then forced herself awake. "Danoph. Is he all right?"

Balfruss's smile vanished. "The war left terrible scars on his people. The wounds of his body have been healed, but I'm not sure his mind will ever recover. We'll do what we can to help him."

Tianne drifted away into the warm, comfortable darkness. When next she woke the first thing she smelled was fresh bread. Next to the bed someone had left a plate of warm bread, cold chicken and some greens. She tucked into it with relish, smearing fresh, creamy butter onto the bread. She overheard voices coming from the room next door as someone had left the door slightly ajar. Tianne was certain she wasn't supposed to listen but she couldn't help overhearing. The Grey Council were having a heated conversation.

"It must be done," Garvey was insisting. No one except the other members of the Grey Council ever stood up to him. Tianne thought the other teachers were more than a little afraid of him. "You both know it will happen," Garvey was saying.

"Then we have failed," said Balfruss. "Despite everything we've accomplished in the last ten years. It has all been for nothing."

"All is not lost. There's still time," said Eloise, her gentle voice calming them both. "If we start tomorrow and do it gradually, there's still a chance."

The three of them were quiet for a minute and Tianne thought the conversation was over. She focused on eating and kept her eyes on the food in case someone came to check on her. Eventually Balfruss spoke again and Tianne was so surprised by his tone of voice that her fork paused halfway to her mouth.

He was afraid.

"Are you sure we have to do this?"

Even Garvey's laugh was a harsh, cynical thing. "I'm sorry, my old friend, I'm not mocking you. You know there is no other way." Balfruss said something but it was muffled and Garvey laughed again. "I wish I had your optimism. People will need it in the days ahead. And you, Eloise, dear heart. You are the soul of this place. The Red Tower would not exist today if you had not rebuilt it."

"You both understand what we may have to do?" asked Eloise.

Garvey's sigh seemed to go on for a long time. "I do. I'm ready."

"Then may Elwei bless us and keep us safe," said Balfruss.

"There's no need to be so dramatic," scoffed Garvey. He didn't sound worried but the other two did. After all they had accomplished, what could possibly scare them?

Tianne heard the shuffling of feet and quickly lay back down and closed her eyes. She heard someone approaching and feigned waking up and yawning. When she opened her eyes she found Garvey staring at her from across the room. His unwavering stare was unnerving and she felt her mouth go dry. Without saying a word he turned and stomped away down the corridor.

"Are you feeling any better?" asked Balfruss, coming into the room.

"Much better, thank you," she babbled, clutching the blanket to her chest. It was difficult to talk to him without feeling as if her tongue filled her entire mouth.

"I wondered if you wouldn't mind doing me a favour," he asked with a smile that made her stomach churn.

"Anything for you," she blurted out, then looked away to hide her embarrassment.

If Balfruss noticed her blush he didn't say anything. "There's a new student joining us tomorrow. Would you look after her? Maybe you could show her around and help her settle in. Would you do that?"

"I'd be happy to," she managed, proud for almost sounding normal.

"Thank you, Tianne."

It was only when she was halfway back to the dormitory that she wondered what was so special about the new student. Why had Balfruss taken a personal interest in her?

It wasn't yet dawn and already the day was proving to be one that Tianne wouldn't forget for a long time.

CHAPTER 3

Tammy never felt more at home than when she was walking the familiar corridors of Unity Hall. As a Guardian of the Peace, her work over the last ten years had taken her across the world and every time she came back to Perizzi, the capital of Yerskania, it seemed different. Each small change in the city made it feel less welcoming. At least here, in the headquarters of the Guardians, time appeared to be standing still as the decor never changed. It was never updated to suit a change in fashion. The heavy wooden furniture was stained with black lacquer that seemed to absorb the light, while the polished wooden floors were the colour of freshly spilled blood. Black and red dominated every room and every corridor. The building was a solid and immovable rock in the river of time.

On her way to the Old Man's office she passed many Guardians, all of them dressed in the famous jackets that were also black and red. Tammy still owned one, but she'd not worn her uniform for a long time. It was a lot easier to blend in if they didn't know why she was there ahead of time.

Although Guardians were predominantly responsible for investigating crimes in Yerskania, their reputation was such that other nations often sent requests for assistance with difficult or unusual cases. In the course of her work Tammy had travelled all over the west, from Shael to Zecorria, Morrinow and even once to Drassia. It had been difficult and often exhausting work but, sadly, coming back to Yerskania didn't feel like a home-coming. A child of two nations, Seveldrom and Yerskania, she'd grown up feeling as if she belonged to both and yet to neither. Perhaps that was why she felt most comfortable on the road.

The Khevassar, known simply to many as the Old Man, was the head of the Guardians. As she stepped into his outer office she received an unpleasant surprise. Instead of seeing Rummpoe, the Old Man's curmudgeonly secretary, a young woman with a pinched faced was sitting behind his desk. The rest of the room looked exactly the same as before. The walls were covered, floor to ceiling, with shelves that were filled with hundreds of identical red leather journals. They were the hand-written account of all crimes in the city going back decades, penned by the Old Man. A history of blood and violence. As their leader she guessed he must have seen it all. She wondered if anything ever surprised him these days, or was it all cyclical?

Two novices sat waiting for their first interview with the Khevassar and they looked nervous. They had every right to be. It was all part of the traditional initiation every Guardian had to endure. While investigating crimes they had to delve into the private lives of victims and their families. They were required to ask the most personal questions in pursuit of justice, but first they had to understand themselves and be able to accept who and what they were.

Tammy still remembered her interview with the Old Man and the cutting remarks he'd made. Everything had been laid bare. It was as if he'd been able to see inside her mind.

As Tammy approached Rummpoe's desk, the young woman looked up, clearly annoyed at the interruption.

"Yes?" she asked.

"Where's Rummpoe?" asked Tammy.

"I am Rummpoe," said the secretary, rolling her eyes. Unimpressed, Tammy crossed her arms and waited, looming over the desk. When the young woman realised she wasn't going to go away her arrogance receded a little. "He was my great-grandfather. I took over the job and the name, in honour of him."

"I'm here to see the Old Man."

Rummpoe shook her head. "First, as you well know, he is to be referred to only as the Khevassar. Second, you can't just turn up whenever you like and ask to see him. That's not how it works."

"That's exactly how it works," said the Old Man standing in his office doorway. Tammy watched as a teary-eyed novice scuttled out of the waiting room. No doubt the novice had been forced to come face to face with some unsettling truths about himself. Her interview had been equally brutal, although she'd managed not to cry in his presence. That had come later.

"Sir, there are protocols to follow," Rummpoe began to argue. "I thought—"

"That was your mistake," snapped the Old Man. "You are here to follow my orders. Disobey me again and I'll demote you to the Watch. You'll be scraping up drunks on the docks and be knee deep in shit and vomit every night for the rest of your life. Is that clear?"

Rummpoe had the good grace to look suitably ashamed. She kept her eyes on her desk and muttered something under her breath.

"Speak up. I'm going a bit deaf in my old age," said the Old Man, cupping a hand to the side of his head.

"I said, yes Sir, I understand."

"Your grandfather used to tell me you were clever. Start acting like it."

Tammy followed the Old Man into his office and closed the door behind her. He sat down behind his desk and heaved a long sigh. "Why did he have to go and die on me, the old fool?"

Rummpoe and the Khevassar must have been friends for decades. Tammy had always found him irritating but the Old Man was clearly missing him.

He'd never been a big man, but the Khevassar looked smaller and more frail than she remembered. Most of his hair was gone and his uniform seemed ill-fitting, as if he'd borrowed it from someone larger. His normally steady hands trembled and even his sharp blue eyes had lost some of their sparkle. Now they were rheumy and turning yellow. In the past he would have noticed her studying him but today he seemed lost in thought.

"How did your last job go?" he asked, returning to the present.

"As expected. Nothing went as planned. The locals in Zecorria didn't cooperate."

"But you got the job done," he said, stating it as fact.

"I did. Do you want the details?"

Much to her surprise he waved it away. "I'll read it in your report. I know you've only just got back, but something else has already come up."

"I'm ready, Sir."

His smile was brief but in that moment she saw a spark of the man she remembered. "It's a missing person case. I need you to look into it."

Tammy had to work hard to conceal her disappointment. The last ten years had seen her mostly working on cases that threatened hundreds or thousands of lives. Political kidnappings, religious splinter groups, magic-related hate crimes and politically sensitive jobs that only a few people were allowed to know about. The scale of what she had been dealing with was always significant. A missing person seemed like a grand departure and a waste of her abilities.

"My eyesight may be fading, but even I can see you're disappointed."

"Why do you want me on this case?" she asked.

Instead of answering he tossed a letter across the desk. "Read it."

Even before she opened the letter Tammy recognised the distinctive wax seal. A stylised tower surrounded by a sea of stars. The letter was from the Red Tower in Shael.

"It was addressed to you?" she asked.

"Yes, but there's a separate letter inside with your name on it."

The letter to the Khevassar was brief and she quickly scanned the contents before turning to her envelope. The seal was intact, not that she was surprised. The Old Man's integrity was one of many things she admired about him.

From the first word she recognised the handwriting. The contents were similar to the other letter, but there was also some personal information unrelated to the case. Both letters were unsigned. She glanced up at the Old Man when she was done but his expression was unreadable.

"Been keeping secrets?" he asked, then held up a hand before she could answer. "It doesn't matter. Let me guess what's in it," he said, gesturing at her letter. "Someone has gone missing from a village and they want you to investigate."

"Yes."

"Who is it from?"

"An old friend," said Tammy, touching the hilt of the unusual sword she carried on her belt. It had been a gift several years ago from Balfruss during their voyage to the remote city of Voechenka in Shael.

The Old Man glanced at her sword and grunted. He knew all about her journey with Balfruss and what had really happened there. Only a few people knew the whole story and only the Old Man had taken it all in his stride. Maybe nothing could surprise him any more.

"When will you leave?" he asked.

"Tomorrow. The village isn't far. I can reach it in a couple of days."

"Take whatever supplies you need and report back when it's done."

As she left the Old Man's office, Tammy felt a stab of pity for him, buried beneath a mountain of paperwork, working all hours in service of the people. He was too old to be doing this and should have retired years ago. His family should be caring for him, but when he took on the mantle of the Khevassar he'd given up everything, including his name, his past and his family. She wondered if, looking back over the last few decades, would he think it was all worth it?

Tammy flopped down on the bed beside Kovac and it took her a while to catch her breath. Her skin was slick with sweat and loose strands of hair clung to her face. She needed a bath and at least ten hours' sleep. She also had to be up early in the morning to get back on the road and ride south. All thoughts of that had vanished an hour ago when they'd been tearing off each other's clothes.

Tammy rolled out of bed, pulled on some loose trousers and a shirt then tied back her long blonde hair in a ponytail. She filled two cups with water and brought them back to bed.

"You were trying to tell me something when you arrived," she said.

Kovac gulped his water and poured some into his hand before wiping it across his face and greying beard. There was less black in his hair than she remembered. He didn't like her mentioning it. No one wanted to be reminded they were getting older, but she thought it made him look distinguished.

"Last month I was up in Zecorria. I heard some rumours about a smuggler who used to work for a crime boss here in Perizzi."

"What kind of rumours?" she asked.

"This was a few years back, but apparently he robbed one of the Dons and took a lot of money." Tammy knew from first-hand experience that was never a good idea. They hadn't achieved their positions from being kind and forgiving. "The smuggler thought he'd covered his tracks, but when the Don found out, he came to a nasty end. The problem is, no one ever found the money. They think he hid it somewhere in Perizzi. Mercenaries love the idea of finding buried gold."

"So, are you here because of the money?" she asked.

Kovac gave her a withering look. "No, I'm not."

"Sorry," she said, touching his face. Despite earning a living with his sword, she knew Kovac was better than that. He had morals which, in her experience, many mercenaries seemed to lack.

She would pass the information on to the Old Man. If more mercenaries turned up in the city hoping to find the treasure, there could be a spike in the number of burglaries. As well as making money mercenaries also liked spending their gold on food, drink and a companion for the night. Also they weren't afraid to get into a fight with each other or strangers. Depending on the number of treasure hunters in the city they might need more squads of the Watch to patrol the docks.

Tammy saw how Kovac was looking at her and suddenly felt cold inside. He hadn't told her the story because she was a Guardian. "Who was he?" she asked, although part of her already knew. "Who was the smuggler?"

"He was your husband."

The old pain that she thought was gone suddenly returned. She'd tried to lock it away in the dark corners of her mind and forget all about it. She'd hoped that by doing so it would disappear in time, but it was still there. She'd been carrying it around for all these years. After all this time she was amazed at how much it still hurt.

"Why would you tell me that and risk what we have?"

Kovac sighed and looked away. "Because there's a distance between us. You haven't fully let go of the past. Part of you is still living there with him."

Tammy wanted to argue but she knew he was right. Her life had radically changed the day her husband had been murdered almost fifteen years ago. She'd gone from working for one of the crime lords in the city to preventing crime in the Watch and then the Guardians. That was not all she'd given up in search of a new life. She didn't want to think about that right now as her mind was reeling from Kovac's revelation.

"If you want me to stay away from it, just say the word. I'll never mention it again," he promised.

Part of her wanted to tell him to leave it buried in the past where it belonged, but she'd never been one to shy away from a difficult decision. Besides, as a Guardian it was her job to solve cases and bring people to justice. Sometimes that included solving murders and giving family members closure so that they could move on with their lives. Perhaps it was time she was granted that same measure of peace.

"When are you heading back to Zecorria?"

"Three days," said Kovac. "Protection for a merchant train."

"Find out who murdered him. Get me some answers."

"Are you sure?" asked Kovac.

"Get me a name, but be careful," said Tammy, touching him on the cheek to show that she wasn't angry with him. That would come later, when she found out who was responsible.

Despite the hour, Tammy didn't have to wait long for someone to answer the door. Her twin sister, Mary-Beth, looked the same as when she'd last seen her a few years ago. Without saying a word she hugged Tammy and ushered her into the house.

The kitchen was still a tidy haven where everything was in its rightful place. From the neatly labelled jars of herbs, to the freshly scrubbed pans hanging from the ceiling, the room was incredibly neat. In a house with several children that was a considerable feat. Despite their differences, they both had methodical minds that liked order.

Something spicy was bubbling away in a large pot on the stove. The tantalising smells reminding Tammy that she'd not eaten that morning. Her stomach growled and without being asked Mary put a plate of fresh bread, cheese and fruit in front of her. As Tammy started eating Mary resumed chopping more vegetables for the stew, her knife moving so quickly it flashed in the air. Tammy had no doubt she would have made a deadly swordswoman and Guardian. As twins, when they looked in a mirror, she suspected they each saw the road not taken.

"Where is everyone?" asked Tammy, realising the house was remarkably quiet.

"Asleep. They'll be up in an hour or so. You're going away again, aren't you?"

"Yes, but that's not why I'm here. I've heard a rumour about how Kurne was murdered. A friend is looking into it for me."

Mary's knife paused and she briefly bowed her head before the chopping resumed.

"When you find the person responsible, are you going to kill them or bring them to justice?" she asked.

"Right now, I'm not sure."

Mary put down the knife and clasped one of Tammy's hands in both of hers. "I really don't care which you choose. As long as it helps you move on."

Tammy raised an eyebrow. "That's not what I expected you to say. I thought you were going to preach about forgiveness and the Maker's justice."

Mary snorted and went back to her stew. "There's no point. You'll do it your way, no matter what I say. You could teach mules lessons about being stubborn. I just want you to get on with your life."

"What does that mean?" asked Tammy.

"You've had a restless spirit for years. It's why you've been travelling abroad so much. Here, you have a family, a job and a man who loves you, not that he'd ever say it."

"Do you mean Kovac?"

"I know all about him," said Mary, dismissing it with a wave of her hand. "Maybe finding Kurne's killer will bring you peace. If it does, we'll all be here, waiting for you."

Tammy wasn't sure what to say. She ate the rest of her breakfast in silence, lost in thought. When she was done Mary walked her to the door and they embraced again. Noises above their heads told Tammy the children were starting to wake up. If she didn't leave immediately she'd have to face them and that was something she couldn't deal with at the moment.

Mary was far better suited at being a mother than Tammy had ever been. It was why she'd asked her sister to look after her son all those years ago. At the time finding who had killed

Kurne was all that mattered and she'd no room for a small boy in her life. Her old boss, Don Lowell, had done everything in his power to help her but she'd never found those responsible. Back then, she couldn't have given him a good home. Now, she couldn't take him away from the only family he'd ever known.

"He's well and I think he's happy," said Mary, sparing Tammy from asking about her son.

"Thank you, Mary."

"Be careful."

"Always."

Without looking back Tammy set off down the street, leaving her sister and son behind, as she went in search of a missing Seeker.

CHAPTER 4

Munroe took a deep breath in a vain attempt to calm the storm raging inside. Her mother was dying and there was nothing she could do about it.

She crossed the courtyard, barely glancing at the massive red needle that loomed over everything.

The Red Tower.

Hearing about it was one thing but seeing it for the first time was always an experience. Almost in spite of themselves every visitor stopped what they were doing and stared. They couldn't help it. Most were awed by its size but a few had screamed. The very idea of something so massive terrified them. It was as if their minds couldn't contemplate how such a tall building could exist.

When she'd first arrived years ago, Munroe had wondered how the tower could be so high and yet so narrow. A second later she'd wondered which poor bastard had the awful job of cleaning it. As it turned out the answer was no one.

For some reason no birds dared go anywhere near it, and not one scrap of moss or fungus grew on the blood-red stones. The building was ancient and yet the colour had never faded from its original grisly hue. Its architect, and the technique used to create such a monstrosity, was lost to history. Perhaps that was for the best if its mere presence could unsettle and scare some to the point of wetting themselves. People still laughed about that particular merchant, but he'd never been back and she didn't think it was because of embarrassment.

Some claimed that centuries ago the first Grey Council had built it by communing with an ancient being from beyond the Veil. It had whispered secrets in their ears in return for blood and human sacrifices. Others said that they'd summoned it from beneath the earth and the tower had risen into the sky fully formed. That it had been lying dormant until it was called upon. One or two people had even told her that it was a relic from another world. Wherever it originated, Munroe knew that it was unique and she doubted there would ever be another like it.

Munroe realised she'd stopped in the courtyard and was staring at the tower like a fresh pupil. She was stalling because fear twisted inside her belly like a fat, angry snake.

Wiping tears from her face she doggedly pressed on, ignoring everyone on her way back to the visitors' tavern.

A warren of buildings had sprung up around the tower over the years to house the staff and students, but at one time supplicants had also been common. For centuries people had sought the wisdom and expertise of the Grey Council. To cure terrible diseases. To act as mediators between intractable enemies. And sometimes to fight for kings and queens, defending the lives of innocents by shedding their own blood. These days, with so many now afraid of magic, the number of supplicants were few and far between, but the small visitors' town, a mile away from the school, was still there.

Now the nameless town was occupied by many of the people who worked with the Red Tower, but had no magical ability.

The farmers, millers, bakers, cooks, farriers, fletchers, coopers, blacksmiths and dozens of others who supported the Tower. It took a lot more than magic and the Grey Council to run the school. And with every tanner and brewer there was a husband or wife and several children. A renewed community had sprung up in the long shadow of the Red Tower. There were also signs that the town was growing with the skeletons of several new houses on the outskirts. After all, there was nowhere safer in all of Shael than right next door to a school full of mages. Only a blind, deaf idiot would try to start trouble in town.

She'd hoped the walk would calm her down, but somehow Munroe maintained the same level of panic all the way. It was a bright day but an icy wind froze the tears on her cheeks, bringing with it the smells of the town. It was a strange mix of metal, cooking vegetables and cow shit.

There had been a long period in her life when she and her mother had barely spoken, but that had changed in the last ten years. Now it was difficult for Munroe to think about a future without her.

When she reached the tavern she took a moment to wipe her face again, not that it would make any difference. She pushed open the front door of the White Hart and paused on the threshold. What she saw made her smile, despite how she was feeling. It was her whole world, everyone she loved together in the same room.

Her husband, son and mother were sitting on the floor in front of the cold fireplace. Little Sam was playing with some of his toys on a blanket while Choss and her mother were talking.

Looking at her, it was hard for Munroe to believe that she was ill. She looked a little pale and tired, but that might have been from spending too much time indoors and not getting enough sleep. Part of her wanted to believe that Eloise had made a mistake, but the moment her mother looked up and their eyes met, Munroe knew it was true. A silent message passed between them and Munroe felt as if she was falling down a well while standing still. She had to grab hold of the doorframe to stop her knees from buckling.

Samara doted on her only grandson and spoiled him rotten, but she still had her own life. It was only now, as she thought back over the last year, that Munroe realised her mother's visits had become more frequent. She wondered how long Samara had known.

"We'll be back soon," said her mother, kissing Sam and touching Choss fondly on the arm. Munroe quickly crossed the room and followed her mother upstairs, not stopping to talk to Choss in case she began to cry again. She was afraid that once she started she wouldn't be able to stop. Right now she didn't want to cry. She wanted to find a solution. Just giving up and waiting for the inevitable was not acceptable.

"Shut the door," said Samara, before Munroe had a chance to speak. Once the door was closed she couldn't let go of the handle and was afraid to turn around. Afraid to hear what she already knew in her heart. "Come and sit down, girl."

Munroe swallowed the lump in her throat and sat down opposite her mother by the window. It was a bright day outside with a clear blue sky, completely at odds with how she was feeling.

"I can tell by your face that you've spoken to the healer," said Samara. Munroe wondered if she would look as good as her mother if she reached the same age.

"Is that why you've been visiting more often?"

Samara sighed and took out the small tin she always carried

with her. Inside was a neat row of long black cigars with white tips. "I knew before they did that the magic wasn't working any more. They'd heal me and I'd feel better for a while, but then I'd start to get tired again. No matter how much I slept or ate, I was still tired. I always thought these would kill me," she said, tapping her cigar tin.

"Can't they do something?" asked Munroe.

Her mother shook her head. "It's a part of me, somewhere deep inside. They can push it down for a time, but then it just grows back again."

Samara looked at her flint and tinder and then held out the cigar towards Munroe. She embraced the Source and channelled a trickle of power into a small flame on the end of her thumb. Her mother used it to light her cigar.

"I never get tired of seeing you do that," said Samara.

They sat in silence for a while as her mother took a few long drags. Normally she would have complained about the smell but it hardly seemed to matter now.

It took Munroe several attempts but eventually she managed to ask. "How long?"

"A few months. Maybe a year. The other healers want to keep trying, but the smart one, Eloise, she knows it's pointless. So I'm not going far from the Red Tower for a while. I'll still be here when you get back."

"Get back?"

Samara looked at her as if she was an idiot. "From your first job. Isn't this what you've been asking the Grey Council for?"

"I can't abandon you."

"Munroe, when you first came here and started studying, I thought you wouldn't last a month. I thought you'd get bored and run away. You proved me wrong and for a while you seemed happy. But now all you ever tell me is that you want to get out. To do something with your magic, instead of being stuck in a classroom all day."

"I do."

"Then go and do this job for them. Prove to the Grey Council, and especially that bastard Garvey, that you're ready for this. I'm not going to die overnight." Samara seemed so calm about her impending death it was unnerving. Munroe just wanted to start screaming until everyone in the world felt like her. The grief inside was gnawing at her like a living thing.

Munroe shook her head. "I can't leave."

"So, it's all right for your husband to see his Vorga mistress, but not for you to leave on a mission. Is that right?"

"She's not his mistress," said Munroe. They'd had this argument dozens of times before and her mother refused to believe what she was told. The idea of any human being in a relationship with a Vorga would normally sound like the start of a bad joke. Until a few years ago Munroe wouldn't have thought it possible either. "She's his . . . friend."

Samara snorted with derision and part of Munroe couldn't blame her for that. "Friend" was an inadequate word to describe the bond between Choss and Gorraxi after what they'd been through. She'd not spent much time with the Vorga over the years, mostly because, like all of her kind, Gorraxi was fairly terrifying, but Choss understood her like no other. Most people knew little about the Vorga, other than they weren't human and originally they came from the sea. This allowed them to breathe on land and under water through their gills. All Vorga were tall, liked to fight and they believed in strength above all else. Although different in many ways from other Vorga, Gorraxi could still rip a man in half with her bare hands if she was in the mood.

Choss had explained that there was so much more to them but what he described made little sense to her.

But there was one thing about her that Munroe knew for certain. Gorraxi loved her husband and would do anything for him. She didn't have to worry about Choss and trusted him to remain faithful. He'd cut off his own arms before he did anything that would hurt her.

"Do you really think you're ready for this?" asked Samara.

"That's what the Grey Council asked me," said Munroe. Eloise had been in favour of her leaving on her first mission. Garvey had been completely against it, leaving the deciding vote with Balfruss. After listening to both sides he had eventually voted in her favour.

Being older and more aware than many of the other students, she knew the school needed money to keep it running. That meant the Battlemages and Sorcerers had to take paid work. Sometimes Balfruss or Garvey would leave the school for a couple of weeks or a month at a time. When they returned they were always tired and fresh rumours of their accomplishments would circulate around the school for weeks. Soon after a caravan of wagons laden with supplies would arrive at the front gates, paid for by their hard work.

"What did you say to them?" asked Samara.

"That I've been studying for six years. How long will it be before they say I'm ready? Ten years? Twenty?"

None of them had been able to answer her, not even Garvey. The Red Tower itself was ancient, but the new Grey Council had only been working together for a few years since reopening the school. They were still working things out and sometimes that meant making them up as they went. She was the first student even close to being ready to graduate and they didn't really know what to do with her.

Munroe was among the oldest students at the school and she knew there were only a handful who had the potential in the next few years to become Battlemages, never mind Sorcerers. That was a title and level of understanding that would take decades to master and no one had the patience for it. Not when they could be out there exploring the world and using their magic outside of a classroom.

Many of the older students who'd learned to conceal their magic were taught how to stay in control, to keep themselves safe and prevent accidents in their communities. They were often middle-aged men and women, approached with discretion, so as not to alert their friends and neighbours. Most had no desire to learn more, didn't want to become a Battlemage and wanted nothing to do with the Red Tower. These days it was becoming too dangerous with so much anti-magic sentiment.

Those few who did make discreet visits to the school quickly went back to their lives and none of their neighbours were any the wiser. Sometimes that was the last anyone at the Red Tower ever heard from them. Sometimes they took a gold mask home with them and became a Seeker. That way any children in their local area with magic ability came to the Red Tower, before they hurt themselves or disappeared in suspicious circumstances. It wasn't a perfect system but it was better than nothing.

Even by Munroe's conservative guesses, it would be at least another five or six years before the most accomplished students would be ready to graduate. That meant years of finding a lot of money to prevent the school from falling into ruin again. Sooner or later the Grey Council would have to turn to people like her to help them.

"I'm ready. I have to be," said Munroe.

"Be careful," said Samara, grinding the stub of her cigar onto a plate.

"I can take care of myself."

Samara laughed. "I know you can, but no matter how old you get, it doesn't stop me from worrying. You're still my child. Give it twenty years with Sam and then you'll understand."

As they walked back to their rooms at the school, Munroe felt a pang of guilt. She knew her mother would be safe while she was away, but she was still having second thoughts.

Dusk was approaching and Sam was dozing as he rode on Choss's shoulders. There weren't any lights out here so Munroe summoned a magical globe to help them see in the gloom. It was one of the first things they'd taught her when she'd come to the school and she still used it almost every day.

"Spit it out. I can hear you grinding your teeth," said Choss.

"I'm feeling guilty about going away."

"You should go," said Choss, surprising her, something which didn't happen often. She loved him dearly but he was nothing if not predictable.

"Why do you say that?"

Choss checked that Sam was asleep before easing him off his shoulders and carrying him like a baby in his arms. "I know that lately you've been feeling cooped up. It's made you difficult."

Munroe raised an eyebrow. "Difficult?"

Choss must have known by her tone of voice that he was on thin ice, but still he pressed on. As a former champion fighter he knew when to pick his battles but this time he wasn't backing down. "When you worked for Don Jarrow, you were a prisoner, of sorts."

"We both were," said Munroe, thinking back to what felt like an entirely different life in Perizzi. Don Jarrow was the head of one of the major crime Families in the city. Munroe, and, to a lesser extent Choss, had worked for him. After six years in Shael she felt like an entirely new person. Her old life seemed like a nightmare that continued to lurk in the dark corners of her mind. Back then she'd been lonely and isolated because of her uncontrollable magic, which she had thought was a curse. Most of the time she'd been drunk to numb the pain and boredom. The only bright spot in her life had been Choss. Now she had a family of her own, control over her magic and a real home.

"We were both prisoners, but now this is my home," Choss was saying. "The Red Tower is an amazing place. I've seen the wonderful things they can do with magic. They can help so many people, but I know you still feel trapped. You should be out there, not stuck here," he said, gesturing at the wider world around them.

"I like being here and I love you both," said Munroe, being careful not to wake up Sam.

"I know," said Choss, giving her a squeeze. "That was never in doubt. But you don't belong in a classroom. They're training you to be able to do something with your magic, not teach others. So go out there and do it. Just promise me you'll be careful and come back to us."

"I promise."

"Good. Then it's settled."

"You can be very persuasive when you want to," said Munroe, appraising him.

"I learned from the best," he said.

"Keep talking like that and you'll get a night to remember," she promised him.

The next morning all three members of the Grey Council were there to wave her off. They'd agreed Sam was too little to understand so he was being kept indoors with her mother. She pulled Choss down towards her for one last kiss, not caring that the others were watching, before climbing onto her horse.

When she passed through the gates Munroe expected to feel free. Instead she felt homesick. She just wanted to get the job done as quickly as possible and return to her family. Now all she had to do was find a missing Seeker.

CHAPTER 5

Wren tried not to stare as they approached the Red Tower but despite her father's warning she couldn't help it. She'd never seen a building so tall and strange. It was monstrous and so narrow it looked more like a huge splinter of fresh blood than a building. She hadn't been sure what to expect but her imagination had not prepared her for this. A building that, even at this distance, felt as if it didn't belong.

Wren wondered if anyone actually lived inside it and how they could bear it.

Her father, riding beside her on the wagon, was still preaching ". . . must respect your teachers. I know this school is different from what we know, but they are still your elders and you will listen."

"Yes, Father," she said by rote. Most of their conversations had been like this since they'd left home. At times it had been a long and tedious journey from Drassia.

"Learn as much as you can and try to do . . . well."

Wren smiled and patted his knee. He was trying so hard. She was amazed he'd managed to say even that much. Her father knew almost nothing about magic and how it worked, which was a great deal more than her mother. In fact, none of her people could speak about it with any real authority.

Magic had no functional place in Drassi society. Any child unfortunate enough to have the ability was effectively exiled. Not by their family or the village, but simply because no one in Drassia knew what to do with them. There was no shame or embarrassment, merely indifference.

Wren knew other nations in the west had more severe reactions to children with magic. The introduction of monthly visits from a Seeker had been carefully negotiated. In Drassia there had been no need to walk on eggshells. Every community wanted the children found and taken away as soon as possible so that life could continue as normal.

Her culture was built on skill, tradition and patience. From the weavers and tailors to the bladesmiths and martial arts masters. Any person learning a craft remained an apprentice for a minimum of ten years, while in some cases it could be as many as twenty. There was no shame in this. It was necessary and the time taken to acquire such knowledge could not be rushed. However long it took to achieve, a master of their craft was highly regarded throughout the nation.

To someone from Drassia, magic seemed like the worst kind of shortcut. It was a way to create something quickly and cheat the craftsman. From the little that she knew, Wren understood the ingrained Drassi attitude showed their general ignorance. It took a long time and considerable skill before a mage could effectively wield magic. It also required several more years before one was allowed to use the title of Battlemage. Beyond that only a handful in history had ever attained the mantle of Sorcerer.

Others before her had tried to argue the point, but no one in Drassia wanted to listen, so the level of ignorance remained the same today.

Wren remembered a boy from her village who had left home

two years before to study at the Red Tower. No one really spoke about him any more. No Drassi who went to the Red Tower ever returned home once they were fully trained. There was simply no point. Some Drassi mages became Seekers and others travelled the world as Battlemages, lending their skill and strength to those in need. Beyond the borders of Drassia magic had a purpose and, like everyone, Drassi mages wanted to belong.

She wondered if one day she would be able to call herself a Battlemage. It seemed a tall order and so far away. At the moment all she had was a crude understanding of magic and how it worked.

Her ability to turn the power she summoned into a physical force had seemed like a great achievement. The Seeker visiting her village had been less kind, saying this was the first thing students were taught. The physical manifestation of will was merely the beginning and the easiest skill to master. Wren had felt deflated ever since and had not experimented by herself any further.

The journey to the Red Tower had given her some time to think about what she wanted. Her old life was gone and she could never go back. She was still coming to terms with that, but if magic was to play a large role in her future then she wanted to excel at it.

"Are you listening?" asked her father.

"Yes, Father."

"Then repeat the last thing I said."

"That I should try not to embarrass our family and undermine everything mother has built."

Her father grumbled but let it pass. In truth she'd only been half listening, but he'd said something similar a dozen times already. It was much the same lecture she'd heard all her life. Only now she had one more thing with which to embarrass and disappoint her mother. After all, it was only Wren's great-great-grandmother who had created the thriving business empire that she had passed down to her daughter and so on through the generations. Her family's silk clothing was renowned and worn by kings and queens across the world.

From the moment of her birth it was expected that Wren would inherit and run the business after her mother, but now that honour would pass to her cousin. Apparently that was the worst thing that could ever have happened in the world to her mother and her business empire.

"She does love you," said her father, somehow reading her thoughts.

Wren laughed at the idea. She'd never experienced any displays of affection from her mother. Mostly it was irritation for not being the best in her school at everything. Her mother also blamed her for being shorter than average, enjoying her food a little too much, having stubby fingers and no artistic eye for design. All of these were grave sins, far worse than a crippling injury or even an untimely death.

"We're nearly there," commented her father, gesturing at the gates ahead.

Someone in the nameless town had given them directions to the Red Tower and this last mile on the road felt incredibly long.

Magic had changed the course of her life and Wren felt enormous relief. Her gender had locked her into one path and much had been expected of her. Any ambitions of her own had been irrelevant. Until now. She was determined to become a great mage. Not because it was expected or that she wanted to make her parents proud. She was doing it for herself. Her magic belonged to no one else and with it she would carve out her own future.

The most terrifying part of her great plan was that there was nothing to fall back on. Failing would not mean Wren would be sent home in disgrace. No child in Drassia who left for the Red Tower ever returned. It made her wonder what would happen if she couldn't master even the basics? How long would they give her? Would she be cast out into the street? Or did they have a way to burn the magic out of her for ever? She had so many questions and no answers.

The seed of fear in her stomach grew tendrils that began to spread.

The gates to the Red Tower were not as impressive as Wren had been expecting. They were tall and looked well made, but they were quite ordinary. Some might say plain. The wall surrounding the school was three or four times the height of a grown man, but it too was simply made from ordinary grey stone. Wren considered that perhaps she was being arrogant. Maybe this work was all they knew in Shael and it was the height of their stonemasonry skill. Staring more closely Wren noticed the wall didn't look that old in comparison with the tower itself. She wondered if the original wall had been destroyed in the war ten years ago.

The rest of the school was hidden from view, but waiting for her at the gate was a tall Zecorran girl about her age. When she'd first seen one of the northerners as a small child Wren had assumed the man's eyes were dark brown. It was only later she realised the irises were totally black and featureless, just like every other Zecorran.

The girl had pale skin, long black hair and a friendly face that lit up when she smiled. "You must be Wren."

"Yes, that is me." She hopped down off the wagon and stretched her legs. The air smelled different here, dry and crisp like the moment before a heavy storm. Perhaps it was all the magic.

"I'm Tianne." When the girl held out a hand it took Wren a moment to realise she was supposed to shake it. This was how they greeted people outside Drassia. It was another foreign custom she would have to become familiar with. She'd only just arrived and was already feeling a little out of her depth.

"It's kind of you to meet me." Wren wasn't sure if it was normal for only one student to greet a new arrival at the school. She tried her best not to seem disappointed in case she offended Tianne. Wren saw her father looking around in bewilderment as well. Such a thing would never have happened if they were at home. All of the senior figures in the community would normally have been waiting. Thoughts like those did not belong any more either. Wren was starting to understand that she would have to relearn what was normal for people from other countries, as well as how to use her magic.

"The Grey Council asked me to give you a tour. They're busy at the moment, but you'll have a chance to meet them later."

Wren pulled her bag down from the back of the wagon and then held out her hand towards her father. He gave her a wry smile, touched two fingers to his lips and turned the wagon around.

"Is he a friend?" asked Tianne, watching as the cart slowly trundled away through the gate and then back down the road.

"He's my father."

Tianne was visibly puzzled but Wren ignored her. This moment was for remembrance. For her to think about the many things her father had done for her over the years.

When she'd come home from school angry or in tears, it was her father who had consoled her and made her laugh with his silly jokes. He was the one who had nursed her through a scare with the damp lung while her mother had been travelling abroad. A letter had been sent, but of course her mother had not cut her trip short. Through every scraped knee, every tear and heartache, her father had been someone she could rely on and trust. Her mother had merely been a vague presence in the house, constantly disappointed by her lack of excellence at school. Wren had realised a number of years ago that, no matter how hard she tried, it would never be good enough for her mother.

At least she had been blessed to have one parent who truly loved her.

Wren whispered a brief prayer to the Blessed Mother to look after her father on his return trip and then turned back to her guide.

"Didn't you want to say goodbye?" asked Tianne.

"We'd already said everything on the journey here. Anything more is wasted breath."

"I heard you praying. Is it true everyone in Drassia prays to the Mothers of Summer and Winter?"

Wren wasn't sure if Tianne was joking or not, but she decided to take her question at face value.

"Most people in Drassia follow the teachings of the Blessed Mother, but a few follow the Maker. Every summer we give thanks for a good harvest with a festival."

Tianne looked disappointed. "Oh, we do the same thing back home. Most people in Zecorria follow the Lady of Light these days. Come on, I'll show you around."

Tianne led her away from the gate and then along a narrow path between several buildings. They emerged in an open grassy area with a large paved training ground on one side of the square and six long buildings on the others.

"Those are the dormitories," said Tianne, gesturing at the buildings. Their construction was different from the outer wall and finally Wren saw something familiar. Although they'd not been constructed by her people, she could see the dormitories were incredibly well made. Huge slabs of black stone had been used to fashion the walls and the seams between the blocks were barely noticeable. When she touched the stone Wren saw it had been worn smooth over many years.

"They've been here almost as long as the tower," said Tianne, gesturing at the red needle that loomed over everything. It lurked at the corner of her eye and the weight of it seemed to press against her mind. Wren wondered if she would ever get used to the sense of unease.

Trying to put it from her mind she followed Tianne to one of the buildings. The inside of the dormitory was plainly furnished with rows of bunk beds and foot lockers for their belongings. The space inside was only two-thirds full, suggesting that in the past there had been many more students. The washroom was located at the back of the main room and Wren was alarmed to discover that boys and girls were housed together in the dormitories. Tianne explained the dormitories were organised by age group, allowing classmates to spend time together and become friends. Her twitching eyebrows also indicated it was sometimes more than that.

"There seems to be very little privacy," said Wren, struggling not to make it sound like a criticism.

Tianne shrugged. "There are always quiet places if you need to get away. Especially if you meet someone you like," she said with a wink. When Wren didn't respond in kind she covered her mouth in horror. "I'm so sorry. Was that rude? Are you not allowed to kiss before marriage in Drassia?"

Wren took a deep breath before answering. It seemed as if she was not the only one who had a lot to learn about foreign cultures. "Kissing before marriage is permitted, but I'm not here for that. I want to learn about magic."

Tianne relaxed and chatted on about nothing of consequence while she helped Wren unpack her belongings. She seemed to have an unusual interest in other students and who she'd witnessed sneaking away late at night together. Wren smiled and nodded, pretending to listen to the gossip, but in truth her mind was elsewhere.

The thrum of energy at the edge of her perception was much stronger here. If she concentrated she could almost feel it, like a ghostly hand running across the surface of her skin. The air was alive with wild magic from so many children in one place. Wren could feel an untamed echo of it every time they passed another student. Only the older students and adults radiated an odd sense of calm.

She sought the same tranquillity and control of her own magic. For now it felt as if all she was doing was holding it in check and slowly releasing it, like steam from a boiling kettle. Wren sought to understand the nature of magic and how to control it, not be at its whim. Once she had mastered that she would be in charge of her own fate. No one would be able to control her.

For the next hour Tianne showed her around the school and Wren was disappointed at how mundane much of it seemed. The stables, dining hall and exercise field held no surprises, but when they returned to the training ground Tianne was once more surprised by her answers.

A group of unarmed students were practising in two lines, grappling and throwing one another, under the scrutiny of a large, bald man from Seveldrom. The bluff-faced man moved lightly on his feet in a way that Wren recognised from home. By comparison most of the students clomped around as if their shoes were full of lead.

"As well as magic, they teach us how to fight hand to hand

and with swords," explained Tianne. "I'm not very good without a weapon, but I guess you'll be much better than everyone else."

"Why do you say that?"

"Aren't you taught how to fight from birth?"

Wren shook her head, disappointing Tianne once more with a boring dose of the truth. "Drassi boys learn how to fight from a young age. In Drassia the women lead and organise the country. We govern the cities and run the businesses. If a man survives several years in service, then he may give up the mask and become an apprentice in a profession."

"Why aren't you in class?" said a new voice, startling them both.

Wren turned to find a burly man with a shaggy red beard watching them. Her first impression was that he was not a kind man. His eyes seemed cruel and, from the way Tianne reacted, Wren knew he was someone she feared. Even without reaching out to embrace the Source, she could sense a deep well of power within him. Anger clung to the man, wrapping him in its embrace like a thick cloak. From the clenched jaw to the white knuckles on each fist, he seemed on the verge of violence.

Tianne was stammering, unable to meet his gaze. "I was told to show Wren around, by Master Balfruss. She's just arrived today, from Drassia."

Wren kept her chin up and stared into his wintry blue eyes when he looked her way. She did her best not to seem intimidated and was only partially successful. The man simply harrumphed and stalked away without saying another word. Tianne didn't relax until he'd gone around a corner and was out of sight.

"That's Garvey. He's one of the Grey Council."

"He seems very fierce," said Wren, wiping sweat from her forehead.

"He's a rotten bastard."

"Don't say that," said Wren, aghast at the slur. "He's our teacher and should be respected."

Tianne shook her head. "Just wait. See how you feel after a few of his classes. You'll soon change your mind about him."

By the time Wren had completed her tour and then eaten with Tianne in the dining hall, it was early evening. Throughout the day Tianne explained the rules of the Red Tower and Wren committed them to memory. Most were common sense, such as staying away from private areas and only using her magic when supervised by a teacher.

To her relief Wren discovered she wouldn't be expelled from the Red Tower if it took her a long time to grasp the basics. She would be allowed to progress at her own pace and, since she would be a student for an indeterminate number of years, a few more made little difference.

Unfortunately her relief was short-lived when she discovered another reason expulsion never occurred. Accidents with magic often resulted in either a crippling injury or death. Having come very close to losing control a few times, Wren appreciated the explosive power of magic if left to run wild. She also understood why the nameless town was a mile away from the Red Tower. Perhaps that was why the walls of the school looked relatively new. They could have been ripped apart countless times by new students learning how to tame the magic within.

At least finding out she couldn't be expelled had answered one of her many questions, but it didn't lessen her apprehension. She had nothing to relate it to from her past experience. Magic was a total unknown. At least she had that one thing in common with all of the other students. It made her feel slightly less isolated than when she'd first arrived.

"If you'd like, I can still be your guide," offered Tianne. "Just until you find your way around," she added.

"That's very kind. Thank you," said Wren feeling that she couldn't refuse, despite having memorised the layout of the grounds. Besides, it made Tianne smile and it was clear to Wren that she needed to feel useful. She seemed lonely and they both needed a friend. Finding herself alone for the first time in her life, far from home, she was more than a little scared and Tianne's easy manner was making it easier.

Throughout the day Wren had seen how most of the other students had looked at Tianne. They still blamed her people, the Zecorrans, for all those who had died during the war and somehow that meant it was her fault as well. It was the worst kind of prejudice and Wren had no time for such idiocy.

"I hope that we also become good friends," said Wren, trusting she didn't sound needy.

"I'd like that," said Tianne. "You're very easy to talk to."

After their evening meal they had a little free time before bed. In need of some solitude Wren went to the temple devoted to the Blessed Mother. Temple was a grand word for the cramped room with two benches and a small idol. But it was quiet and peaceful. The other student, a young boy of eight or nine, said nothing the entire time Wren was there, for which she was grateful. At times silence was a blessing.

Wren prayed for courage, to see her through the days ahead, and strength to keep the despair at bay that was welling up inside. Her father had always been there for her, but now she had no one to turn to for comfort. She'd never felt so alone in her life.

The idea of a fresh start was still appealing, but as she prayed in the temple on her first night, all her thoughts were of home and everything she'd lost. Silent tears traced their way down her cheeks and the misery inside made her gasp. After a while it began to subside leaving her feeling hollow. When Wren looked up she realised she was alone. The young boy had slipped away unnoticed at some point. In need of company she wiped her face carefully before leaving the room.

When she returned to the dormitories Wren was amazed to see a dozen lanterns fixed to the walls shining with a magical blue light. None of the other students seemed to notice or care. It was only Wren who paused to inspect them.

Peering closer at the lanterns she narrowed her eyes and focused on the swirl of energy within. At first she saw nothing unusual, just a pulsing blue glow. After a few seconds she could see beyond the surface to the matrix within. Wren was surprised at its incredible simplicity and elegance. A glowing strip was decorated with a collection of circular nodes. These glowing elements flew around the tiny magical pathway, only to loop back on themselves, unable to escape and thus maintain the light without the need to feed more energy into it from the Source.

Wren studied the light for a while longer, trying to picture it in her mind. She hoped that eventually she would be able to create something similar.

Moving away from the lanterns she noticed the other students were sitting around their beds in pairs or groups, talking, laughing, reading, telling jokes or playing cards or a game of Stones.

"Wren, this is my friend, Danoph," said Tianne. The tall boy from Shael had the familiar golden skin of his people and their lithe build. He also seemed burdened by a terrible weight and the sadness behind his eyes was palpable. This tragic element also seemed common to the few people she'd met from Shael. All of them had been refugees, unable or unwilling to stay in their own country after all they'd endured. Their suffering during the war had been the worst. Many towns and cities had been utterly destroyed when the country had been invaded by an army of Morrin and Vorga. She'd heard stories about the death camps and fire pits full of bodies that vomited thick clouds of black smoke into the air for days. They were a broken people trying to rebuild their country from the ashes.

When Danoph held out her hand Wren was pleased with herself for not hesitating. As they shook she felt a peculiar tingle on her skin and yanked her hand free. It felt as if she had been stung by an insect.

"Sorry, I'm still learning how to control my magic," apologised Danoph. "Are you all right?"

Wren inspected her hand and found no marks. "I'm not injured."

"They put the lights out soon. You should get ready for bed," said Tianne.

Feeling conscious of her body, Wren changed into her night-shirt in the washroom and quickly slipped into bed beneath her sheets and blanket. She felt several sets of eyes watching her and few of them seemed friendly.

Not long after she'd settled down the other students quickly packed away their belongings and slipped into their own beds. A moment later a figure appeared in the doorway and silence filled the room. Wren couldn't see him very clearly from her bed, but she could just make out a tall man with dark hair. He clapped his hands once and all the lanterns were extinguished. The room was plunged into darkness but as Wren's eyes adjusted she could see some light filtering in from around the edges of the curtains.

Just as she was settling down to sleep light flared behind her eyelids and she sat up, looking around in alarm. Half a dozen students had summoned light globes of their own and some were resuming their previous activities, playing cards or Stones. The magical lights were muted compared to the fixed lanterns, no doubt to avoid detection. Wren guessed from the lack of surprise from those around her that this happened often at night. Determined to get some sleep, she rolled over and closed her eyes.

A second later she was flung out of bed and found herself sliding across the cold stone floor. She only stopped when she collided with one of the walls and the back of her head cracked against the stone. The shock quickly faded as the chill from the floor seeped into her hands and buttocks. Instantly awake she scrambled to her feet.

A crowd was gathering and somewhere towards the rear she could hear Tianne and Danoph trying to reach her. More muted globes flared into being until the whole area was flooded with washed-out blue light. It made all of those wielding them look pale and sickly, like fresh corpses. A tall boy stepped forward from the crowd. He was grinning and full of bravado. Arrayed behind him she could see more like him, loyal minions doing their best to look tough and keep others back. The faces of the other students were already troubled.

"Leave her alone, Brunwal," hissed Tianne. Her voice was muffled and Wren assumed someone was keeping her back.

"Come on," said Brunwal, gesturing for Wren to approach. "Show me how strong you are." When she didn't respond Brunwal grinned and flicked his left hand towards her. Something slapped her across the left cheek hard enough to sting. Wren touched a finger to her lip and it came away with blood.

"You've made her angry now," said one of Brunwal's cronies.

"I will not fight you," said Wren. People booed but she ignored them, focusing on Brunwal. Rather than getting angry he seemed genuinely puzzled.

"Why not?"

"It's against the rules," she explained. If anything he seemed even more baffled by her response.

"So?"

Words and thinking were clearly not important to him. Rather than confuse him further with logic she chose to say nothing. Brunwal balled up his right hand before gesturing towards her with it. Something crashed into her stomach and Wren fell back against the wall, gasping for air.

"Fight me," he shouted. When she'd regained her breath she stood upright and waited. Her inaction seemed to taunt him and he lashed out again, catching her on her right cheek. "Fight me."

Wren said nothing and did not fight back. She did not reach for her magic or attempt to ward off any of his blows.

"Fight me, coward," said Brunwal, growing more annoyed by the second. "Fight me," he shouted over and over again. Each time he said it another invisible hand slapped her across the face or punched her in the torso. Blood ran freely from her face and one eye was starting to swell shut. Her chest and ribs ached with every breath and still he continued to beat her.

Soon she couldn't stand upright so he hit her in the back instead. Brunwal was still shouting when Wren fell, her face pressed against the ground. It was soothing and didn't seem that cold any more. Her eyes started to close and her body felt so heavy.

Somewhere else, Wren thought she heard a commotion and raised voices. Her head was full of wool and all of her attention remained focused on the blood which trickled from her mouth across the floor. She watched it spread into a pool and wondered if Brunwal would beat her to death while the other students looked on.

She heard shouting and crying, there was a loud crash and then silence. Darkness rushed in and she felt nothing.

CHAPTER 6

Habreel had no interest in the architecture of Herakion, the capital of Zecorria, but even he paused in front of the First Church of the Holy Light. It was a massive building that dwarfed every other structure in the city, even the church of the Maker.

Once the enormous cathedral dedicated to the Lord of Light had been a gleaming jewel at the centre of the city. Now, while the outside looked mostly the same, the interior had been transformed from a place of worship for the wealthy into a refuge for the poor. Rededicated to the Lady of Light, the faith, much like the church, had dramatically changed.

Every bit of gold leaf inside the church had been stripped from the walls, melted down and sold. Every commissioned painting had gone to specialist collectors and every piece of exotic furniture now decorated the homes of the wealthy.

A line of beggars and homeless stood outside the church, patiently waiting for whatever food the priests could provide. The rich didn't come here to pray any more, which was a shame, as the church needed their donations.

A spindly figure in a white frayed robe approached Habreel with a wooden plate. It took him a moment to realise the man was a priest of the Lady of Light and not another beggar.

"Can you spare any money for the poor?"

"Of course," said Habreel, fishing out a few coins and then simply emptying his pouch onto the plate.

The priest's eyes widened at the silver coins and started to fill with tears. "Bless you, Sir. May the Lady of Light shine on you."

Habreel shook the man's hand and moved on before anyone else tried to thank him.

The other sights of the city were lost on him, although he was grateful for the tree-lined avenues, which offered patches of shade on such a warm day. The expensive shirt and jacket itched but they were necessary for his audience with the Regent.

The palace gates were guarded by six men and women dressed in colourful yellow and blue striped armour. Their silver breastplates were gleaming and the bright cotton sleeves would have been comical if not for the owners' reputation.

The Zecorran Royal Guard were famed for their weaponry skill. Trained since early childhood they were an elite unit which the Regent had re-established after the Mad King had banned them in his paranoia. All of the Guards held their halberds casually and seemed relaxed, but Habreel had the impression they were waiting to pounce.

Four of the Guards casually studied him while the other two inspected his papers. Habreel was thoroughly searched before one of them escorted him to the next gate where he was passed off to another Royal Guard. He had a brief glimpse of the palace before he was ushered inside the building and down a gloomy and sparse corridor. He soon realised this part of the building was designed for servants and visitors. The broad, well-lit and beautifully decorated parts of the palace were elsewhere.

Habreel was searched twice more before being deposited in a well-furnished room. Three other people sat waiting, two richly dressed merchants and a minor noble. Despite their plush surroundings none of them looked particularly comfortable. Perhaps they resented being treated like everyone else.

An hour later a servant appeared at the door and one of the merchants was led away for his appointment. Taking it as a good sign that it would soon be his turn, Habreel checked his appearance in the mirror. It was another two hours before the second merchant was led away. By that time he and the remaining noble had drunk all of the water and were starting to feel a little cooped up. Conversation seemed like an obvious solution to pass the time, but the noble had stared down his nose when Habreel had asked for his name. After half a dozen more questions were met with nothing but snorts of derision he gave up. Instead he rehearsed again in his mind what he wanted to say and all of the possible arguments he expected from the Regent. He knew the man was powerful and Habreel carefully chose his words. Any suggestion that he was trying to manipulate or influence the Regent would be dangerous and possibly deadly.

Eventually the door opened again and Habreel sighed, expecting that the noble would be led away next.

"Come with me," said the servant, gesturing at Habreel. The nobleman started to protest but the servant closed the door in his face.

Using the servants' corridors again Habreel was led on a long winding path through the palace to a room much like the one he'd just come from. Only instead of the Regent he found a tall Zecorran woman waiting for him behind a desk that was laden with scrolls, books and papers. She was dressed conservatively in a grey dress with a high neck and long sleeves. Her face was lean and her mouth pinched, as if she'd found life far too sour for her liking.

"Sit down," said the woman, gesturing at the seat in front, while she finished writing something. Reading it upside down was difficult but it looked like a letter from the Regent which she then signed. Dipping the end of a wax stick into the flame of the candle on her desk she sealed the letter and then stamped it with the royal crest.

"The Regent doesn't have time to sign everything personally," she explained. "I apologise for the wait, but the palace receives a lot of requests for an audience."

Habreel was confused. "Will I be able to meet with the Regent today?"

"There seems to be a misunderstanding. I'm Bettina, one of the Regent's clerks. I will assess your request and if I think it's worthy of his time, I will send for you on a separate occasion."

"Very well," said Habreel, trying to collect his thoughts. None of his rehearsed conversations had included this. "I wanted to speak to the Regent about the growing problem of magic. In particular the Seekers who are roaming across the country."

Bettina scribbled down a few notes, dipped her pen in the inkpot and gestured for him to continue. "I'm listening," she said, her pen poised above the page.

"Recently there have been some worrying incidents. A number of children have been taken away to the Red Tower."

The clerk looked up from the page. "Isn't that what they're supposed to do?"

"Before the war, few children were being born with magic. As I understand it, the school in Shael had been abandoned for nearly twenty years. A few years ago someone moved in and started to rebuild. Then the tests with Seekers started up again."

"Every nation in the west and Seveldrom signed a decree allowing them monthly access."

Not wanting to get into the legality of Seekers, Habreel continued as if she hadn't spoken. "Now, whenever a Seeker visits a town or village, they normally come away with at least one child who has the spark of magic."

Bettina raised an eyebrow. "What exactly are you accusing them of doing? Abducting children? Or lying about them having magic?"

"It's possibly the latter, but I think it's something more sinister. I think they're giving magic to children."

Silence filled the room as Bettina mulled it over.

"And how would they do that?" she asked, putting down her pen. "Why would they do it?"

"I don't know, but until a few years ago the Red Tower was a ruin. Now that it's been reopened they need students. Over the last six years, they must have taken several hundred children to the school."

"I will admit that my knowledge of magic is limited," said Bettina, "but I thought a child was either born with magic or not. I was told it manifested during, or just before, puberty."

"If that's true, then how do you explain the increase in the number of children being taken away to the school?"

Bettina laughed and Habreel felt a trickle of sweat run down the sides of his face. "I can't, but that doesn't mean the Red Tower is conspiring to steal children and somehow give them magic."

"If a child is born with magic and does nothing with it, then eventually it withers and fades away. It is my belief that the Seekers are waking this dormant magic with their monthly visits. However," said Habreel, forestalling another argument that he could see coming. "Whatever the cause, if we do not get rid of the Seekers, then the number of children with magic will continue to grow. I'm sure you've heard about accidents where children have lost control. But let's pretend every child with magic is found by a Seeker before there are any more incidents. That means the Red Tower will continue to grow in strength. In just ten or twenty years' time they will have an unbeatable army of mages." Bettina's eyebrows lifted in what he thought was surprise so Habreel decided to press on. "You saw what half a dozen mages did during the war. Imagine what a hundred or a thousand fully trained mages could do."

"You have no proof—"

"Magic is dangerous," he said, cutting her off. "It must be eliminated and if we do nothing, everyone will suffer."

Bettina crossed her arms and leaned back in her chair, her expression souring even more. "And what would you suggest that the Regent should do?"

He knew she was baiting him and just playing along, but he had waited all day and would not miss this opportunity to say it aloud. "Ban all Seekers from entering Zecorria. They are dangerous and they make children unstable. The number of children with magic will decline and they may disappear altogether. If any children are born with magic then let their families deal with it. They've done it that way for decades."

A nerve twitched in the side of Bettina's face. She knew what he was talking about. It had been common twenty or more years ago. It normally involved drowning the child in a river, burning them at the stake or stoning them to death. Either that or they ran and were never seen again. Sometimes the parents were weak and the whole family packed up their belongings and left in the night. "You have no proof, just theories and paranoia," said Bettina.

"The threat is real," insisted Habreel. He knew it was the

truth. He felt it right down to the core of his being. In that moment, if he had believed in fate or prophecy, he would've said it spoke through him. "Magic will destroy us all. What happens if another mage goes rogue like the Warlock? Who will stop them? Do you want another war?"

"Guard!" shouted Bettina, glaring at him. A moment later the door opened and one of the Royal Guards appeared. "Escort him to the gate."

Habreel wanted to say something more but he knew it would be pointless. He'd pushed her too far, too soon. She wasn't ready to listen. By now stories of Seekers being banned in a few towns in Zecorria would have reached the palace, but he doubted such information had been passed on to the Regent. It was too soon.

"Thank you for your time," said Habreel, smiling at Bettina and leaving without an argument. The Guard kept an eye on him, as if expecting trouble, but he offered no resistance and even thanked her at the gate.

By the time he made it back to the house he was renting, Habreel felt calm again. He'd been too eager. It was a small setback but it was certainly not the end.

A few of his people were busy in the cramped room downstairs, writing letters and collating information from contacts across the west. Several of his most trusted allies were sowing seeds of their own, ramping up the existing fear of magic and Seekers. Dannel, one of his lieutenants, met him at the foot of the stairs.

"She's waiting for you upstairs," he said with a sour twist of his mouth.

Habreel patted him on the shoulder and went up to his office. Akosh was sitting in his chair behind the desk, idly playing with a dagger. She gave him a wolfish smile and gestured at the visitors' seats in front, as if this was her office.

"I take it by your delighted expression that it went well?"

"It was too soon," he admitted. "Next time they'll be desperate and come to us."

Akosh put away her blade and leaned across the desk, as eager as a hunting dog pulling at its leash. "Is it my turn to play?"

"Are you sure you can find one?" said Habreel.

"Of course. As long as you hold up your end of the deal."

"You'll get your money."

"Then I can find one," Akosh leaned back in her chair, looking smug. "In fact I've got one all lined up. He's young and impressionable and so desperate to please," she said, licking her lips salaciously and giving him a wink.

Habreel wasn't aroused but he pitied the young man who would soon be the sole focus of her attention. He wouldn't stand a chance.

"How bad do you want it to be?" asked Akosh.

"No children," he insisted and Akosh pouted. "I mean it. And make sure a few adults survive. We need them to spread the word, remember?"

"That will make it more difficult."

"I thought you liked a challenge?"

"That's true," admitted Akosh.

"The children will grow up hating Seekers and anything to do with magic. They'll pass that message on to their children and so on. It will be the next two generations that shape the future."

"Give me a few days and I'll get it done," promised Akosh. "Have my money ready for when I get back." She said it lightly but he heard the promise of steel in her words if he didn't deliver.

"Have I ever let you down?"

"Not yet," she admitted. "But I look forward to our conversation when it inevitably happens."

She sauntered around the desk and as she passed Habreel turned to watch her progress. Akosh glanced over her shoulder, fully aware that he was watching her rear. Habreel shrugged. He was only human after all and it didn't hurt to look.

A few minutes after she'd gone Dannel came up the stairs looking flustered. Akosh must have spoken to him. "We can't trust her."

"I know, but we can use her, just as she's using us for her own ends."

"We don't know what she really wants. She's dangerous."

Habreel could only agree. "True, but she's a means to an end. Once she's no longer useful then we'll get rid of her."

"Do you mean kill her?"

"I hope not," said Habreel. "I would like to believe we could both walk away from this arrangement, but I doubt she takes rejection very well."

"But, how would we do it? Isn't she—"

"There are ways," said Habreel, cutting him off. "That's all you need to know. She's only focused on tomorrow. What we're doing will last for decades, perhaps even longer. Are you having doubts?"

Dannel sat down and scrubbed a hand across his face. He had bags under his eyes and there was a touch more grey in his hair than Habreel remembered. "No, but it's more challenging than I imagined."

"Anything worthwhile is difficult. I cherish every life, but if a few have to be sacrificed in order to save thousands, then so be it. There will be a price but I'm prepared to pay it." Habreel was under no illusions. He knew some would think him mad or evil for what he was planning. One day they would come for him in the night but he was at peace with that. Future generations would remember him as a catalyst for change, perhaps eventually he would be called a hero. This was the only way to ensure that people remained free. If he did nothing it wouldn't be long before they were all slaves to the Red Tower and its might. Magic had to be eliminated, once and for all time.

CHAPTER 7

Munroe's arrival in the town of Morheaton in Yerskania passed without incident, which she hoped was a sign of things to come.

She wore no unusual clothing, had not asked any questions and arrived mid-afternoon along with several other travellers. After securing a room in the nicest of the three taverns, she decided to explore the town.

The Seeker had apparently disappeared without a trace but she was confident one of the locals knew what had happened. Now all she had to do was find out who was responsible without killing anyone, unless it was absolutely necessary and couldn't be avoided. It was going to be a challenge.

Morheaton was set high in the hills, half a day's ride from the main road, making it fairly remote. It was surrounded by miles of rolling peaks and valleys where the locals grazed their huge flocks of sheep. Standing in the middle of town she could see and hear them on the hills even though they were miles away. As she walked around Munroe saw no fewer than four shops selling woollen clothing and because of the cool weather all were busy with passing trade.

People went about their business, working in the quarry,

felling trees or tending their sheep. Merchants haggled with shopkeepers over the price of meat, timber and wool. Everything seemed normal. She even saw groups of children running around playing a game. The only thing that slightly worried Munroe was the nature of the game.

As a girl she'd played Lurgy, where one person pretended to have an awful disease. All they had to do was catch someone else to spread it and the game ended when everyone was "infected". The children in Morheaton were playing something similar, but in their game the odd one out pretended they had magic.

After eating her evening meal in the tavern, Munroe relaxed at her table nursing a glass of wine. The room was full with locals and travellers mostly consisting of merchants, their Drassi guards and a few craftsmen. Much to her surprise none of the men in the room tried to chat her up and take her to bed. She wondered if she was losing her touch. Maybe they could tell that she was married.

No one seemed to be on edge. There were no nervous glances or sly looks her way when people thought she wasn't watching. No one was particularly unfriendly and yet Munroe felt an awful prickling across her scalp. She'd come to trust her instincts and right now they were warning her that something was very wrong at the heart of Morheaton.

Not one person, in any conversation, ever mentioned magic or Seekers. Not once. Even now, ten years on, people still talked about the war and the Battlemages who were involved. Everyone loved hearing stories of bravery and tales of wonder where the Battlemages made the impossible a reality. Stories of Titan holding back an army by himself. Eloise rising from the dead and healing herself. Or Balfruss breaking the earth in his final battle with the Warlock. At the very least someone here would have lost a friend or family member during the war. She would even have preferred a negative reaction and an argument about magic compared to this absence. The room was utterly silent on the subject. It was as if the war had never reached the town.

As the night wore on it was becoming increasingly obvious that magic was taboo by its very omission. When Munroe tried asking some general questions about the war at the bar, the owner, a gangly man with one droopy eyelid, didn't even reply. He simply put his glass down and went into the back room.

"What's his problem?" asked Munroe, nudging the person beside her. The man in question was a burly fellow with the weather-beaten face of someone who spent his life outdoors. He smelled fairly ripe and his boots were covered in mud and sheep shit.

"He doesn't like strangers," slurred the shepherd.

"That's not good for someone who runs a tavern."

"Maybe he just doesn't like your face."

"But my face is lovely," said Munroe, fluttering her eyelashes at the man. "Who wouldn't want to spend time with me? I'm adorable."

"I like you, girl," said the man, slapping her on the shoulder hard enough to nearly unseat her. "If I wasn't married and twice your age, I'd buy you a drink."

"If you were half your age and twice as handsome, then I might let you."

The shepherd laughed so hard he bought her a drink anyway. After an hour of talking to Murray, her new best friend, she knew far too much about the lives of various people in Morheaton. She knew about one family with a teenage boy that wouldn't stop stealing. She knew which farmers were arguing about land boundaries and grazing rights, and she knew how the local apothecary had been getting a bit too friendly with the wife of his neighbour. And yet there was not one word about the war, Seekers or children being born with magic.

"So, Murray," said Munroe, feeling safe enough to ask him something more important. "Have you had a Seeker come around here?"

Murray put his drink down on the bar and his shoulders slumped. "Now why did you have to spoil things by asking that?"

"It's just a question."

"Fine, but I'm not talking."

"We had one come to our town a while back," said Munroe. "He took two teenage girls away with him to the Red Tower."

"Good riddance."

"Why do you say that?" asked Munroe.

Murray opened his mouth to say something else but then changed his mind. He glared at Munroe then focused on his drink. The room behind them was still full of noise but now she had the distinct impression someone was watching her. She could feel their eyes on her back as she had an awful itch between her shoulders. Murray drained the last of his beer and went out of the door without saying another word.

A short while later another man sat down on the vacant stool, but this one smelled much better than its former occupant. From the corner of her eye Munroe could see his hands were smooth and without cracks or calluses. When the barman finally made an appearance he ordered an expensive wine instead of cheap beer.

"My name is Burelle and I'm the Mayor of Morheaton. I make it my business to know who is visiting my town and why. This is a peaceful place and I'd like to keep it that way." Munroe expected him to threaten her next. Instead he sniffed his wine before swirling it around the glass.

If anyone stuck out in the room as a sore thumb it was Burelle. The locals were hardy folk who mostly worked outdoors. Burelle was plump with rosy cheeks and a thick nose covered with broken veins, probably from too much wine. His clothes were finely tailored and his silk shirt probably cost more than most people in Morheaton earned in a month. Even his silvery hair was finely coiffed, flowing away from his face and down to his shoulders in waves.

Burelle drained his glass in a few gulps and gestured at the barman for another.

"That makes sense," said Munroe, realising he was just going to wait until she said something. "If I was Mayor I'd want to know who was visiting my town."

"I'm not sure who sent you, but I know why you're here." Burelle seemed incredibly confident given that they'd just met.

"Really?"

"Oh yes," said Burelle, favouring her with a wry smile. "There's nothing here for you to find. You should just move on in the morning."

Munroe sat back in her chair, the very picture of someone at ease. "I've nowhere to be in a hurry."

"You're wasting your time."

"I like it here. As you said, it's so peaceful. In fact, a friend of mine visited Morheaton, not long ago."

"I haven't seen him," snapped Burelle.

"That's strange," said Munroe tapping her lips with one finger. "A minute ago you said you make it your business to know about who visits this backwater shithole."

Burelle sneered. "What did he look like?"

"It was a woman. She was very distinctive. You'd definitely remember her. She wore a long robe, gloves and had a gold mask."

"I never saw her," said Burelle, far too quickly.

"She came through here at least once a month. In fact, she was here only a couple of weeks ago."

It wasn't a warm night and yet Burelle was sweating. He mopped at his hairline with the sleeve of his expensive coat, staining the material.

Burelle stubbornly shook his head. "Doesn't sound familiar."

"Now we both know you're lying. The last time she was here, I heard she took two children with her to the Red Tower."

"Whatever you've been told it isn't true. We don't have any of that filth around here," he said, slamming his empty glass on the bar. Conversation still flowed around the room but now Munroe felt several pairs of eyes watching her and Burelle. "You should leave and never come back. You don't belong here."

As Burelle walked towards the door Munroe looked over her shoulder. Most of the locals were still talking, but many were watching the rich Mayor with hatred and resentment.

Dressing all in black and sneaking out of her room via the window took Munroe back a few years. The last time she'd done something like this it had been as part of her initiation to join the Silent Order. Allegedly centuries old, the mysterious league of assassins was responsible for the death of many rulers, changing the fate of entire countries. Unfortunately her trial hadn't gone to plan as her innate magic had caused a few incidents, such as accidentally burning down a house. But all of that was behind her now and it had eventually led to better things, like studying at the Red Tower and marrying Choss.

Peering down into the street below she could see the common room was in darkness but lights showed in a few of the other windows to either side of her. Moving as quietly as possible to avoid drawing attention to herself, Munroe swung her legs out into mid-air. Placing her hands and feet securely before putting any weight on them, she slowly descended to the ground.

That was the easy part. Not for the first time Munroe wished she'd been able to master camouflaging herself with magic. She'd tried for six months but the subtlety of it evaded her. For now she would just have to rely on more traditional methods for going unnoticed, together with a little of her own style of magic.

It was well after midnight and the whole town was asleep. The streets were empty and almost all of the houses were silent. Candles burned in a few windows but these were few and far between, making them easy to avoid. Anyone who did glance out of their window would only see a dark shadow flitting by. She'd had the forethought to bring a long black scarf which she'd tied around her hair and face.

During the day Munroe had studied the layout so it didn't take her long to find the Mayor's house. It was significantly bigger and more ostentatious than the others, more evidence that Burelle was lining his pockets. Much to her relief there was a light in one window, but a few minutes later it was extinguished. Munroe settled in, hoping that she hadn't arrived just in time to see Burelle go to sleep. If there was no movement in an hour she planned to go to bed herself and try again tomorrow night.

A short time later she heard a door open and close and the sound of receding footsteps. Flitting from one shadow to the next Munroe followed at a distance, always staying just within earshot. She never moved to where she could see Burelle, but she guessed it was him by the heavy steps and breathlessness. If it wasn't him, then the man she was following was equally unfit.

There was a brief murmur of conversation and then a door closed. As she peered around the final corner Munroe was faced with a row of silent and dark houses. There was no movement inside any of the buildings on either side of the street. Staying calm she sneaked around the back of one line of houses, looking for lights and listening for conversation. When she crossed the street and slipped behind the other side it was easy to spot which was occupied. They'd done their best to conceal the light with heavy curtains across the window, but with no other sources of light even a tiny crack was nearly blinding.

Even though Munroe knew she was missing part of the conversation, she approached with caution. She may not have passed all the tests required to join the Silent Order, but she'd learned the lessons well. It was far better to hear a little and escape with her life than be caught by rushing in.

Climbing over numerous objects she couldn't see, and stepping in things she didn't want to identify, Munroe inched closer. The murmur of conversation swelled until she was close enough to hear the voices.

"—going to find out what we did with the Seeker. It's only a matter of time," someone was saying. The man had a whiny voice that immediately grated on her nerves.

"Calm down," said Burelle. "She doesn't know anything. Did you do everything we talked about?"

"Yes, but—"

"Then there's nothing to find. There's no body."

There was a long, pregnant pause before a new female voice joined the conversation. "She's not the only one snooping around."

"What?" asked Burelle.

"There's another stranger in town. One who doesn't belong with the usual crowd of visitors."

"Have they been asking questions?"

"No," admitted the woman, "but it doesn't smell right. I don't believe in coincidences."

"Neither do I," said Burelle. "So, we stick to the plan."

"What if she doesn't leave? If she stays here long enough, someone will talk."

"Then it will be their word against ours," said Burelle. "There's no proof, remember?"

Munroe had heard more than enough. The conversation wasn't over but she knew it was time to leave.

Just as she was starting to turn away someone grabbed her from behind, clamping a hand over her mouth. Their other arm went around her waist and both squeezed tight before she had a chance to scream.

CHAPTER 8

Wren came awake slowly. At first all she could feel was the bed. It was soft and the sheets were warm and smelled of jasmine. As she took a deep breath the aromas of fresh bread and something spicy tickled her nose. Her stomach growled and a fierce hunger seized her body, forcing her eyes open.

"Easy, girl," said a rough voice. She tried to sit up but her arms were so weak they wouldn't bear her weight. Someone gently helped her sit up, before easing her back against some pillows.

It took a few seconds for her eyes to adjust to the light but eventually Wren could see. She was lying in a small room that contained only a bed, a table with a tray of food and a chair. The room was flooded with sunlight from behind her but Wren couldn't see a window. The wall looked like solid stone and yet it glowed. The only door into the room was made of dark metal that was covered with unusual symbols which seemed to be moving. After a few seconds the writhing glyphs started to give her a headache.

"Don't look at them too long," said Garvey, setting the tray of food down on her lap. There was big bowl of some kind of stew and some thick slices of bread smeared with butter. "Eat," he said and Wren didn't wait. She tore into the bread and started dipping it into the stew.

"Am I a prisoner?" she asked, around a mouthful of stew. It was chicken and vegetable and a bit too spicy for her taste, but she was famished and didn't complain.

"Why do you say that?" asked Garvey. She noticed he had heavy bags under his eyes and his beard was wild and unkempt.

"The bare walls. The plain furniture. The thick door. Magic wards, perhaps."

"Well, at least there's been no permanent damage to your head," he said, not answering her question. She had the impression that was his way. He asked much but told people little. Perhaps she had to earn the answers. "What's the last thing you remember?"

Wren paused, the spoon halfway to her mouth. "There was a boy in the dormitory. He wanted me to fight him. He kept beating me and then I blacked out."

Garvey grunted. Turning his face towards the bright wall he closed his eyes. He seemed to be soaking up the light like a cat warming itself in a sunbeam.

"Students have been duelling in the dormitories since before I came here as a boy. It's against the rules and we dissuade students, but it still happens. The strong always want to test themselves."

"Can't you stop it?"

"We can't watch you every hour of every day. This is a school, not a prison."

Wren wiped the bottom of the bowl with her last slice of bread. "And yet this is a cell," she noted.

Garvey finally relented. "It used to be. Now it's a quiet room for convalescence. The door is open if you want to walk out." They both knew she barely had the energy to sit upright never mind walk unaided. "Your strength will return. Healing takes something from both people. Your body needs plenty of food to rebuild itself."

"Did you heal me?" asked Wren.

"No. My abilities lie in other areas." She noticed again he didn't say what those areas were. "I'll send for some more food. You should be able to go back to the dormitory tomorrow." Garvey got up and moved towards the door.

"What about that boy?" asked Wren.

"What about him?"

"Is he in a cell?"

He paused and turned around, leaning against the doorframe. "No."

A seed of dread formed in the pit of Wren's stomach. She had to clear her throat twice before she managed to ask "Is he dead?"

Garvey considered it and a worrying smile crossed his face. The seed blossomed and fresh tendrils made her flesh break out in goosebumps. "Do you think the Grey Council would do something like that?" he asked. Wren wasn't sure. From what she knew about the others she didn't think they would do such a thing. However, Tianne had said he wasn't a good man and her first impression about him being cruel had not changed. "Do you think I would?" he asked.

"No," she lied.

Garvey's smile unnerved her more than the writhing symbols on the door. "No, the boy isn't dead. We've spoken to him about what happened. We don't think he'll attack you again." He didn't sound certain or that he particularly cared.

"What should I do if he does?"

The smile vanished. "You have two choices, Wren. Let him continue to bully you or fight back."

Garvey seemed to be waiting for her to say something. Perhaps this was a test. "What if he's stronger than me?"

That unsettling smile returned and he came back into the room and sat down again. Suddenly Wren felt uncomfortable with him being so close. She was also conscious that they were alone. If she screamed would anyone hear her?

"You won't know how strong he is until you fight back. But, really, that doesn't matter."

"It doesn't?"

Garvey shook his head slowly. "The old Grey Council lied. One of the first things they used to tell new students was that a mage's strength never changes over time. It can and it does. If you push yourself to the limit and then go beyond, just a little, you can stretch your ability. Over time the amount of power you can channel from the Source will grow."

"Isn't that dangerous?"

"If you push yourself too hard, you will die. Most likely you'll explode." Garvey sounded indifferent to the idea.

"Are you saying it's worth the risk?"

Garvey looked disappointed by her question. "If you were a prisoner held in chains, would you sit back and wait to die, or would you try to break them?" Before she could answer he walked towards the door again. "You have to decide. Are you happy to live under someone's boot heel?"

"What if I die?" asked Wren.

Garvey paused with his back to her. Wren couldn't see his face but felt that somehow she'd let him down again. "Then you die. It's better than being a slave."

He went out of the door, leaving Wren with only the writhing symbols for company.

She spent the rest of the day sleeping and waking up to find trays of food had been left for her. Wren wasn't sure she would be able to eat all of it, but every time she had a few mouthfuls it wasn't long before she had cleared the plate. Her first day at the Red Tower had not been the one she'd hoped for, but at least the food was tasty.

Thinking of her father and his approach, Wren tried to see the positives of her situation. The Grey Council were aware of the bully and had already warned Brunwal, so perhaps he wouldn't risk another fight. Then again he seemed to think the rules didn't apply to him. Next her father would tell her to simply ignore the bully, but that wouldn't help either if he attacked her a second time.

She could hear people moving around in the corridor and had the impression that if she cried out someone would be there, but they left her alone to rest. If she claimed to still be in pain they might let her stay in the hospital for another day or two. But pretending to be ill would only delay the inevitable, not make the problem go away.

With nothing else to do when she was awake Wren thought about what Garvey had told her. She had come to the school to learn, not be intimidated by an ignorant boy. He was responsible for missing her first day in a classroom and Wren did not want to miss any more.

A few times she tentatively reached for the Source, feeling its power flood her body, which made her feel slightly drunk. It also made the underlying fatigue vanish and her senses became more acute. It allowed her to hear the whisper of a person's sandals as they roamed the corridor, checking on other patients. She could feel their presence as well. Their connection to the Source created an echo in her mind.

Deep beneath her, in the earth and all around, Wren felt something else. Magic that was both alien and familiar. It was older and far stronger than anything she'd ever known. Reaching towards it with her senses she saw the glyphs on the door of her room start to glow. The moment she stopped they faded and the sense of the other magic in her mind vanished. Wren glanced again at the solid wall behind her and knew that she was inside the Red Tower itself. It was the source of the ancient and peculiar magic.

Late at night, after another meal, she drowsed and thought about tomorrow. They would put her back in the dormitory and Brunwal would be there. She doubted that being reprimanded by the Grey Council would cower him for long. He might pretend it had worked and claim to be sorry, but instinct told her it wouldn't last.

She was alone. Her father couldn't help her now and, as Garvey had said, the Grey Council couldn't watch over them all day and night. It was up to her to fight back or be crushed.

In Drassia a girl was treated as an adult at sixteen. With the emergence of her magic, Wren's special birthday had gone unnoticed. It seemed as if here in Shael she was also expected to deal with her own problems.

Wren embraced the Source and drew power into herself. Its infinite warmth filled her being until she felt as if her skin was stretched tight across her body. Slowly, she reached for a little more, testing her limit. Her head swam and she felt sick, even lying in bed. Letting go was a relief and she felt sweat trickling down the sides of her face from the effort.

Twice more she tried and each time felt as if the limit of her ability was impermeable. It was possible Garvey had told her a lie, but that seemed far-fetched. Even if he didn't have her best interests in mind, she trusted that his knowledge of the Source was greater than her own.

Gritting her teeth in determination Wren took a deep breath and readied herself. She had not travelled all this way, and lost everything in her life, only to be defeated by an idiotic bully in her first week.

She tried one final time, channelling power until she could barely breathe. Until her lungs felt swollen and her vision blurred. Until she felt as if she was a hair's breadth from death. She pictured a cell and chains holding her in place. The chains could be broken and she would be free. All she had to do was hold on and push just a little bit more.

The room whirled around her but she gripped the sides of the bed and held on as if amidships during a storm. The Source thrummed in her veins, a loud drumbeat in sync with the pounding of her heart. She teetered on the threshold and reached for just a little more. Wren realised she was holding her breath but couldn't stop herself. There was a stretching sensation and then a spike of agony in her mind.

With a loud gasp of air she let go of it all and collapsed onto her pillow, drenched in sweat. Eventually her breathing slowed and exhaustion flooded her body. Sleep pulled at her and before she fell into the black Wren didn't know if she'd achieved anything or not. Tomorrow would be the real test.

By mid-afternoon the following day Wren was allowed to return to the dormitory. Her physical strength was fully restored and the intense hunger had faded. She spent a few hours nervously reading some books that had been left on her bed before the other students began to return.

Danoph and Tianne greeted her warmly and she sat with them in the dining hall. Tianne talked almost non-stop the entire time, updating her on what she had missed which seemed like very little of worth. Garvey had been tough in his class, as usual, pushing them all so hard that three students had fainted. No one had seen Balfruss for a few days, suggesting he was away on a mission for the Tower and Eloise remained busy running the school. Tianne commented that she never seemed to stop and was seen at all hours, organising people to make sure everything ran smoothly. Apart from that Tianne had only rumours about Seekers going missing.

Wren appreciated her enthusiasm and attempt to keep the conversation flowing, but a dark cloud hung over all of them. Danoph said very little as well, but she saw him watching the other students with a thoughtful expression. Across the room Brunwal and his group of six friends were having a loud conversation peppered with coarse laughter. She expected him to leer or look in her direction, but he seemed to be ignoring her. Despite his apparent indifference as time wore on she was filled with a growing sense of dread.

When they returned to the dormitory Wren used the washroom as normal but climbed into bed fully clothed. Modesty seemed unimportant when her life was at risk, but she couldn't help it. The lanterns were doused on schedule and a few minutes later some of the students created lights of their own. Lying in the gloom with her eyes closed, Wren waited for the inevitable.

A few times she nearly fell asleep and had to force herself awake or pinch her skin. If he came for her tonight Brunwal would not catch her unawares. Perhaps an hour passed before she sensed someone approaching. An intense echo of power told her a student nearby was embracing the Source. Cracking one eye open she saw Brunwal stalking towards her, flanked as ever by his group of friends.

Wren rolled out of bed and waited with her back against the bunk beds. A crowd began to form and conversations trickled away until silence filled the entire dormitory.

Brunwal stared at her with disdain but said nothing. His friends made jokes and urged him to beat her again and teach her a lesson. Some made crude remarks and Brunwal finally smiled, sizing her up in a way that made her skin crawl.

She knew there was no honour here. He was brutish and ignorant. Subtlety would be meaningless against one so blunt.

Not waiting for him to attack Wren embraced the Source and lashed out. There was no art to her attack. It was simply a solid block of force shaped by her will.

A wall slammed into Brunwal, throwing him backwards and scattering his friends. He skidded across the floor until this time he collided with the far wall. Dazed but unhurt he quickly got to his feet and tried to retaliate with his own magic.

Despite being a student at the school for much longer than Wren it seemed as if he'd learned very little. The physical manifestation of a person's magic was the basest use of power from the Source. Instead of creating anything complex, Brunwal simply pushed with his magic, trying to outmuscle her.

Wren drew more power from the Source and met his attack full on. There was a loud crack as their magic collided and it became a battle of will. Brunwal cursed and spat as he strained against her. On her peripheral vision Wren could see other students watching and cheering her on. Some were taking bets and she saw money changing hands. Many of them must have seen Brunwal do this before with other students. Perhaps he had attacked them as well in his attempt to prove his dominance. Only his friends were supporting him, but their voices were lost amid the din. Noise and movement flickered all around, but in front of her Brunwal was perfectly still.

Sweat started to run down his face from the strain. He fell silent, no longer having the energy for curses, and she sensed him drawing more power from the Source. The air crackled between them as she matched his strength, rendering another stalemate. No matter how hard he pushed he couldn't move her, not even a little.

As he struggled against her, Wren became aware of two

things. First that Brunwal was at the limit of his ability, unable to channel any more power, and, second, that he was afraid. He was throwing everything he had against her and it wasn't enough. Her strength was significantly greater than his. She could feel him trying to reach for more, clawing and stretching, but they both knew even a drop more would be fatal.

Wren thrust her open hands towards Brunwal and his feet came off the floor. His connection to the Source evaporated as he hung in the air, choking for breath. She watched his face turn red and then purple as he clawed at the invisible noose she'd fastened around his neck. Pointing at his chest she flung him against the wall where he stayed, his feet dangling off the ground, gulping in air. All cheering had stopped. The dormitory was silent except for his choking. Wren eased the noose a little, allowing him some air.

"You are weak and I am strong," she said, choosing her words carefully. She needed to make sure her message was clear. "Say it." When Brunwal hesitated Wren marched up to him and slapped him hard across the face, leaving a red handprint on his cheek. "Say it," she repeated.

"You are strong," said Brunwal, but she knew it wasn't enough. Beating him wasn't enough. Shaming him wasn't enough. She needed to render him powerless and that meant taking away their fear of him.

"And?" she pressed, holding up her hand again.

"I am weak," he whispered. In the silence of the room every student heard him. And with those words something changed. The air of menace around him evaporated. He was no longer a terrifying thought that plagued her mind. He was just a stupid boy. Wren released him and Brunwal fell to the ground, sobbing quietly.

Looking at the crowd she noticed his friends had disappeared, returning to their beds as if they'd never been part of this.

When she looked at the faces of the other students she was startled to see fear in their eyes, but not of Brunwal. He had been the strongest and scariest student in the dormitory but he was broken. Wren had beaten and embarrassed him.

Now they had someone else to fear. They were scared of her and what she might do to them.

CHAPTER 9

"Don't struggle," said the woman holding a hand over Munroe's mouth. "Or the sentry will hear us."

If her arms hadn't been pinned to her sides Munroe would have stabbed her assailant with a dagger. Instead she started reaching for the Source when the woman's words finally penetrated her panic.

"To the right," whispered the woman.

The sentry was difficult to see but eventually Munroe picked him out. He was standing in the shadows at the end of the row of houses. She'd come from the other direction but now she wondered if this had been a trap. If she tried to retrace her steps, would she find they were boxed in on both sides?

"Don't scream," said the woman, slowly easing her hands away from Munroe's mouth and body. In the gloom she couldn't make out much about the other woman except that she was tall and freakishly strong. "There's another guard behind us," said the woman. "Can you distract the one in front?"

"Who are you?"

"Tammy Baker. Balfruss sent me to keep an eye on you."

"He did what?" hissed Munroe. "Why?"

"Do you really want to talk about this now? Here?" said

Tammy. Munroe hated to admit it, but she had a point. "Can you distract the sentry?"

Munroe swallowed her irritation and embraced the Source. Power flooded her body and her senses became more acute. She couldn't see in the dark, that Talent was beyond her abilities, but the shadows had peeled back a little. Now the sentry was more than just an inky outline. She could make out that he wore armour of some kind and carried a sword on his belt. Although he looked relaxed, she noticed he was constantly scanning the area for trouble, his head turning this way and that.

Focusing on the roof above the sentry's head, Munroe extended her senses towards the tiles, looking for imperfections. She felt moss, rotting leaves, bird shit and scattered seeds before finding what she was after. There was a dull crack and three tiles slid off the roof. The sentry moved away from the edge of the building and lifted his head in time for the first tile to hit him in the face, breaking his nose. The second hit him on the crown of his head and the third on his left temple. He dropped to the ground in a silent heap, bleeding but alive.

"Let's go," said Munroe, not waiting to see if Tammy followed. She crept past the window and then scuttled along more quickly. Once they were back on the main street she let go of the Source and there was a distinct dulling of her senses.

She was tempted to run, putting some distance between her and the unconscious man, but knew that would look suspicious. Instead the two of them casually walked back to Munroe's tavern as if they'd been out for a midnight stroll.

"Can you climb up?" said Munroe, gesturing at her first-floor window. The front door of the tavern would be locked by now, so this was the only way in without drawing attention. The rest of the windows were dark so they had to do this quietly.

"You go first, I'll follow," said Tammy, keeping an eye on the street.

Retracing her route and digging her fingers into the pitted stone, Munroe scampered up the wall like a squirrel. Once inside her room she lay on the floor for a minute, listening to the rest of the building for any sounds of movement. There was nothing, just the occasional snore and squeaky fart from neighbouring rooms.

With a couple of grunts of effort Tammy climbed up the building and through the window. Once the window was closed and the curtains drawn, Munroe lit a lantern and got her first real look at her large new friend.

"Have we met before?" asked Munroe, eyeing up the other woman. There was something familiar about her, but she couldn't place it.

"I'm a Guardian of the Peace. I used to live in Perizzi."

Munroe grunted. That made sense. She might have seen her around the city at some point over the years. She would be hard to forget, being nearly as tall as Choss but not quite as wide. Tammy had the pale skin of someone from Yerskania but the height of a Seve, indicating a mixed heritage. Almost immediately Munroe noticed the scarring on her hands and sunken knuckles, also just like her husband. Others might find it peculiar, that a fighter had become a Guardian, but Munroe had seen far stranger things in her life. A Guardian who could talk to the dead. A mage who could transform his flesh and absorb someone else's memories. A hole torn in the fabric of the world to another place she still couldn't fathom.

Who would have thought that she, as someone who had once worked for one of the crime Families of Perizzi, would end up a mage at the Red Tower.

Life was fucking weird.

"How do you know Balfruss?"

Tammy sighed and touched the sword on her belt. "We worked together in the past."

"That's nice and vague."

"It was in Voechenka. It's a city in Shael. He gave me this," said Tammy, resting a hand on her sword again.

"I've heard the name before," admitted Munroe, "but Balfruss won't talk about it, at all. But I know something important happened there."

There were a lot of rumours but Balfruss wouldn't even admit he'd been there when she'd asked him about it. Voechenka had been destroyed during the war, but that was not why it had a reputation. Balfruss, and apparently Tammy, had been sent there a few years ago to deal with something lurking in the shadowy ruins.

"What happened there is better forgotten," said Tammy. "It was a dark time."

"So why are you following me?" said Munroe, crossing her arms. She was trying her best not to get annoyed, but was struggling. She didn't like the fact that, despite having lived at the Red Tower for years and spoken to Balfruss almost every day, Tammy seemed to know more about him than she did.

"Balfruss told me this was your first mission for the Red Tower. He also said you're not very subtle."

Munroe wanted to argue but really she couldn't disagree with that assessment. Still, she didn't like being kept in the dark. "Did he tell you anything else?"

"Only that a Seeker had gone missing and that you're a powerful mage."

Munroe wasn't sure if Balfruss had really said that or Tammy was attempting to pay her a compliment but she let it go for now.

"So what do you think has happened to the Seeker?"

"I heard part of Burelle's conversation. It ties in with what I've seen."

"Which is what?" asked Munroe.

"Guilt."

Munroe agreed. It seemed as if her worst fear had come true. She'd arrived too late and the Seeker was already dead. "From what Burelle and the others were saying, it sounds like they killed her and hid the body. They were confident we'd never find it."

"Then it's time to leave," said Tammy, gesturing at the room. "Pack up your belongings."

"Leave? Burelle and the others need to be punished. Preferably with an axe to the head, or a sharp knife in the groin."

"Munroe."

"I thought you were a Guardian?"

"I am, and justice will be served. But if we don't leave now, we could also end up buried in unmarked graves. Then no one will ever know what happened to the Seeker and they'll never find our bodies either."

"I can take care of myself," said Munroe, willing someone to come through the door. She could kill them all with a glance before they took two steps towards her.

"So can I against a few, but not a whole town. You've spent the day here. Tell me what you've seen."

Munroe thought about how the locals had reacted to her presence. Everything appeared normal on the surface and yet she'd felt on edge. Her new friend Murray had been willing to talk to her right up to the moment she'd mentioned the Seeker.

"They're scared. But I can't believe the whole town was involved in murdering the Seeker."

Tammy shook her head. "I think some of them were there

when it happened and the rest were told to mind their own business. Some may even have known what was going on, but they did nothing to stop it. Guilt is keeping them quiet. You've seen how Burelle runs this town. I think he's threatened everyone if they talk."

"How could someone just stand there and do nothing?" asked Munroe, struggling to understand. Morheaton was a small town and the people who lived in such places were not like those in the city. She wasn't naïve. She'd lived in Perizzi and seen people inflict horrible cruelties upon one another. But in a place like this with a small community, where everyone knew each other, it seemed impossible. "We can't let them get away with this."

"What would you suggest?" asked Tammy.

"I don't know."

"If no one will talk, how do we prove that anyone was murdered? Can you raise the Seeker's spirit like Guardian Fray?"

Three times a year Fray came to the Red Tower to study. He also let the Grey Council watch him as he used his rare Talent which allowed him to speak with the dead. They had been trying to unravel it for over six years and were only just starting to understand it.

"No, I can't do that."

"Then do you want me to just arrest Burelle and wait for him to confess? They'd never let us leave town with him."

"I can stop anyone who gets in the way," insisted Munroe, confident in the strength of her magic. She could hold off dozens of people if necessary with a solid wall of force.

"I'm sure you can. As long as you see them coming. I also know that eventually you'll need to sleep."

Munroe didn't need her to spell out the rest. Even if they somehow managed to grab Burelle and make it out of town his friends would follow them at a distance. At some point she would fall asleep and, as competent as she thought Tammy was, not even she could hold off a dozen armed thugs.

She hated it. Hated it deep down in her guts, but she knew there was only one choice.

Moving quickly around the room Munroe shoved her belongings into her saddlebags. She was angry at the people of Morheaton. She was angry at Burelle and his friends for getting away with murder. And she was angry at herself that, despite having powerful magic, there was nothing she could do about it. She couldn't even find the body so that the Seeker's family had a sense of closure.

"I asked a few merchants some questions about other towns in the area," said Tammy, glancing out of the window at the street. "Someone has been riling the locals. Preaching to them about the dangers of magic and that all Seekers are evil."

"Then this wasn't just about Morheaton."

"No," said Tammy, "This isn't an isolated incident. I think it's the start of something." She pulled the curtain closed and doused the lantern. "Someone is coming."

"Who?"

"Four armed men. I think Burelle has decided not to wait. They're coming for you."

"I think it's time for a little payback," whispered Munroe.

"Can you do it subtly?" asked Tammy, moving to stand behind the door.

"Maybe."

"Try not to kill them, or burn down the whole tavern."

"How—"

"No time," said Tammy.

Munroe ground her teeth and climbed into bed, fully clothed. Beneath the sheets she held a knife at the ready while Tammy pulled on a pair of leather gloves.

In the deep silence of the night, Munroe heard the rattling of the lock downstairs as the thugs forced open the front door. She tracked their progress through the building as the stairs creaked under their weight. There was a lull and silence briefly returned before the door flew open, nearly hitting Tammy in the face.

Two men came into the room carrying daggers. One of them held a lantern which he set down on the table. The men were burly and had the bearing of street thugs. That meant men who had plenty of muscle and were good at following orders. A glance at their faces told her they weren't good at thinking. It probably wasn't an important attribute for them.

"You need to pack your things and leave town," said one of the men, looming over the bed and waving his dagger in a threatening manner.

"I'm all packed and ready to go," said Munroe, gesturing at her saddlebags. The thug stared at them and seemed lost for words. Perhaps he'd been expecting her to argue rather than just agree so quickly. He was baffled and clearly hadn't been given any instructions on what to do if Munroe complied. "I'm leaving in the morning."

"Oh. That's good then," he said, putting away his dagger. "Thank you. That's lovely. We'll leave you to get some sleep."

The bedroom door slammed shut. As one of the thugs turned around Tammy slugged him in the face. The thug went down and stayed there. Thinking Tammy was the greater threat the other turned towards her, just in time for Munroe to jump out of bed and smash the lantern into the back of his head. He dropped to the floor in a heap with a muffled grunt.

When the door flew open a second time Munroe was ready. She leaped onto the third man and started beating him about the face. From the cries of pain behind her she knew Tammy was taking care of the fourth thug. Screaming as Munroe gouged at his eyes the thug slammed her into the wall. She was tempted to use her magic, but right now Burelle had no reason to connect her directly with the Red Tower. Using magic would only add to their problems.

Releasing her grip she dropped to the ground and slammed an elbow into the man's groin. He stopped struggling and stared at her for a few heartbeats, frozen in place. A moment later the pain hit him and he started to screech like a bird. As he started to curl up in pain Munroe punched him in the face, just as Choss had taught her. The jab was well timed but the thug didn't fall. Instead he stumbled backwards, tripped and fell down the stairs, landing in a tangled heap at the bottom. The ruckus would have woken up half of the building and yet no one had opened their door to investigate. It seemed as if the locals were willing to look the other way for just about anything.

"Was that you trying to be subtle?" asked Tammy.

"It wasn't my fault," said Munroe, wondering how many times she'd said that in her life.

"Maybe we should take the backstairs," suggested Tammy.

After collecting her belongings they went out the back and around the side of the building to the stables. Munroe expected to find more men lying in wait, but Burelle had underestimated her. They retrieved Tammy's horse without any issues and rode out of town without seeing another person. At first she wondered if they'd just been lucky, but soon realised it was something else. Ignorance was bliss in Morheaton and the people thought they were safer not knowing and getting involved.

Seething with anger, Munroe rode away from the town and made a promise to herself. One day she would return to deal with Burelle and whoever else had been responsible for the Seeker's murder. Then she'd show them what her magic could do.

CHAPTER 10

Choss's attention was drawn away from the sparring pair of students as another laden wagon headed out of the main gates. That was the fifth he had seen in as many days. Normally they came into the Red Tower full of supplies and left empty with happy merchants. It took a lot to keep all the students fed, clothed and washed. As he'd learned over the last few years, magic could only do so much.

When he'd first arrived at the school it had been as Munroe's husband and he'd sought work in the nearby town. In return for helping the town warden keep the peace, especially at night, he'd been given a room and his meals. After only a month he'd moved into the school and started teaching the students how to fight with their bare hands and weapons. He and two other members of staff were trying to teach the children how to protect themselves in all circumstances.

Balfruss came into the courtyard with Garvey. The two men were in mid-conversation and, despite being too far away to hear what was being said, Choss could see Balfruss wasn't happy. He kept shaking his head and Garvey kept insisting on something, but the Sorcerer would not be moved. They were as stubborn as each other, like iron and granite. Neither would back down.

If not for Eloise to act as a mediator the Grey Council would never make any decisions.

Occasionally Choss would sit with Balfruss and they'd drink and talk about their lives. Sometimes they'd tell stories, but they were not tall tales about Balfruss the Sorcerer, or what he and Munroe had done in Perizzi a few years ago. These were smaller stories about their family, their hopes and dreams.

Not once, in all the years he'd been at the Red Tower, had Choss had a personal conversation with Garvey. Sometimes they would speak about the students, or the stables or another aspect of keeping the school running. Beyond his name, Choss knew nothing about the other man. Whoever he had been before coming here, and whatever he'd done, Garvey didn't want anyone to know about it. Balfruss and Eloise were aware, as they had vouched for him and asked for his help in running the school, but they weren't talking either.

Choss knew there was a deep well of anger in him because it was all too familiar. Perhaps that was why they'd never got along. Choss had overcome his demons and learned to control the anger that had haunted him throughout his life, whereas Garvey seemed to feed on his rage. Whatever the horrors or tragedies in his past, they still fuelled him to this day.

"Speak to her if you want. I will not change my mind," said Garvey, as he walked away from Balfruss. "It must be done. These days, difficult choices are all that's left to us."

Choss and Balfruss watched the other Sorcerer cross the courtyard and disappear through the main gates. A few students had noticed the exchange as well but Choss quickly turned them back to their practice. He walked up and down the line, correcting postures, straightening backs and raising elbows. Some didn't see the point of learning how to fight with steel and their bare hands. They thought that their magic made them untouchable, but he knew otherwise.

Every couple of years a demonstration was needed where Choss would flatten a student using only his fists against their magic. Now when he said it, most of them listened and stopped complaining.

A mage could die just as quickly as someone else with a foot of steel in their belly. Everyone knew that one of the Battlemages had died with a knife in his back during the war. Only a few people knew the Battlemage in the stories, Darius, had been Eloise's late husband and a close friend of Balfruss. The Warlock had walked up behind Darius when no one was looking and stabbed him to death. Magic required an enormous amount of willpower and concentration, which wasn't always easy to summon at a moment's notice. Sometimes a sword or a fist would do the job just as well.

"Swing with your whole body," said Choss, touching Tianne on her shoulder. "Use your hips to throw the punch. You'll get more power behind it." The girl tried again and this time got it right. Her partner, the new short girl from Drassia, only had to be shown how to do something once. After that all of her movements were precise and exact, time after time.

"How are they getting on?" asked Balfruss, coming to stand beside him.

The Sorcerer's presence unsettled the students and a few fell out of sync with their sparring partners. "Eyes on your partners!" said Choss, and the pupils twitched as if they'd been slapped.

They moved a short distance away so they could talk privately while Choss could still keep an eye on them.

"I didn't mean to disturb your lesson."

Choss waved it away. "They're easily distracted. They still have a lot to learn."

"How is Samara?"

"In good spirits. She doesn't seem to be in much pain."

"She's stubborn. I can see where her daughter gets it from," said Balfruss. He could only agree, not that he'd ever say that to his wife or out loud to his mother-in-law. "Tell her to visit Eloise before the pain gets unbearable."

"I will suggest it but . . . " Choss trailed off and shrugged his shoulders. They both knew neither Samara nor her daughter could be made to do anything they hadn't already decided for themselves. "Have you heard from Munroe?"

"Not yet. I will let her know you were asking after her."

"Thank you."

Balfruss clapped him on the shoulder and went inside the tower itself. The building still made Choss feel uncomfortable. Even though he knew it didn't move, it always seemed to be lurking at the corner of his eye. He'd never been inside and didn't want to either. Some of the pupils thought it mysterious and wonderful. Others were unnerved by it. Like most things that were dangerous, Choss had a healthy regard for it and that meant keeping his distance.

Putting the Red Tower from his mind he turned his attention back to the students and noticed several were sneaking worried glances at the new girl, Wren. It seemed that not all of their discomfort had been because of Balfruss.

With no classes to teach that afternoon, Choss took a horse from the stables and rode east at a gentle walk. After an hour the ground began to dip and he followed a well-worn trail down to the river. In truth it was only a small branch of the mighty Suzoa, a vast, churning river that was so wide and powerful it could only be crossed in a few locations with enormous stone bridges. It ran north to south all the way from the mountains down to the coast.

It was so deep in places it was a challenge even for a Vorga to reach the bottom. Or so he'd been told by Gorraxi over the years.

Choss tethered his horse to the post he'd set up beside the small cabin and went inside. The floor was dry and nothing seemed to have been moved since his last visit. The main room wasn't large and it held little in the way of furniture, just a table, a few chairs, cupboards for storage and a small wood stove which was mostly for his comfort in winter.

They'd built it together, not as somewhere for either of them to live, merely a place to meet. His home was at the school with his family while she mostly lived in the river and the ocean. But sometimes she spent a few days on land and they would meet. Other times when he visited the cabin she was away, so he would fish and enjoy the quiet and solitude, a stark contrast to the constant bustle at home.

There was no bedroom but a wide set of steps in the middle of the room descended into a large stone cellar beneath the house. It was split into two rooms and was large enough for him to stand upright, making the ceiling nearly seven feet high.

Some of the cheese he'd left in the cold larder was gone and he presumed it had been eaten by Gorraxi. In its place sat a stack of salted snapper fish which were his favourite. He emptied his bag, leaving a few items in the larder before taking some fish in their place.

Just as he was coming out of the front door he heard the creaking of the wooden pier and the thump of heavy footsteps. In response his horse whinnied and tried to pull free from where he'd tied it up. No matter how many times he came here, or even which horse he chose, they never got used to being close to Gorraxi.

"I was just about to leave," he said to the Vorga as she walked up the pier towards him. "You nearly missed me."

Gorraxi was dripping wet and seemed to be shining with an inner light. Being in seawater revitalised her people in a way that he still didn't understand, but he knew it could heal her wounds. Most people would be intimidated by seeing a hulking green Vorga walking towards them, showing its teeth and armed with a net and spear. Choss just smiled back and embraced his friend, being careful not to jab himself on one of the bony ridges around her jaw.

Vorga were not human and as such most people didn't understand their behaviour or their culture. Their customs were alien, they prayed to Nethun, god of the sea and storms, and their warring nature appeared abrupt and unfriendly to outsiders. There were a few Vorga merchants who visited human cities across the west, but no human ever went into their homeland.

"I'm glad to see you," said Gorraxi, offering him another toothy smile. "Can you stay a while?"

"Of course," said Choss, noting that the net was full of spiky lion fish. They were poisonous to humans and vicious looking creatures, but to Gorraxi they were a delicacy. She went inside to dump her belongings and came out nibbling on a wedge of the goat's cheese he'd left behind. After a few years he was finally starting to get the knack of making it. Not that she'd complained when his first attempt had been tart and all but inedible. He also noticed she was dressed in a kilt and vest, a tradition she'd adopted when on land, even around him. There was no need for clothes in the ocean and they would be a hindrance, but on dry land she'd realised it made humans feel more comfortable in her presence. Gorraxi had been around humans for many years now and was starting to pick up a few habits without realising.

"You are tense," said Gorraxi, reading his body language. She'd always been able to do that with ease. There were no secrets between them and she spoke freely about what she observed. Over the years he'd realised she was a lot more astute than he appreciated. Gorraxi sat down on the bench beside him and he smelled the ocean on her skin.

"I'm worried about Munroe. She's been gone for a couple of weeks now."

"But you were expecting this."

"I know, but I still worry," admitted Choss.

"Your wife is small, but mighty," said Gorraxi, popping the last bit of cheese into her mouth. "Her magic is powerful."

"It is."

"So is her mouth," said Gorraxi and Choss laughed. "It is good that you worry. It tells me that your love for her is still true. The bond is still strong here," she said, tapping herself on the chest. "Is there something else that worries you?"

Choss knew he could trust her but he still hesitated because it was just a feeling in his gut. "Yes, but I don't know what it is. But I feel it," he said, touching his heart and then his head. "There is tension in the air at the Red Tower. It's probably nothing."

"I will be nearby for a while, if you want to talk," said Gorraxi. "And if you need me for anything, call, and I will be there."

"Thank you," said Choss with a smile. They were so different and yet she was probably his closest friend.

"I am going to roast the lion fish," she said, gesturing at the fire pit. "Do you want to stay and try some?"

"I should be getting back. Samara is watching over my son, but she tires easily."

Gorraxi nodded and busied herself clearing the ashes. "Can I ask a small favour?" she said, her eyes on the task at hand. One of her sail-like ears flipped away from the side of her head and back. He knew it meant she was nervous.

"Of course."

"Would you bring your son to visit me again? It was good to meet him."

Their first meeting had not gone well as Sam had cried and run screaming the moment he saw Gorraxi. Subsequent visits had been a little better, but sometimes he still had nightmares about green monsters from the sea coming to get him. Choss knew that Munroe blamed the Vorga but she'd not forbidden further visits. Gorraxi was an outcast from her own people and had no family of her own. Choss and his family were the closest thing she had. Perhaps it would be better to bring Sam for another visit soon, before Munroe returned.

"I will bring him soon for a visit. I promise."

"Thank you," said Gorraxi with a shy smile.

Choss embraced his friend and then untied his horse. She stayed back, seeing how nervous the animal was, but remained outside to wave him off.

The peace of his visit was slightly spoiled on the ride back as the growing sense of foreboding returned. When the Red Tower came into view above the trees Choss felt himself reaching for a weapon, but he'd not worn one in years. Perhaps now would be a good time to start again.

CHAPTER 11

This time when Tammy entered the Khevassar's outer office his assistant, the new Rummpoe, didn't hesitate to tell the Old Man immediately of her arrival. She sensed a lingering tension in the air but Rummpoe seemed a lot more contrite than on her previous visit.

As ever the Old Man sat amid a mountain of paper scattered across his desk. "Report," he said, gesturing at the chair opposite. She'd come straight from the stables and was stiff and saddle-sore. Tammy gratefully sat down and stretched out her long legs, massaging her calves while the Khevassar sipped at his tea.

"The situation in Morheaton isn't good. It's the worst news in some ways." She went to tell him about Burelle, the murder of the Seeker and the town's attitude towards magic.

"I've been hearing some interesting rumours from some of Queen Morganse's agents in the north," he said, tapping a stack of papers. Like most of her counterparts in the west the Queen of Yerskania had a vast network of spies. "One girl in Zecorria killed herself, rather than be taken to the Red Tower. After that, the town banned Seekers from ever visiting them again. So far it's fairly peaceful towards them, but other towns in Zecorria are starting to adopt the ban. I expect it soon will happen elsewhere."

"This isn't a coincidence."

"Any theories?" asked the Old Man.

"I listened to conversations around Morheaton, and someone had been there a few weeks before, stirring up the locals. People have been afraid of magic for a long time and the war only made it worse. Someone is building on that fear and blaming the Seekers, even though their job is to help the children."

"Did you know that the Warlock studied at the Red Tower?" he asked.

"No, but it makes sense. He was once a student."

"That story is also popular in taverns at the moment. It's souring people on the Red Tower."

Tammy could see where this was going. "So whenever someone sees a gold mask they inevitably think of the Warlock."

The Khevassar nodded sagely. "Anyone could be under that mask. Any child taken away could become the next Warlock."

"This is being carefully orchestrated."

"My reports from the north say much the same thing," mused the Old Man. "My fear is the murder of the Seeker in Morheaton is only the beginning."

"I agree."

"So, what would you suggest we do?" he asked.

Tammy tried to ease the tension in her shoulders as she thought it through. "We need to find the other Seekers and warn them they may be targets. Perhaps get them into hiding for now. If we can get ahead of any assaults or another murder, we might be able to find out who is pulling the strings."

"The golden masks make it difficult to identify Seekers," said the Khevassar. "Keeping them anonymous was a good idea at the time, but how do we find them?"

"My guess is Balfruss will have the same idea as us. He'll want to protect his people. Munroe can help us find Seekers here in Yerskania."

"What about other countries?" he asked.

Tammy ticked them off on her fingers. "There are no Morrin or Vorga mages, so we don't have to worry about them. We'll leave Shael to the Red Tower, since it's on their doorstep. Mages have no place in Drassian society and they've always sent children to the Red Tower. Besides, all foreigners stick out like a sore thumb."

They weren't xenophobic, but visiting Drassia always involved an awkward dance of being overly polite, so as not to cause offence. A simple break in protocol was enough to do that. Tammy couldn't see an outsider being allowed to remain in the country long enough to stir up trouble. They simply wouldn't tolerate it and the offender would be firmly, but politely, escorted to the border.

"And the rest?" asked the Old Man.

"Zecorria will not allow us to send Guardians into their country uninvited, but we still need up-to-date information about what's happening there."

The Khevassar scribbled down a note. "I'll speak to Queen Morganse. See if some of her agents in the north can be persuaded to help. I'd like to send in a few Guardians, too, undercover of course."

"I can suggest half a dozen names," offered Tammy.

"Good, leave them with Rummpoe."

"So that leaves Seveldrom."

Despite Seveldrom and the west being on opposite sides during the war, Queen Talandra had become a good friend of their Queen, Morganse. The two of them were determined to ensure that nothing divided their two nations in the future.

The Old Man grunted. "I'm sure Queen Talandra will have something to say about people trying to commit murder in her country. Especially as she was an early advocate of bringing Seekers back. I know Queen Morganse has recently been in touch with her, but I'll make sure Talandra's network gets everything we have. Her people will have to do their best to protect Seekers in Seveldrom. So that just leaves Yerskania in our hands."

"It all sounds so easy when you say it like that," said Tammy with a wry smile. "Because everything always goes according to plan."

The Khevassar smiled briefly. "It's going to get bloody," he warned her. "There will be some tough choices ahead."

"What are you saying?"

Some of the steel crept back into his rheumy eyes. "You had a taste of it in Morheaton, letting them get away with murder—"

"For now. Justice will be served," she reminded him.

His grin was wolfish. "Yes, it will, but not just yet. However, soon you'll be faced with a situation where there are only difficult and unpleasant options. I hope you can live with those decisions on your conscience."

"That sounds ominous." She also didn't think it sounded like the Khevassar she knew.

"I'm just trying to prepare you," he muttered, almost to himself. "Get some rest and keep me updated on your progress with the Seekers and Munroe."

"Yes, Sir," she said, moving to the door. Pausing on her way out Tammy looked back over her shoulder and wished she hadn't. The Khevassar looked so old and frail, all alone in his office. She felt a stab of pity for him and hurried out, wiping at her eyes.

CHAPTER 12

Taking another deep breath, Munroe tried to calm her frantic mind. Worries about her mother and family were flying around, preventing her from finding any kind of inner peace. Meditating with her eyes closed wasn't working, so instead she lit the huge candle she'd brought with her. It was almost as fat as her forearm and would burn for several days if left unattended. Hopefully she wouldn't need it for long tonight.

The flame danced and flickered until she closed the window. It felt peculiar to be back in Perizzi and it was not at all like coming home. It had taken years but eventually she'd escaped the city. To come back voluntarily felt like a betrayal and a step backwards. But the job wasn't done and there were other Seekers that needed protecting.

So far she'd not seen anyone she recognised and she wanted to keep it that way. She wasn't the same person any more. Munroe wanted to leave Perizzi and go back to where she belonged as soon as possible.

The tavern she was staying in was popular with visitors and located in the bustling heart of the city. That meant the streets were regularly patrolled by the Watch and, beyond a few pickpockets, there were few criminals from any of the crime Families. Trying to rob someone here just wasn't worth the risk and aggravation that would follow. The people she had dealt with in the past tended to stick to the shadows and avoid the bright lights. The odds of her running into them were very small.

Realising she was getting distracted again Munroe focused on the flame. With the window closed the flame didn't waver. Staring into the heart of the fire she focused on the tiny blue centre and tried to let go of her anxieties. Her shoulders eased and her breathing deepened as her mind started to drift.

Lifting her eyes from the candle she stared at her reflection in the standing mirror. Minutes passed in silence as she did nothing except stare at her twin and the candle in the glass. With her mind finally at peace she summoned an image of Balfruss in her mind and drew power from the Source. The magic thrummed in her bloodstream and all of her senses became more focused. She heard scratchy, uneven music from a few streets away as a child practised on the fiddle. Her room at the tavern had been well aired when she'd first entered, but now she could smell old food that had been spilled on the floor. A tiny spider was silently spinning in the far corner behind her while several flies vainly struggled to break free of the sticky web.

Keeping her eyes open Munroe concentrated on the picture of Balfruss in her head and brought to mind all the little details she could remember. The three scars on his jaw that he refused to let anyone heal. The greying beard and thinning hair. The tribal tattoo around one of his wrists and the deep sadness behind his eyes.

Even before arriving at the Red Tower she'd heard stories about him and not just those about how he had defeated the Warlock. After the war he'd travelled across the Dead Sea to distant lands most people thought were only myths. Sometimes

Choss mentioned something Balfruss had told him during one of their drinking sessions which left Munroe with her mouth agape in amazement.

Staring at her reflection Munroe trickled a little bit of magic into the mirror and pictured Balfruss sitting on the floor opposite her. The glass rippled once like the surface of a pond and then was perfectly still. Sweat began to trickle down the sides of Munroe's face and her knees were aching, but she gritted her teeth and tried to ignore it all. Reaching out with one hand she pressed her fingers against the surface which now felt unusually warm to the touch.

The glass turned cloudy and then black before returning to normal. Instead of seeing herself in the mirror the reflection showed Balfruss sitting in a room she didn't recognise. He looked more tired than she'd pictured and his clothes were rumpled and mud-spattered from travel. On the floor beside him she saw a candle like her own but also a wicked looking axe.

"Focus," he whispered and she concentrated on her connection to the Source. The power thrummed in her veins and Munroe knew there was so much more she could summon. Power enough to flatten the entire room or destroy the whole tavern if she wanted. It was intoxicating and alluring, to draw more power and use it to shape the world to her will. Her strength was almost without equal, but when it came to subtly wielding magic she struggled enormously.

Munroe concentrated on her breathing, on the slow steady trickle of power she fed into the mirror and Balfruss's image. She felt the surface of the glass bend and her fingers sank into it until she gripped his callused hand.

"What did you find in Morheaton?" asked Balfruss. His voice was clear and sharp in her ears. His lips were slightly out of sync with the words but she tried not to focus on that. She could sense his urgency. Neither of them knew how long she could maintain this connection. They had practised a few times before she'd left the Red Tower and she'd only managed to keep it going for a few minutes. There was an easier way to communicate over long distances, but she'd refused as it bonded her with the other person in an intimate way. They would be able to hear every surface thought and feel every emotion, making them closer than lovers. The only man Munroe wanted to be that familiar with was her husband.

"The Seeker is dead. Murdered by the town Mayor, a man named Burelle, and some of his people." Munroe quickly told him what else she and Tammy had found. "Tammy spoke to her boss, the Old Man, and he said there have been attacks on Seekers across the west. One town in Zecorria banished the Seeker and told him they never wanted to see another ever again."

"A few others have fallen silent in the north," said Balfruss. "All of this is not a coincidence. Someone is making a concerted effort to undermine all that we've done in the last few years."

"What do you want me to do?" asked Munroe, trying not to think about how she could feel the warmth of Balfruss's hand against hers.

"Where are you?" he asked, glancing over her shoulder.

"Perizzi. I came here with Tammy."

"That's good. Focus on Yerskania. We need to warn the other Seekers there. I can tell you where they live."

"Do you want them to return to the Red Tower?"

"Not unless they have to," said Balfruss. "Tell them to forget about the monthly tests for the time being. They're to stay hidden, stay safe and keep an eye on their communities. Someone is poisoning people against magic and the Red Tower, and we need to know who is doing it."

"What if a child with magic starts to manifest and lose control?"

"They're to use their discretion, but if they intervene and even one person talks, it could put their life at risk."

Either option didn't sound appealing. Let a child struggle with their wild magic and risk them hurting themselves and other people, or save the child and risk exile and being attacked. Balfruss ran through a list of towns in Yerskania where the Seekers lived and she repeated it back to him, committing the names to memory.

A headache was forming at the back of her skull and Munroe could feel her damp shirt clinging to the base of her back. They were almost out of time.

"I spoke to your husband," said Balfruss, startling her so much she almost lost control. "He's worried about you."

"Tell him I'm safe and I'll see him soon."

"I will."

"Why did you send Tammy to keep an eye on me?" asked Munroe.

"It's not about trust, Munroe, it's about control. You might be the most powerful mage I've ever met. You have the strength and the will, but you're far from subtle. She's an experienced investigator, trained to spot small clues and read people's body language. Tammy can find out who is behind this. She's also my friend and I trust her with my life." Munroe was stunned. She couldn't remember him saying that about anyone, apart from Eloise. Then again, for some reason he'd also said the same about Garvey.

The surface of the mirror flickered, turning black for a second, and Munroe felt her connection waver. "Find out who is doing this," said Balfruss in a rush. "Contact me again in seven days."

"I will."

"Garvey said you weren't ready for this, but I disagreed. My vote gave you this opportunity to go out on your own. Prove me right. Save our people."

Pain flared in Munroe's head and she felt Balfruss release her fingers. She pulled her hand away from the mirror and her connection to the Source evaporated. Her senses contracted again and she fell backwards breathing hard. For a few minutes she just lay there until her heart had slowed down. Her clothes were drenched with sweat and a bone-weary exhaustion was pulling her towards sleep.

Rolling onto her side Munroe slowly pulled herself to her feet. She blew out the candle and glanced at the mirror. It was whole and the image was hers again. Stumbling across the room she flopped down on the bed and managed to pull the blanket over herself before falling into a dreamless sleep.

CHAPTER 13

Wren felt the occasional glance of other students in her class, like an ant crawling across her scalp, but she did her best to ignore them. It had been over a week since she'd embarrassed Brunwal and yet she was still being ostracised. They were treating her like a frenzied animal that might attack at any moment. If not for Danoph and Tianne she would have been totally isolated. Her hope of creating a different life for herself was proving far more challenging than she realised. Yet she was still determined to succeed. Magic was now the centre of her life and, once she'd achieved a certain level of skill, she could go anywhere and leave such petty concerns far behind.

Wren returned her attention to the teacher, a kind man from Shael named Rue Yettle. He was busy demonstrating the basics of healing, but it was so complex she couldn't really follow what he was doing.

It was the final lesson of the day and she was already feeling quite tired and hungry. Her stomach rumbled loudly, reminding her that lunch had been a long time ago.

On the surface it looked fairly easy. He simply placed a golden net of energy over a patient and through it healed them with power from the Source. The only problem was upon looking deeper into how he'd constructed the net she realised its complexity. Healing a cut on the skin seemed simple. The weave of diamond-shaped nodes was uniform, like sewing a line of thread in a shirt. At the very least Wren thought she might be able to heal the skin.

When he moved on to healing bones she saw the net was constructed of multiple layers, each slightly different from the other and yet all working in unison. It required an understanding of not only magic, but how the body worked and the importance of different organs. If you attempted to heal someone without such knowledge, you could end up doing more harm than good. That meant she would have to spend more hours in the library reading books on anatomy.

Over the course of the class Master Yettle had explained the theory of healing in great detail, but no one had shown an affinity or an innate Talent.

As Danoph had told her earlier, each teacher at the school was proficient in at least one Talent. These were areas of magic most mages found difficult to master, even with years of study and training. But every now and then a student would instinctively understand a Talent and be able to repeat it almost immediately. Some Talents were so peculiar and rare, people had not considered such things possible. Tianne had even told her of one mage who could talk to spirits of the recently deceased. She had doubted the story until Danoph had confirmed it, having seen the mage visit the school months earlier.

Despite thinking she would be able to heal a cut on her finger Wren failed every time. It looked easy, moulding the energy into the diamond weave, but each time she managed to create one node it soon fell apart.

So far neither Danoph nor Tianne had found an innate Talent, but they were both still looking. Thankfully there were hundreds of Talents catalogued in the library, inside the tower, and a few more were added every year.

Some students believed everyone had at least one Talent and that everyone was special, but to Wren it sounded like child-ish wish-fulfilment. Some of the students in her class seemed unwilling to work hard to accomplish anything. They wanted simply to have a unique ability that set them apart.

Although she came from a society of artisans, where master-ing a trade took many years, she'd encountered such laziness before. The more she learned about the culture in Shael and other nations in the west, the more disappointed she was by their depressing similarities.

By the time they reached the last part of the lesson, Wren was exhausted from practising and couldn't even pull together one healing node. With a sigh she realised it was not going to be her area of expertise.

"The odds were always small," said Master Yettle, with a slight shrug of his shoulders. He didn't seem surprised that no one in the class was instantly proficient in healing. They would all have to learn it the hard way and that meant it would take years of study and practice.

"Well, thank you, Master Yettle, for demonstrating healing to the class," said Master Jorey, their current teacher. It was Master Yettle who had healed Wren after her fight with Brunwal and whose presence she'd sensed patrolling the halls while recuperating. According to Tianne's gossip he was rarely seen outside the tower as there was always more than one patient in the small hospital.

Apart from the circumstances, Tianne had been jealous of her visit to the hospital as few students were allowed beyond the fourth floor of the tower. The ground and second floor were taken up by the expansive school library which was managed by

Master Ottah, a waspish man with a vicious glare. He was not a mage and yet not a single student dared cross the diminutive librarian. His tongue was sharp enough to cut through steel and in his eyes, which saw everything, mistreating a book was worse than murder.

The hospital occupied the next two floors of the tower and beyond that several floors were taken up by the private rooms of the Grey Council and senior teachers. No one was really sure what was above that as the floors were off limits and no one except the Grey Council had ever been to the top. Tianne suspected it was where they kept the most secret and dangerous books that were not stored in the library.

There was a polite round of applause for Master Yettle who waved and returned to the hospital.

Master Jorey, who some pupils had unkindly nicknamed Stump, was a short, rotund woman in her sixties. Wren had overheard some of her classmates wondering why she was a teacher when her connection to the Source was so weak. Reaching out with her senses, Wren could barely feel an echo between herself and Master Jorey.

She thought that Master Jorey resembled a fish wife rather than a teacher with her weather-beaten face, red hands and homespun woollen clothes. Whatever she'd done before coming to the Red Tower, it had involved spending a lot of time out-doors. Wren realised that another difference between her and the other pupils was that she would never treat one teacher differently from another. They were in a position of trust and authority and she firmly believed they had earned the right. It was not her place to judge their worth.

The more she learned about the other students the more Wren worried about fitting in as she was so different. Many of them had little respect for teachers and from listening to their conversations at meal times they showed no deference to their elders. It was so different at home in Drassia where age and wisdom were respected at all times. For the first few days Wren had struggled to contain her shock at other students openly making fun of their absent parents and older relatives.

"As you saw from Master Yettle, healing does not require brute force," Master Jorey was saying. "You don't even need to have a strong connection to the Source. It's incredibly delicate work that requires skill and patience to learn."

"Maybe that's how she became a teacher," muttered someone behind Wren. She frowned at them but either they didn't notice or simply didn't care. "They'll let anyone into the Red Tower."

The two students sniggered and somehow Master Jorey seemed to hear them. Her welcoming smile quickly faded and all whispered conversations faded until silence filled the classroom. The stillness of Master Jorey was unnerving and every eye in the room was drawn to her like a magnet.

"Students often wonder what each teacher did before coming to the Red Tower. Can anyone guess what my job was?"

"Butcher."

"Seamstress."

"Blacksmith."

"Cook."

A dozen other ideas were shouted out and each time Master Jorey shook her head. She let it continue for a while until the number of ideas dwindled.

"I will tell you," she said, pausing for dramatic effect. "I was a merchant captain. I spent my life at sea, transporting goods around the world. I owned a fleet of vessels and was one of the most successful in the business. I have three sons, two daughters and fifteen grandchildren. A few years ago my eldest took over the business and I came here to teach."

"Why?" asked a wealthy student from Yerskania. Wren had noticed he always wore silk shirts and his clothes were the latest fashion. Ironically, he was someone her mother would have liked. Most of the other students thought him foppish and shallow for caring so much about his clothes. "Why give up all of that?"

Master Jorey perched on the end of her desk, a wry smile on her face. No one was whispering or laughing at her now. Every face was rapt with attention. "Tomorrow it will rain."

Her comment struck Wren as peculiar and everyone else seemed equally puzzled.

"You have the Talent of second sight," said Danoph, leaning forward intently.

Master Jorey smiled at him and nodded. A few of Wren's classmates looked sheepish, wondering if perhaps Master Jorey had already seen this day and overheard their nicknames and snide comments.

"A kind of second sight. I can predict the weather for up to a day in the future. I can tell you when a storm is brewing, or if it will be bright and sunny. It was how I never lost one ship from my fleet. Not one," she said with obvious pride. "If I focus my Talent and think about something other than the weather, I can peer into the future, but only a little way. A few heartbeats at most. If you flip a coin I will be able to call it almost every time. But ask me what will happen in an hour or tomorrow, and I cannot say. The Grey Council have tried to study my Talent, but as with many others, they have no idea how it's done. But it's as simple as breathing for me. I don't have to think about how I do it. All of the teachers came here from other lives and we all have one or more Talents. In time, you may discover yours and few require a strong connection to the Source."

Silence filled the classroom until it made Wren's ears ring.

Some had been visibly bored at the start of Master Jorey's class on Talents, but she knew that next time everyone would be paying close attention.

"Does every mage have at least one Talent?" asked someone.

"We don't know," said Master Jorey and a few students looked deflated at her words. "Today Master Yettle showed you healing, but imagine if you'd never seen it before. How would you know if you had an innate ability for it? You may discover a Talent while at the Red Tower or you may not. It might come to you years from now when you're out in the world. Or you may never discover one, but that shouldn't stop you from studying as hard as possible. Time for dinner," she said, hopping off the desk and waddling out of the classroom ahead of the students.

"I would never have guessed that about her," said Tianne, coming to stand beside Wren's desk on one side. Danoph lurked on the other, a thoughtful expression on his face. He said little and was often elsewhere in thought. Still waters run deep, was something her father sometimes said. "I always thought she was a fish wife," whispered Tianne. Wren felt a stab of guilt at having the same unworthy thought about Master Jorey.

Lost in thought, Wren followed the others in silence through the brightly lit corridors, barely glancing at the mage lights fixed to the walls. Part of her mind idly wondered who was responsible for lighting them each night.

Normally in the dining hall there were at least ten people serving food, but for some reason there were only five this evening. It took Wren and her friends longer than normal to get their meals, but eventually they sat down to eat in their usual spot. A pool of space was left around them which Wren pretended not to notice. She'd hoped all of this would go away, but nothing had changed since that night when she'd fought back. Others might have tried in the past, but Brunwal had been the strongest in their dormitory until now.

"Do either of you have any advice on how to fix this?" asked Wren, hoping they might have an idea she'd not considered.

"Well, you wanted him to stop bullying you, and it worked," said Tianne, trying to see the good in the current situation. Sometimes her positive attitude was refreshing. This was not one of those times.

"I didn't want to become the bully," said Wren. "Even though I've not hurt anyone else, they're all scared of me. I need to find a way to regain their trust."

"That's not easy," said Danoph, around a mouthful of beans. He was always hungry and ate every meal as if it was his last, often scraping his plate clean. "It will take time."

"Maybe you should do something nice. Then people will like you," suggested Tianne. Wren frowned and chose not to comment on Tianne's idea. She knew her friend wanted to be liked by everyone which seemed both an impossible and senseless goal. Wren didn't want all of the students to like her. She just didn't want to be feared and ignored.

"Perhaps I should ask a teacher. This cannot be the first time something like this has happened."

"Isn't that what got you into this?" said Tianne. "Listening to Garvey." She dropped her voice and looked around the hall. There was no one close enough to overhear them and, besides, Garvey never ate his meals with the other teachers.

A handful of teachers took their meals in their rooms, but some of them came into the dining hall on most days. No food of any kind was allowed in the library and before every meal Master Ottah pulled on a pair of leather gloves. Food smears and crumbs found inside a book were another crime he considered punishable by a slow death.

Occasionally Balfruss would sit with Master Jorey or Choss during their evening meal and Wren would hear a rumble of laughter coming from their table.

Today the teachers' table was empty which she assumed meant they were all busy.

"The fault was mine," said Wren, thinking back to her conversation with Master Garvey. "I must have misinterpreted his instructions."

"I doubt it," said Tianne. "I think he likes seeing people get hurt."

Her friend's disrespect had gone far enough and Wren could not ignore it any longer. "Tianne, I know you don't like him, but he's still a teacher, and a member of the Grey Council. All of the teachers only want the best for us. He was trying to teach me something and I misunderstood."

It was clear from Tianne's expression that she disagreed, but this time she bit her tongue and sullenly went back to her meal. Wren cleared her plate and passed it through the hatch to the kitchen. Even the student working there this week couldn't meet her gaze.

"Be careful," said Danoph, as he walked past. "Perhaps the lesson Garvey was trying to teach is not one that you want to learn."

Wren frowned and pondered his words as she searched for Garvey. At this time of night students were not allowed inside the tower without being accompanied by a teacher. All three members of the Grey Council had rooms inside, but asking for him at the front door was the last place to try on her list. She'd noticed that when she and the others left the dining hall at night, Garvey was often walking around the grounds smoking his pipe. Using her nose she walked around until she saw a small cloud of blue smoke. He was leaning against the back of one of the dormitories that surrounded their training ground.

"Master Garvey, could I speak to you for a moment?" she asked, not wanting to intrude if he was hoping for some privacy. He beckoned her closer with his pipe and took a few more drags. "I wanted to ask your advice on how to deal with the other students."

"Has something else happened?" he asked, staring up at the sky. It was a cool evening and the night sky was awash with a sea of glittering stars, but Wren had no time for stargazing. She heard enough about stars and their spiritual meanings in Master Farshad's lessons on religion.

"Nothing new," she said, "but the other students are now afraid of me. What can I do to reassure them that I'm not a threat?"

Garvey tapped out the bowl of his pipe and ground the contents under his heel. "You were stupid."

Wren was so shocked she didn't know what to say. He seemed content to wait for her to find her voice. He crossed his arms and leaned back against the wall.

"I thought that was what you wanted me to do," said Wren, ignoring the insult. "To stand up to him."

Garvey shook his head. "I told you to fight back. Instead you lashed out without any planning or forethought, making you just as stupid as him. Before, you had one bully and a few of his friends who did nothing, just watched and jeered. Now you have five or six enemies that are plotting their revenge. Not only for beating Brunwal, but also for embarrassing him in front of everyone. You can't beat that many enemies at once."

"I don't understand," said Wren, not seeing where he was going. She'd thought he was going to offer her advice, but instead he was only succeeding in scaring her.

"What you should have done is bided your time. Waited until Brunwal was alone and beaten that idiot until he was scared of you." Garvey's contempt for the boy was palpable, as if he'd been personally hurt. "Then the next time they spotted you, Brunwal would have found an excuse to ignore you and moved on to bullying someone else."

For a second time Wren found herself speechless. Normally she could control her anger, but his solution was so callous she ignored decorum.

"I came to you hoping for wisdom, but your advice is to let him hurt someone else in my place."

Garvey shrugged. "You can't fight everyone's battles for them. Otherwise I could have thrashed that boy after he attacked you. But what would that have accomplished?" he asked and Wren didn't have an answer. If anything she now felt more confused about what to do next. "I'm disappointed in you, Wren."

He tapped his pipe on the wall one final time and walked away leaving her feeling twisted up inside with anxiety. "What should I do?" she called after him.

Without turning around he spoke over his shoulder. "Stick close to your friends, and sleep with one eye open."

He moved around a corner and Wren felt her knees begin to buckle. She'd thought the situation with Brunwal was over, but if Garvey was right this was merely the calm before the storm. She'd never considered he would have a vendetta against her. Perhaps it was not fear that kept the other students away. Maybe none of them wanted to be seen with her in case Brunwal and his cronies turned their attention towards them as well.

Realising she was alone and hidden from view, Wren hurried back towards her dormitory, wiping her face and trying to compose herself. Thankfully Brunwal and his friends were not lying in wait for her, but that didn't mean they wouldn't be another time.

For the first time since arriving at the Red Tower, Wren wondered if she had made a grave mistake.

CHAPTER 14

A kosh rode into town and tied up her horse outside the first tavern. She'd visited many times in the past few months and moments after she entered the main room a drink was waiting for her on the bar.

"Go and take care of her horse," said the owner to the stable hand. The adolescent boy blushed and raced off while the sweaty-faced owner mopped at his balding head. He'd told Akosh his name at some point in the past, but she'd not bothered to remember it, so in her mind he was simply the owner.

Ever the professional and willing to play her role to a fault, she smiled at his inane grin and even went so far as to enquire after his family.

While he prattled on about his offspring, regaling her with their tedious accomplishments, Akosh nodded along in all the right places, but her mind remained elsewhere. Occasionally she'd wondered what it would be like to settle down. To find a small town, somewhere out of the way, and just live a normal life. Working at an ordinary job every day. Coming home to the same house every night. Buying things she liked to decorate it. Maybe even marrying a big, strong man and growing old together. As ever, whenever she idly thought about it, Akosh came to the same conclusion.

She'd be bored within a week and murderous after two. It wouldn't take her long to tire of her husband and bury a kitchen knife in his chest, just to stop him flapping his mouth. Maybe she'd even kill a few of the neighbours, just for some peace and quiet.

Such a life would definitely not suit her at all. A more nomadic approach was much more interesting. Safer as well, for everyone else.

When the owner had finally finished talking about his wretched children, Akosh asked for her usual room and he waddled off to take care of it personally. She wondered what that meant and hoped it wasn't something perverted. He thought he was being clever, staring at her cleavage when she was looking elsewhere, but she always noticed him doing it. Then again, she couldn't really blame him. The owner's wife replaced him behind the bar, glaring at Akosh as if she were responsible for her being born with a face like a sow's diseased arse. Akosh thought it amazing the owner had managed to look past his wife's ugliness and have one child with her. That he had fathered more than one was miraculous. Perhaps he closed his eyes and pictured someone else. Probably Akosh and her cleavage. She smiled at the wife who sneered and scuttled away, no doubt to spit in the food.

In the afternoon Akosh went to the boy's house in time for her weekly appointment. She knocked loudly on the front door and was greeted by his long-suffering mother, a child on one hip and two more clustered around her feet. The whole house smelled of boiled cabbage, feet and unwashed children.

Forcing a smile was difficult but Akosh eventually managed it by grinding her teeth together. "Is Yacob home?"

"Yes, would you like to come in and wait for him?" she asked. Akosh felt her smile waver. She was willing to do many things to fulfil her role, but going inside the stinky house was pushing her to the limit.

Before she had a chance to reply she was saved by Yacob appearing. "I'm ready. Let's go," he said, coming towards her across the room. Akosh heaved a sigh of relief as his mother fussed over him, straightening the collar of his shirt.

"You're getting so tall now," she said, embarrassing the boy who at sixteen was almost a man. Or so he believed.

Yacob hurried out of the front door and Akosh followed, delighted to be away from the smell. In the centre of town the Mayor had arranged for several tables and benches to be set out for various events.

They sat down to one table, out of the way of passing traffic, so that they were not disturbed during the boy's lesson.

Without being asked Yacob took his pens and paper out of his satchel and laid them out on the table. There were few career options available for people in this small town. Most ended up working in the mine and a few left as soon as they could to find their fortune elsewhere.

Yacob was intelligent and had an aptitude for writing and numbers. With some schooling from her, and if he was very lucky, he might become an apprentice scribe or bookkeeper. He was desperate to have a future beyond the town and its population of inbred miners. Akosh thought if he was very unlucky then Yacob might become a tax collector for the Regent. She was sure his family would see the funny side when he came to collect and they couldn't pay their debt.

After their lesson, as was part of their routine, they went for a walk together around town. They moved beyond the houses and headed into the surrounding forest. A few people were felling trees damaged by a recent storm for firewood.

"Do you see that plant?" said Akosh waving her hand towards

something at random. "If you grind up the petals of the flower they can be used to make ink. The stem also numbs muscle pain if you chew it."

Yacob frowned because he knew she was just making it up, but he played along until they were out of earshot. As far as everyone knew he was a student and she was just his tutor. They both had roles to play when other people were present.

A few minutes later they stepped off the path and went deeper into the trees. Akosh stopped in a small clearing and before she had a chance to speak Yacob was pressing her against a tree, his mouth on hers.

She let it continue for a little while as he slobbered on her before easing him backwards. "Slow down."

"You don't know what it's been like," he said. The whine in his voice made her wince, but of course he didn't notice. "The house is suffocating me. No one ever thinks about what's out there, beyond the town. I feel like I'm sleepwalking except when I'm with you."

He lunged towards her again with his eyes closed and Akosh dodged out of the way. The swelling in his trousers was significantly pronounced already but it started to fade when he walked face first into the tree. Once his nose had stopped bleeding she gave Yacob a brief kiss to placate him before peeling his roving hands off her again.

"What's wrong?" he asked.

"Have you been practising, like I asked?"

"You want to talk about that now?"

Swallowing a sarcastic retort Akosh forced another smile. "Yacob, my sweet, the Seeker will be here tomorrow morning. You need to be ready."

Yacob frowned when she mentioned the Seeker. "People in town have been talking. They think Seekers are corrupting children and cursing them with magic."

Akosh forced herself to smile. "Who cares what they think? Are you cursed?"

"No."

"Besides, I thought you wanted to be different from everyone else."

"I do," said Yacob, nodding emphatically.

"Good, because if you impress him, you'll immediately leave town, and never have to come back. Ever."

That finally cooled his libido as a thoughtful expression crossed his gormless face. "Never?"

Akosh shook her head. "Why would you?" she said, not hiding her contempt for the town and its inhabitants. "They all live small, tedious lives. Day after day they're grinding away underground, burrowing in the dirt. You could travel all over the world as a powerful mage. Kings and queens pay mages a great deal of money for their services."

"How much?" he asked.

"A lot," she promised, touching him on the chest to distract him. "You would have money, power, and who wouldn't find that attractive?" she asked rhetorically, sliding a hand up to his neck. Her hand spasmed and she almost crushed his throat but fought down the impulse.

His eyes drifted away and she could imagine where his teenage mind was wandering. She let him contemplate the fantasy of being a famous mage for a while before dragging him back to the present, gripping his jaw firmly in one hand.

"None of that will happen if you can't impress the Seeker," she promised. "You'll end up back here, working in the mine."

"No," he said, trying to pull free but her hand was like a vice.

"You'll marry one of your fat neighbours and then have lots of fat squalling children. After that you'll spend the rest of your life stuck here until you die of old age or the damp lung. Then you'll be just like your parents and grandparents before them."

The horror in his eyes made her smile but he didn't notice. "No. I can't. I won't."

"Then show me," she said, shoving him backwards. Red marks from where her fingers had pressed into the side of his jaw stood out against the white of his skin.

Fumbling along Yacob reached for the Source and slowly drew power into his body. The tide slowed from a rush to a trickle until she felt the power radiating from him like sunlight against her skin.

Akosh shook her head in disappointment. "Is that it? You said you'd been practising."

"Wait," said Yacob, as she turned away. He was sweating from the pressure already, but she felt him stretch as another small trickle of power seeped into him. "Is that enough?" he asked, gasping for breath.

"Maybe," she said, not promising anything. Before she could push him any further he released his connection and slumped to the ground in exhaustion. "You know I've been teaching Jelkin as well. I think he's a bit stronger than you." A different kind of heat flushed Yacob's cheeks. "I'll see if he needs some extra tuition tomorrow, after the test."

"I'm stronger," shouted Yacob as she walked away. "I'll prove it!"

The following morning when the Seeker came to town most of the people stayed away. They were too busy, working down the mine, washing their clothes or boiling cabbage, which was about the only thing they seemed to eat.

The crowd was not quite what Akosh wanted, numbering barely a hundred, but it would have to do. Dozens of women with their screaming children, a few dying miners with the damp lung and one or two nervous parents stood waiting for the Seeker to stop talking. The woman was rambling on about the honour of going to the Red Tower, but no one was really listening. A few locals were muttering and casting dark glances at the woman in the gold mask. Akosh heard a few people whispering about the Red Tower stealing their children for their private army. It seemed as if Habreel's people had been busy indeed.

Most of the people in the crowd stood with eyes that had glazed over. She wondered what they were thinking about. Probably cabbage.

When Yacob was called up Akosh moved through the crowd to stand beside Jelkin, the other teenage boy she'd been coaching. She waited until Yacob saw them together and then whispered a promise of what she would do to the boy when they were alone in her room. Yacob was too far away to hear the words but Jelkin's inane grin was enough. Yacob clenched his jaw and fists so tight his knuckles turned white.

Akosh walked at a steady pace until the crowd was out of view around a corner and then ran the rest of the way back to the tavern. She could feel the build-up of energy in the air as she climbed onto her horse and rode out of town at a gallop. Behind her there was a loud whistling sound, as if something had flown right past her ears, and then a detonation. She felt the earth shake and quickly dismounted, leading her skittish horse along the road.

Somewhere in the distance behind her she could hear screaming and a grin stretched across a face. She was just about to mount up again when she felt a persistent tugging of a different kind. Her smile faded.

Moving to the side of the road, she quickly tied the reins of her horse to a tree. She didn't want him wandering off while she was distracted.

Akosh closed her eyes and bowed her head. When she opened her eyes again she was standing inside a long banqueting hall. The walls were fashioned from huge slabs of white marble and at regular intervals were fireplaces tall enough to walk into without stooping.

A huge table ran down the middle of the room and on either side were two rows of identical looking chairs. But each was vastly different from its neighbour and no one would accidentally sit in the wrong chair. At the head of the table was a huge chair that was far too big for even the largest man at the unusual gathering.

There were no visible doors into the hall, and despite the lack of lanterns the room was filled with a warm glow. In this place, many of the usual rules did not apply. Apart from the table and chairs, everything else was an elaborate illusion.

Dozens of people, all shapes and sizes, were appearing out of thin air. No two people resembled each other and yet this was a family gathering of a kind. Akosh knew that appearances were deceiving, especially here, and it was a good idea not to underestimate anyone. If she really wanted, Akosh could look beyond the masks everyone was wearing and see their true faces, but she resisted the urge. Some of them, in particular the eldest, were terrifying to look upon.

There were a few faces which she acknowledged but those she considered friends were noticeably absent. Others didn't seem aware as even here a hierarchy existed and those towards the far end of the table had no idea about her and others like her. They were too far removed and believed themselves involved in more important matters.

The old sailor, Nethun, made his way towards the far end of

the table and Akosh made sure to give him a wide berth. She also kept her eyes averted when he looked in her direction. He was almost timeless and infinitely more powerful than her. Fear was a natural response and quelling the terror in her gut took some effort. As one of the oldest there, he called the meeting to order and Akosh took her seat, nodding politely to the two people on either side of her.

One was enraptured by Nethun, staring at him with adoration, while the other was looking at the Lady of Light with a puzzled expression. She had grown significantly in power over the last few years. That was the reason she still sat towards the far end of the table. Akosh remembered when the Lady of Light had been just a mewling girl, doing as she was told, desperate to go unnoticed. Now she had so many devout followers it was hard to believe the Lord of Light had ever existed. No one ever talked about him any more and every one of his images had been erased from all churches of the Holy Light. It showed Akosh how much could change in a short space of time. All it required was patience and cunning. Or a lot of luck. The Lady of Light didn't have the intelligence to have orchestrated her rise to power, but now that her star was in ascendance she was doing everything to hold on to it.

It also confirmed what Akosh had long suspected. Someone at this table was pulling strings behind the scenes.

Over time many of those gods around the table would naturally fade when their star waned. The loyal shrank in number. The churches crumbled and became ruins that were eventually torn down. The new was built on top of the old and their names became nothing more than a line or two of text in a dusty history book.

But others disappeared suddenly, ahead of time, for overstepping their bounds. The Lord of Light was one. He'd been on the rise, sat at the far end of the table, and a few years ago had vanished. Akosh glanced at the large empty chair at the head of the table. It was possible. But it seemed more likely that some-one else was responsible. It meant her caution was warranted. She was right not to trust a single one of them.

Vargus, the Weaver, and Nethun were talking about magic and Seekers, but Akosh wasn't really listening as she already knew everything. It was necessary that she attended these meet-ings but they were an exercise in tedium. Those on her level were never called upon to express an opinion and yet they were required to be here. If she didn't attend her absence would be noted and that would prompt an investigation which she wanted to avoid. She had the feeling that was why several others showed up every time, looking equally bored as her. Everyone had secrets they preferred stayed hidden from those around the table.

Akosh felt a prickle across her scalp as if she were being watched. Glancing up the table she saw the meeting was car-rying on as normal, but one of the more powerful beings was looking in her direction.

The conversation flowed around Elwei but the old pilgrim said nothing. His face was partially hidden in shadow inside his headscarf, but Akosh could see one of his eyes gleaming in the dark. She knew almost nothing about him, except that he was very old and, most important of all, very powerful. Nethun and Vargus sometimes asked for Elwei's opinion and they seemed to respect him which told her to be wary around him.

Akosh politely inclined her head but he didn't react. His focused attention unnerved her and she tried not to fidget. Doing her best to ignore him she turned her attention back to the discussion. They were talking about the growing tide of hatred and fear directed at the Seekers, and in turn any magic user, but were at a loss to identify its source. As usual they directed Vargus to investigate while the rest did nothing and were reminded not to interfere with the fate of the mortal races. Eventually Akosh risked looking at Elwei and was relieved to see that his attention had moved elsewhere.

Taking it as a reminder that there were beings far more powerful than her, who could snuff her out with little effort, Akosh knew she would have to be extremely careful moving forward. Her plan, and her survival, depended upon it.

CHAPTER 15

The town of Maldorn in Yerskania was not one Tammy had visited before but, after half a day of walking its streets, she had a sense of it. The townspeople lived fairly comfortable lives, situated on a main trade route and not too far from the southern city of Rojenne, which generated lots of opportunities. In remote towns and villages, young people often felt they had only two choices. Stay at home, and labour in the industry of their parents, or leave behind everything familiar and risk it all. For those living in Maldorn a city was only a few days' ride and the young could get a taste of what was available without the all or nothing approach. All of this gave her hope that when the Seeker returned the townspeople would treat her differently.

This was the second Seeker she and Munroe had sought out together. The first had been located without difficulty and advised to hide his mask and avoid the monthly testing of children in the area. He didn't like it, especially as it could put children at risk, but he saw the wisdom in keeping a low profile for the time being. He'd also promised to watch for outsiders causing trouble and send word to the Red Tower and the Khevassar if he saw anyone.

Striding around the town in her Guardian uniform during

the day Tammy had received admiring looks and greetings from everyone. The people of Yerskania respected her station and several young people in town had questioned her about becoming a Guardian of the Peace. Living on a trade route they were more aware of other countries and customs than in a remote town. She took their interest in other people as another encouraging sign of a community with an open mind.

When night fell she made her way to the Black Lion, the tavern where she'd booked a room. As she sat at the bar nursing a mug of ale the general mood of conversation in the room proved to be troubling.

While the locals had not personally experienced any issues with magic or Seekers, there was still a general air of concern and fear. The latest stories, which had arrived earlier in the day with passing merchants, had now spread throughout the town. A whole village in Zecorria had apparently been destroyed. Allegedly every house had been levelled and every stone crushed, as if beneath a giant's hand. No one said a child was responsible for the destruction, but every tale involved wild magic being unleashed in the presence of a Seeker. People were certain of that much.

Magic was unnatural. There was also widespread agreement on that. When a dissenting voice in the room mentioned that magic could be a good thing, they were quickly shouted down by others. People reminded them of the war and all that had happened. How easily the Warlock had used his dark arts to manipulate the rulers in the west into uniting for war. How thousands had died in the conflict and the resulting effects were still being felt to this day, ten years later. The civil war in Morrinow continued to rumble along and parts of Shael remained lawless or utterly abandoned. It would take decades for the world to recover and some of the scars would never heal.

In such a hostile room in the west no one dared speak of the Battlemages and all that they had done to save lives in the same war. Tammy wondered if conversations in the taverns of Seveldrom were any different. Did they celebrate and honour the Battlemages who had died to protect them? Or were they also cursing their names and anything connected to magic? For years the name of Balfruss had become a curse that few would say out loud in case it drew his attention. The display of power he'd used to kill the Warlock had frightened people. Afterwards Balfruss had voluntarily gone into exile, but if he'd chosen to stay, who could have stopped him?

Inevitably conversation in the tavern turned to the Seeker due to return to Maldorn the following morning. People were afraid of what might happen during the test. They were afraid for their children, in case they had the curse of magic, but also for themselves. Many had heard stories about people being injured during a test. One or two stories might be labelled as fanciful, but when tales of children dying were sprouting up all over the world like weeds, they could not be ignored.

For thirty years no child in Maldorn had been cursed with magic. Since the tests had restarted a few years ago four children had been taken away to the Red Tower. It wasn't hard for Tammy to see why they might blame the Seeker instead of the ingrained fear and hatred of magic. When someone suggested banning the Seeker from the town no one at the table disagreed.

After a quick meal and more conversation that left a sour taste in her mouth, Tammy went up to her room. Munroe was waiting for her inside, hunched in a blanket in a comfy chair by the window. It was pouring with rain and in the distance there was the occasional rumble of thunder. Wet strands of dark hair clung to Munroe's face and she irritably brushed them aside. Her whole body was rigid with tension.

"That bad?" said Tammy, sitting down opposite her.

"Almost everyone in town is scared. They're trying not to show it, but it's there, below the surface."

Walking around in uniform meant that people would talk to Tammy, but only in a certain way and not about everything. It also kept them focused on her while Munroe went unnoticed as she chatted to people in town. She could pass for just another curious visitor trying to catch up on the news as she travelled through.

"Every time I heard a story being retold, it's grown worse," said Munroe, shaking her head. Stray drops of rain fell from her hair onto the blanket. "First it's ten people dead in Zecorria. Then twenty. By tomorrow it could be a hundred. I looked for the source and it turned out to be a couple of merchants who'd recently passed that way. They'd heard the stories from other merchants. They gossip worse than teenagers."

In this instance, malicious or not, news of the accident was spreading fast.

"Everyone is nervous about tomorrow."

"We should go and see the blacksmith tonight. To warn her," said Munroe, shrugging off her blanket and standing up. As far as everyone in town was aware, Leonie was only a blacksmith. However, she also took regular trips to other communities to test the children in her other role as a Seeker for the Red Tower.

"I think that's a bad idea," warned Tammy. "We might draw unwanted attention to her."

"I can sneak in. No one will see me."

"Are you sure? Can you guarantee that?" asked Tammy.

"Of course not."

"Then we should wait until morning. So far I've not seen anyone suspicious, but there are a lot of strangers in town. Any of them could be involved in spreading the paranoia about magic. Or they might be watching for anything unusual."

Munroe wasn't convinced. "She needs to know what she's walking into."

"We'll go first thing in the morning," said Tammy. "The testing isn't until midday, so we'll have a few hours to talk with her."

Munroe finally relented, sitting down again and folding her legs up onto the chair. She looked cold and pulled the blanket tight around her shoulders. They'd been riding for a few days now, travelling from one town to the next, and Tammy could see that she wasn't used to long days in the saddle.

"Maybe you should get some sleep. You look exhausted."

"I'm fine," said Munroe, stifling a massive yawn. "All right, maybe just a little nap."

She insisted on staying in the chair so Tammy covered her with another blanket. Munroe was asleep in moments but when Tammy lay down she found sleep evaded her. Worries about not only tomorrow but where all of this was leading preyed on her mind. Eventually she fell asleep but her dreams were equally troubled by images of terrified children being pursued by mobs of adults waving weapons.

Inevitably her thoughts strayed to her son and she wondered what would happen if one day he developed magic. In her dreams he became the child being chased by a bloodthirsty mob.

After an early breakfast, Tammy and Munroe made their way to the nearest smithy. There were two blacksmiths in Maldorn and the one they sought had just returned from a trip to the southern city of Rojenne.

Despite arriving home late the night before, they found the front doors of the smithy wide open and the smith and her apprentices hard at work. Two tall lads, who looked like twins, were busy working together on a huge lump of something. One held the metal on the anvil with a set of tongs while the other swung a huge hammer. A short distance away a burly woman with short, dark hair and broad shoulders was directing the striker. She left them to it, tucking thick gloves into her belt, as Tammy and Munroe came in through the front door. The heat from the forge hit Tammy like a wave and a layer of sweat formed in her hairline. She could see why the smith and her apprentices were only dressed in thin cotton trousers and shirts. They also had on thick aprons and gloves but despite their precautions Tammy could see they all had several burn scars. Every window and the back door was thrown open and still the building felt like they were standing inside a giant oven.

"Something I can help you with?" asked the smith, glancing at her Guardian uniform. A frown briefly wrinkled the smith's forehead. Tammy couldn't blame her. She and Munroe made an odd couple.

"Is there somewhere we could talk in private?" asked Munroe, having to shout to be heard over the constant clanging.

The smith frowned again but led them down a short corridor to a cramped office. There were multiple charcoal drawings pinned to the wall of weapons and an intricate set of metal railings. Beside each drawing was a set of measurements in precise handwriting. A workbench with a few small, half-finished items and several ledgers sat at the back. The rest of the room was filled with floor-to-ceiling shelves overflowing with tools which were all labelled. It spoke to Tammy of an organised and practical mind.

There was no door on the room so Tammy leaned against the frame, effectively blocking anyone's view inside. In the background they could still hear the clang of the apprentices, but they were far away enough that their conversation couldn't be overheard.

"You're in danger, Leonie," said Munroe, starting the conversation in her usual abrupt fashion. "I've come from the Red Tower to warn you."

The smith said nothing and just stared at Munroe. Then she glanced over at Tammy and raised an eyebrow. "Is this a joke?"

"I can feel your connection to the Source," whispered Munroe, although there was no need with so much noise in the other room. "Can't you sense the echo in me?"

Leonie rubbed a hand across her shorn head and heaved a long sigh. "What do you want?" she asked.

Tammy noticed she'd not admitted to anything and was still being cautious.

"This is ridiculous," said Munroe and Tammy saw blue light flare up between her fingers, filling the room with its pale glow. The smith's eyes widened in alarm and she quickly moved to cover the ball of light with her hands. The light faded and Tammy glanced back along the corridor. She could see the two apprentices were still hard at work. When Leonie looked her way Tammy just shook her head.

"They didn't notice."

"Seekers are being attacked across the world," said Munroe, keeping her voice low. "Balfruss, from the Grey Council, sent me to warn you. You have to stop the monthly tests for the time being. It's too dangerous."

Leonie rubbed the heavy knuckles of her left hand. "I've heard stories on the road. Children combusting while being tested. Such a thing has never happened to me, and it's very rare. That has nothing to do with the Seekers."

"You know that. I know that," said Munroe, clearly exasperated. "They don't," she said, gesturing at the wider world around them. "If you go out there today, in your mask, the crowd might turn on you. Seekers have been chased out of towns and villages across the west. A few towns in Zecorria have banned them for ever. We even visited one town where they'd murdered the Seeker. It's safer for you to hide the mask for now."

Leonie stubbornly shook her head. "That's Zecorria—"

"It's happening all over the west," said Munroe, interrupting her.

"It's different here. I've lived in this town my entire life. The people here know me. They're my friends and neighbours."

"That doesn't matter to them," said Munroe. "People are scared of magic and what you might do to them."

"They don't understand magic and what it can do to help people. All they've heard recently is that it can kill them and their children," said Tammy, drawing all eyes in the room to her. "You wouldn't invite a friend with a disease into your home, no matter how much you liked them."

"They won't hurt me," insisted Leonie. Tammy could see Munroe was about to argue, but she stepped over her protest.

"We'll stay in town until after you've tested the children," said the Guardian. "For your safety."

"It's not necessary."

"We insist," said Munroe, smiling through her teeth.

The smith quickly realised they were not going to change their minds. "Then I'll see you both in the square at midday."

Once they'd left the smithy and were a few streets away Munroe rounded on Tammy. "Why did you agree to let her test the children?"

"Nothing we said was making a difference. Either everything will be normal, or it will go badly. I would rather be here to help her in case of trouble." Tammy rubbed a hand over her face. She was tired and the images from her dreams still plagued her mind. "It's not an easy thing to hear. That your friends will turn on you because of a secret. It's been ten years since the war, and, despite everything Balfruss and the others did, most people still think of magic as a curse."

"But not you?" asked Munroe. It was clear she was itching for an argument to get rid of the tension that had built up but Tammy was not about to oblige.

"I've seen what magic can do, good and bad. On reflection, I think it's a gift. Without the Red Tower and its Seekers, the situation could become much worse. As bad as it was in Voechenka."

Munroe frowned. "What did you see in that city?"

In the darkest and loneliest hours of the night, when dawn seemed an eternity away, Tammy's worst nightmares were filled with memories of Voechenka. She didn't need her imagination to invent something horrific to haunt her. She had seen it up close and had lived to tell the tale.

"True evil," said Tammy.

At midday the square was busy with people, all of them focused on the green in the middle. The Mayor was there, a tall man in his fifties with thick arms wearing a white apron. Tammy had bought some fresh bread from him the previous morning.

As they waited for the Seeker to arrive she studied the crowd and listened to the conversation flowing around her. She said nothing and tried to go unnoticed, but it was a little difficult with her size and uniform. Meanwhile Munroe moved through the crowd, pausing here and there to listen before moving on. Her grim expression told Tammy everything she needed to know. They were scared. The risk of magic to their lives was becoming something real that could not be ignored indefinitely. In the past it was seen as someone else's problem, but now it was here. A deadly secret that lurked in their homes and possibly within their own children.

When the Seeker appeared a strained hush fell over the crowd. There were four children standing with their parents towards the front. Without speaking the Seeker beckoned them to approach and eventually the children shuffled forward with reluctance. The parents stayed back, as if magic was a contagious disease.

The Seeker moved to stand in front of the first child, raising a hand towards her. After a few seconds she shook her head and the girl's relief was clear. She burst into tears and ran back into the welcoming arms of her parents. Moving down the line the Seeker tested each child and, perhaps mercifully on this occasion, all four of them were without the potential for magic. If any had proven positive Tammy wondered how quickly the mood of the crowd would have changed.

It should have been over, but the people didn't disperse. The Mayor came forward again to stand beside the Seeker.

"The risk is too great," he said, addressing the Seeker. "You need to leave town and never return."

"I'm not the cause," said Leonie, her voice slightly muffled by the mask. "I'm here to help. Without me any child born with magic might hurt themselves, or someone else."

"It's not working!" shouted someone, and several others agreed. A prickle of worry ran across her scalp. Looking around the square Tammy realised she'd lost track of Munroe.

"Children are dying," said the Mayor. "It's been worse since your kind came back."

"You don't understand," said Leonie, but the Mayor wouldn't listen.

"It's too dangerous for you to be here. You must go."

The Seeker remained silent while the crowd cheered the Mayor's words for her to leave. The safe thing to do would be to walk away. To bury the mask and wait for the storm to pass. It was one thing to be spurned by strangers, but to be turned away by friends and neighbours was something else entirely.

"Tomorrow, if one of your daughters fell ill," said Leonie to the Mayor, "you'd visit the doctor or apothecary. And you, Saul," she said gesturing to a man in the front row. "If your plough breaks, you'd visit the smith to get it repaired. But what happens if a child comes into their magic? Without a Seeker and the Red Tower, to teach them control, it could be dangerous. If you ban us, then you put your own lives in danger."

All eyes were watching the Seeker in rapt silence, but that seed of worry had blossomed and Tammy felt her heart begin to race. The crowd's silence had become something else. Something fraught with the possibility of violence. With a grimace she pulled on her gloves and readied herself for a fight.

"We've not had any cursed children for a long time. It's only in the last few years they've started appearing and that's your fault."

"Really?" asked Leonie. "What do you think happened to Lamm Fisher? Where do you think he went?"

The Mayor was staring at the Seeker. "How do you know about him?"

"He didn't have a disease, Hap. His fever was because of his magic. There's been half a dozen other families that have moved away and given similar excuses."

"Who are you?" asked the Mayor.

When Leonie reached towards her face with both hands there was movement in the crowd. Munroe was shoving her way through the people, but they weren't giving way fast enough. Tammy knew she was going to be too late to stop the smith from unveiling herself.

"No! Don't do it!" shouted Munroe but the Seeker ignored her. Leonie lowered her hood and then took off her mask.

"You all know me," said Leonie, looking from one stunned face to another in the crowd. "I've lived here most of my life. I've watched many of your children being born. The last thing I would do is harm them. I want to protect them and you."

The silence was deafening. It felt like a pregnant pause but she didn't know which way it was going to go. Violence or acceptance.

Munroe had reached the front row but she was far too late.

"How long?" asked the Mayor, breaking the silence.

"What?" said Leonie.

"How long have you been lying to us?" he said.

In that moment Tammy saw something fade behind Leonie's eyes. Her face turned towards the crowd, hoping to see something, but whatever it was – hope, love, even just under-standing – it was lacking in their collective gaze. The smith's broad shoulders slumped in defeat.

It was over.

"Get out!" someone shouted.

"We don't want you here."

"We've known her for years," someone was saying to their neighbour in the crowd. "We can trust her."

"It's your fault!" said a third voice, ignoring everything Leonie had said. "Our children are getting sick because of you."

Tammy started moving towards the front of the crowd as well, easing people aside if they didn't move fast enough. One or two started to protest until they saw her Guardian uniform and then the look on her face. Perhaps they thought she was going to arrest the smith and take her away.

"You should go," Tammy heard the Mayor saying to the smith. The noise level started to rise and more people began to shout and boo. "Please."

Munroe appeared at her elbow and a quick glance told Tammy

that she was furious. "Don't do anything rash," she hissed at the diminutive mage. "Go and get the horses. We'll need to leave in a hurry." Munroe had to be distracted into doing something useful before she acted on impulse and made it worse.

"What about Leonie?"

"I'll stay with her," promised Tammy. "Meet us at the smithy."

With a final glare at the crowd, that thankfully went unnoticed, Munroe stomped away. Given how powerful she was the people of Maldorn didn't realise their lucky escape. Tammy stepped up beside Leonie where she and the Mayor were having a heated conversation.

"You've known me for over fifteen years, Hap," she was saying. "You know this is wrong."

"I'm sorry, Leonie, but it would be better for everyone if you left town. Just for a little while. I'm sure if what you say is true, then this will all blow over." He did sound genuinely apologetic but the smith continued to glare. It was also very clear she didn't think this problem would go away in a few days or even weeks. It meant exile.

"Arrest her!" someone shouted behind her back.

"We need to go. Now," insisted Tammy.

The pain in Leonie's eyes was there briefly before it turned into anger. Tammy could see that she felt both betrayed and let down by their response. She'd exposed herself and shared her best-kept secret, risking her home and career, only to be rewarded with fear. It was as if she'd never truly known the people she'd been living with all these years.

Tammy followed the smith back to her forge, still hot with residual heat from earlier in the day.

"You should pack a bag. Only whatever you can carry," suggested Tammy.

"Who's going to look after the forge? What about all the work that's half finished?" Leonie stood in the middle of the room, utterly despondent. So far the street was empty but Tammy wondered how long it would remain that way. The people of Maldorn were not as aggressive as some had been, but then none of the previous Seekers had revealed their identity to the crowd.

Guiding the smith by her elbow Tammy helped her to her room where they packed a bag together. A few minutes later the sound of horses outside drew Tammy to the window where she saw Munroe waiting with three mounts.

They rode out of town in a hurry, not waiting to see if anyone followed them. Leonie was accustomed to riding and despite being distracted she guided her horse with ease. She remained silent, her face a mask of misery. They kept to a canter until Tammy felt the danger of pursuit had passed and then slowed to a walk.

"It's getting worse," Tammy said to Munroe. "We need to split up to cover more ground." There were still several names on the list Balfruss had given them. She knew it wasn't ideal, given that she had been tasked with accompanying Munroe, partially to keep her in check, but they were running out of time.

Despite what had happened Tammy knew they'd been lucky. The story of what Leonie had done in Maldorn would spread and with it people would begin to wonder who else was hiding behind the golden masks. Previously the identity of the Seekers hadn't mattered to anyone, but now suspicion would grow and with it the level of fear would increase.

They needed to get to the other Seekers before it was too late.

CHAPTER 16

Regent Choilan of Zecorria settled himself into his chair, taking his time to arrange the tails of his jacket artfully, before gesturing for his clerks and Ministers to be seated. He thought the frock coat made him look ridiculous but his third wife, who stayed up to date on fashion, assured him it was extremely desirable. Since first wearing it a week ago Choilan had noticed four of his Ministers had adopted the style, although their jackets were not nearly as ornate, as was proper for their station.

For the next hour he closely followed his Ministers' reports, listening to what they were saying and also what went unspoken. The clerks at the edges of the room made notes and offered further details when called upon to clarify a point of interest. When the Minister of Trade finally started to wind down Choilan offered the man a generous smile. He wondered how dense the Minister must be to think that his dalliances with a mistress had gone unnoticed by his wife, and, in turn, his Regent. For betraying her and breaking his sacred marriage vow she had called for his head, or at the very least his balls. Choilan was still debating which would have the least impact on his Minister's ability to carry out his duties.

With a wave of his hand he dismissed his Ministers who shuffled out of the room backwards.

"May the Lady of Light bless you," said the Minister of Trade, the last to leave, closing the doors behind him. Perhaps his wife would make a better Minister. Her loyalty would be unquestionable and she wouldn't be nearly as distracted. The Regent made a mental note to discuss it with his first wife and seek her counsel.

Now that the Ministers were gone most of the clerks took their turn to file out, until only ten remained who moved forward to sit at the central table. These were the hidden eyes and ears that worked for him in plain sight. Their primary role was that of clerks, but each was vastly overqualified for the position. Their secondary role was to watch, listen and report directly to the Regent about news the Ministers had failed to share, out of ignorance or an attempt at deception.

"Bettina, what's the latest development with Seekers from the Red Tower?"

"Regent, the trend has continued both here and abroad. With the backing of their Mayor, several towns and villages in Zecorria have exiled them. When questioned, the Mayors said the people would take care of any children with magic in the future by themselves."

The Regent held out his cup and it was instantly filled by a waiting servant. The watered-down wine was light and crisp, sweetened with fresh fruit. He took a sip and grimaced, not at the taste but the current situation.

"Tell me about the town."

Bettina had a number of papers on the table before her but she didn't need to look at them. The details of what had happened were etched into her mind, as they were his. His people had interviewed the survivors and the report was one of the most troubling he'd ever seen.

"A teenage boy was being tested by a Seeker. Something went wrong and during the process he exploded." There were a few gasps in the room. Some of the clerks were hearing this for the first time. Choilan made a note of those who showed no obvious surprise or signs of dismay.

"How many are dead?" he asked.

"The latest guess is ninety to one hundred and twenty people, including women and children." He suspected the grimace on Bettina's face came from the ambiguity of not having a precise figure, not the actual loss of life. She was icy and loved nothing except numbers and order. If she hadn't become a clerk he suspected she would have made an excellent assassin.

"Other towns in the area responded by instantly banning Seekers. They too have made declarations about dealing with their own children."

"I remember the bad old days," said Choilan, setting down his cup, suddenly no longer thirsty. "As a boy I saw them drown my cousin in the river. He screamed then he choked to death, while his parents watched and did nothing. We are not going back to that."

He didn't know if Seekers posed a genuine threat or not, but since the Red Tower had reopened there had been fewer incidents of children being drowned or burned alive. Choilan had assumed this was a result of those children with magic being identified early and sent to the school for training. Or perhaps the number of incidents had not declined and communities had become better at covering up what they were doing.

Fear of magic sat like a stone in the stomach of every Zecorran. They all remembered the war and how the Warlock had led Zecorria astray. The corrupt wizard had confused the mind of an already troubled King and perverted the faith of an entire nation. It had taken them years to root out all of the religious zealots, the Chosen, and see that they were eliminated.

Despite all his resources, Choilan had only rumours about the Seekers and the level of danger they might pose. The Red Tower claimed they were reactive, simply finding what was already there in a child. Others were now claiming magic was more widespread than it had been a few years ago. His agents reliably informed him that over the last six years hundreds of students had walked through the gates of the Red Tower. So where had all of the potential mages come from? Had they simply been hiding, doing their best to control their magic without supervision? Or was there something more sinister going on?

He needed reliable information so that he could make a decision, but it had to be done soon. His people were dying and they needed to see decisive action from their Regent or their faith in him would begin to waver.

"Find me someone with some answers."

Bettina grimaced. He'd become adept at reading her moods and knew this one signified personal distaste. "I know of someone. A man recently came to the palace, asking for an audience. He has some ideas, although I'm sceptical."

"Bring him to me," said the Regent. It was better than nothing and so far his own network of contacts had not produced anything.

"Yes, my Regent."

The following morning Regent Choilan sat in one of his private audience chambers, nibbling at some slices of apple and coconut cake. Two guards were stationed just outside the door as a precaution, but Bettina was confident the man, Habreel, posed no threat to him. When Habreel arrived, bowing low alongside his clerk, Choilan took a moment to study the man.

Descended from Yerskania, with their paler than pale skin and blue eyes, there seemed to be little of note about him. He stood of average height, his features were bland and he carried himself with neither arrogance nor the bold carriage of a man confident of a great destiny. Habreel resembled a shopkeeper or an accountant. It was only later, when the Regent thought back over their conversation, that he noted Habreel came alive when he mentioned his goal. In those moments a fire burned behind his eyes that spoke of passion and, perhaps, a hint of madness.

"Regent, thank you for agreeing to see me."

Choilan gestured at the seat opposite, deciding to take a generous approach for the time being. Bettina remained standing, moving to the far corner where she scribbled notes in her journal while listening to their conversation.

"Bettina tells me you have some thoughts on the current situation with the Seekers."

"Yes, Regent."

"Tell me."

"I believe it began during the war. Zecorria, as a nation was led astray. As you know the Warlock tricked the people here. He confused their minds with his magic and with it led this country into a dark time."

Habreel paused, perhaps waiting to see what impact his words had and whether or not he would be hanged or cheered on for such a bold statement. The Regent remained impassive and gestured for him to continue.

"The war was ten years ago, but people in other countries still regard Zecorria with scorn. They blame Zecorrans for all that happened and ignore the facts. They ignore that many other nations in the west were also led astray by dark magic."

"I am aware of the false assumptions. Quickly come to the point," advised the Regent.

Rather than grow angry or frustrated at the interruption, Habreel quickly adapted. "I humbly submit that now is the time for Zecorria to lead the way. If you were to establish a nationwide ban on Seekers, it would send a clear message to the people here, and to the Red Tower."

"Bettina tells me you also have a theory. That Seekers are waking dormant magic in children, providing them with more soldiers for their army of mages."

Habreel's smile held no warmth. "Whether my belief is true or not, the facts speak for themselves. Magic is destructive and dangerous. The few good deeds carried out by one or two mages do not outweigh the number of dead when compared to those who abuse its power. They did nothing to earn it. I've been told it occurs at random in children. That it's not passed down in the blood."

Choilan glanced over at Bettina for confirmation and she reluctantly agreed with what Habreel had said so far.

"People are angry and afraid," he continued. "Here, people are tired of being blamed for all the ills in the world. Children everywhere are dying in grisly ways and somehow magic is involved. That is a fact."

"It is my belief that banning the Seekers will not solve the problem. In fact it could make it worse," said the Regent, daring Habreel to question his idea. But he was too sharp and didn't take the bait.

"That is possible, but I believe a decision needs to be made in Zecorria. I've spoken to many people who believe taking matters into their own hands is acceptable. I make no pretence about liking the Seekers, or their Masters, but I do not condone murder and mob rule."

Choilan grunted but said nothing. His thoughts of where this would inevitably lead were similar to those of Habreel.

Failure to act on his part could lead to a dangerous situation where he had to bring in the army to make sure that his decrees were enforced. Working against the common will of the people would also put his position in jeopardy. He held the reins of the country through his continuing popularity. Choilan had no birthright or noble ancestry like those before him. He knew Habreel was not telling him everything, and yet he agreed that doing nothing was not an option.

"If you ban all Seekers and then all mages in Zecorria, the magic in children will go unused and wither away." Habreel spoke with confidence but Choilan had his doubts. "I know some doubt my assuredness, but since the Seekers returned, far more children are being found with magic than before. If the same number were being born every year before that, what happened to them all?"

The answer to that question worried Choilan a great deal. In the last twenty years there would have been dozens of stories about children going missing or accidents, both at home and abroad in the west, but there were almost none. Not every child born with magic would have been able to control it by themselves. Perhaps a small number could learn it without training, but what about the rest? What had happened to them?

Or there was the possibility that what Habreel claimed was true.

"You've given me much to consider. I may call on you again," said the Regent, dismissing him with a wave. Bettina saw him out of the room and then returned a short time later. He couldn't decipher the sour expression on her face which made her look as if she had been sucking on a lemon.

"Speak."

"I do not like or trust that man," said Bettina.

"Neither of which is a concern if he is right."

Bettina chewed her lip and some of the prideful scorn eased from her features. "A nationwide ban on all Seekers would be a popular move. It would send a bold statement to the people." Choilan could see that admitting Habreel's idea could work pained her.

"And?"

"If properly phrased, it would show that we, as a nation, are in control of our own destiny. That we will not allow history to repeat itself. We won't be led around by the nose by the likes of the Warlock and magic of any kind."

"But?" he asked, sensing the trap.

"If the number of children with magic does not fall, we'll know the Seekers had nothing to do with it."

"But if they do then it could be the start of something new. This ban would be a temporary measure at best. But it could have wider implications if it works here." The thought of being the start of a wave that spread across the world appealed to Choilan. Too often the kings and queens of Zecorria had either been tame, achieving little during their rule, or they had been driven by insane passions. To change the course of events, even in a small way, would be a good way to be remembered by the historians.

"I will consider Habreel's idea. In the meantime I will speak in public about magic and the latest atrocity with the dead boy." It would give him the opportunity to gauge how a proclamation would be received. "Arrange for my second wife to visit the village and speak to the people. Give them some money to help with rebuilding and so on. Also begin drawing up the paperwork for a ban on all Seekers in the meantime."

"Yes, my Regent."

"And Bettina," he said, making her pause as she retreated from the room. "Be very clear in the document that any Seekers are to be escorted to the border and asked to leave. I will not tolerate any violence towards them." He would not sanction widespread murder of any kind against people who might not be responsible for what had happened. It also wouldn't do to be on bad terms with the Red Tower if this turned out to be the wrong decision. One mage had torn the world apart. A whole school full of them, unsupervised except by their own kind, greatly troubled him.

"Yes, my Regent."

"And have someone find out more about this Habreel. Who is he and where did he come from?"

Bettina offered a rare and genuine smile which disturbed him as it was so alien an expression for her. "I took the liberty of starting an investigation after his first visit."

"Of course you did," said the Regent, dismissing her. Events were in motion that he could not control. Now all that remained was to see if he would be another victim or witness to what transpired, or if he would become one of the architects of the future. Choilan hoped for the latter so that his legacy would outshine that of the Mad King.

CHAPTER 17

Tianne closed her eyes, turned her face towards the sunlight, and for a moment she forgot about everything. Every fourth day they were given some time to themselves, for prayer and study, but today she was using the time to catch up on her sleep. This was the third time in a week they'd been given a few hours to themselves, something that had not happened since she'd arrived almost a year ago.

To her left Danoph lay dozing in the sun. When the clouds parted and sunlight touched his golden skin it seemed to shimmer. Even asleep it looked as if he were carrying a heavy weight. His shoulders were hunched, his forehead creased and eyebrows drawn down. Perhaps he was worrying about his country, Shael, and the future of his people. They had lost almost everything, but, unlike most, he didn't blame her personally, or all of Zecorria, for what had happened during the war.

On her right Wren could have been sleeping, but instead she was reading a book on Talents she'd borrowed from the library. So far she'd been able to stay on Master Ottah's good side, but if she stained the pages with grass that would be the end of his leniency.

Tianne could see her lips moving as she went over something

again and again, trying to squeeze meaning from the vague text. There were no half-measures with her. Wren pushed herself in all of their classes and had earned the admiration of her teachers for her tenacity, even when she failed.

Tianne only wanted to learn enough to get by. She'd just about given up on finding a Talent and was getting used to disappointment. Wren seemed to take each failure personally and would try even harder the next time. So far she'd had three nosebleeds and had passed out twice from overexerting herself. Tianne thought some of the other students were afraid of her because of this, not what she'd done to Brunwal.

Wren had already proven that she was the strongest in their dormitory, but that wasn't enough for her. As Master Jorey had said, much could be done with even a weak connection to the Source. You just had to know how. Despite being told it might never happen, she was determined to prove she was proficient in at least one Talent. Tianne watched as Wren studied the next Talent in the list and then tried to weave together what was described. She could feel her drawing energy from the Source and it created a faint echo between them like a second pulse.

Tianne still remembered the first time she'd drawn power into herself from the Source. It was a feeling unlike anything she'd ever experienced and still had trouble describing.

At times, when growing up in Zecorria, she'd felt disconnected from those around her. The moment she'd reached towards that disturbance on the edge of her senses, everything had changed. The hollow spaces within were filled with light. Everything she saw became clearer, the colours more vibrant, and she felt connected to something greater than herself.

Every week she'd gone to church with her parents, but no matter how hard she prayed Tianne never felt what the priests and other people spoke about. The benevolent presence of the

Lady of Light. To fit in she had pretended, but here at the Red Tower there was no need to lie any more.

The Source gave her a sense of belonging. Her family was her blood, but Tianne felt connected on a deeper level to other mages, and her friends even more so.

"I can feel you staring," said Wren, without looking up from the page. "Did you want to ask me something?"

"No," said Tianne, quickly looking away. She pulled up a few blades of grass and started twisting them into a chain. A minute later she was studying her friend's profile again. With a sigh Wren put the book down and turned towards her.

"You have something on your mind?"

Tianne shrugged. "Don't you find it strange that we've been given free time again? The last time was only two days ago."

"It's not free time. You're supposed to be studying or at prayer."

"Fine, study time. But it's never been this often. Once a week at most."

Wren frowned. "I will admit, it is peculiar."

"I met a girl yesterday, and she said her class on Talents was cancelled. Apparently Master Jorey was called away on urgent business. I've seen other teachers riding out of the gates in a hurry and now we're here, again." Tianne gestured at the space around them. Not far away other groups of students were lounging in the sun, sleeping, reading and playing cards. The oldest students, those eighteen and above, were noticeably absent. She guessed they were at the nearby town, trying their luck at buying ale from one of the taverns. Most of the owners knew not to sell to students, but there were a few who didn't care as long as you had money and didn't cause any trouble.

"Perhaps we should ask one of the teachers," suggested Wren. "They may have some answers."

"Who could we ask? Garvey?" joked Tianne.

Wren fiddled with the front cover of her book, opening and closing it before she answered. "I would prefer not to ask him."

"I told you he was a bastard," said Tianne. Much to her surprise Wren didn't disagree and tell her off for speaking ill of a teacher. Her silence spoke volumes. "What happened? Did you talk to him?"

"After what happened with Brunwal I sought his advice. His suggestions were troubling."

"You can't trust him," said Tianne. "Did you know that both Eloise and Balfruss fought against the west during the war?"

"I don't see the connection."

"The King of Seveldrom sent out a message for powerful Battlemages to defend the country against the Warlock. Where was Garvey?"

"I don't know."

"No one does," said Tianne. "There's a rumour he was too far away in the east to help, but I don't believe it. I think he stayed away because he was afraid."

Wren smiled at her in a way that Tianne found more than a little condescending. "He is many things, dangerous, cruel and unlikeable, but I do not believe him to be a coward. You know how strong he is. You can feel it."

Tianne disagreed and still thought him a coward, but she said nothing further. She was confident that time would prove her right, but at least Wren knew that Garvey was dangerous. Hopefully it would be enough to make her stay away from him in the future.

"Perhaps Balfruss might be willing to talk to us about what's happening," suggested Wren.

"He's not here," said Tianne. "He left two days ago in a hurry. Just before guests arrived to visit Eloise."

"How is it that you know so much?"

Tianne was aware some people called her a gossip but she preferred to know what was happening around her at all times. The more information she had the more difficult it was for someone to deceive her. She would not fall into that trap again.

Back home some of the local children had used her naïveté against her. They told her stories so often, and with such confidence, that she'd believed them. She would repeat the outlandish tales as facts, leading to public humiliation and a reputation for lying that was impossible to shake.

Sometimes she thought coming to the Red Tower had been one of the best things to happen to her. It gave her a fresh start as no one here knew what she'd done in the past. She was a blank slate without a reputation. Her dark eyes marked her apart from most, but she was not the only student from Zecorria. And, despite everything, she'd found a few friends who liked her for who she was now.

"I just like to know what's going on," said Tianne with a shrug. She turned her face away so that Wren couldn't see her wiping at her eyes. It annoyed her that the pain of what had happened during her childhood could still get to her so easily. Wren must have sensed something as she grasped Tianne's hand.

"Who were the visitors?" she asked gently.

"They looked like Jhanidi."

"What are those?"

Tianne smiled, feeling a little smug that Wren didn't know what they were. "They're warrior monks from the desert kingdoms in the far east. They accept children into their temples and train them to fight with blunt weapons as well as magic. I don't know why they can't use swords. It might be a religious thing. But when their training is complete students can choose either to return home to their old lives, or serve the King. Anyone who serves gets a tattoo on their face and wherever they go they're treated as honoured guests."

"That would be a nice change," said Danoph, propping himself up on one elbow. "To be welcomed and not shunned for being a mage."

"You saw these priests?" said Wren, sounding doubtful.

"Two women. They both had a tattoo here," said Tianne, tracing a vertical line down from her forehead across her right eye to her jaw.

Danoph's frown deepened. He was probably wondering the same thing as Tianne. Why had they come to the Red Tower? And why now?

The sound of heavy footsteps made everyone who was dozing sit up suddenly and pretend to be reading. The decks of cards disappeared and an unnatural silence fell across all the groups. Choss came around the corner and marched on without looking around or noticing. Tianne thought he looked tense. He had one hand resting on a short sword that he had recently taken to wearing.

She knew from some of the older students that it wasn't just stories about Balfruss that people discussed in taverns. There were a few about him and Munroe being involved with a war between criminal Families in Perizzi five or six years ago. The details were sketchy but every tale put him and Munroe at the heart of them.

Judging by his level of wariness it seemed like the rumours she'd heard were true. Seekers were being attacked in villages and towns across the west when they went to test children. People seemed to think they were responsible for a few children losing control of their magic. It would explain why all of the teaching staff seemed so on edge. She'd thought about telling her friends, but they had enough to worry about. Danoph with his woes about his people and Wren with her ongoing issues with Brunwal.

"I'll be right back," said Tianne, feeling a tightness in her belly.

"You have a bladder the size of a walnut," said Danoph, lying down and closing his eyes again. Tianne tossed her book at him which landed on his stomach, making him gasp.

As she came out of the washroom Tianne found the dormitory was completely empty. It was so tempting. She just wanted to lie down on her bed and sleep away the rest of the afternoon. The teachers had relaxed the rules a little but she didn't think they'd go that far.

With a sigh she marched to the front door and then stepped back quickly, reaching for the Source.

"I just want to talk!" said the boy who'd suddenly appeared in the doorway. Tianne didn't know his name but she'd seen him following Brunwal around like a lapdog. He was one of the group who had been there when Brunwal had beaten Wren unconscious. It didn't matter to her that he was from Zecorria as well. That hadn't helped her when she'd first arrived and Brunwal had bullied her until she'd lost in a duel. The boy had been jeering along with all of the others.

"Get out of my way," said Tianne, drawing more power into her body until it thrummed against her temples. She could attack him first and everyone would believe it had been in self-defence. He and the others who hung around Brunwal had unpleasant reputations.

"I'm not here to fight," he said, glancing around. She backed away from the door and braced herself for his friends to rush into the dormitory after him. Instead he followed her in and closed the door. "Please, I just want to talk."

So far he hadn't reached for the Source, but Tianne wasn't as gullible as she used to be. She wouldn't be caught unaware. She would fight him with everything she had.

For now she decided to play along. "Then talk."

He moved away from the door to the far corner and she followed him in parallel, making sure there was plenty of open space around her. If he tried anything, or anyone tried to come at her, she would see them before they were within arm's reach.

"I'm Mozell."

"I don't care. What do you want?"

Mozell ran a hand through his hair and stared out of the window. For a moment he seemed to have forgotten she was even there. "He's not going to stop."

"Who?"

Mozell looked at her briefly and lowered his voice, as if afraid of being overheard. "Brunwal. He's going to go after your friend again."

"Why?"

"I don't know. I thought he just wanted to scare her, like he did with the others."

Tianne noticed he didn't apologise for his part or say how many others there had been in the past. She wondered if he even knew how many people Brunwal had beaten and intimidated. "Is this because she embarrassed him?"

"Yes. No. I don't know." Mozell was sweating and he kept swallowing and rubbing his throat. It was only then Tianne realised he was afraid of Brunwal. "We've all tried to talk him out of it, but he just won't listen. He's obsessed with her."

Tianne finally released the Source but he didn't notice. A horrible clammy feeling began to creep across her skin. "What is he planning to do?"

Mozell finally looked at her. "He's going to kill Wren."

Tianne was speechless. She had known that Brunwal wouldn't

let it go, but she hadn't thought he would go that far. "What do we do?"

"No one can stop it." Mozell's eyes were haunted, as if he was already watching it happen.

"There must be something we can try."

"He wants us there, to keep you and anyone else off him. I've spoken to the others in the group. We've all agreed not to fight, if you'll do the same."

Finally it all started to make sense. She should have seen it coming. "This is a trick. You're trying to fool me. You want me to stand idle while you all beat my friend to death."

"Tianne, I swear by the Lady of Light and the Maker himself. May they both strike me down if I'm lying. This is not a trick." He was pleading and the desperation in his eyes seemed real. She could see he was trapped. If he tried to leave the group he would become just another victim. But if he stayed he was protected by the person he feared the most.

"I promise we will not fight for him," repeated Mozell.

Tianne still wasn't convinced. Experience had taught her to be extremely cautious. "Why come to me?"

"We're both from Zecorria. I thought you might agree because of that. We should stick together."

"Do I look that stupid?"

"Fine. I can't be seen with Wren and your friend, Danoph, is weird. His eyes are creepy."

"You're afraid," said Tianne.

"Of course I am. And you should be, too. Brunwal is out for blood." He glanced out of the window again and moved to the door. "Remember what I've said. Leave it to Brunwal and Wren to sort it out. This isn't going to end until one of them is dead. I don't want to get caught in the middle and neither do you."

"I still don't trust you," she said as he opened the door.

"I wouldn't expect you to. Just keep an eye out. It's going to happen soon." He raced out of the door and Tianne heard his footsteps recede into the distance. The silence of the dormitory was normally soothing but standing alone in the empty room it began to feel eerie. As if she was standing inside a crypt.

Tianne hurried outside and headed back towards her friends, but even when she was standing in bright sunlight the chill inside didn't fade.

CHAPTER 18

Akosh walked into the church of the Maker and lazily made her way towards the front pews. Unlike everyone else who entered the vast cathedral, she was neither amazed by its beauty nor overwhelmed by its size. She felt no sudden awareness of a great benevolent spirit. In fact, quite the opposite. The whole place felt abandoned, as if she'd walked into an empty house that had been left to rot for years.

There was no powerful spirit lurking in the rafters. No magnanimous presence bestowing gifts and answering the prayers of its faithful. Only a large, echoing building that would otherwise be a decaying shell, home only to pigeons and rats, if not for the deluded followers of a dead god.

Part of her wanted to spit on the floor but she resisted the urge because it was childish. She had no fear of reprisal. She knew very well that the Maker had abandoned his followers as he had abandoned the world. No one had seen him in centuries and, despite their continued reverence and fear, she knew he had gone somewhere beyond the Veil.

Akosh contemplated leaving something more permanent in her wake. Something baffling and, perhaps, slightly mystical for the priests to try and untangle over the next decade or two. On second thoughts she changed her mind. Such a mystery would only be twisted by the priests until it served their continuing mass delusion. They would use it as a form of proof to convince the people that the Maker still existed.

There was a lot of empty space but Akosh chose to sit directly behind one of the parishioners. The man in front of her was whispering but she could hear him asking for strength and forgiveness.

"He's not listening," she said in his ear. Akosh was delighted to see Habreel recoil and exclaim in surprise, his voice echoing around the vast tomb-like hall. She cackled and slouched back on her pew, piling up some of the cushions behind her until it was reasonably comfortable. She stretched out and put one boot on the pew in front, smearing mud everywhere.

"What are you doing here?" he said, lowering his voice to a whisper.

"I'm here for one of our exhilarating meetings."

"At my office, not here." Habreel was furious and swept her foot off the back of the pew onto the floor. Akosh smiled, pleased to have finally found something to get under his skin.

Normally he was so in control of his emotions that nothing seemed to knock him off balance. It made their talks rather tedious. It was as if he'd written them down beforehand and spent time rehearsing his answers. "Go to my office. I will meet you there," he hissed.

"I'm not one of your idiot followers that you can order around." Akosh refused to lower her voice even though she knew it was attracting stares from other people scattered around the church. Even the balding priest was glancing in their direction and looked ready to give them a stern telling off. Akosh winked at the priest and blew him a kiss, completely flustering the idiot. "We need to talk."

"I will not discuss our affairs or anything else in this church. I am here to pray."

He was going all stiff again and stubborn. It seemed as if a little reminder was necessary of who was in charge. "You know that I could easily kill you, even here in this holy place, and nothing would happen." Akosh held her arms out wide towards the distant arched ceiling, daring the Maker to do something, anything. As usual, the only reply was a dead silence.

"I know," admitted Habreel.

"Do not forget who holds the power in our relationship," she said, grabbing him by the arm. Habreel slowly pulled it clear of her grip and she rolled her eyes. He was being boring and retreating into his shell again. The walls were going back up inside.

With a dramatic yawn she walked out of the church and into the first tavern she found. The woman behind the bar gave her the first drink for free, but when Akosh turned on her dazzling smile she left the bottle.

After an indeterminate amount of time, enough for her to sip her way through half the bottle and lose most of the feeling in her toes, Akosh stumbled out of the front door. The fingers on her right hand were tingling as well, which probably wasn't a good sign, but she ignored it and waited for it to go away as she drifted through the city.

Herakion was a dull place. The people were so stiff and defensive. You couldn't say anything to one of them without someone mentioning the war. What followed was a strident protest about it not being their fault before someone inevitably apologised out of some misplaced sense of guilt.

Everyone blamed them for their previous King going mad and starting the war. Most people in Zecorria said it had nothing to do with them, but somewhere down the line it seemed as if some of them had started to believe it, too.

The city had once been rife with intrigue and political games as noble families backstabbed each other in a variety of inventive ways to gain favour with the King. When the Mad King had taken the throne from his father it had been even more interesting for a time and business for Akosh had thrived. No one knew if the King would grant them a boon or stab them to death on a whim. The whole city had been balanced on the edge of a blade. One false step and a person could topple off or split themselves in two. It had been delicious.

Much had changed over time and Akosh had been slow to realise that her survival depended on remaining adaptable. It was the mortals who had taught her that with their fickle nature.

A fad in clothing could become incredibly popular overnight. It might start with a powerful noble, or merely someone making a bold and outlandish statement. The following day every tailor and person in power would be scrambling to imitate the design. They needed to be noticed and wanted to feel like they mattered. They were all so desperate to feel valued that they scrambled around, with their noses in the dirt, instead of looking towards the horizon and tomorrow.

Of course fads could disappear as quickly as they arrived. And quite often those chasing the trend managed to get the desired garment just as it went out of fashion. Then they looked like an idiot and the tailors were left with bolts of cloth that no one wanted to buy any more.

So it had been with Akosh and who she used to be.

She stared with disdain at the giant domes and towers of the old religions that dominated the city's skyline. The Maker. The church of the Holy Light. Temples devoted to the Blessed Mother. They were all set in stone, unable to change or evolve over time. She would never be like them.

Who she'd been at the beginning, when she'd first become aware, was a long way from who she was now. Interference was forbidden but they all bent the rules to ensure their survival.

Rather depressingly, she felt quite sober again and with nothing else to do made her way to Habreel's office. She waved at those downstairs as she went past and entered his office without knocking. On the surface he looked calm but she could see fire dancing behind his eyes.

"What did you do?"

Maybe she was still a little drunk after all. "Is this about interrupting your prayers?"

Habreel was livid. "What did you do in Faulkner's Quarry?"

It took Akosh a moment to remember that was the name of the village where Yacob was from. She shrugged. "Only what we discussed."

"You killed over a hundred people."

"I didn't kill anyone. The boy got too excited and exploded early, which often happens."

Habreel was in no mood for jokes. "Women and children died."

"I did you a favour. If only a few people had been killed, no one would have cared. But now, everyone is talking about it."

"This is not what we discussed. I cannot condone your actions."

"It worked, didn't it?" she said, raising an eyebrow. "How was your meeting with the Regent?"

Habreel opened his mouth to answer but then stopped himself. She saw that his rudimentary intelligence was starting to join up a few dots and he began to wonder. How did she know he'd met with the Regent? Had one of his people told her? Or did she have spies of her own in the palace?

"The Regent is a moderate," he said eventually, his tone calm. She could see he was studying her now, looking for clues and facial tics that might give away what she was thinking. "Even with other incidents abroad, he won't take drastic action. But the number of dead at home cannot be ignored. The people of Zecorria are watching and they expect him to do something. I think he'll agree to a national ban on Seekers."

"It sounds like we should be celebrating. Do you have anything to drink?"

"It's a good beginning," he conceded, "but getting rid of the Seekers will not stop children being born with magic. We need to cut it off at the source."

"And I've told you, over and over again, it doesn't run in family lines," said Akosh. They'd had this conversation many times. Even if he drowned the parents of every child born with magic it wouldn't help. Another child would be born with magic at some point. She'd told him magic was not connected to bloodlines, but he still doubted her.

"Then we need a complete ban. Drive them all away. Anyone who has any magic needs to be exiled. Every single mage."

Some heat was coming back into his voice which caught her attention. "And where would you send them?" she asked.

"I don't care."

Akosh pursed her lips. "Tell me. Who did you lose during the war? Did one of the Battlemages blow up your dear wife and little children?"

Habreel chuckled, but his eyes were cold. "That would make it nice and easy for you, wouldn't it? That I'm doing all of this for revenge because of a personal slight. My poor dead wife and darling children."

"Well, aren't you?" she asked. Habreel liked to think he was different from everyone else, but deep down she'd assumed he was a simple man with base needs. Up to now she hadn't cared about his motivation, but he'd piqued her interest.

"No. I didn't lose anyone. I don't have any family. I'm doing this because it has to be done. I saw first-hand the destructive power of magic and how it taints everything that it touches. From the Mad King to the Queen of Yerskania. Magic is dangerous and unnatural. People should be afraid and want to distance themselves from it. You've said anyone can be born with magic. That it's random and a quirk of birth."

"That's true."

"That kind of destructive power should not be in the hands of anyone. It cannot be tamed and the Red Tower is untrustworthy. Why should they be allowed to make decisions that affect all of our lives? Why are they the only ones to govern mages from across the world? They have a private army that could rule every nation."

"You think they're going to try and take over?" Akosh was losing interest. Insanity wasn't nearly as interesting as people believed.

"Think of it this way," said Habreel. "You wouldn't let a simpleton make decisions that could affect the lives of those around them. So it is with magic. A complete ban, in every country, is the only way to protect ourselves."

"Then we should continue with the plan. It's too late to back out now anyway," said Akosh. She expected Habreel to protest. Then she would have to talk him around on the subject until his morality allowed it, but instead he stayed silent and immobile, turning it over in his head.

"What would you do next?" he finally asked. Akosh smiled to herself. He wasn't so different after all.

"There are plenty more teenagers on the cusp. All they need is a little push, and the right motivation," she said, winking and gyrating her hips.

"May the Maker forgive me," he muttered. "Find another child and this time make sure a few more witnesses survive. It does no good if no one is alive to spread the stories."

"I'll take care of it. Which reminds me, you still owe me payment for the last one."

Habreel's sneer was not unexpected but she ignored it. He thought he knew why she asked for money, to spend on indulgences, but the real reason would never cross his mind. "Speak to Dannel. He'll give you the money."

Downstairs Dannel and two other young men were busy scribbling in notebooks, but they all paused when she entered the room. Akosh could feel the heat behind their stares, but Dannel kept his eyes averted and was both polite and efficient. She offered him a smile of thanks when he gave her the money but he didn't reciprocate.

Akosh walked purposefully towards the most run-down part of the city in the east. Here, the homes were modest and some of the oldest, which meant they were in desperate need of repair. Those with money had moved to other areas, sometimes leaving behind huge empty buildings that seemed far too grand when compared to those around them. With no money to maintain them they had become empty shells stripped of anything that could be sold. Like the skeleton of a vast beast that had been picked clean of meat.

In these rotting shells lived the refugees, the poor, the desperate and the needy. Akosh stopped in front of a wide three-storey building that had once been the home of a noble who had died over fifty years ago. She remembered him as a sweaty man who was constantly stuffing shellfish into his face. He'd bought a new home elsewhere, taking his growing brood of children with him, leaving this behind to charity. As Akosh recalled he'd choked to death on a fishbone.

A small crudely painted sign by the front door told Akosh she was in the right place. In the entrance hall she found a small boy and in the next room four more children playing a game with coloured pebbles. All of them looked underfed, but they were clean and dressed in ill-fitting clothing that had probably been passed on to them. There was little furniture in any of the rooms, but she could see the floors had been scrubbed.

In the room beyond that she found a group of six small children listening in rapt silence to a woman read them a story from a battered old book. A seventh child was sitting on the woman's lap, reading along and mouthing the words as he traced them with his finger. The woman was in her thirties and as thin as a rake. Her face was drawn, heavy bags sat under her eyes and her lank black hair was badly cut. All of it made her look much older than her years.

"Children, we have a guest," said the woman. Another helper, a young man, came into the room, taking over the story. Akosh followed the woman through a warren of empty rooms to a basic office at the back of the building. It had a scarred and worn desk that wobbled, a pair of mismatched chairs and several musty books. As she sat down the woman pulled a thin blanket around her shoulders. Despite everything the smile she offered was warm and generous.

"My name is Jille. How can I help you?"

"Actually, I'm here to help you," said Akosh, putting a heavy pouch of money on the table. It was everything she'd been given from Habreel.

"We happily accept donations. The children are always hungry and more arrive all the time."

"I would like to be more than just a donor," said Akosh and at this the woman met her gaze for the first time. Recognition sparked behind Jille's eyes for a moment. "I would like to become the patron of this orphanage."

Jille's smile faltered. "And what would that mean?"

"I would make regular donations. In return, I will visit on occasion, to ensure the money is being well spent."

"Everything we have goes to the children," swore Jille. "We take nothing for ourselves."

"I'm not accusing you of anything," she said, softening the words with a warm smile. "I'd just like to see how the children are getting on from time to time."

Despite the promise of regular donations Jille was still wary. "Is that everything?"

"No. There's one more thing. Do you have an idol or a prayer corner?"

Jille nodded slowly. "Devoted to the Maker. We teach the children about him once a week."

"It must go and in its place you'll teach them about their new patron." Akosh took a small stone idol from her pocket which she put on the table beside the money. It was crudely made, which was in keeping with such a humble orphanage, and showed a caring mother looking after a child.

"I've heard of you," said Jille. "You've done this before, with other orphanages."

Akosh nodded. "Many times." Even then Jille hesitated. "There are others in the city. Go and speak to them. You'll see that with my help they've flourished over the years. They have plenty of money for food, fuel in winter, clothing and books to give the children a good chance. One of them hires a tutor to teach them to write. What more could you ask for?"

"And you'll impose no other rules? Demand nothing in return?"

"I ask only that you look after the children. But, before you can do that, you must also look after yourself. Have you been skipping meals?"

"There's so little food. They need it more than me," said Jille.

"That must stop. They rely on you. If you fall ill, who will look after them? I'll have your promise on that," insisted Akosh. "You must look after yourself as well." She waited until Jille had promised before picking up the idol but leaving the money. "Whether you accept my offer or not, that's for the children. I'll return in a week for your answer. I'll see myself out."

Akosh left the orphanage and had barely gone the length of the street before she was approached by a young man in his twenties. He didn't look familiar but when he smiled it was as if he'd known her all of his life.

"Mother," he whispered reverentially, bowing his head ever so slightly.

She looked around but no one had noticed. Akosh took him by the arm and moved out of the middle of the road to be less conspicuous. "Hello, my child. Please, speak to me normally. What is your name?"

"Adem."

"Do you have some news for me, Adem?"

"Yes, Mother. I live a few days south of here, close to the border. A man came to our town asking questions about children and magic."

"What sort of questions?"

"He was asking about where we heard our news. We've all listened to stories about children hurting themselves and other people. He was very persistent. I think he wanted to find out who was spreading the stories."

That ruled out one of Habreel's people. They were the ones perpetuating the stories about the dangers of magic. And it wasn't one of her children as someone would have let her know.

It was possible the man was in fact not a man at all, but one of her peculiar siblings.

"Describe the man. Was there anything unusual about him?" asked Akosh.

"Not really. He was from Yerskania with pale skin and he was cross eyed. I think he might have been a soldier at some time, but it must have been years ago."

It didn't sound like anyone she knew. As expected, other mortal parties were curious and trying to find answers of their own. She knew most of the rulers had spy networks that operated in other countries. Yerskania sent Guardians of the Peace abroad on jobs, so it could have been one of them. The Red Tower would be investigating as well.

"When you get home I want you to keep an eye out for other strangers," said Akosh. "If you hear anything, send word to me. Our time is approaching and very soon I will need you, and all of the others, for what lies ahead."

CHAPTER 19

"You have no right to keep me here," said Grell, crossing his arms.

Tammy wasn't impressed and chose not to comment. Over the last few hours she'd heard more than enough from him, all of it unpleasant.

She'd travelled by herself to Morby Dale, a tiny village on Munroe's list, in the hope of finding the Seeker before he was injured or exiled. She hadn't anticipated coming across one of those responsible for spreading fear of magic.

Grell was from Yerskania, but didn't live close to Morby Dale. From speaking to locals earlier in the day she'd found out he'd turned up in the village a few days ago. Since then he'd spent most of his time drinking and talking to anyone who would listen. A Seeker was due to visit in a week's time and Grell's goal seemed to create a hostile atmosphere. People were already nervous of magic, but Grell wanted to make sure they were terrified of it and anyone connected to it.

She'd overheard him spreading stories of children exploding in graphic detail because of a visit from a Seeker. With tears in his eyes he'd nearly wept as he described the women and children who had died in a horrible accident in Zecorria. He'd even claimed to have helped dig some of the tiny graves for the children and a mass grave for the mixed body parts that were recovered.

It was all an act. The tragedy was real, but almost everything else he said was a lie. After listening to him talk with different groups, Tammy noticed how he adjusted the tone and facts of his story depending on the audience and their initial response.

If they showed disinterest he focused on the Seeker's pending arrival and the threat it would pose to them, even here in a tiny village. If they replied with disbelief that Seekers were responsible for children dying, he focused on how he'd seen it happen. He provided so much detail that it sounded credible rather than pure fiction. If the person was a woman he started by telling them his sob story about dead children.

After a while she'd been unable to bear the sound of his voice and had dragged him out of the tavern and locked him in the storage room. Morby Dale was so small that any official business was normally conducted in the Mayor's front room. In his absence, and with nowhere secure to keep Grell, she'd been forced to improvise. The storage room at the back of the tavern was normally used to store vegetables for the kitchen, but she'd borrowed it from the owner. She'd been only too happy to help as Tammy wasn't the only one tired of Grell's voice.

Grell sat in front of her with a smug grin, confident that she would have to let him go as soon as the Mayor returned. There was a sly cunning behind his small brown eyes. Overweight with a sparse straw-coloured beard and balding head, Grell didn't look like much of a threat. But she knew he was a menace. He reminded her of the type of bully she'd seen growing up who carried out horrible tricks on smaller children then played them all off as a joke. In Grell's mind he believed what he was doing was noble.

"Who gave you the power to keep me here?" asked Grell, tiring of the silence.

It was Tammy's turn to smile. "The Queen of Yerskania and the Khevassar when they appointed me a Guardian of the Peace."

Grell's smile faltered. "I'm not wanted for any crime. I've broken no laws."

"I'm sure I can find a few."

"Such as?"

"How about inciting hatred and violence? Or disturbing the peace?"

"I've not disturbed anyone, just shared a few true stories. People like to hear news from the outside world. After all, Morby Dale is a small place." If not for his patronising tone what he was saying would sound reasonable. That was what made him so dangerous. He was like a greased pig running through a crowd. Counting the number of chins he had, it was an apt comparison.

"The Queen of Yerskania gave the Seekers permission to travel anywhere in the country and test children once a month."

"We're supposed to trust her? After what she did during the war? She's not fit to rule," scoffed Grell.

Tammy stopped herself from getting drawn into an argument. As a Guardian, and therefore perhaps a patriot, he expected an emotional response by going after the Queen. When she didn't rise to the bait a smile briefly flickered across his face. It had probably been a while since he'd met someone who could see through his façade so easily.

"How long have you been sharing your stories?" she asked.

Grell shrugged. "A few days."

"And what were you doing before that?"

"Working here and there."

"Doing what?"

"These are troubling times and people need protection."

Tammy couldn't help scoffing. "You're a mercenary?"

"We come in all shapes and sizes."

"Not many are your shape," she said, gesturing at his lumpy physique. "Have you ever held a sword before?"

"I didn't earn these working in the fields," he said, showing her calluses on his right hand.

"So why were you kicked out of the Watch?"

Grell started to answer but then stopped himself. He clamped his mouth shut, glared at her and folded his arms again. Two could play the same mind games.

Tammy had been a member of the Watch for years before being promoted to becoming a Guardian of the Peace. Only the best were chosen and Grell did not represent them. There were too many people in the Watch for her to know them all, but she'd seen plenty of calluses like his in the past.

"Let me guess," she pondered, tapping her chin. "You were dismissed for gambling? Drugs? Blackmail?" When Grell didn't react she snapped her fingers. "I've got it. You were just too lazy and stupid."

"How long are you going to keep me here?"

Tammy shook her head, ignoring his question. "No, it was probably something more sinister. Perhaps you were paid to look the other way for one of the Families." The crime Families in Perizzi knew better than to try and bribe a Guardian, but sometimes they found members of the Watch with vices that could be exploited in return for small favours.

"I chose to leave," said Grell, which they both knew was a lie.

"To pursue a higher calling."

"What we're doing is important," he said, ignoring her mocking tone. "We will change the future."

Tammy dismissed him with a wave. "We? You're nothing but a peon, following orders."

"I make a difference!" shrieked Grell.

"You didn't come up with this plan. Don't pretend anyone listens to your opinion."

"I'm valued."

"You're deluded."

"Habreel trusts me!"

Tammy's grin stretched from ear to ear. The colour slowly drained from Grell's face as he realised what he'd said. "So, it was all Habreel's idea."

Grell didn't move. Not even an eyelid twitched. She knew that for now he wouldn't say another word, no matter what she said. A heavy silence settled on the room and Tammy used the quiet to ponder Habreel's identity and where Grell knew him from.

A short time later a loud knocking at the door surprised them both. A short bearded man squeezed into the room, closing the door behind him. In his middling years, with grey speckling his black hair and a friendly, open face, Tammy guessed he was the Mayor of Morby Dale.

"I'm Cobb. What's happening here?"

"I'm being illegally held by this woman!" shouted Grell. He started to stand up, as if about to leave, until Tammy kicked out one of his feet. Grell fell back into his chair and it rocked backwards on two legs before he was able to rebalance it.

"I'm a Guardian of the Peace. This is all legal. Do you have a moment to talk?" she asked.

Cobb's pale green eyes studied her. She noticed his right eye was covered with a milky white film. A faded old scar ran through his eyebrow onto his cheek. "Let's step outside."

She followed him out of the room, making sure the door

was securely bolted, before stepping into the street. The day was bright and sunny with fluffy white clouds ghosting past above them silently. Nearby she could hear children playing and see people in the village going about their business without any worry. It felt a long way from the world she knew with its dangers.

"Walk with me?" he asked, and she nodded, shortening her stride to match his pace. "Life here is very quiet," said Cobb, gesturing at the village and its people. "As Mayor the biggest problems I have to deal with is someone getting drunk and starting a fight. Or someone's dog accidentally killing one of their neighbour's chickens. We get our news from passing merchants, but most traders don't bother coming here as we're too small."

They passed the smithy where a sweaty, red-faced man and his two apprentices were hard at work. The smith wiped at his brow and waved at Cobb as they walked past. The Mayor raised a hand but they didn't stop to talk to him. A little further down the road two similar-looking women, she guessed mother and daughter, were in lively discussion over a bolt of silk. Cobb steered Tammy away from the two women, moving down a parallel side street.

"It's my eldest daughter's wedding," murmured Cobb. "I brought the silk back for her dress. She and her mother are having a disagreement about the style. Do you have a family?"

Tammy's mind turned to what she had left behind in Perizzi and Kovac's quest to find her an answer. She'd been so busy lately there hadn't been time to think about it, but the old pain was still there deep inside. She wondered if it would ever go away.

"No," she lied. "Have you lived here a long time?"

Cobb glanced up at her and touched the scar on his cheek.

"I got this as a member of the Watch. A fight on the docks in Perizzi got out of hand. No one died but it was close and I lost my sight in one eye. Been here ever since. Nearly thirty years now."

They paused at the end of the muddy track and Cobb led them to a small bridge that crossed a narrow stream. The water was so clear Tammy could see the bottom where a few small fish were swimming around lazily in the sun, their scales glistening red and purple. Cobb paused on the middle of the bridge and Tammy realised he'd led her to a secluded spot where they could speak without being overheard.

"I'm not here to cause any trouble," said Tammy.

"I know, but nonetheless your presence will cause ripples," he said, gesturing at the water below.

"Do you know what's going on out there?"

"Some," admitted Cobb. "Tell me about the man you've locked up."

Tammy explained what Grell had been doing and the wider implications. Cobb had heard about the child in Zecorria killing some people while being tested, but not the impact.

"Grell, and whoever he works for, are intent on spreading fear and hatred. Anyone with magic could soon find themselves driven out of town or worse. A golden mask might protect a Seeker's identity, but right now it makes them a target."

"You're worried that people here will attack the Seeker next week," said Cobb, sitting down on the bridge. Feeling that she was already looming over him, Tammy sat down next to him and he smiled at the gesture. Despite having only one good eye, he saw plenty.

"If people like Grell continue spreading hatred of anyone who's different, then I think it's possible." Yerskania had always taken pride in trading with every other nation in the world.

She could walk down the streets of Perizzi and see faces from Zecorria to Morrinow to the desert kingdoms. "This intolerance is a sickness. If it's left to fester it can poison good people."

"I will speak to the people here. Find out what they really think."

Tammy looked around and still lowered her voice before speaking. "Don't test the children next week. The Red Tower has said you should stay safe and hidden for now."

What most people in Morby Dale didn't know was that, as well as being the Mayor, Cobb was also the local Seeker. No one raised an eyebrow when he made regular trips to other villages in the area. In fact it was expected. As far as they knew he was speaking to other Mayors, not testing the children for magic.

"Do you want to see the sum total of my magic?" he asked. Tammy was going to say no, but there was something in Cobb's voice that changed her mind.

"Yes."

Cobb leaned over the side of the bridge and gestured at the water below. As she watched the surface of the trickling stream slowed and then began to part around a patch of ice that had formed. The pebble-sized ball of ice was held in place for a moment and then Cobb's shoulders slumped. With that it slipped free of its mooring and floated away. It began to break apart almost immediately and in the warm sun it would be gone in moments.

"Not even my wife knows," said Cobb. "Not because I don't trust her, but once someone finds out they always look at you differently. If I'd told people what I can do, I would never have been allowed into the Watch, never been injured, and never come here. They would never have made me the Mayor and I wouldn't have a wife and two beautiful daughters."

Cobb looked despondent, staring into the distance, perhaps

wondering how his life would have turned out if he'd gone to the Red Tower as a youth.

It made Tammy wonder where she would have ended up if her husband was still alive. Would she still be working for Don Lowell in Perizzi? Would she have been running one of the Families by now, instead of working as a Guardian?

"Although I'm worried about the children, I will bury the mask," he said, coming back to the present. "Perhaps in time, people's attitudes towards magic will change."

"Let's hope so," said Tammy, feeling some of Cobb's melancholy rub off on her. She had regrets as well but it was too late to change the past. All she could do was try to keep moving forward and hope to leave her old life far behind.

"Enough brooding. Let's go and get something to eat. Are you hungry?" he said, forcing a smile.

"I could eat, but then I'll be heading back to Perizzi."

"What about your prisoner?"

"He knows a lot more about what's going on than he pretends. Once I get him back to Unity Hall, and he sees the cells, he'll talk. It's a long road and I'll need all my strength to cope with Grell and his mouth on the way."

Cobb offered her a sympathetic smile. "Perhaps you could gag him?" he suggested. She shared a smile with him as they set off towards the tavern.

It was still warm under the trees in the sun, but Tammy shivered despite herself. She was worried about what was coming and if they would be able to stop it before someone else was murdered.

CHAPTER 20

G roaning with effort, Munroe pulled Denke a little higher as he was slumping towards the street again. She had one arm around his waist and the other gripping his blood-slicked hand over her shoulder. He moaned in pain but didn't cry out. She admired Denke's grit, less so his faith in the people of Rojenne. After all, they had just tried to kill him for being a Seeker.

"Just a little further," she murmured, although she'd been saying that for a while. Not for the first time in her life, Munroe regretted being a little on the short side. Denke wasn't a big man but he was at least twice her weight. Sweat had already soaked her shirt from the short walk and the muscles in her shoulders and arms were burning. He couldn't walk and she wouldn't be able to carry him much further without some help. The crowd were not pursuing them yet, but she knew it wouldn't be long before someone followed.

Glancing around, she checked the street and then embraced the Source. Using a steady trickle of power Munroe shored up Denke, easing most of his weight off her shoulders. To an outsider it still looked as if she were carrying him, but now they were walking more quickly and his feet were barely touching the floor. Gritting her teeth against the pressure she scanned the streets for what she needed.

On purpose she'd taken them away from the busier streets and nicer areas, descending into a more run-down part of the city. Rojenne wasn't big compared to Perizzi, the capital, but even here she knew where to find a certain type of person.

Munroe turned down narrower streets and eventually came to a neighbourhood where a lot of the shops were closed and boarded up. There were a few legitimate businesses struggling to survive, a baker's, a couple of drinking holes and a butcher's selling questionable meat. She went past all of them without stopping but could feel a few sets of eyes following her progress with keen interest. Eventually Munroe spotted what she was after. A teenage boy lurking on a corner, doing nothing, or so it seemed. When he noticed her watching he slunk away and she followed at a sedate pace. Beside her Denke murmured something as he drifted in and out of consciousness. She couldn't make out the words and didn't know if he was asking her to do something important or was just rambling. Either way it wasn't a good sign.

Holding onto the Source made the power thrum inside Munroe, but it also heightened her senses. Tilting her head to one side she followed the quiet patter of the boy's feet. She'd gone down two streets and along a narrow alley, walking sideways with Denke, before she stopped at a crossroads.

A broad man with a shaven head stood waiting for her with his beefy arms crossed. The boy lurked behind him. From the look of the thug's face someone had used it to test their fists over a period of many years. His nose was a broken, scarred mess. One ear was gone, probably torn off, and the other stuck out in a comical fashion, twisted and gnarled like a piece of cauliflower. However, despite his rough exterior she noticed that his cool,

calculating eyes were watching her closely. They flickered once
to Denke before settling back on her.

"What do you need?" asked the thug, his gravelly voice so
deep she could almost feel it in her bones.

"Doctor."

"Show me your coin."

Moving carefully, so as not to rip open the wound in Denke's
side any further, she lowered him to the ground. His eyes flut-
tered and then stayed closed. As she stood up Munroe's back
cracked and she winced. The thug hadn't moved but now she
saw one hand drop to his belt which made her smile. He was
smarter than he looked. Despite her size, he hadn't underestimated her and still regarded her as a serious threat. It would be
a shame if she had to kill him.

"No need for any trouble," she said, offering him a smile
before throwing her money. His eyes never left her face but
he caught the pouch and weighed it before tossing it over his
shoulder to the boy.

"A bit of silver, couple of gold," said the boy and the thug
slightly relaxed.

"Who runs your crew?" asked Munroe.

"Cannok. You know him?"

"No. Have the Families extended down here?"

The thug raised an eyebrow. "You work for one of them?"

"Used to. Don Jarrow."

Whether he was impressed or not it didn't show on his battered face. "Bring him," he said, gesturing at Denke. With a
pretend grunt of effort Munroe lifted him up again, noting the
patch of blood on the street where he'd been sitting.

"I'm Munroe." She didn't think the thug was going to answer
but he seemed to be weighing something up. Eventually he
bobbed his head.

"Tok," he said, shoving the boy ahead.

"Just Tok?" she asked, making conversation as she followed him down a small side street.

"It's short for Tok-ram-Gara," chirped the boy.

"Shut up, Eel," said Tok.

After that neither of them were willing to talk and Munroe focused on carrying Denke. She was still sweating a little, but not as much as before. Nevertheless she made sure to grunt every now and then from the apparent effort of carrying a dead weight.

A short time later they came to a boarded-up building that looked very much like those neighbouring it. The only difference she could see was a small painted symbol, a triangle with an open eye at its centre. Tok knocked on the wooden shell and waited. One of the boards opened to reveal a sturdy door and behind it a scarred Morrin.

Like all of her kind the woman on the door had impenetrable yellow eyes, a slightly wedge-shaped face and pointed ears. Her white skin was marbled with seams of blue and her uniformly black hair suggested she wasn't that old. Morrin were a hardy race that, if left unmolested, could live for two hundred years or more. If things didn't go well in the next few minutes Munroe might have to test the limits of her endurance.

"Is Doctor Silver in?" asked Tok.

The Morrin just grunted. "Bring them. Get lost, Eel." Words seemed to be at a premium for the Morrin, who stared at the boy until he rolled his eyes and shuffled off.

Inside the old shop Munroe had expected to find dust and grime. Instead it was a warm, homely room decorated with lots of overlapping colourful rugs on the floor. Bright watercolours of forests and the sea hung on the walls and a tidy kitchen sat off to one side. A wide set of stairs in the middle of the room led down into the basement. It felt more like someone's home than a surgery. The Morrin sat down on the chair beside the door, immobile and silent. Apparently her job consisted solely of opening the door.

Tok gestured at the basement stairs and she raised an eyebrow, shuffling Denke again, and remembering to wince in pain. Not all of it was fake as her arms and shoulders were still hurting. Moving with care, Tok gently picked up Denke and carried him down the stairs.

"Such a gentleman," she murmured, earning a brief smile.

In the basement three beds sat off to one side, but only one of them was occupied by a man with bandages around his torso. Asleep in a chair beside him was an elderly woman with long wavy grey hair and a deeply lined face.

"Patient for you, Doctor," said Tok, setting Denke down on one of the empty beds. The doctor came awake, blinking rapidly.

"Out of the way, oaf. Wait upstairs," said Silver, shooing everyone away. "You, girl. You can stay. I'll need another pair of hands."

"All right. What do I need to do?" asked Munroe.

"Start by telling me what happened," said Silver, cutting off Denke's shirt and then slowly peeling the cloth away from the wound in his side.

"Angry mob. They threw some rotten fruit and then it turned nasty. Someone knifed him in the side."

"That explains this," said Silver, picking a bit of tomato out of Denke's hair. When his shirt was clear of the wound she hissed and shook her head. "Hold him steady, I need to see if they've nicked anything."

Munroe held Denke by the shoulders while Doctor Silver forced her fingers into the wound. He'd been drifting in and out of consciousness but now his eyes flashed open. A scream began to build up somewhere in his chest. Before it had time to emerge Denke's eyes rolled up and he collapsed, limbs dangling loose.

"He's not dead," said Silver, wiping her hands on a towel before taking a long metal spike from a nearby table. It was tapered at one end and seemed to be hollow. "Just passed out from the pain."

"What are you going to do with that?" said Munroe, as Silver picked up a small hammer.

"If you're squeamish, I suggest you wait upstairs," said the doctor, positioning the metal spike against Denke's side. Munroe wasn't bothered by a bit of gore, but she needed a chance to sit down and collect her thoughts. She'd been so focused on helping Denke that she hadn't considered her next move if successful.

"I'll wait upstairs," said Munroe, excusing herself.

It should have been so easy. She'd found Denke before he spoke to the crowd but much like the others he'd insisted on testing the children. Thankfully he had not intended to reveal his identity if they rejected his offer of continued help. As it happened he'd barely made it onto the stage before the gathered crowd tried to chase him out of the city with rotten fruit and the promise of violence. Denke was lucky she'd been there to spirit him away from the mob before they beat and stabbed him to death.

On the ground floor Tok was sitting on one of the tall stools in the kitchen area. Across the room the Morrin remained by the door, saying nothing, doing nothing. For once silence suited Munroe. She flopped down on one of the stools beside Tok and rested her head on the table for a moment.

A rough hand shook her shoulder and she came awake to find Tok and another man waiting. There was a faint pulse in her head, the echo of pain, but it quickly faded. The newcomer was dressed in colourful silks and had long black hair and an immaculate oiled beard. The dark-skinned man seemed completely at ease, his green eyes sparkling with humour as he watched her wake up. A smile tugged at the corners of his mouth, but she had the feeling it could quickly fade. Rarely had Munroe seen a man so pretty and so aware of it.

"Cannok?"

"Yes, indeed," he said, accepting a mug of something from Tok who moved to stand behind the boss off to one side. The message was clear. It was them against her.

"I'm not here to step on anyone's toes. I'm not representing anyone or getting into anything. My friend and I just got into a bit of trouble. Once the doctor patches him up, we'll be on our way."

Munroe didn't want to get dragged into the underworld politics of Rojenne. At the same time, however, she wasn't about to bow down and kiss Cannok's boots. He might be the equivalent of a Don in these parts, but she'd left all that behind and owed him nothing. And, besides, she was so much more than what she used to be. She never had to bow down to anyone in her life ever again.

"Where did you come from?" asked Cannok.

"South. A village not far away."

"Lie," said a new voice. Turning on her stool Munroe saw a tall teenage girl, all awkward elbows and big knees. Munroe embraced the Source and extended her senses towards the girl. It was just as she thought. The faint pulse wasn't a pending headache but an echo of power coming from the girl. Judging by her bored expression Munroe was confident the girl had no idea she had a Talent or that she wasn't the only one in the room with magic. In a peculiar way, she reminded Munroe of herself at the same age. Full of vinegar, with a sour mouth and a know-it-all attitude.

The girl was twisting a strand of her hair around her finger over and over. Keen to test her theory that the girl was able to tell when someone was lying, a cruel thought occurred.

"You know, if you do that all day, your hair will end up greasy," commented Munroe. The girl stared at her and then let go of her hair with a grimace. A wry smile crept across Munroe's face as she turned back to face Cannok.

"Let's try that again. Where did you come from?" he asked.

"It doesn't matter. I'm not staying," said Munroe, waiting for Cannok to tell her otherwise. To her surprise he didn't. Instead, a frown briefly creased his forehead.

"You're not afraid, are you?"

"No. I can walk out of this room any time I want. There's nothing anyone here could do to stop me."

Cannok glanced over her shoulder at the girl and the jovial spark in his eyes faded. He probably thought she was mad or well connected to be so confident. "Who are you?" he asked.

"It doesn't matter. A mob took offence at my friend and now I need to get him out of the city."

"Is this going to bring trouble for my people?"

"No."

"Lie," said the girl once again.

Munroe sighed. "If the people in this room can keep their mouths shut, then it will be fine. There'll be no trouble for you. If someone finds out I'm here, there might be."

The girl remained silent and Cannok relaxed his clenched jaw. "Did anyone else see her?" he asked Tok.

"Just the boy, Eel," said the big man.

Cannok rolled his eyes. "Dox, go and find Eel. Tell him not to speak to anyone until I find him. Sit on him if you have to, but keep him silent."

"Why do I have to go?" whined the girl.

Cannok's less than friendly stare settled on her. "Dox, if you don't go right now, I will make you very, very sorry."

Without having Dox's Talent they all knew he wasn't lying. The girl hurried out of the door without any more lip. Cannok ran a hand across his face, suddenly looking tired and annoyed. "Can you at least tell me what happened, so I'm not in the dark?"

"I will if you give me a mug of something," promised Munroe.

The crime boss laughed and gestured for Tok to fetch her a drink. In the basement she could hear Doctor Silver shuffling about, muttering to herself, and two other people breathing. One of them was quiet, as if asleep, and the other had a peculiar whistle, probably from having a giant spike driven into their chest. At least Denke was alive for the time being.

"Have you heard about some of the recent trouble with Seekers?" asked Munroe, accepting the mug of ale from Tok. The big man's expression hadn't changed but she sensed he was revising his previous opinion of her. She was far more dangerous than even he realised.

"People are blaming them for children dying and exploding."

"Denke is the Seeker for Rojenne. I warned him there might be trouble, but he didn't believe me. Someone in the city got the crowd excited before he arrived and rotten fruit turned to violence. I managed to get him out of there before they tried to string him up."

"They won't find him here," said Cannok.

"As soon as it's safe for Denke to travel, we're leaving the city."

"He's not going anywhere," said Silver, coming up the stairs. "The puncture in his lung isn't life-threatening any more, but he shouldn't be moved. There was some trapped air, but I've dealt with it."

Munroe shrugged, not really sure what Silver was talking about. "Will he live?"

"With plenty of rest, he'll recover. But he shouldn't travel anywhere for a few weeks."

"We don't really have a choice," said Munroe. "We need to leave."

"Then he's as good as dead."

"People will come after him."

Silver shrugged. "No one knows he's here. He'll be safe if he doesn't leave this building."

Everyone turned to look at Cannok. She didn't think for a second he would let Denke stay here out of the goodness of his heart. There was no profit in such a move for him.

"He was asking for you," said the doctor. Munroe took the hint, giving them some space to talk without her in the room.

Denke was pale and sweat covered his body, but at least he was awake. Munroe tried not to look at the spike sticking out of the side of his chest but she couldn't help wincing.

"The doctor told me I'll get better, as long as I don't move for a while."

"You were lucky," said Munroe.

"No, I'm alive because of you," said Denke. "I'm sorry I didn't believe you. I thought they'd listen to me."

"It doesn't matter. We need to get you out of here, as soon as you're able to travel." Munroe started considering different options on how to get out of the city. If only she'd been able to learn how to camouflage herself with magic she could've walked them both out of the gates. Subtle had never been her way and unfortunately that extended to her use of magic as well. Her teachers had insisted it was simply in her mind, but so far she'd not been able to move past that particular mental block.

"I'm not leaving," said Denke.

"Why?"

"My family is here, my friends. My life. If I suddenly disappear, people will notice. If they can't find me they could go after my family."

"How are you going to explain that?" she said, gesturing at his injury.

"I'll come up with something. I can even say I was injured today in the crowd. They don't need to know I was the one in the mask."

"Are you going to keep testing children?" asked Munroe.

Denke shook his head. "You were right. It's too dangerous. I dropped the mask on the way here and won't be going back for it. I'm done for now."

Munroe was relieved, but she also knew staying in the city could be dangerous for him. Getting rid of the mask and pretending he had nothing to do with the Red Tower would keep him safe from most people. But Cannok hadn't risen to his position because of his kind heart and generous spirit. There would be a price to pay, either now or later, for his silence. If he ever revealed that Denke had been a Seeker, a secret he'd kept from his own family, then it would put his life at risk again. She was afraid that if she left now Cannok might try to blackmail Denke once he was well. Perhaps force him to use his magic to further Cannok's ambitions.

She would have to make a deal before she left to protect Denke. Munroe had a feeling the price was going to be rather steep.

As she came back upstairs Munroe was surprised to see five new faces waiting for her with the others. Even more surprising was that all of them were armed with loaded crossbows pointed at her chest. On the far side of the room Cannok sat at the table casually sipping his ale. Beside him stood Tok and the ageing doctor, both of whom wore identical frowns. Neither were keen on this idea, but they knew it was probably not a good idea to object or else they might be next.

"I was about to say we should make a deal," said Munroe.

"I'm ready to deal," said Cannok. "Let's start by discussing what you're going to do for me."

CHAPTER 21

A scream ripped through the air. Wren opened her eyes and rolled out of bed, coming awake without her usual sluggishness. She'd been on edge for days and had only just fallen into a light sleep.

Moving on instinct she walked towards the thrashing figure. Tianne was already there, shaking Danoph by the shoulders and gently saying his name over and over again. Nearby she could hear other students groaning and complaining. She saw a few burying their heads under pillows, but no one else had got out of bed. The feeling of being watched made Wren turn around.

Across the dormitory she could see Brunwal sitting up in bed. She had the feeling he was staring straight at her. There wasn't much light in the room, just what Tianne had summoned and ambient light from gaps in the curtains, but it was enough to show his outline. Part of her wanted to pretend it was just her imagination. At this distance there was no way to be sure. He might have been staring at something else, but deep down she knew. She could feel the weight of his eyes resting on her.

She was already exhausted from days of waiting. But so far all he'd done was watch. He was waiting for the most opportune moment to strike, when she was at her weakest. Wren believed he grinned at her before lying down again.

"Help me," said Tianne, struggling to get Danoph out of bed by herself. He was almost awake but seemed unable to stand unaided. Supporting him on either side they shuffled towards the washrooms. Wren worked the pump while Tianne filled a bowl with water and threw in a washcloth. Holding a wet cloth against Danoph's forehead seemed to help. The first time this had happened Wren had thought he was burning with fever, but apparently being so hot was a typical side effect of his nightmares. Not that there seemed to be anything normal about his night terrors. Even when he didn't wake up screaming Danoph didn't seem to sleep very well. It was as if all his dreams were plagued with images that left him weary in the morning.

"Thank you," murmured Danoph taking the cloth from Tianne. He took a deep breath and dunked his face into the cold water. He came up a few seconds later, dripping wet but smiling. "I'm sorry this keeps happening."

"It's not your fault," said Tianne. "And we don't mind."

As usual Tianne didn't want to say a bad thing about anyone, despite the inconvenience. "Have the Grey Council said if they can help you?" asked Wren, trying to be more pragmatic about finding a solution. This could not continue indefinitely.

Danoph shrugged. "They tried something, and it seemed to help for a while, but the dreams have come back, just as strong as before. They're so clear. I can see every detail."

"Once I dreamed that all my teeth fell out," said Tianne, putting a hand to her mouth as if to check they were still there. "Do you think dreams mean anything?"

Wren realised they were both looking at her for an answer. "I don't know. None of my dreams have ever come true, but then neither have my nightmares."

"You should both get some sleep," said Danoph, running a hand over his uneven scalp. "I'll stay up a while and cut my hair."

Wren noticed he always kept it very short and preferred to do it himself. Her own hair was getting long, almost to her shoulders. Normally she kept it much shorter, but hadn't found anyone she trusted to cut it. Maybe she would ask Danoph to do it one day.

Taking his advice, she returned to her bed but couldn't get back to sleep. Lying awake, listening to the snoring of other students, she considered her situation again.

Apart from her two friends Wren was starting to realise there wasn't anyone else she could rely on, not even the teachers. Recently they'd all been preoccupied and far too busy dealing with larger issues to concern themselves with what might happen to her. There were numerous stories swirling around the school, brought to them from merchants and senior students allowed to visit the nearby town. Rumours about children dying while being tested for magic. There were stories about whole villages being destroyed and Seekers getting the blame. Wren had heard six different versions of one story about a boy who had exploded, killing at least fifty people in his village. With each retelling the details varied but the underlying message was the same. There was a rising tide of fear and prejudice against those with magic, which also meant anyone connected to the Red Tower.

What was happening beyond the walls of the school concerned her, but right now she couldn't spend too long focused on it. Her immediate problem with Brunwal had not gone away. Even thoughts about what she would do when she left the Red Tower were pushed to the back of her mind. Survival was her most pressing concern.

Turning over in bed Wren tried to rest but her mind was too agitated and she didn't sleep for a long time. When morning came she was sandy-eyed, sluggish and her head felt as if it had been stuffed with wool.

The next few days passed in a dazed blur in which Wren was simply going through the motions. She ate her meals, attended her classes and every night she tried to sleep, waking at the slightest sound before eventually passing out from exhaustion a few hours before dawn.

During a break between classes she found herself dozing on the grass outside in the sun. Whispering voices lurked on the periphery of her senses and in a panic she scrambled away from them, coming awake gasping for breath. Wren frantically searched for the danger but saw only Danoph and Tianne sitting beside her.

"I heard whispering," said Wren, trying to catch her breath.

"We didn't want to wake you," said Tianne. "You look so tired. You should get some rest."

Knowing she wouldn't be able to sleep again Wren dismissed the idea with a wave of her hand. "What were you saying?"

"Some of the teachers have already come back from their trips. They've only been gone a few days."

"Then they stayed local," said Danoph.

"I think they've been warning Seekers here in Shael."

"It would make sense if the stories are true."

"There are a few new adults in the school," said Tianne. Wren nearly asked her how she knew when they spent most of their time together, but she bit her tongue. Her exhaustion was making her snippy and she couldn't afford to lose one of her two allies. "I think some of the Seekers from abroad are here, but I don't know why. I asked a couple of teachers about the rumours, but they wouldn't tell me anything." One of Tianne's feet was twitching, as if she was nervous. When she saw Wren watching she turned away and her foot stopped moving. "No one is talking."

"We'll find out eventually," said Danoph. "Right now we have more pressing matters to worry about."

They all watched as Brunwal and his cronies walked past. He didn't speak to Wren, didn't even glance in her direction, but she felt other people watching them both expectantly. They were all waiting for it as well. Oddly, one of Brunwal's cronies looked over his shoulder and much to her surprise Wren saw fear in his eyes. Perhaps when she'd beaten Brunwal she'd scared his friends worse than she'd realised.

In their next class Master Jorey had returned from her trip and was attempting to teach them how to channel small amounts of energy to control the weather. Drawing power from the Source into herself felt so natural to Wren, like breathing. It was what she did next that was proving difficult. So far she seemed to be faring better than Danoph who struggled with all but the basics. If not for the echo she felt between them Wren would have questioned him being at the school. Thankfully it wasn't just her who had difficulty with the class as Tianne couldn't master it either.

During sword training Wren felt so tired that she ended up with a number of bruises on her arms and shoulders. She saw the blows coming and tried to block them but her tired limbs were just too slow. Master Choss pulled her out of line and they walked a short distance away.

"Are you unwell?" he asked, one hand resting on his belt. Wren had noticed that he'd taken to wearing a sword, even at meal times, but when she'd first arrived he'd not carried a weapon.

"No, just very tired. I've not been sleeping."

He stared down at her and although his expression remained impassive she could see his eyes were troubled. "If you can't sleep, perhaps you should pay Master Yettle a visit. He may be able to help."

"Are you sleeping, Master Choss?" she asked, noting the deep shadows under his eyes.

He raised one eyebrow but didn't dismiss her. At home a student would never dare ask a teacher such a personal question. There were clearly defined lines but here in Shael it was different. "No, I'm not," he admitted. "But I can have a drink of something to help with that. You're a little young. Sit out the rest of the class, maybe doze in the shade," he said striding back towards the line of students. Wren noticed he'd not said why he wasn't sleeping.

By the time they'd finished their classes and eaten their evening meal, Wren was practically asleep on her feet. Tianne came back to their table bubbling with new gossip as Danoph was scraping the last few mouthfuls off his plate.

"Balfruss has gone away on a trip, and Eloise left the school yesterday with the Jhanidi. Only Garvey is here from the Grey Council," said Tianne. Wren had noticed there were only a few teachers eating at their table tonight.

As her eyes roamed around the room Wren felt as if someone was watching her. Turning her head she saw Brunwal staring from across the room. This time there was no doubt. The whole room continued to move around them, full of noise and motion, but for a moment the two of them were trapped in a bubble of silence. His lips moved and she heard the words. A promise of pain and suffering.

"It will be tonight," she said, more to herself than the others.

"What's tonight?" asked Tianne, hungry as ever for fresh news.

"Brunwal will come for me."

Danoph and Tianne exchanged a look. "Are you sure?" asked Tianne.

The message had been clear. "Yes."

"Then we should hide, or tell someone," babbled Tianne, suddenly flustered. Oddly, despite the fear in the pit of her stomach, an icy calm fell over Wren.

"You said it yourself, Tianne. There's no one else I can trust. I could hide, but that would just delay it."

"Say something!" said Tianne, pleading with Danoph. He was staring at Brunwal with his head tilted to one side and a puzzled expression.

"All paths lead to this moment," he said, patting Tianne on the hand. "You can rely on us, Wren. We'll be there with you."

The lights had barely dimmed when Wren heard a scuffing sound in the dark. She lay on her bed fully clothed and had told her friends to do the same. A faint blue glow filled the room as several magic lights blossomed around the dormitory.

A few students seemed to have no idea what was happening but the majority scrambled out of bed, heading for the relative safety of the washrooms. Word spread and they all realised what was about to happen.

Wren rolled to her feet and moved away from the bunks to the clear space towards the front of the room. Tianne and Danoph moved to flank her on either side and she felt reassured by their presence. Whatever happened she would not be facing it alone. Danoph's face was without expression, while Tianne was visibly scared, making Wren realise her friend was braver than she'd thought.

Across the room Brunwal and five of his friends watched her in silence. They seemed to be waiting for something. One of his companions, a boy from Zecorria, seemed particularly on edge and he kept staring at Tianne. Perhaps he had been instructed to attack her first.

This silence wasn't what she'd expected from Brunwal. Perhaps a speech about embarrassing him and that she deserved this. Maybe threats about what he was going to do to her. She had not anticipated the icy silence that now filled the dormitory. When it began to stretch out so much that it echoed in her ears, part of Wren wondered if he'd lost his nerve now that the moment had finally arrived.

"Oh no," whispered Tianne, her voice seeming loud in the silent dormitory. A fire was building behind Brunwal's eyes. Wren could see it growing. A rage that would not be quenched by just another beating.

With the speed of thought Wren drew power from the Source into herself and shaped it into a series of threads. She wove these together into a shield in front of her, layering them over and over like folding metal in the forging of a blade. Others preferred a solid block of force to stop an attack, absorbing all of the energy, but the jarring impact could still cause an injury if they were not careful. Her shield would bend and keep bending as it absorbed and reflected energy away from her.

Brunwal hurled something at her with a shout. A fiery spear shattered against her shield with enough force to drive her back a few steps. To Wren's relief there was little real damage to her shield beyond destroying a few of the outer layers. Nevertheless, moving her left hand in a series of twisting gestures, Wren repaired her shield while she waited for his next attack.

Brunwal was screaming incoherently now, a sound of pure rage. Every now and then he'd curse her as he hurled bolt after bolt of energy laced with fire towards her. Wren could see he was expending so much energy she knew he wouldn't be able to sustain this level of attack for long. The Source was infinite but his stamina was not.

Bending her knees and bracing herself against the assault, Wren held her ground, biding her time and waiting for an opening. On the periphery of her vision she saw Tianne pulling Danoph away from the fight. Across the room Brunwal's friends had also moved elsewhere to give them space, but they were also not interfering. They simply watched in silence.

When his first attacks failed to break through her defence Brunwal changed tactics, pulling together something she'd never seen before. Even when the teachers did something she couldn't copy, Wren had a vague inkling of what they were doing. She could see how the pieces fitted together in her mind, changing power into heat or light, but this was alien. An oily black sphere of nothingness began to swell between Brunwal's hands. It throbbed in time with her connection to the Source as if it were alive. She heard shouting and angry voices, but didn't dare turn away in case she lost concentration.

When she looked deeper into the weave of Brunwal's magic, Wren felt her stomach lurch in revulsion. All his attacks until now had been organic and, while destructive, they were natural; mostly weaves of force and fire. This was something utterly alien, so much so that Wren couldn't understand what it was or how he'd done it.

Instead of using brute force he'd switched to something forbidden and corrupt. Somehow he'd delved into magic that had been banned or perhaps it was conjured from his imagination. No teacher had ever taught him how to do this.

The growing darkness in his hands twitched and stretched like a chrysalis, as if trying to give birth to something monstrous within. Wren could feel and smell it from across the room. The rotten stench of it filled her nose. Nearby she heard someone retching, their vomit spattering onto the stone floor.

At the edges of her perception she could feel a raging torrent that was the Source. A limitless river of energy that ran through all living things, nurturing them as it, in turn, was replenished. The aberration that Brunwal was creating caused barely a ripple on the surface, but nevertheless she felt it enough to make her gag.

To combat this feeling Wren stretched towards the Source with her senses and drew more power into her body until it felt as if she was bursting at the seams. The weariness from not sleeping for several days instantly vanished and her senses became heightened. Time seemed to slow and she was very aware of her heartbeat. It sounded so loud, as if it were filling the entire room. The energy fizzed as it coursed through her veins making her skin tingle, and her chest swelled as she was overcome with a sense of euphoria.

With adrenaline coursing through her body, and her life on the line, channelling energy from the Source had never been so addictive. Wielding so much power made her feel immortal. But as Wren revelled in the feeling of being more than human, a part of her knew it was a lie.

If she pushed herself just a fraction more, the power would burn her alive from the inside out, consuming her flesh and bones in the blink of an eye. Perhaps that was what Brunwal wanted. To panic her into destroying herself as she was much stronger than him.

It was time to take the initiative and attack Brunwal, not wait for whatever he was creating. She felt him pulling together a shield, but instead of an attack Wren simply wrapped him in a shield of her own making. Working with both hands outstretched, fingers twitching as if she were controlling a pair of marionettes, Wren enveloped him in a cocoon denser than any she'd created before. Nothing would be able to penetrate it and with every passing second she added more layers on top. Then she began to squeeze.

At first nothing happened but as she brought her will to bear, Brunwal began to sweat. He couldn't maintain his own shield and keep feeding the thing hovering above his hands. A loud crack echoed around the room as Brunwal's own shield shattered like a pane of glass. The moment it disappeared Wren squeezed again.

"Help me!" he screamed at his friends. He couldn't finish what he was doing and stop her at the same time. The Zecorran boy said something to the others and with some reluctance they all moved further away, distancing themselves from Brunwal. He cursed them and struggled vainly against Wren who now held his limbs in place until he became a living statue.

She could feel him trying to regain control of his body, flexing his will, but her connection to the Source was stronger and she held him in place with ease. Brunwal must have lost concentration as the swirling black mass wobbled on its axis and then broke apart into a thousand pieces. As the first shard touched the shield she'd created around him Wren felt it from across the room, as if someone had dug a knife into her flesh. With a scream she fell back, staring in horror at the swollen cut that had opened up on her forearm.

The shield around him vanished. Her cry of pain was lost in the noise coming from Brunwal as dozens of black motes touched his skin. He fell to the ground screeching so loudly it hurt her ears, but worse was what she saw. Each piece smouldered and then sank into his flesh, leaving a burning trail behind as if it were molten lava. The smell of scorched meat filled the room and she heard the bubble of fat as the corrosive substance ate its way through his body, dissolving flesh and melting muscle and bone with ease. She could see holes burned into his body and beneath that white bones and purple organs.

It seemed to go on for ever, with Brunwal thrashing about on the floor keening in agony. She'd never known a human being could make such terrible sounds. Slowly he was being consumed by the darkness he had summoned. It ate through him and then sank into the stone floor beneath. She wondered if anything would stop it.

A final wheeze made Brunwal's body shudder and then he was finally still. His remaining eye stared at her accusingly.

One of Brunwal's friends moved to stand beside the body, the expression on his face unreadable. With a sudden howl of fury he drew a dagger from the small of his back and launched himself at Wren. Tianne was ready and easily tripped the boy, kicking out one of his legs. The blade went skittering away across the floor. Before he could try anything else Danoph tapped the boy on the side of his head with an open hand.

The bully's eyes widened in surprise, his jaw stretched open and he collapsed. Before Wren could ask what he'd done all of the lanterns in the room flared into life and Garvey came striding into the dormitory. He took one look at Wren and her friends before moving to stand over what remained of Brunwal.

After everything that had happened she wasn't sure what to expect from him. Anger would have been her first thought, or disappointment. Garvey hid it quickly but for a second Wren was sure he'd been smiling.

CHAPTER 22

The Khevassar did his best to make an impression as he marched down the corridors of the palace. Time, it seemed, was robbing him of everything, piece by piece. The Yerskani Royal Guards noticed him but paid little attention. They were all young, strong and had their whole lives in front of them. In their eyes he was just another old man, probably wandering the halls in a daze. None of them thought of him as a commanding presence. None of them were intimidated by his glare and no one stood at attention when he walked past.

Pausing in front of an old portrait of Queen Morganse, he wondered where the time had gone. He clearly remembered walking down this hallway to her office on the day it had been painted. Instead of being seated behind her desk as usual, the Queen had been perched on an uncomfortable chair, wearing an elaborate dress. That was twenty years ago and yet sometimes it seemed as if so little time had passed.

"Can I help you?" asked a kind voice.

"No, I'm fine," he said, trying to recall details about that day for just a little longer. It had rained that morning, he remembered. All the streets had been shining in the sunlight as if someone had painted them black in the night. Or perhaps the

Maker had washed away all the blood and filth, giving the city a clean slate. A poetic image and definitely not his usual. Perhaps time was mellowing him after all.

"Are you lost?" the voice asked again.

Startled from his reverie, the Old Man turned his glare on the person interrupting his thoughts. The Khevassar found himself face to face with one of the Royal Guards who was looking at him as if he were senile. "Young lady, I have been navigating the corridors of this palace since before you learned to walk. Now stand aside."

He gave the guard his fiercest glare and was pleased to see her recoil as if she'd been slapped. Feeling smug he moved on, letting his feet guide him, not even thinking about where he was going. In the Queen's outer office he received his second unpleasant surprise of the morning. The Queen's ageing herald and assistant was absent and in his place sat a rotund, sweaty young man. The Khevassar didn't even need to ask what had happened. The new secretary seemed at home and familiar with everything around him, reaching for objects on the desk without looking up from the page.

He continued scratching out a note as the Old Man came to stand in front of his desk. Thinking he would have to educate this new secretary, just as he was doing with his own replacement for Rummpoe, the Khevassar loudly cleared his throat.

The secretary glanced up and immediately came to his feet. The Old Man would've liked to believe he saw the other man sweat a little at having him so close, but it was difficult to tell. Sweating seemed to be his main hobby.

"Please take a seat, Sir," he stammered, gesturing at several of the chairs around the room. "I will let her Majesty know you are here. Immediately."

Thinking he had perhaps misjudged the man, the Khevassar let his glare fade a little. "What's your name, boy?"

"Dorn, Sir."

"I like a young person with manners."

"Yes, Sir. Thank you, Sir," he said, knocking loudly and then slipping inside the Queen's office. The Old Man harrumphed and sat down, resting his legs for a minute.

He noted how the boy had swallowed and wiped at his face before knocking. He should have known. Queen Morganse was not one to suffer fools gladly. The boy was terrified of her, not scared of an old codger like him. Pride, it seemed, was something that had not been taken from him just yet.

Morganse had always been headstrong and determined. It was one of the many things he admired about her. Perhaps he should have taken a firmer hand with the new Rummpoe from the beginning.

Dorn emerged a few minutes later and held the door open wide. "Her Majesty will see you now, Sir."

As he entered the room Queen Morganse stood up and came around from behind her desk to shake his hand. She didn't need to do it, and etiquette dictated that he should bow or salute, but it was a sign of her affection for him. They'd known each other for so long that he thought of her like family. "That will be all, Dorn," said the Queen, dismissing her secretary. Once the doors were closed and they were away from prying eyes she kissed him on the cheek and gave him a hug.

As ever she was impeccably dressed, her hair tied back from her face and her sapphire silk dress was both flattering and elegant. He sometimes forgot that she was already a grandmother.

"Please, sit down," she said gesturing at the chairs in front of her desk. "Tea?"

"I should be the one to serve you, Majesty."

"Nonsense," said Morganse, pouring two glasses before sitting down in the chair beside him.

"I was thinking about your portrait out there," he said. "Sometimes it seems like yesterday. You've barely changed."

"If only," laughed Morganse, touching her hair. There was still plenty of colour in it, even if there was some white around the ears. "We're all a little more grey and saggy than back then."

For a little while they merely sat together, sipping tea and talking of happier times. Since he had no family to speak of they talked about her children and the latest achievements of her grandchildren. Far too soon their levity faded as the conversation inevitably returned to the present and more sobering events.

"One of my people sent me a report last night about another incident in Zecorria," said the Queen, setting down her glass. "It was a young girl this time. She exploded while being tested, killing herself and thirty people in her town. The Seeker was injured, but he managed to escape before the locals turned on him."

The Khevassar took a deep breath and rested his head against the back of his chair for a moment. He ran through the possible repercussions in his mind and could see only one likely outcome. "Has the Regent been in touch?"

Morganse gestured at a letter at the front of her desk. The seal on it was broken but he recognised the Zecorran crest. "In a few days' time he's going to make a public announcement. There will be a national ban on Seekers in Zecorria."

On the one hand he couldn't blame the Regent for making such a decision. He was neither rash nor insane, two traits the previous two rulers had possessed. However, he was also a popularist who had a tenuous grip on the crown. Far too often it seemed as if his decisions were based on what he thought the people wanted. Of course he believed that would ensure his continued stewardship of the throne until a suitable descendant came of age. The Khevassar wasn't sure how long the Regent could manage to keep walking the tightrope before he fell.

On the other hand, the national ban would put children with blossoming wild magic at risk. Looking beyond that everyone was at risk from the fear of magic. Someone with a grudge could accuse another of performing a mystical act and, without a Seeker to test the child, the outcome would depend only on who was the most convincing. That led to the bad old days of superstition before the war. Exile, public drownings and hanging over running water.

"Did the Regent say anything else in his letter?"

"It was quite the emotional appeal," said Morganse, rubbing her temples to ease tension. "He has asked that I make a similar declaration here in Yerskania."

"Can I assume a similar missive has been sent to Queen Talandra and the others?"

"I would think so. I'm sure I'll hear from them very soon."

He didn't think she would have invited him to the palace and served him tea only to ambush him. There was no requirement for her to consult with him, or anyone else for that matter, before making a declaration, but in all the years he'd worked for her, she'd yet to do it. Morganse always listened to the sage counsel of her advisers before making a decision, no matter the personal cost.

Even so, something made him ask, "Have you already made a decision?" Her only response was to raise an eyebrow. "I apologise, I shouldn't have asked."

She waved it away. "It's all right. I will admit to having spent a great deal of time thinking about Seekers and the Red Tower of late. Have you seen this?" Morganse fished a report off her desk from the scattered papers and passed it across. He quickly scanned the contents and then set it aside. His own people had provided him with a more detailed version of events.

"I've seen similar reports."

"It's not only happening in Zecorria. If it were, I might be able to ignore the Regent's appeal. There have been three incidents of Seekers being banned in villages, here, in my country. Today I received two more reports. One where a Seeker was chased out of a town after an explosion that left three dead and another where a Seeker was drowned in a river. The poor man didn't even say anything. He was set upon by a mob, dragged from his horse on the road and killed."

A heavy silence settled on the room. Both of them were locked away in their minds, contemplating the future. That it was happening abroad was one thing. It was slightly removed and didn't feel real. But for the Yerskani people to have gone against a royal decree, for them to ban Seekers, was a slap in the face. Even worse, a form of mob mentality was taking over here where the rule of law had always been respected.

Eventually Morganse spoke again, but this time in a whisper, as if she were afraid that someone might overhear. Her words were clipped and she sounded tired.

"I've received appeals from several city representatives. They want me to ban all Seekers from coming to Perizzi. Ban them, from my capital city."

Despite her best efforts to remain calm he could hear the heat creeping into her voice. The Khevassar knew that Morganse's declaration of support, together with Queen Talandra, had led to Seekers restarting the monthly testing of children across the west and Seveldrom.

At the beginning, so soon after the war, people had been worried about magic and the return of Seekers to their towns and villages. Morganse had taken suitable precautions to keep the peace. Members of the Watch had been discreetly stationed during every test, but, over time, when no accidents occurred they had become unnecessary. Now she was being asked to repeal her own declaration.

"I've heard about another incident," he admitted. Since she had been so honest and open it seemed churlish to hide one more violent incident. "A Seeker was attacked by a mob in Rojenne. There are mixed statements from witnesses, but several mention that he was bleeding quite badly when he fled."

"When did this happen?"

"Yesterday. I have someone looking into it," he said. One witness reported the Seeker being helped away from the scene by a short woman, but he was waiting for confirmation that it was Munroe.

"The people of Perizzi believe there is a real danger."

"As I said when we last met, there is more to this situation." He had shared reports from several Guardians that mentioned strangers visiting towns and cities with the intent of stirring up trouble. With so much of it happening at once, in different places, there was no doubt in his mind that this was not a coincidence. There was a network of people behind it. He wasn't sure how they were connected to one another, but he suspected they all had a personal reason to hate magic. The number of people who generally disliked magic users had only increased in the last ten years. Many in the west had died at the hands of the Warlock and his experiments, but many more because of the Battlemages.

"Have you found anything more about who is behind it all?"

The Khevassar wasn't sure how much to tell her at this stage, but, given the appeal from the Regent of Zecorria, he could see time was running out. She would be forced to make a decision soon unless he could provide her with some convincing evidence.

"One of my people apprehended one of the rabble-rousers. She's bringing him in now for questioning and should be here any day."

"Well, that's some good news."

The Khevassar licked his lips. He hated rumours, but right now that was all he had. "We also have a name. Habreel."

"I know that look," said Morganse. "You know who this Habreel is, don't you?"

"I have a suspicion."

The Queen crossed her arms and sat back in her chair. "Well, tell me who you suspect."

Perhaps he should have kept his mouth shut but it was too late now. "I think he might be Torran Habreel. He used to be a Guardian."

Morganse was stunned. "A Guardian?"

"He left during the war, when the Chosen were in control of Perizzi. Habreel quit and shortly after I released a few others from their service. They didn't like what was happening in the city at the time and felt powerless. That's the official story."

"And the unofficial one?"

"After we regained the city, stories started to emerge. When the city was in chaos, they were accused of collusion with the Chosen, corruption and bribery. They were bad eggs so I got rid of them."

"And now you think they're working with Habreel."

The Khevassar shrugged. "Perhaps. He would need a network of trustworthy people to create such widespread chaos. I'm gathering their names and I have people looking into their whereabouts."

"Keep me informed. I want to know what the rabble-rouser has to say."

"And in the meantime?" he asked.

Morganse shook her head sadly. "I will have to seriously consider the Regent's request."

The Regent had her over a barrel. If she did nothing then

she would be seen as ignoring the plight of her people. While her hold on the throne was not as unstable as his, Morganse had plenty of detractors who would use this as another opportunity to remind the people of her decisions during the war. When she had refused an order the Mad King had sent thousands of her troops against a well-defended, heavily armoured enemy. To prevent further needless slaughter, and to protect her other children after the maiming of her only son, Morganse had abdicated the throne and announced the Mad King as Regent in her place. The difficulties that followed were eventually resolved, and, while most people understood her reasons, there were some who were still angry about what she'd done.

The Khevassar knew that, whatever she decided, Morganse would not allow the current situation to continue for long. People openly defying her rule by taking the law into their own hands would not be tolerated.

"I've sent birds to Olivia and Talandra, but I may have to make a decision before I hear back from them. I can't wait too long."

"I understand," he said, slowly getting to his feet. Even that was getting more difficult every day. He took a moment to regain his balance. "But I hope you appreciate that if you also bring in a ban, you could be making an enemy of the Red Tower and the Grey Council."

Morganse's expression turned grave. "I know, and I also know who sits on the Grey Council and what they did for everyone during the war. But unless you can prove that Seekers aren't involved, I don't have much of a choice. I must protect the people, even if it puts children at risk."

He knew the thought of it sickened her because he felt the same. There was no way to know which child would be born with magic. One of her own grandchildren could have it and if she agreed to a national ban, it could put them in grave danger.

Unfortunately maintaining the status quo and hoping things got better was not an option. In the short term banning Seekers would ease international pressures, appease the people and give the Guardians some time to find answers and those responsible. But without the Seekers the old ways of dealing with special children could return. Children simply disappeared and were never mentioned again. Don't ask, don't tell, and no one wanted that.

"I'll keep you informed," said the Khevassar, marching out of the room. He hoped to return to his office and find some good news waiting, but hope seemed to be in short supply.

CHAPTER 23

Habreel straightened his collar in the mirror and contemplated his reflection. The long navy jacket was a far cry from his old uniform, but these days it was all he had. Despite no longer being a Guardian he still maintained a certain level of discipline and he expected his followers to do the same. Whether that was being smartly dressed or not drinking during the day, he led by example and so far those closest to him were doing the same.

He concentrated on his clothing and studiously avoided looking his reflection in the eye. After recent events he was finding it difficult. He may not have killed the children himself, but he'd given the order to Akosh. He'd always known the task ahead was never going to be easy and that lasting change required considerable sacrifice. What he hadn't understood was how many compromises it would require and how often he'd have to break his own moral code. In the past prayer had helped soothe his conscience, but lately it had given him little comfort. Habreel threw his old jacket over the mirror and left his room.

He hoped a walk through the city would remind him of what he was fighting for, but by the time he reached his office he felt no more at ease with himself. To make matters worse he knew from the expressions of those downstairs that she was already waiting for him.

Akosh was sitting on his chair, both feet resting on his desk, a bottle of something in one hand and two glasses in the other.

"Ah, Habreel, come in," she said, gesturing for him to sit as if this were her office. "Come and celebrate with me." She poured two generous measures of what smelled like whisky and slid one towards him across the desk. Habreel caught the glass before it fell on the floor but he didn't drink.

"What are we celebrating?"

"The national ban, of course," said Akosh. "A little bird in the palace has told me the Regent is preparing to make a public declaration in a few days."

"Is this a joke? Are you playing a trick on me?"

Akosh sat upright and set both glass and bottle aside. Resting both hands flat on the desk she leaned towards him. "It's true. The Regent is going to ban all Seekers in Zecorria. Messages have been sent to other rulers in the west and to Queen Talandra in Seveldrom, asking them to bring in a ban as well."

There didn't seem to be any hint of mockery in her expression. Deciding to believe her until his own sources confirmed it, Habreel sat back in his chair, idly rolling the glass back and forth between his hands.

Akosh frowned. "I thought you would be more excited. Isn't this what you wanted?"

"It's a good start, but I want the Regent and the others to do more."

"I could arrange a few more accidents," suggested Akosh.

"No. It wouldn't help," said Habreel. "The Regent is a moderate. If two didn't sway him to take more decisive action, more deaths won't change his mind. The best we can hope for at the moment is that other countries will follow suit. After that we can start to move things towards a total ban on all magic."

Just as she opened her mouth to ask a question they heard an argument downstairs, followed by the sound of heavy feet on the steps. The office door flew open and Dannel appeared, trying to restrain a Yerskani woman from entering. Habreel vaguely recognised her as part of his network, but he didn't know her by name.

"I'm sorry, Sir, she refused to wait," apologised Dannel. "I told her you were in an important meeting."

"I must speak with you," insisted the woman. "I have urgent news."

"What is your name?" asked Habreel, gesturing for Dannel to ease back. He released the woman but remained standing right behind her.

"Jaine. My sister works for you. She lives in Maldorn. It's a town in southern Yerskania."

Habreel glanced at the others but they were none the wiser. "Has something happened there?"

"My sister sent me a letter. She said the townspeople in Maldorn banded together and exiled the Seeker."

"That's wonderful news. My friend will take a statement which I promise to read later," he said, gesturing at Dannel to escort her out of the room. Akosh had already lost interest and was now drinking directly from the bottle.

"The Seeker was a local woman," said Jaine as Dannel tried to drag her out.

"What?" asked Habreel, slowly getting to his feet. "Say that again."

"She lived in Maldorn. She's a blacksmith who's lived there for years until they kicked her out."

Dannel released her again and Habreel guided her into one of the two chairs in front of his desk. With a wave of his hand he dismissed Dannel who closed the door behind him. Across the desk Akosh was fixing the newcomer with a penetrating glare.

"Start at the beginning," said Habreel. "Tell me what happened."

"Spare no detail," said Akosh, drawing Jaine's focus which seemed to unsettle her.

"The Seeker tested the children as normal and all of them were clean. Then the Mayor came forward and spoke for the people. They asked the Seeker, Leonie, to leave and never come back, but she argued."

"I'm not surprised if she'd lived there for a long time," commented Akosh. "To be exiled by strangers is one thing, but to be made an outcast by your own friends and family is something totally different."

There was a tone in her voice that made Habreel think she was speaking from personal experience. He made a mental note and filed it away for later. "What happened next?"

"When the Mayor wouldn't change his mind, she took off her mask in front of everyone."

"By the Maker," hissed Habreel. "Did it change their minds?"

Jaine shook her head. "It made them angrier because she'd been lying to them for years. Pretending to leave town on business only to ride back the following day wearing a Seeker's mask. In the end she fled town and that was the last anyone saw of her."

Habreel saw Jaine to the door, asked her to leave her address with Dannel and thanked her. Once she was gone he sat down and seriously contemplated drinking his whisky despite the hour.

"Have we really been so blind?" he said, asking himself as much as Akosh.

Up to now, along with everyone else he'd always assumed

Seekers travelled across the country, going from one village to the next before returning to the Red Tower. That was how it had been in the old days. But what if everyone was wrong? What if Seekers were living among the very people they tested, hiding in plain sight?

If the Seeker in Maldorn was not an isolated incident then it meant the Red Tower had people everywhere.

"Why would they need such a network?" said Habreel, thinking aloud.

"Control," said Akosh. She had set her glass aside and suddenly looked sober. "They have an invisible network of people who see everything. With spies everywhere, in every country, the Red Tower hears everything. Every word is probably reported back to their leaders."

It seemed unlikely and more than a little paranoid. Habreel raised an eyebrow. "Why?"

"Are you really so naïve?" snapped Akosh. "Don't you want to destroy them? Get rid of the Seekers and all magic?"

"I do."

"Then we will use their own people against them."

"What if this was just an isolated incident?" asked Habreel.

Akosh sneered at him. "As if that matters."

"More innocent people could be hurt."

"We are far beyond that now," she said, her voice utterly devoid of mercy. "Spread news of this throughout your network. Every person in every village and town across the world should know that the Seeker could be someone living among them. Their friends, their neighbours, maybe even someone in their own family could be working for the Red Tower. They will tear each other apart trying to find a spy." The delight in her voice was terrifying as she contemplated the widespread violence that would follow. Habreel knew that fear and paranoia would spread like wildfire. Hatred of magic and the Red Tower would reach new levels.

"We can't," he said, but she didn't hear or most likely didn't care.

"This could be exactly what we need. Every ruler will be forced to ban all Seekers. Perhaps even take it a step further and ban all magic."

"We can't," said Habreel, more loudly this time. He slammed his glass down on the desk, splashing whisky everywhere. "It would be chaos."

He could see it so clearly. Mob rule. Friends and family turning on each other for no reason. People being dragged out of their beds and accused. All it would take was the discovery of a golden mask among their belongings. It wouldn't be difficult to make one and plant it on someone you didn't like. People wouldn't wait to see the spy punished by the law, they would act. No one would be safe. No one.

Mages were the real enemy. If the violence had to continue, then let them be the target. His ultimate goal had always been a total ban on magic. That was the only way to be safe. One mage had torn the world apart and he could not allow it to happen again. He would not.

Until now the targets and sacrifices had been carefully selected. But this could cause widespread violence on a scale they'd not seen in ten years.

"I will not allow you to do this," he said.

The fury in Akosh's eyes was so great he thought she was going to leap across the table and kill him. A moment later it was gone and the seductress returned. She sauntered around the desk and sat down on the edge close to him. When she spoke her voice was calm and her smile inviting. Habreel preferred her anger. At least it was honest. "This gives us an opportunity. It's everything you've been working towards for years."

"But the cost—"

"How long did it take you to build up your network of followers? How many years? How much have you personally sacrificed to reach this moment?" she asked, leaning forward. Habreel shied away from her as if she were a venomous snake. Realising seduction was pointless she quickly changed tactic, settling for brutal honesty. "We're so close. If you don't do this now, we may never get another opportunity like it. When there are no more accidents, a ban on Seekers could quickly disappear. If we don't reveal this, then all of your hard work will have been for nothing. We must act now."

Akosh crossed her arms and waited for his decision.

Not long ago Habreel would have prayed for wisdom, but now it seemed as if his faith had abandoned him as well. He felt utterly adrift.

More than the famed coat, the rule of law had been his armour when he'd been a Guardian of the Peace. During the war, when the Chosen had left him feeling powerless, he'd walked away from everything he knew in search of something better. Over time he'd found others like him, the dispossessed and those cast out for daring to think differently. Hope that change would come in time had quickly evaporated. Habreel had slowly come to the realisation that the only way things would improve was through direct action.

As he wrestled with his decision Habreel wondered if Akosh had planned this all along. When they'd first met she claimed to want the same thing, an end to magic, but he'd doubted her from the start. Her own secret agenda had not conflicted with his until now. She was useful and had been reliable, but now he was beginning to wonder if it was time to get rid of her. Akosh had powers and influence he didn't understand. Perhaps she was trying to control him even now.

He was faced with an impossible choice. The danger to others was clear. Spreading news of this among his followers would result in violence and murder. There was no way to know if what emerged after the dust settled would be better. Part of him also wondered if it could be any worse.

Perhaps this was why he had been unable to look himself in the mirror that morning. Some small part of him had instinctively known he would cross this line.

"Send word to everyone. Let them know the truth about the Seekers," said Habreel. "But make sure they know who to blame."

Her smile was chilling. "A wise decision, but I think there needs to be a final push. Something more to make sure they lose all faith in the Red Tower and its people."

"Do I even want to know?" he asked, more than a little afraid of what the answer might be.

"Leave it to me," said Akosh. "It will be a surprise!"

She went out of the door in a hurry, a passionate servant of chaos.

Habreel picked up his glass and drained it in one gulp. It burned all the way down his throat and the fire spread from his stomach. It wasn't enough to extinguish the terror that ran through him at her words.

"May the Maker forgive me," he whispered in the empty room.

CHAPTER 24

Danoph had rarely spent this much time inside the Red Tower before and the longer he sat in the hospital room, the more uncomfortable he became. So far he'd managed to avoid any serious injuries and had only seen Master Yettle in the classroom when he demonstrated healing. Now the slight man was studying him very closely as they sat together in a strange room inside the tower.

The nightmares were getting worse again. Whatever the Grey Council had done previously had worn off and now every night he dreaded going to sleep.

As Yettle stared intently at him, and somehow beyond his skin into him, Danoph studied the runes on the back of the door. The writing was ancient, from a dead language, but somehow it seemed familiar. Perhaps he'd read about it in the library or seen something similar in the past. He felt if he concentrated hard enough it might just be possible to decipher them.

"Don't look at the runes if they make you feel queasy," said Yettle, his eyes returning to the present.

Danoph didn't feel sick at all. He was going to ask what Yettle meant, but changed his mind. The door didn't concern him. It was the tower itself that made his bones ache. Standing close to it made him feel as if he were walking naked through a blizzard, icy daggers pummelling his flesh all over. By comparison being inside the tower was agony.

New arrivals often spoke about it being unnerving, but he'd never heard anyone say that it hurt them. Pain blossomed somewhere behind his eyes. This was also why he spent as little time as possible in the library.

"Do you see anything?" he asked Master Yettle, gesturing at himself.

"No. You're a healthy young man. Everything is as it should be," said Yettle, sounding confused.

"Is something wrong?"

"Hmm, oh no. I was just wondering why you don't have any scars."

Danoph knew what he was referring to and his mind immediately shied away from the memories. The war. It always came back to the war. Especially for his people who had suffered so much during the occupation. Yettle had been here, safe behind the walls of the Red Tower, where no army dared approach. Danoph had not been so lucky.

He could still smell the huge graves full of rotting bodies and see the hills made of bones. In some ways they were the lucky ones. Their deaths were often painful, but at least it was usually quick. Other prisoners, whose only crime had been that they were hungry, had it worse. They were often staked out and left to die of starvation. Carrion eaters picked at them, taking the tastiest morsels first before other less choosy wild animals came for the rest. After that all that remained was a collection of bones held together with sinew and gristle.

One of his jobs in the camp had been to collect what remained of those staked out and throw them into one of the mass graves. This was so that someone else could be staked out in their place.

The guards had also given him a hammer to crack every skull. He'd barely been big enough to lift it, but that hadn't mattered to his captors. They enjoyed watching him struggle and placed bets on how many hits it would take him with the hammer.

If he didn't do it he would be tied out instead and wouldn't eat. As it was they only gave him scraps from their meals, but it was a lot better than nothing. At one point, when he'd dared rebel, they had starved him for days to teach him a lesson. After that he ate whatever he was given and never once complained. He tried not to look at it, to think about what it was, and forced it down, willing his stomach to accept it. Survival had been everything.

"The Morrin in charge of our camp was patient and without emotion," said Danoph, his voice low. Even now it still hurt to talk about it. "She never became angry, even at the end when we rebelled. She never let any of her people use a whip on us. Not even a knife. Instead she used ropes and weights. People strung upside down until they choked to death. A cairn of stones piled on someone's chest until they suffocated. Stretching limbs with ropes until they came out of the sockets. She was very inventive."

Danoph rubbed his wrists, remembering the burning of the ropes. Those who had survived the camp had scars on the outside that healed fairly quickly, but the wounds within still festered and stank with rot.

"What happened to her?" asked Yettle.

"When we rebelled she took her own life. I was there when they found her. She'd rather die than let one of us touch her. In her mind we were not worthy."

Yettle laid a hand on Danoph's shoulder and he tried to smile, as if the memory didn't still burn. As if he didn't daydream about choking the life out of her with his own hands. "But she is gone now."

"Yes."

"Do you still dream about her?" asked Master Yettle.

Danoph shook his head. "Not her, but sometimes what the guards did to us in the camp. Recently I've just been having nightmares about a terrible fire. It's so bright. I can hear the screams and see the bodies writhing in the flames. They're in so much pain I can't describe it. But I can feel the heat of the fire on my skin. I can smell burning hair and hear meat sizzling. Why can I feel it?" asked Danoph, running a hand down his arm.

"I'm not sure, but I have a theory. Would you like to hear it?" asked Yettle.

"Please."

"Your mind is making it real. At the Red Tower we deal with the remarkable every day. We use the power of creation to mould energy into wonderful abilities. We can read the weather, heal the sick, create fire, ice and light. We can talk across great distances that would take days to ride on a horse. This and so much more is possible, but most of it is done when we're awake. There are a few abilities that live on the border, somewhere between being awake and asleep, like dreamwalking. I think yours is something like this."

"Then, I'm doing this to myself?"

Yettle nodded slowly. "Yes. Some small part of you. A part that still hurts and agonises over what happened. You wish you could have done more. You wish you'd developed your magic earlier, so that you could have fought back and saved our people."

He'd only been a young boy of seven at the time. It would be years before he felt the first stirrings of magic and a connection to the Source. Danoph knew it wasn't his fault and yet it still hurt to think about all of those lives that had been lost. All of those he'd seen murdered in barbaric ways, just to satisfy the desires of a warped mind. Even revenge on the worst of their torturers had been denied when the Morrin had killed herself with a smile. A terrible fury about the evil that had been committed still raged inside. Perhaps this was what fuelled his mind while he slept, creating horrific visions of people burning to death.

"You've given me much to think on. Thank you, Master Yettle."

"There are some techniques I can teach you, to quieten the mind before you go to sleep," he said. "They will help you to rest, but only if you are at peace with what happened."

"I don't know that I will ever be at peace with it."

"I misspoke," apologised Yettle. "If not at peace then at a new level of understanding." Danoph knew what he was going to say next but he still didn't believe it. "It wasn't your fault, Danoph. You couldn't have done more. You survived and many others did not. The guilt of that, and feeling powerless, is what's eating at your sleeping mind. You must forgive yourself."

Danoph wiped at his face and tried to swallow the lump in his throat that would not go away. "I will try."

"One more thing. Can you tell me what happened to the boy you touched?"

It had all happened so fast. The fight between Wren and Brunwal had been brutal but he'd never had a chance. That much was clear to Danoph from the start. Tianne had been scared for Wren but he'd known how it would turn out. As expected, she had bested him, although not in a way Danoph had anticipated, turning Brunwal's own twisted creation against him. Once he stopped screaming that should have been the end. Then one of Brunwal's friends had tried to interfere and without thinking Danoph had moved to intercept him.

"He was going to stab Wren. I could see it so clearly and feel her warm blood on my hands. There was so much of it, all over me. I just wanted him to stop."

"Do you remember what you did to the boy?"

Danoph tried to recall, but it had all been on instinct. "No, I'm sorry, Master Yettle. I can't remember."

"That's fine, Danoph. You can go back to class."

"Is he going to be all right?"

Yettle smiled. "He's resting. I'll know more in a few days."

A short time later Garvey and Balfruss came into the room where Yettle was still sitting, turning it over in his mind. Balfruss had only just returned from his trip and looked weary, but Yettle didn't avoid telling him the truth.

"Well?" asked Garvey, abrupt as ever.

"He doesn't remember."

"Do you believe him?"

Yettle sighed. He felt wrung out and sleep tugged at him. "Yes, Garvey. Danoph reacted instinctively to protect his friend."

"And what of the boy?" asked Balfruss.

"He's barely alive. His mind has been shattered into a hundred pieces. There's nothing I can do to help him."

"How long does he have?"

Yettle shrugged. "Perhaps a few days, maybe less."

Balfruss muttered a brief prayer then asked. "Did you tell Danoph?"

"No, I will not add to his burdens. I told him the injured boy is resting."

"And what about his dreams?" asked Garvey. "Did you tell him the truth about them?"

"Not all of it. He's not ready."

"You know what's happening out there," said Balfruss, pushing in his own subtle way.

"I'm sorry, Balfruss. It's too soon," insisted Yettle. "He needs more time."

"Then I hope he gets it," snapped Garvey, before storming off. Balfruss rolled his eyes and went after his old friend.

After everything that had happened to Danoph, including recent events with Brunwal, shielding him from the truth was the right decision. If they told him too much too soon, he might crumble under yet another weight. He was already struggling with a lot of guilt from his early childhood. It was not the right time to tell him about his magic, but he would have to be told soon.

Yettle hoped that when they did have that difficult conversation Danoph would understand the repercussions and avoid doing something rash, for all their sakes.

CHAPTER 25

Ignoring the five crossbows pointed at her, Munroe crossed the room and sat down at the table opposite Cannok. If the crime boss expected her to be intimidated he was in for a rude awakening.

"I'm not surprised, but I am disappointed," admitted Munroe, sipping her ale.

"Really?" said Cannok with a smile.

"I used to work for a crime Family in Perizzi, so I've seen it all. Whatever piss-poor operation you've got here in Rojenne, it's going to be tame by comparison." If anything Cannok's grin broadened at her insult. She would have to work much harder to get under his skin. "So, what do you want?"

"Are you representing your friend?" said Cannok, gesturing at the basement where Denke was recovering.

"Forget about him. He's off the table."

"Really?"

"Really," insisted Munroe. "Tell me what needs doing and I'll see that it's done. In return you'll leave him alone and never go near him, or his family, ever again."

Cannok ran his finger around the rim of his mug as he mulled it over. "But he has magic, and that could be extremely useful to me."

"He can't be the first person with magic you've ever met."

"No, but most of the time their magic ability is small and specific, like Dox, who can tell when people are lying. Do you know what your friend can do?"

As it happened Munroe didn't know, but she was able to sense that Denke's connection to the Source was fairly weak. It was possible he had a rare and unusual Talent that would make him useful to Cannok, but it seemed unlikely. Even so, the crime boss had found a way to use Dox and she suspected he would do the same for Denke if given the chance.

"He's not part of the deal. You will leave him alone," she insisted.

"From where I'm sitting, it doesn't seem like you have much to bargain with," said Cannok, crossing his arms. Doctor Silver stood up and started towards the stairs. "Where are you going?"

"To see to my patients," said Silver.

"Sit down, Doctor."

"You're not half as clever, or witty, as you think you are, and I've no time for this nonsense."

"Unless something has changed, you still work for me, Doctor. So sit down and shut up," said Cannok. He hadn't raised his voice but there was a definite chill to his words. It seemed as if the crime boss liked to perform for an audience. He waited until Silver had sat down again before turning back to Munroe. All humour had now drained from his face. "Let me make your situation very clear, since the obvious seems to have eluded you."

"Oh, please, enlighten me," said Munroe, sitting back and hooking one arm over the back of her chair. Over Cannok's shoulder Tok raised an eyebrow, surprised at her relaxed posture but he said nothing. Cannok and the others assumed it was bravado. Munroe struggled to keep the grin off her face but couldn't help winking at the big man which unsettled him even more.

"You brought an injured man into my building, to my doctor—"

"Whose time I paid for, generously," said Munroe.

"But, you haven't paid any of us to keep his identity a secret. I hear Seekers are very unpopular these days."

Munroe started to laugh. At first it was just a chuckle but as Cannok's expression soured it just made her laugh even harder. "Money. Is that all you care about?" she asked between chuckles. "Now I'm *really* disappointed."

"I'm beginning to think your quiver is short of a few arrows," he said, tapping the side of his head. "You seem to have a peculiar delusion of grandeur. I rule this city and I have more than a hundred people working for me. Five of them have crossbows pointed at your back. You, on the other hand, have an injured friend with a target on his back and a purse half full of silver. You have nothing to barter with. I am in control and I decide if you live or die."

"Do you follow him because he pays you well, or because he's the only crime boss in the city?" she said, addressing her question at Tok. The big man didn't answer but he did squirm a bit. Doctor Silver just laughed and crossed her arms while Cannok glared at them both. "What about the rest of you?" said Munroe, turning in her chair to look at the five men with crossbows.

"It seems as if a demonstration is required. You seem to be having some trouble understanding the danger," said Cannok.

"A demonstration is an excellent idea," said Munroe.

"Tok, teach her some manners," said Cannok. The enforcer glanced at his boss and then back to Munroe, who smiled at him sweetly. "What are you waiting for?" snapped Cannok, when the big man didn't move.

"What are your instincts telling you?" she asked Tok, ignoring the seething crime boss.

"That you're dangerous. And you're not afraid," he replied, watching her closely.

"Look at the size of her!" scoffed Cannok. "Doctor Silver could probably best her, and she's ancient."

"Do you have a family, Tok?" asked Munroe.

"A wife. Two boys, aged five and three."

"And what would you do to protect them?"

"Anything." The way in which he said that one word told Munroe a great deal about him. It was neither threatening nor aggressive. But she also had the feeling he would be utterly implacable if anyone stood between him and his family. He would never, ever stop and would fight until his last breath. They had a great deal in common.

"I have a husband and a son. There is nothing in the world that I love more and nothing I wouldn't do to get home to them."

"I understand."

"What are you two talking about?" asked Cannok. "Tok, if you won't do anything then someone else will. Farrell," he said, pointing at the bowman on the far left. "Shoot her in the foot."

Farrell had less intuition than Tok as he pointed his crossbow at one of Munroe's feet and pulled the trigger.

With the speed of thought she embraced the Source, raised her hand and stopped the crossbow bolt in mid-air. It hung there, as if trapped in amber, neither swaying nor twitching. Without looking, and with a casual wave of her hand, Munroe redirected the bolt's trajectory so that it lodged into the far wall instead.

"I would suggest you don't try that again," she said, glaring at Cannok. His face had turned pale and his eyes kept flicking between the bolt and Munroe. She'd been unpopular before, but the atmosphere became even worse at the realisation she was a mage.

"All of you, fire! Kill her now!" screamed Cannok, scrambling back out of his chair. As Munroe turned to face the other bowmen the Morrin by the door drew her sword as well.

"Let's dance," said Munroe, grinning at them.

Twisting her left hand she unleashed her Talent, manipulating the odds and breaking all of the crossbows into pieces. The shattered weapons sprayed bits of wood and wire everywhere. One man fell to the ground clutching his ruined hands which now had pieces of metal sticking out of them. The others had fared better, but they quickly discarded the bows and drew a variety of blades.

"Put your weapons down and I won't hurt you," said Munroe. "If you don't then I'm not going to be gentle."

One man snarled and ran at her with his sword raised, quickly followed by two more. Lifting him off the floor slightly she increased the swordsman's momentum and stepped aside. He flew through the air and hammered into the wall with a sickening crunch of bone before sliding to the floor in a bloody-faced heap.

Another had thrown a dagger which she stopped in mid-air, turned it around and sent it flying back towards the owner. The dagger impaled the man in his right shoulder and he stumbled back out of the fight.

The other two, and the Morrin, were slightly smarter as they muttered something and then all attacked together. Raising both hands and focusing her will, Munroe stopped them all at once, freezing their limbs until they became living statues. All six had no control over their bodies except for the movement of their eyes. Even their jaws were clamped shut. A few strained against their invisible bonds but nothing happened. She was simply too strong and there was nothing they could do.

Across the room Cannok finally realised he was not in control of the situation and never had been since the start. Beside him Doctor Silver was grinning but Tok seemed troubled.

"If you'd thought about it, even for a moment, you might have asked yourself, who would the Red Tower send to warn its Seekers?" said Munroe. "A stable boy? A cook? An innkeeper? Or maybe, just maybe, a Battlemage."

With that Munroe raised her left hand and behind her all six thugs were lifted off the floor and slammed into the ceiling. She let them fall naturally to the floor where they lay groaning in pain, before lifting them up again and creating more dents in the ceiling. Then she let them drop a second time before pinning them to the floor, unable to move and barely able to breathe.

"Now, let me make your situation very clear. You're no longer in charge."

"But—"

"I've heard enough from you," said Munroe, pinching his mouth shut. Cannok squawked and tried to open his jaw but his struggles were feeble against her magic. "So, why do you work for him?" she said, directing the question at Tok.

The big man glanced at his boss and this time he answered. "It's like you said. He's the only crime boss in the city. He doesn't even pay that well."

"Well, you're in charge now."

Tok raised an eyebrow. "Me?"

"Sure. Why not?" asked Munroe.

"I'm not sure they'll follow my orders."

"Let's see if anyone objects to my suggestion," said Munroe, looking at the others in the room who were either injured or unconscious. All of them were glaring at her but said nothing.

"There, you see, it's settled. Besides, you've got better instincts than these idiots," she said, including Cannok and the others in her scowl. Doctor Silver chuckled and sat back in her chair, enjoying the show.

"So, Don Tok-ram-Gara of Rojenne. My friend is in Doctor Silver's care, which I've paid for. Now all I want to do is leave here and finish my work so that I can go home to my family. Do I need to worry about my friend?"

"No," replied the big man, without hesitation. "He'll be well cared for and then sent home. His secret is also safe. You have my word."

"Excellent," said Munroe, offering her hand to the new crime boss. He paused, glanced at her nervously in case she did something with her magic, but then shook it gently. "I'm not going to have a reason to come back here, am I?"

"I certainly hope not," said Tok and she grinned at him.

Cannok had been embarrassed in front of his people and his power usurped in a matter of minutes. Although he was unable to speak he could still move. As Munroe was pondering what to do with him, Cannok grabbed a dagger from Tok's belt and launched himself at her across the table. She reacted without thinking, bringing her old power to bear on the former crime boss. There was a loud crack and he screamed before collapsing face down on the table. A trickle of blood ran from the corner of his mouth. It crept across the wooden surface before pattering on the floor. His sightless eyes stared at her, accusing and angry.

Part of her wanted to apologise, to say that he'd given her no choice, but Munroe bit her tongue and had to work hard to keep her expression neutral. Showing compassion at such a time wouldn't help her. It would be seen as weakness and it might erode their fear. Taking a deep breath, she stared down at Cannok without compassion and then lifted her eyes to Tok.

"Do we have a problem?"

The big man shook his head but didn't reply. Doctor Silver wasn't smiling any more but she did have a slightly smug expression. Cannok had been far less popular with his own people than he realised. Everyone was now staring at her and she could smell their fear. Magic like Dox's was seen as useful and it was so slight it didn't really count in their minds. She'd just given them a glimpse of real magic and, in doing so, confirmed all of their worst fears.

Munroe crossed the room, walking on the backs of those pinned to the floor before pausing at the door. With a flick of her hand she released them and they started rolling about, groaning and gasping for air. No one would look her in the eye any more.

"I've left you a little reminder," she said to those recovering on the floor. "If you ever think about trying to get even for this embarrassment, or perhaps to seek revenge, look there."

Everyone in the room stared at their former boss and she hoped that had quelled any thoughts of retaliation. With a final wink at Tok, Munroe went out of the door, one step closer to going home.

CHAPTER 26

W ren stared at the runes on the back of the door, trying to find a pattern amid the writhing chaos. They continued to squirm, but the motion no longer gave her a headache. It had at the beginning, but she'd been staring at them for quite some time. She wasn't sure how long. It must have been at least a few hours.

Wren was aware that she was in one of the hospital rooms inside the Red Tower, but she couldn't remember how she got here. Looking herself over, she couldn't see any blood or obvious wounds. Her memory loss must be the reason why she was here. It was the only logical explanation.

If the symbols would just stop moving she might be able to decipher them. It had to be some kind of ancient language but Wren didn't recognise a single letter. Nothing even looked vaguely similar. Without a key it would be extremely difficult to decode, but she was determined. There wasn't anything else to do.

Glancing at the wall behind her she noticed the light was slightly muted. From around the edges of her door she could see a soft blue glow from the lanterns filled with mage light. That meant it must be night-time. The man who wandered the hallways in sandals always briefly stopped outside every room and she felt a brief surge of power as he embraced the Source. Wren had seen others create mage lights so often she was confident she could do the same. It would just take a bit of practice.

As she embraced the Source and drew power into herself, the glyphs on the door flared to light, glowing orange in response. The more power she drew the brighter the runes became, changing in colour from orange to ruby-red. The glow was so intense that she could still see them through her eyelids when she closed her eyes. A different kind of headache began to form at the back of her skull. Tendrils of pain began to stretch out and as soon as she tried to channel any power she felt a jolt of energy run through her entire body.

Wren woke up lying face down on the floor in the middle of her room. The symbols on the door were black again, but they continued to twitch and squirm as if alive.

The door opened and Master Yettle came in. For such a slight man he was surprisingly strong as he lifted Wren off the floor and helped her settle back on the bed. She felt a pleasant warmth envelope her whole body, starting at the back of her head, easing away the pain, before spreading down her torso and along her limbs. She felt safe and her eyelids drooped shut.

When she woke up next Master Yettle was sitting on a chair reading a book at the foot of her bed. The door to her room stood open and beyond she could see the corridor. The peculiar wall behind her was bright with golden light, suggesting it was already morning.

"What time is it?" asked Wren.

"Breakfast time. You've slept for most of a day and a night. How do you feel?"

"I feel fine. Why am I in the hospital this time?"

"What is the last thing you remember before waking up here?"

She was about to say being asleep in the dormitory when she remembered the fight with Brunwal. Her heart began to race, a groan escaped her lips and she started scratching at the skin on her arms, looking for where the black mote had burned her flesh. She'd felt its corruption seeping into her bloodstream, even though it hadn't directly touched her bare skin.

"You're safe," said Master Yettle. "The inversion is gone."

"What was it?" said Wren, remembering the swirling darkness Brunwal had summoned. To use the Source to create something so grotesque and tainted felt like the worst sin a mage could commit.

"Something forbidden. I don't know how he learned about it."

Part of her didn't want to ask but she had to know. "Is he . . . dead?"

Master Yettle's sad smile told her everything. "There was nothing we could do to help him. It was too late."

"What's going to happen to me now?"

"Well, that depends on my assessment. The Grey Council wants to speak to you about what happened, but they're not allowed until I've declared you healthy."

She had thought all the teachers deferred to the Grey Council in every matter. It made her smile to think of Garvey trying to bully his way in here, only to be turned aside by the calm and kind face of Master Yettle.

"Do you feel well enough to talk about what happened?"

Part of her was tempted to say no and hide a bit longer, but more time wouldn't change the facts. Even though it had been in self-defence, she had killed another student.

Once, Wren had seen a murderer passing through her town on his way for trial. He'd seemed so ordinary and unassuming. It had been so difficult for her to bring together in her mind the terrible things that had been done to the victims with the quiet, affable man she'd seen. He was nothing like she'd expected. There'd been no malice in his expression or outward sign of the evil that lurked within. Even after, when they'd found him covered in blood and entrails, he'd not changed into a snarling lunatic. Whatever passion or rage had consumed him in that moment was gone. He'd remained calm, polite and happy to oblige. It was as if nothing unusual had happened.

Her father had told her that such an event changed a person. Sometimes the changes were slight and at other times it was as if something inside had snapped and could never be mended. Over time their outside transformed to match the new person within they saw when looking in the mirror.

Wren wondered what she would see when she looked in the mirror. Would there be a new version of herself staring back? Was there something festering inside her that would grow over time and remake her in its image?

"I can't hide in here for ever," said Wren, shaking her head in a vain attempt to dislodge thoughts of what she might become.

"How much do you remember?"

"Everything. Do you want me to tell you what happened?"

"There's no need," said Master Yettle. "We've spoken to the other students who were there. I just needed to know if your memory was impaired. Sometimes the mind can obscure such a traumatic event to protect itself."

There would be no hiding for her, within or without. She would have to look at herself and other people in the eye and cope with whatever happened next.

"Do you remember how you came here?" he asked, gesturing at the room.

"I was in the dormitory and people were screaming and crying. Then I remember a sense of falling. I was lying some-where and I overheard part of an argument between Master

Garvey and Master Balfruss. They both seemed so angry. Was that recently? Did that actually happen?"

"Anything else?" said Master Yettle, avoiding all of her questions.

Wren closed her eyes, trying to recall what had happened after that but there was nothing. Just darkness and silence. A featureless void in her thoughts.

"The next thing I remember is being in this room."

"If you're feeling hungry, I'll have some breakfast brought to you."

"Thank you, Master Yettle." Wren didn't know how she could feel hungry after what had happened but her stomach was growling. "Why did he choose me?"

That wasn't what she wanted to ask but the other question wouldn't come easily. Master Yettle could see she was struggling with something. He sat back and waited patiently for her to find the courage. Finally she managed to blurt it out. "What will I become?"

"I don't know," he said. Much to her surprise he'd not offered her platitudes or false hope about the future. Such honesty was refreshing, although it did sting. Wren didn't notice she was crying until tears began to drip off her chin. More than anything she wished her father was there to console her. He would have known exactly the right thing to say and make her laugh. But she'd said goodbye to him, perhaps for the last time, and was on her own. "I won't lie and say this won't change you," said Master Yettle. "It must and it will change you over time, but how it changes you is the real unknown. That depends on you, Wren. Can I offer you one piece of advice?"

"Please." At this moment Wren needed something to hold on to. She felt adrift. She wanted nothing more than for Master Yettle to put his arms around her and tell her everything was going to be all right. But he was not her father and she was no longer a child.

If she were still at home in Drassia she would be regarded as a woman. Society would treat her with the same respect and responsibility as any other woman, no matter their age.

For all of the good that came from it, Wren knew there was a loss of innocence. She had seen a friend of hers set apart from other girls, unable to play any more. Childish antics and temper tantrums were no longer tolerated. Even though she was only a few months older than Wren, her friend was expected to remain indoors at work.

If she were still in Drassia by now Wren would have been given responsibilities by her mother. The future was rigid and set. Now, she felt like a child once more, cut off from everything familiar that might guide her through such a murky time. She had no idea what might happen tomorrow, never mind a week or a year from now. For a time such freedom had been exhilarating, but now it was starting to terrify her.

"Be honest with yourself," said Master Yettle.

"I don't understand," replied Wren.

Master Yettle stared at the far wall as if he could see through it but it was clear his mind had travelled elsewhere. "As the days pass, and you think over what happened, don't shy away from anything. Let yourself feel all of it. If you lie to yourself, if you censure parts of it, then you will suffer. I can mend a broken bone. I can heal bruises and cure diseases, but I cannot heal your mind. Only you can do that."

After breakfast Wren spent the rest of the morning alone, thinking on her future. Master Yettle had left the door to her room open but she didn't try to step outside. There was no point. Right now she needed to be away from other people.

A few hours later there was a loud commotion in the corridor followed by the sound of raised voices. Just as she was getting up to investigate Garvey came into the room. A second behind him came Balfruss, who tried to pull the other Sorcerer out of the room by the shoulder, but Garvey shook him off.

"Are you well, girl? Can you answer a few questions?"

"Leave her be, Garvey," said Balfruss. "We don't have to do this now."

"Time is the one thing we lack," snarled Garvey. As soon as they set foot in the room Wren felt the familiar thrum of power echoing in her mind. Both men had such strong connections to the Source it felt as if she had a second pulse. It was so intense it thumped against her temples as if someone was tapping her on the side of the head.

"Gentlemen," said the calm voice of Master Yettle. The tension eased with his presence, but there was still some friction between the two Sorcerers. "I said you could speak to Wren, but only when she had recovered."

"She looks fine to me," said Garvey.

Master Yettle ignored both men and came into the room, standing at the foot of Wren's bed, blocking her view of them. "Do you feel well enough to talk, or shall I send them away?"

Wren was confident Garvey would argue again but much to her surprise he remained silent. Part of her would have liked nothing better than to see him dismissed and sent away like an errant child. It would serve him right, but it would also be petty and childish of her. She might not be in Drassia any longer but she couldn't pretend to be a girl any more.

"I'm happy to speak with them."

"Keep it brief," said Master Yettle, looking directly at Garvey. "She still needs some rest." The healer waited until Garvey agreed before stepping aside and letting them further into the room.

"Can you tell us what happened last night?" asked Balfruss. "Take us through the events from the beginning."

Speaking slowly and trying to keep her voice calm, Wren laid out what had happened. She started with Brunwal's unprovoked attack on her the first night and what had happened when next they'd duelled in the dormitory. Even though she hadn't mentioned going to visit Garvey for advice, Balfruss seemed to know as he glared at the other Sorcerer. Garvey said nothing and merely listened, leaning against the wall with his arms folded. Wren was unable to read anything from his body language but she could feel constant waves of rage radiating from him. It seemed to be seeping from every pore in his body. Something truly awful must have happened to him in the past to make him so bitter and angry all the time.

Eventually she spoke about her final confrontation with Brunwal. Balfruss gently questioned her about what he had summoned and the effects.

"I've never seen anything like it before. It was horrific. A festering darkness that smelled awful. A few people were physically sick just from being near it. I looked into the weave and what I saw made no sense."

"You did what?" asked Garvey, exchanging a quick look with Balfruss.

"I tried to understand what he'd done and how, but there was an absence. Normally everything created from the Source is filled with light and colour. Beads and diamonds on translucent threads. Glowing embers in a pattern made of light. By comparison what he'd made was just a void filled with darkness and despair."

"Can you always see how something is created with magic?" asked Balfruss.

Wren shrugged. "As long as I'm able to focus and I have a little time. Why? Is that normal?"

Again both Sorcerers said nothing but a silent message seemed to pass between them.

"What happened next?" asked Balfruss, dodging her question.

"I wrapped Brunwal in a shield, trapping the thing inside with him. I thought he would dispel it but he didn't, or he couldn't, and it consumed him." Wren's stomach flipped over as she thought about the noises he'd made as the first black mote touched his skin. The smell of his burning flesh seemed lodged in her nose.

"Do you regret what you did?" asked Garvey, earning another glare from Balfruss, but he ignored it. From the way he asked the question he made it sound as if she had been the perpetrator and not the victim.

"He wanted to kill me. I would have died if I'd not fought back. I didn't have a choice."

"We know that," said Balfruss. "Master Garvey didn't mean to make it sound like an accusation."

"Am I a prisoner?"

"No, we brought you here as a precaution. So that Master Yettle could make sure you weren't injured."

"You heard her. She had no choice. It was self-defence. We're done here." Garvey pushed away from the wall, ready to leave, but Balfruss didn't move.

"Why didn't you come to one of us for help?" he asked.

Garvey slowly turned around until they were both watching her very closely. She wanted to tell Balfruss the truth about everything that had happened, but she couldn't say it with Garvey standing in the room. It was as if he knew what she was thinking as a sly smile crept across his face, daring her to say something against him. It would be her word, as a new student, against that of a respected teacher and member of the Grey Council.

In the end she settled for a version of the truth.

"Recently you've all been so busy. Almost every teacher has taken sudden trips and the other members of staff seem distracted. We've all heard rumours about the Seekers and have seen unusual visitors coming and going from the school for weeks. Something important is happening out there. My problems seemed small and unimportant by comparison."

"There's nothing more important to us than the students at the Red Tower," said Balfruss and even Garvey agreed.

"Everything we do here is for you and the other children," said the grizzled man. Wren was so surprised she was rendered speechless. He was a far better actor than she realised. He sounded genuine and as if he really cared about her and the other students.

Master Eloise appeared at the door and Wren started to feel overwhelmed with all three members of the Grey Council standing in her room. The echo of power coming from two of them had been intense, but with all three so close it felt as if someone were beating a huge drum in her head.

"We're overwhelming her," said Eloise. "Come, there is important news we need to discuss."

"The students will hear about it soon enough. I'd rather she hear it from us, than a version of the truth through the grapevine," said Balfruss.

Eloise glanced at Wren with an unreadable expression and she had the sense of being assessed. "Very well, but shroud us, before we give her a migraine."

Balfruss made a peculiar circling gesture with one hand and she felt a brief flare of magic. It was too subtle and had been too quick for her to follow, but immediately after Wren couldn't sense the others any more. They were still standing in the room, but now hers was the only connection to the Source she could feel.

Eloise passed Balfruss a tiny piece of paper which he unrolled and quickly scanned before passing it to Garvey.

"Following recent events, with children dying during their tests, the Regent of Zecorria has banned all Seekers from the country," said Eloise. Wren noticed the others were disappointed by the news but neither of them seemed particularly surprised.

"Anything else?"

"He made a public declaration announcing his intent. There is a one-week amnesty, at which point any Seekers found within Zecorria will be escorted to the border."

"Or murdered," muttered Garvey, but all of them heard.

"There's something else," said Balfruss, a frown creasing his brow.

Eloise wiped a hand over her face. She looked exhausted and it wasn't yet midday. Wren wondered how long it had been since she'd had a decent night's sleep.

"During his speech, the Regent mentioned that he has called on other rulers to take a stand as well. I knew that he'd sent private missives to several of them, but apparently they're taking too long to respond. Now he's forced their hand."

"What about Queen Olivia?" asked Balfruss.

Eloise held up another roll of paper, this one larger than the other. "A raven just came in from the capital. A child had an accident during a test here in Shael. The Seeker tried to intervene but the crowd misinterpreted what she was doing and attacked. Seven people are dead, and fourteen severely wounded. The Seeker is being blamed."

"How many incidents is that now?" asked Garvey. "How many dead?"

"Too many," said Eloise. "It's all over the west and now here, right on our doorstep. Queen Olivia has always been a strong advocate of Seekers, but this latest incident will force her to respond."

"Is it worth us trying to speak to her directly?" asked Balfruss. "One of us could travel to Oshoa and explain what's happening."

"It's too late for that. They won't want us there," said Garvey. "It would probably just make things worse."

"Sadly, I agree with Garvey," said Eloise.

Wren had heard rumours of children exploding from Tianne, but she'd assumed her friend had been exaggerating. To hear it from the Grey Council, and to see how worried they all looked, was a different matter. Banning Seekers made no sense to Wren. They were the only ones who could help children with their emerging magic, and yet they were being blamed. Something was happening during the tests, but she couldn't believe the Seekers were responsible, which led to the notion of sabotage. But who would do such a thing and why?

Without the Seekers surely it would lead to an increase in the number of accidental deaths, where children didn't receive training in time and lost control. If other countries banned them as well, what would happen?

"It doesn't make any sense," said Wren, mostly to herself. The others heard and Garvey grunted.

"You're right, girl. It's madness that will only lead to more bloodshed. We're not involved, but somehow we still get the blame."

"Hush, Garvey, you're scaring the girl," said Eloise.

"I thought we were being honest," he said. Wren couldn't understand the man. His behaviour was so inconsistent. One moment he was full of anger and giving her poor advice and the next he was treating her like an adult, wanting to include her in their conversations.

"We can discuss this later. Let's leave her to rest," said Eloise, ushering the others out of the room. "Try not to worry too much. You're safe here."

When they were gone she felt slightly relieved but also fears about the future began to creep in. The world was becoming increasingly hostile to those with magic and people were scared of Seekers when all they wanted to do was help.

Wren would have said the Red Tower was the safest place for her, except that even here, behind its walls, someone had tried to murder her. It seemed as if there wasn't anywhere in the world that was safe any more.

CHAPTER 27

Tammy followed the stooped form of the Old Man through the hallways of the palace, trying not to stare too much. It was her first visit to the palace of Perizzi and it was just as she imagined. The interior of the building was even more ostentatious and gaudy than the outside. The high ceilings and elaborate coving looked impressive, but she knew the rooms would be difficult to clean and impractical to heat in winter. The building had the feel of a museum rather than someone's home. Everything was just a little too neat. There wasn't a pinch of dust anywhere. Every surface was highly polished until it gleamed. Moving silently around them she saw an army of staff, tidying, rearranging and cleaning, to maintain the impeccable façade.

The decor of the palace was a horrible mishmash, seemingly without rhyme or reason, with peculiar artefacts from all over the world sitting next to each other on plinths and tables. She guessed they were gifts from visiting dignitaries, but there were very few objects she'd ever want in her house. It was all for show. Nothing felt real. Tammy wondered if the Queen's private rooms were equally as immaculate. If she dropped something on the floor, how long would it stay there before it was picked up by a member of staff and put away? Tammy liked order but this was something else entirely. It was artificial.

"Impressive, isn't it?" said the Old Man, glancing over his shoulder.

"Very interesting," said Tammy, confident he would hear the lie if she claimed to like it. "Do you like it, Munroe?"

"I've seen it before."

Ever since she'd returned from Rojenne last night, Munroe had been unusually quiet. It was more than a little unnerving. She hadn't gone into much detail, but did report that the Seeker was safe. It was clear something else had happened and she didn't want to talk about it, but Tammy knew that was only part of the reason for her silence.

Working together they had managed to warn all the Seekers in Yerskania about the danger. Despite knowing that those responsible in Morheaton would eventually be brought to justice, Munroe remained annoyed. Tammy had thought it was because they had been forced to run, in order to save their lives, rather than stand and fight.

The main reason for her sulk was that, despite completing her first assignment, although not to her satisfaction, Munroe had been ordered by Balfruss to remain in Perizzi and help Tammy. Munroe wouldn't say how Balfruss had been in touch with her, when there'd been no letters or birds, but when pressed had just said "magic". It seemed as if being away from her family for this long was taking its toll.

They entered the Queen's outer office and were greeted by a plump assistant who waved them straight into her meeting room. This was the first time Tammy had met Queen Morganse and her impression was that of a powerful woman in her prime. Tall, with a curvy figure and flawless pale skin, her age was difficult to pinpoint. The weight of her office and its responsibilities showed in a few places, notably the deep ridges between her eyebrows and the dark circles under her eyes. Morganse's dark brown eyes were studying her just as closely and Tammy resisted the urge to rub her hands when the Queen glanced at her scarred knuckles.

"Your Majesty, may I introduce Guardian Baker," said the Khevassar.

Morganse's smile was warm and generous. "I've heard many good things about you."

"Thank you, Majesty."

"Is it true you were the Guardian sent to Voechenka?"

"Yes, Majesty."

Tammy wondered how much the Queen already knew about what had happened there from the Old Man. She doubted he sent the Queen every Guardian report, but she felt confident Morganse would have read about the significant events that took place in the desolate city. It seemed as if the Queen wanted to ask another related question, but she hesitated and the moment passed. Perhaps she wanted to know if the rumours were true about her son, the Crown Prince and former heir to the throne, being in Voechenka.

"And I believe you already know Munroe?" said the Old Man.

"Yes. We've met," said the Queen, her tone crisp and icy. There was clearly a history there but no one elaborated. It was something she would have to ask Munroe about later. "Please, be seated."

Again Munroe said nothing and didn't take the opportunity to make a joke or comment on the decor. The Queen frowned briefly at the diminutive mage, noticing her unusual silence, but she said nothing about it.

"I believe you have news on the Seekers here in Yerskania?" said the Queen once they were settled.

"Yes, your Majesty. Munroe and I have managed to contact all the Seekers based in the country. They've been told to suspend monthly testing of children for the time being."

"What do you mean, 'based in the country'?" asked Morganse.

The Khevassar looked equally puzzled. "Is there something you want to tell us?"

"Seekers don't roam the country like they used to," said Munroe, startling everyone by breaking her silence. "They live in their communities and only travel short distances to test children in the surrounding area."

"How long has this been happening?" asked Morganse.

Munroe shrugged. "Six years. Ever since the Red Tower officially reopened."

"We should have been told about this," said the Queen. "You should have told me."

"I don't work for you any more," said Munroe. This time it was Tammy's turn to stare in surprise. The Old Man shook his head when she glanced in his direction. It was a subject for another time. "It was decided you didn't need to know."

"Why do it this way? Why not have them travel around?" asked Morganse.

"Some people have a connection to the Source that's so weak, they can do little with it. They'd never become a Battlemage or a Healer and most people don't want to. People are more scared of magic than ever before. They just want to go on with their lives. So we teach them how to control it, and, in return, some of them put on a mask and test children for the Red Tower."

"This changes things," said Morganse, shaking her head.

"I don't see why," said Munroe. Tammy knew that after recent events she was being deliberately obtuse.

The Queen folded her arms and sat back in her chair, clearly displeased. "You know that people are scared of magic and they're blaming Seekers for what's happening to their children. If this ever became public knowledge, communities would tear themselves apart. The Regent of Zecorria has already banned all Seekers from his country. Imagine what will happen if people find out their neighbours are secretly working for the Red Tower. The paranoia could trigger catastrophic damage across the west."

"The Red Tower is taking steps to protect all the Seekers," said Munroe. "No one will know."

"It may already be too late for that," said Tammy, taking the lead since the Old Man had fallen silent. He seemed a bit listless and she thought he was having some difficulty following the conversation.

"What do you mean?" asked Munroe.

"Remember what happened with the Seeker in Maldorn?" said Tammy. Leonie had unmasked herself in front of a crowd in the hope of being accepted by them. If news of what happened spread elsewhere, or if other Seekers had tried the same tactic, it was only a matter of time. "Expect the worst if Habreel's people find out what happened."

There was a loud knocking on the door and the Queen's secretary came into the room bearing two letters. "Apologies for the interruption, but I have urgent news, Majesty."

The Queen took the letters and opened the first one. Her eyes flicked over the contents and then she sat back in her chair looking deflated. She passed the letter to the Old Man who read it more slowly.

"The news has broken. A number of riots have broken out in the south."

"Has it reached the capital? Do the people here know?" asked the Old Man.

"It doesn't say," said Morganse. "But I'll order more patrols by the Watch as a precaution."

"We've done our best to protect the Seekers here," said Munroe. "As long as they've hidden their masks they should be safe."

Tammy thought she was being naïve. Paranoia and fear did strange things to ordinary people. They would use this as an excuse to persecute those who were different or unpopular. And it wouldn't be difficult for someone to make a similar gold mask.

"This may force my hand to ban Seekers from Yerskania," said Morganse, unrolling the second letter. "Queen Talandra and Queen Olivia may not be far behind as well in making a declaration."

"You can't," said Munroe. "They've done nothing wrong."

"I know, but if they show their faces they could be attacked or even murdered, like the Seeker in Morheaton. A ban might actually protect them and force them to stay hidden."

As the Queen scanned the second letter the colour drained from her face. She put one hand to her forehead for a moment. "Majesty?" said the Old Man. "What's happened?"

She passed the letter to the Khevassar whose hands began to shake as he read it. "By the Maker," he muttered.

"What's happened?" asked Munroe.

"Morheaton is gone," said the Old Man.

A horrible sinking sensation started in the pit of Tammy's stomach and she felt as if she was going to fall through the floor. "What do you mean, gone?"

"There was another incident with magic," said Morganse. "A Seeker came to Morheaton, perhaps wanting revenge for what happened. The townspeople gathered in the public square and tried to drive him out, but he refused."

"It makes no sense," said Munroe. "A Seeker wouldn't go back there."

"Do you need me to go and investigate?" said Tammy.

"There's no point. The town is gone." The Old Man seemed to age another ten years before her eyes. "Survivors say the Seeker lashed out at the crowd, killing people with his magic. People ran but he cut most of them down. After that he set fire to the buildings. A few escaped and some even fought back, injuring the Seeker, and they eventually cornered him in a building. They rushed inside to finish him but never came out. The building exploded and the whole street went with it."

"Tell them the rest," whispered Morganse.

"That's not the worst?" asked Tammy, shocked there was more.

"Just before the Seeker started killing people, he shouted something at the crowd," the Old Man's voice became a harsh rasp, his breathing loud. "He said 'For Balfruss and the Red Tower'."

"Fuck," whispered Munroe.

Tammy felt numb. Everyone in the room was silent, contemplating what had happened. "I know Balfruss. He'd never do anything like that," she said.

"She's right," agreed Munroe. "Someone else has done this and they're blaming him."

"Right now that doesn't matter. We need to make plans," huffed the Khevassar, trying to stand up, but he flopped back into his chair. He was sweating badly and one of his arms began to shake. "We must . . . " he said but then trailed off as his eyes rolled back in his head and he slid to the floor.

While Tammy rushed to his side Morganse hurried into her outer office, shouting at her assistant to fetch a doctor. The Old Man's skin was cold and covered with sweat. She tried to feel for a pulse, but when that failed she pressed an ear to his chest.

"Is he all right?" asked Munroe.

"I don't think he's breathing."

CHAPTER 28

It was late in the morning but Akosh was still rather drunk from the previous night. It had numbed the anguish for a time, but now she began to feel it again. She quietly slipped out of bed, doing her best not to wake the others who were still deeply asleep. They had also helped her forget about everything, but only for a short time. This morning the pain of her loss struck her anew, raw and red, like an angry, festering wound in her heart. This wasn't the first time it had happened. She should have been used to it by now but she wasn't. It hurt just the same, every time.

After splashing water on her face, she pulled on her clothes and ate a late breakfast in the common room. The owner couldn't look her in the eye and, to be fair, she couldn't blame him. They had been rather noisy last night. Akosh paid him for breakfast and added a couple of coins.

"For the damage to the room," she said. There were a few dents in the walls and most of the furniture had taken a good battering. One chair had been reduced to kindling. Despite his embarrassment he scooped up the money, bobbed his head in thanks and scurried away without saying a word.

When she stepped outside it was almost midday and the day

was bright and cool, the sun hidden behind a haze of thin cloud. Akosh squinted until her eyes adjusted to the light and then set off at a slow pace towards Habreel's office.

All around her the people of Herakion were talking in voices that were too loud. She didn't have to listen very hard to hear what was on everyone's lips. Magic. Seekers hiding among them, spying for the Red Tower. They were pleased at the Regent's decree banning them, but many people spoke about it not going far enough. Here in the capital city at midday it was all polite conversation and huddled groups talking in whispers. That would be as far as it went so close to the seat of power. It would be a very different story in the countryside, away from prying eyes and the long arm of the law. There were villages where the city guard never visited and punishment was meted out by locally elected Mayors. In such places she suspected it was going to get very bloody indeed.

Door-to-door searches for gold masks. Lynch mobs. Drownings. Mob rule and public hangings. Delicious.

It wouldn't take long for word of such incidents to reach the Regent's ears and then he'd have no choice but to bring in a national ban on all magic users. It was just as Habreel wanted and in doing so it served her purpose.

It meant more chaos and distrust where people could disappear without too many eyebrows being raised. In turn it created opportunities for some of her people to fill the void created by such fortuitous circumstances. They would simply be the right people, in the right place, at the right time.

Akosh was happy to let others sit on the thrones and lead the armies. Those people were public figures and targets whose life expectancy was often shorter than most. But just a step down from the leader was a tier of important people with power who saw kings and queens come and go during their tenure. It was here that her people operated out of sight.

By the time she reached Habreel's office Akosh was feeling a little better after her heavy night. She breezed past the front room, waving at the people within who all stared as she went up the stairs unannounced. This time no one even bothered to follow and try to block her path.

Habreel was busy writing a letter as she entered his office without knocking, but he didn't seem surprised to see her. His face was pale, heavy bags sat under his eyes, and she was confident he'd been wearing the same clothes for a few days. The room smelled stale and the remains of several meals were stacked up on plates in a corner. Normally he was fastidious and his office equally tidy and organised. She barely recognised the dishevelled man in front of her.

"What have you done?" he said, setting his pen aside. Rather than return it to the inkpot he dropped it on the desk where it rolled off onto the floor. He didn't notice. His haunted eyes were searching hers, but for what she couldn't say.

"Be more specific."

"I knew you were dangerous, but I had no idea you would take it this far." Habreel shook his head and scrubbed a hand across his stubbly face. He hadn't shaved in a few days either. "I knew a few children would have to be sacrificed. I had made peace with that."

"Did the Maker forgive you?" sneered Akosh. "Your god is dead. He has been for a long time."

Habreel didn't seem to have heard, or perhaps at this point he simply didn't care. "Seekers are dangerous. I know it in my heart and revealing their secret to the world was the right decision. I regret the lives being lost and the unrest, but, in the end, people will be happier. They will be free of magic and its corruption."

"You whine like a spoiled child."

"Perhaps," said Habreel, acknowledging her with a wry smile.

"Perhaps I was spoiled. But I know my sins and I will accept my judgement when the day comes. Can you say the same thing when you meet your end?"

"What are you babbling on about?"

"They're saying it was a rogue Seeker from the Red Tower. That he did it in Balfruss's name, but I know it was you. Somehow you persuaded another deluded fool to blow himself up in Yerskania. Only this time it wasn't a child, but a mage. Did you know he would attack the townspeople? Did you order him to do it?" asked Habreel. When she didn't respond he took her silence for admission, scrambling backwards to his feet, tipping over his chair. "Maker forgive me. You did. You told him to kill everyone in Morheaton."

"You're confused," said Akosh, but he knew she was lying.

"No, no. I'm seeing clearly for the first time since we began our arrangement." His hands were shaking, as if hungover or an addict craving their next fix. It wasn't a good sign and she thought he was going into shock. "I never expected it to go this far. I've sacrificed too much already."

"Sacrifice?" shouted Akosh, her voice echoing off the walls. Habreel winced and she lowered her voice slightly as it made her ears ring. "What do you know about sacrifice? Yes, I did it. I asked one of my people, my children, to do it for me. Someone I took in as a starving orphan decades ago. I shaped him over the years. I did that. I provided for him, gave him a future. The Red Tower might have trained him for a few years, but I gave him life."

"What are you saying?" asked Habreel.

"I asked my child to sacrifice himself for this cause. To help bring about an end to all magic. He did it because I asked him to. So, do not pretend you understand anything about real sacrifice."

Habreel was staring at her as if seeing her for the first time. "I always knew you were strange, but I thought it was just your way. But it's not that, is it?"

"No, it's not."

"I should have known. I should have seen it sooner," he muttered, shaking his head. "You're mad."

Akosh snorted. "What?"

"You're confused. You're not old enough to have raised someone for decades."

"Habreel, are you really that stupid?" she asked. For a moment she'd thought he'd realised the truth but was sadly disappointed.

"This charade has gone on for too long. I tolerated your quirks because I needed you, but the cost is too great. Our arrangement is over. We are finished."

"Really?" said Akosh, laughing at his stern expression. "How are you going to do this without me?"

"It doesn't matter. My followers and I will find a way. This is not what I wanted." Habreel moved to the door and pulled it open, keeping one eye on her as if expecting trouble. "Dannel!" he yelled down the stairs.

"You've got everything you wanted. Don't be a fool, Habreel." Akosh thought it was worth trying one last time. He was a useful figurehead and focus. She had expected he would need replacing but had thought to use him a little longer. Her plan only worked when she remained out of sight, otherwise she might attract the attention of her siblings. She did not want to suddenly disappear like the Lord of Light.

"You're right, I have been a fool, but no longer," said Habreel. "I won't listen to you any more." He was adamant and kept a safe distance, eyeing her as if she were rabid. "I wanted to unite everyone against magic, but normal people are spying and fighting with their neighbours. They're paranoid about an invisible enemy hiding among them. It will take me a long time to unpick this mess and find a new way forward, but I will do it without you. Nothing will change my mind on that. We are done."

"I'm sorry to hear you say that," said Akosh standing up and leaning back against the desk.

Dannel came into the room and paused on the threshold, looking between them. "Give Akosh her final payment and then see her to the door," said Habreel. "Our arrangement is at an end. If she tries to return in the future, send her away."

"This isn't over, Habreel. You don't know what I'm capable of."

Much to her surprise he laughed. "I know what you are, mage. And I know that even you can die like anyone else with a dagger in your back. The Warlock proved it during the war, so do not pretend otherwise."

"But I'm not a mage," said Akosh.

Habreel drew his short sword, and gestured at Dannel to do the same. His assistant slowly drew his weapon as well, but seemed reluctant to use it. "Final warning. Leave now in peace or this will turn bloody."

Akosh spread her arms wide. "Go ahead. I think a little bloodshed is required."

Dannel's fist hammered into the side of Habreel's face, knocking him sideways. He fell against the wall just in time for the pommel of Dannel's sword to break his nose, spraying blood across his face. With a groan he slumped to the floor, dazed and surprised by the attack.

"Are you all right, Mother?" asked Dannel. "Did he injure you?"

"No, I'm unhurt," she said. Habreel had been rendered speechless. His eyes were watering and blood ran down his face from one nostril, but it wasn't the pain that had stunned him. He didn't understand what had just happened and was in shock. "Oh, don't look so surprised. Dannel is one of mine. He was an orphan, too. Didn't you know? Did you ever ask him about his parents or upbringing?"

"I didn't know," said Habreel, wiping blood from his face.

"Of course you didn't. You just needed good little soldiers for your crusade. I may have been part of your plan, but you were a useful part of mine. Change is now required, but no matter. It's not a serious setback." Akosh pursed her lips and pondered his fate.

"Do you want me to kill him?" asked Dannel, readying his sword for a fatal blow.

"Someone downstairs will hear. You'll never get away with this!" protested Habreel.

"He may have a point. And it would create a mess," mused Akosh. It might also cause a scene that would attract unwanted attention from the city guard. She had not remained undetected for so long by being rash. One of the other three downstairs was one of her children, but that left two others. The odds that one of them might escape in a struggle and spread the news didn't appeal.

"I can do it quietly," suggested Dannel, "with minimal bloodshed. We can hide his body up here until tonight, then I can dump it elsewhere. We can say he was attacked on the street by a cutpurse."

The betrayal in Habreel's eyes as he looked at Dannel was delicious. Until now he'd been a loyal friend when they had served in the Guardians and then a strong supporter of his crusade to eliminate magic. It was quite a shock to realise he'd never really known him at all.

"No, we may need him in the future. He was useful for

gaining access to the Regent, and, more importantly, the people around him. When things escalate it will be useful to have a scapegoat. We need him alive, for the time being at least," said Akosh, winking at Habreel.

"On your feet," said Dannel, kicking his former friend.

"I can't," whined Habreel. "I think I banged my head when you hit me."

Dannel sighed and sheathed his sword before pulling Habreel to his feet. He swayed and would have fallen if Dannel hadn't grabbed him by the front of his rumpled jacket.

"Dannel, please don't do this," pleaded Habreel. "Think of everything we've been through together."

"You're wasting your breath," said Dannel. "She gave me life. Without her, I would have died in the gutter as a young boy. There is nothing you can say that means anything. My loyalty to her is absolute."

"Then I'm very sorry," said Habreel.

"It's too late for an apology," said Dannel. His abrupt tone was so at odds with his normally placid nature. "How you treated me doesn't matter any more."

"No, I meant for this," said Habreel. He lashed out with a dagger that must have been hidden somewhere on his person. Dannel was taken by surprise, stumbling back and hissing in pain as he gripped his upper arm. Habreel tried to kick out one of his knees but Dannel twisted his leg and caught it on the thigh. The pain was enough to make him stumble back and Habreel skirted around to the far side of his desk.

"What are you looking for, Habreel?" asked Akosh, as he rummaged through his desk drawers. With a cry of satisfaction he yanked something out and held it up towards her. Akosh stared at the misshapen lump of metal, trying to work out what it was for. It was a roughly made amulet, with six sides and a fine network of wires holding a purple crystal at its centre, like a fly caught in a spider's web.

"Stay back, creature," said Habreel. "I command you!"

Akosh laughed and helped Dannel to his feet. "What's that supposed to do?"

"He bought it to ward off evil spirits and dark magic," said Dannel, checking the wound on his arm. "Some fool conned him into thinking it was real, and I played along."

Disappointed and let down once more, Habreel's shoulders slumped and his arms drooped. He seemed to have given up.

"Put down your dagger and come quietly, or I will make you suffer," promised Dannel.

The amulet whined as it flew through the air. Akosh had a moment to notice how the crystal seemed to sparkle before it hit her in the face, cutting her cheek. She hissed in pain and swore. There was a crash of breaking glass as she blinked away her tears. When she could see again Dannel was standing by the remains of the window, peering down into the street.

"He's going west. Are you all right, Mother?"

"Fine, just don't let him escape."

Dannel raced down the stairs and out the front door. Akosh winced and touched her cheek. It had been a long time since someone had made her bleed. About an hour later Dannel returned looking flustered, his boots and trousers muddy and rumpled.

"I'm sorry, Mother, but he got away. But I promise we will find him."

"I'm sure you will, because you wouldn't want to disappoint me, would you?"

"No, Mother. I'll have some people watch the gates and roads out of the city. He won't escape," swore Dannel.

"Good. Any more news?"

Dannel hesitated. "Yes, and unfortunately it's not good. A report just came in. The Guardians found one of our mouth-pieces, a man named Grell. He's been taken back to Perizzi for questioning."

"Is he one of mine, or one of Habreel's people?"

"He's loyal to Habreel."

Akosh had been happy to let Habreel be in charge so that she didn't have to deal with all the tedious day-to-day stuff. It was far more interesting to be out there rather than be seated behind a desk, telling other people how to solve every single little problem. It had taken her decades to build up her network of orphanages and slowly trickle her people into positions adjacent to those in power.

Habreel didn't know who or what she really was, but he could still prove to be a problem. She couldn't just ignore him and hope that he would go away. His new-found conscience wouldn't allow it. It was the same with Grell. This was one of the reasons why she had followers. It was mundane grunt work.

"Do we know where he's being held?" asked Akosh.

"No, but I would guess inside Unity Hall, their stronghold."

"Do we have any loyal inside?"

Dannel hesitated again. "Yes, but she's the only one. If we do this and she doesn't escape, we won't have any other eyes inside."

"How much does Grell know?"

"Enough about the network to damage it," admitted Dannel. "Habreel trusted him."

"Then we have no choice. Get rid of him and make sure you capture Habreel alive."

"Yes, Mother."

Now she would have to spend more time in the city adjusting plans and getting someone else close to the Regent. She'd need a convincing reason to explain Habreel's sudden disappearance. A version of the truth would suffice and in no time he'd be locked up in an asylum. Her plans in Herakion wouldn't stop, but they might have to slow down a little. But Akosh was patient and careful. It was how she had survived for so long when so many others like her had faded away into oblivion.

None of her children knew what she was planning. A few had sight of small pieces, but only she could see the full pattern stretched across the west like a giant invisible web.

Habreel was just one man who ultimately meant very little. Nothing would stand in her way.

CHAPTER 29

Munroe unlocked the heavy door and stepped into the plain room. She'd never seen the inside of a questioning room before at Unity Hall. Normally they were only used by Guardians to interrogate suspects, but these were special circumstances.

The room had two doors and no windows. One door led deeper into the warren of offices that made up most of Unity Hall and the other to the cells below. The room had plain walls made from granite and the only furniture was a wooden table and two benches fixed to a metal base. Everything was attached to the floor with huge metal spikes making it impossible to move. There was nothing else in the room. No furnishings, no weapons, no tools of torture. Just a featureless, empty room for two people with no distractions.

The bolt clanked on the other door and it opened to reveal the chubby face of Grell. Munroe had been briefed by Tammy about him and he lived up to her low expectations. Despite the grimy clothes, stubble from several days without a shave and generally dishevelled appearance, Grell was still defiant. Munroe was confident that would soon change.

She could see the arrogance in the set of his jaw and the

way he shook off the jailer's hand and sat down by himself. The guard retreated and locked the door, giving her a chance to study him. Grell remained uncowed by his imprisonment. Tammy had been questioning him with little success for two days and today was his fifth in a cell. He smelled a little ripe but that didn't seem to bother him. Grell lounged on his bench as if they were sitting together in a tavern.

Normally she would never be here. Normally a civilian would never be allowed to question a suspect. But these were not normal times. When the Old Man had collapsed Munroe had been frozen at first, scared and worried about him, but also because her thoughts had turned to her mother. The Khevassar was being treated by the Queen's physician, but she knew little about his condition other than he was still alive.

Until he returned to his duties all of the other Guardians were trying to do their best without him. Rather than waste another day, locked in a room with Grell, Tammy was chasing down other leads. It had been her suggestion that Munroe take a more direct approach. A Guardian would never beat a confession out of a suspect, but she was neither a Guardian nor a member of the Watch.

She was also what Grell seemed intent on destroying. When Munroe thought about all of those who might have been injured, or even murdered, as a result of Grell spreading fear of magic, her blood began to boil. It was an effort for her to stay calm but she was determined to try.

"If we're just going to sit here in silence, could you at least fetch me a drink?" asked Grell, breaking the silence.

"I'm not a serving girl."

"And you're not a Guardian, or a member of the Watch," he noted.

Munroe's smile was wolfish. "Oh no, I'm not. But they sent me to speak to you anyway."

Grell crossed his arms. "I'm not going to say another word. You're wasting your time. So tell them to charge me with something or let me go."

"You're not going anywhere," scoffed Munroe. "You'll be staying here for the rest of your life."

"But I've done nothing wrong." It sounded as if he truly believed that as well. The man was either mad or seriously deluded. She suspected it was the latter.

"Do you know the problem with Guardians?" asked Munroe, barely waiting for him to shake his head. "They're so stuffy. Always by the book. They'd never lay a hand on you, even though we both know you're guilty." Grell said nothing and waited, his piggy little eyes watching her carefully. "But as you said, I'm not a Guardian, so I don't have to play by their rules."

Grell looked her up and down and laughed. "Don't waste my time. I could break you like a twig."

Munroe grinned. She loved it when they underestimated her. "You need to understand something, Grell. The situation has changed since you were locked up. The Regent of Zecorria has declared a national ban on Seekers." Grell's eyes widened in surprise but then narrowed again in suspicion. "Oh no, this isn't a trick or a game. He's done it. He made a big speech in public and sent letters to all the other rulers, asking them to do the same."

"That is good news," said Grell, scratching at his scalp. He probably had lice.

Munroe put both hands on the table and leaned backwards on her bench. "Actually, it's bad news, especially for you. There have been more attacks everywhere on Seekers. People are blaming them for all their problems. Queen Morganse herself is under pressure to sign a ban. It might lead to a complete ban on all mages."

"More wonderful news," he said, grinning at her. "We should have a drink to celebrate. Do you have any wine?"

"The problem is, I know that Seekers aren't responsible. I also know that the children and magic aren't to blame. Do you want to know how?"

Grell didn't answer but something crept into his eyes. Doubt and then something more. A hint of fear.

Fire blossomed in the palm of Munroe's hand and Grell fell backwards off his bench. He screamed and banged his head on the floor, but barely seemed to notice. Staring at the fire he scrambled away from her until his head hit the door.

Munroe watched as the blue fire flickered and swirled in her hand. The flames shone so brightly in the gloom, creating peculiar shadows that danced across the walls. This was how stories were told in ancient times. Woven out of thin air and nothing more than shadows. Monsters, heroes and entire worlds were conjured from images in the flames and the intricate moving shapes they created on the wall. Sometimes she told Sam a story before he went to sleep and she summoned flames like this to help with his imagination.

"Help! Let me out!" screamed Grell as Munroe stood up, looming over him. She let the fire spread, moving up her arm to the elbow and then right up to her shoulder. Holding her arm aloft, now completely wreathed in flames, it was almost as if she had become the wick. The undying black strand at the heart of the blaze. The flames were mesmerising, moving with a life and joy of their own, fed by the Source.

Grell was banging his fist on the door but no one was listening. They'd been told to ignore any loud noises coming from this room.

"No one is coming, Grell. It's just you and me," said Munroe, moving her arm back and forth. The flames trailed after her, creating a peculiar double image, blue and yet also black and white when she blinked.

She stalked around the table towards Grell who scuttled backwards until he was wedged into a corner. "Get away from me!" he shrieked, hitting such a high note it made Munroe wince.

"Now, I'm going to ask a question, and you're going to answer. If you don't answer I'm going to set you on fire. Do you understand?"

Grell's eyes were darting around the room for something to help him, but there was nothing. It had been designed to be free of all distractions and there was nothing he could use as a weapon. He was alone in a locked room with a mage. It was probably his worst nightmare come true.

"Last time I'm asking, then I'm going to cut off one of your feet. Do you understand?" said Munroe, reshaping the flames into a short blade. She fed more power into the fire until it glowed cherry-red and then white hot. "The good news is, it will instantly cauterise the wound. So at least you won't get an infection or bleed to death." She wasn't sure if her cheery smile or the words unnerved him the most.

Munroe grabbed one of his legs, yanking it straight and holding the rest of him in place with her magic. He tried to pull free but her will stopped all movement below his neck. She raised the fiery sword and then slowly brought it down towards his ankle. It licked at the material of his trousers which began to smoke and blacken. She smelled the hairs on his leg begin to burn and he screamed again.

"Stop! Please stop," he begged. "What do you want to know? I'll tell you anything."

Munroe moved her arm back slightly but kept the glowing blade close to his outstretched leg. "Let's start with an easy question. Who is in charge of your group?"

"Torran Habreel. He used to be a Guardian. He helped me a few times when I got into trouble. I used to be in the Watch." Grell's eyes were wide with terror, locked onto the glowing blade of fire.

"Where is he?"

"In Herakion, the capital of Zecorria. He has an office there. I know the address."

"That's very kind of you," said Munroe, giving him a friendly smile. "Next question. What was your goal?"

"Our goal?" he asked. She didn't know if he was stalling for time or genuinely didn't understand, but she had no time and even less patience. Munroe touched the edge of the blade to the bare flesh of his ankle and there was a sizzling sound. Grell screamed and desperately tried to pull away from her but it was like a child trying to outmuscle an adult.

"We wanted to get rid of all the Seekers and then all mages," said Grell. "They're dangerous and unclean."

Until now Munroe had been fairly calm but his words made her temper flare. The fiery blade vanished and the restraints on Grell, who curled up into a ball, hugging his knees to his chest.

"Unclean?" whispered Munroe.

"You're tainted. It's in your blood. Magic is a disease." Grell spoke with confidence as if what he said was fact. She didn't know if this was all part of an attempt to make her angry and somehow escape. She really didn't care any more.

With a snarl Munroe picked him off the floor with her magic and pinned him to the wall, feet dangling in mid-air. He flopped about trying to break free but she pressed harder until manacles forged from her will held him aloft. She added a tight band around his torso that squeezed his chest until he wheezed and his ribs creaked.

"You should be afraid, Grell. You should be pissing your pants, because I can torture you in ways that are not possible without magic. I can freeze the water in your blood. I can shatter the bones in your body, one at a time, without even bruising your skin. I can peel the flesh from your body one strip at a time, and keep you awake while I do it."

"What do you want?" pleaded Grell. "I'll tell you anything."

"What else is Habreel planning?"

"I don't know," he said and Munroe squeezed the band around his chest. A rib snapped and he gasped in pain. "Wait, I can help."

"How?" asked Munroe, flexing the band, and he groaned. "You just said you don't know anything."

"Habreel's followers, his network. There are six people, his lieutenants, they work together. They used to be Guardians, too."

"And?" said Munroe, leaning towards him.

"I know where they are." Grell was sweating profusely, his skin flushed and he stank. It was the reek of fear, seeping through his pores.

"Names and addresses."

Grell rattled them off but Munroe didn't move away and ease off on the pressure. He had held on until the final moment before giving up their names. She wondered what else he was hiding.

"What else?" asked Munroe, holding up one hand in front of him, fingers spread. "You're holding something back."

He was desperate. "That's all I know. I swear!"

Munroe shook her head and flexed her fingers, squeezing his chest again until another rib snapped. He howled and thrashed about before sagging against the invisible bonds that held him in place. Munroe slapped him hard across the cheek one way and then the other until he stirred.

"No sleeping just yet," she said, yanking his head backwards. "What else do you know?"

"Water . . . " he said. Munroe held up her hand in front of his face and he recoiled. "There was a woman. An assassin Habreel called on regularly. She had her own connections."

There was a loud knocking on the door behind Munroe but she ignored it. "What about her?"

"Habreel didn't want people to know about her, but we all saw her in Herakion."

The knocking came again, more insistent. "Go away!" Munroe called over her shoulder. "Why did he want to keep her a secret?"

"Because she had some kind of magic of her own."

The door behind Munroe started to open and she released her grip on him. Grell dropped to the floor where he lay in a tangled heap, clutching his ribs. A waspish-faced Guardian swept into the room, staring down her nose at Munroe which immediately made her dislike the woman.

"Didn't you hear me knocking?"

"I'm in the middle of questioning a suspect."

"Well, that's over now," said the woman. "I'm Guardian Brook. I have orders to take him to the palace for questioning."

"I have my orders, too, and they come from Guardian Baker."

Guardian Brook pursed her thin lips and briefly glanced over Munroe's shoulder at Grell. "What happened to him?"

"He tripped and fell," said Munroe, never taking her eyes off the woman's face. "Didn't you, Grell?"

"Yes, I fell," he replied, climbing back onto his bench with some difficulty.

"Who did your orders come from?" asked Munroe.

"The Khevassar."

"Has he recovered then?" asked Munroe. "He didn't look so well the last time I saw him."

Brook smiled, but even that was a harsh thing that twisted her face. "He is as tough as old leather."

"I have just one more question, then he's all yours," said Munroe.

"There's no time," said Brook, moving around the table.

"It's very simple. It will only take a moment."

The Guardian pulled Grell to his feet, wrinkling her nose slightly at the smell before trying to shuffle him out of the door. "It will have to wait."

Munroe held up one arm, blocking the way. "I will be very quick." Guardian Brook grimaced but was starting to realise Munroe wouldn't relent.

"What was the name of the woman?" asked Munroe, keeping one eye on the Guardian and the other on Grell. "The assassin who helped Habreel."

"I can't remember," he said.

"Time to go." Brook tried to shove her aside but Munroe moved to block the door. "He said he can't remember."

"Give him a moment to try. Think very hard, Grell," said Munroe, holding up her hand in front of his face and flexing her fingers. His face turned pale.

"We don't have time for this," said the Guardian, trying to force her way past Munroe. She let her pass but gripped Grell by the arm, stalling them both.

"I think it was Akosh," said Grell.

"Not one more word," snapped Brook. "You have your answer and we need to go."

Munroe followed them into the corridor, still holding onto

Grell's arm. Brook had him by the other arm and he looked miserable in the middle, caught between two enemies. "What's the rush?"

"I have my orders." She kept saying that but Munroe thought she was lying.

"When exactly did you speak to the Old Man?" asked Munroe. The Guardian realised her ruse had failed as she drew her short sword. Grell tried to pull away from both of them but neither released their grip. His eyes flicked between the two women then around the corridor, searching for an escape.

"Don't do anything stupid," said Munroe.

Before she'd finished speaking Brook buried the blade of her sword into Grell's side. With a shove she yanked her sword free and he toppled onto Munroe, knocking them both to the ground.

"Get off me," she said, pushing him aside. Grell was bleeding badly and howling in pain but she wasn't a doctor. There was nothing she could do for him. Brook was already running and Munroe followed, skidding around a corner in pursuit. They went down three corridors before she followed Brook around another corner and collided with a group of Guardians. Just beyond them stood Brook, panting and spattered with Grell's blood.

"That's her, she just attacked me!" said Brook, waving at Munroe.

"Let me pass," she said as the Guardians tried to restrain her. "She just killed a suspect."

"A likely story," said one of the group. Two others were trying to pin her arms behind her back, but Munroe kept wriggling free.

"I'm sorry," said Munroe. The Guardians flew away from her in all directions as she forced them back with her magic, pinning them to the walls, the floor and one to the ceiling. Brook was just regaining her breath but she set off in a panicked run again, arms and legs pumping as fast as she could move them.

Munroe tried to use her magic to trip her up, but every time Brook darted around a corner she lost sight of her prey. Finally the network of corridors in Unity Hall turned in her favour as Brook came to a locked door. Munroe wasn't far behind and could see the Guardian frantically searching for the key in her pockets.

"It's over. Stop running," gasped Munroe, trying to catch her breath. Brook forgot about the keys and instead drew a dagger and unsheathed her short sword. "Steel won't work against me. So let's just talk this through instead."

"Forgive me, Mother," said Brook, throwing her dagger at Munroe.

She instinctively summoned a shield, blocking the weapon. It collided with the unseen barrier and fell to the floor. At the same time Brook cut her own throat with her sword. A torrent of blood gushed from the wound and she dropped to her knees, gagging loudly.

Munroe tried to stem the bleeding but there was so much. She couldn't hold it back and didn't know what to do. The sound of heavy footsteps caught her attention but she didn't think anything of it until she was pulled off Brook and pinned to the floor face down. She could have fought back, could have thrown them all off with her magic, but now there were a dozen Guardians filling the corridor. All were armed, several with crossbows pointed at her. Their numbers wouldn't make any difference to her, but right now doing nothing was easier and safer for them.

Munroe's eyes were drawn back to Brook, convulsing on the floor as rich blood pumped from the jagged wound in her throat. One of the other Guardians was trying to stop the bleeding but she could see it was too late. A short time later Brook's body seemed to collapse on itself and a final breath passed through her lips. Her eyes stared on for ever, looking beyond the Veil.

CHAPTER 30

D anoph wasn't sure how one of the students had smuggled in the whisky. Those with him were a few years too young to buy it, but right now he just didn't care. The bottle went around the circle again and he took another gulp. It burned the back of his mouth and then seemed to scald a good portion of his throat before taking up residence in his stomach. It was cheap and rough, but no one here was a connoisseur. Besides, they were drinking to numb themselves and to forget, not for the taste.

The student next to him, a tall girl from Seveldrom with jet-black hair called Vania, touched him on the cheek, feeling his skin with her fingertips. "It's so soft," she mused. Her eyes were unfocused and she swayed slightly as if on board a ship. She'd never spoken to him before. Never even shown the slightest bit of interest, but now she seemed fascinated by him.

Danoph was pulled towards her and the whole world seemed to swing about. Eventually his eyes settled and now Vania was staring at his skin in the gloom. With a negligent wave of her hand she summoned mage light and he winced at its brightness.

"Your skin sparkles in the light," she slurred, her breath

tickling the side of his neck. She was gripping him around the shoulders with remarkable strength. There were worse places to be, wrapped in her arms, warm and slightly drunk on cheap whisky. As her close inspection continued Danoph let his mind wander.

Normally they wouldn't have had this much free time before curfew, but the erratic changes in their lessons continued. Some teachers were absent for their lessons and notes were left pinned to the classroom doors. Others arrived late to class and left early on urgent business. Every teacher was distracted and, while they made an attempt to focus on the lessons, it was obvious their hearts weren't in it.

In Danoph's final class of the day, on the history of magic, their teacher Master Stenne had droned on about the infinite majesty and power of the Source. Nothing she told them was new as she'd given them the same lesson the week before, almost word for word. When one girl mentioned this a few minutes into the lesson the teacher's expression had turned sour.

"Clearly you didn't learn it well enough the first time, so it bears repeating," she snapped. What followed was an hour of tedium where no one else objected again, just in case they were forced to endure it a third time next week.

What had puzzled Danoph the most, since his first day at the Red Tower, was that no one addressed the duality he sensed within everyone.

Like every other mage in training, he could feel the Source and when he reached towards it the sensation was like no other. Its complexity was such that he struggled to define it and whenever he tried it always seemed inadequate. It was a dozen wonderful things combined and yet none of them. It was more glorious than the warmth of the sun on his face. More refreshing than jumping into a freezing lake on a hot day. It coursed through every part of his body and all of his senses were magnified when he embraced it. He'd overheard others speaking about this, so he knew these feelings were not unique to him.

And yet, no one ever talked about the dual echo of magic within people. Learning how to sense magical ability in someone else was easy. It was also something all students did instinctively to measure their strength against everyone else. Seekers used this technique to test children, where it created an echo between them. An alien and yet familiar pulse that connected them to each other.

Whenever Danoph did this he felt something else that no one spoke about. He wondered if this was part of a new Talent that only he possessed.

Vania had one arm slung around his waist, her head resting on his shoulder. She wasn't quite asleep but he could feel she was relaxed and comfortable. Embracing the Source, he reached out with his senses and studied her.

Once again Danoph was struck by the duality he felt within her. There was the familiar echo of magic that everybody spoke about, but also there was a second pulse. It lived in between the beats. He sensed it almost as dark spots between the light that filled her being with power from the Source. It was a small part of her that seemed insignificant in comparison to the vastness of the Source. But it was there within her. It was within everyone.

Sometimes he thought there were other pulses, but he'd come to believe they were merely echoes. In every lesson, as he tried to better understand how to channel power from the Source, Danoph also hoped to find answers about what he could sense. If it was a Talent then what purpose did it serve? And what was he sensing in other people?

Vania stirred, wrapping both arms around his waist and giving him a squeeze. "Are you friends with the girl who killed

Brunwal?" she asked. The question seemed at odds with her nuzzling his neck.

"Wren is my friend," he said.

"That's exciting," she said, gripping his chin and turning his face towards her. The kiss was unexpected and yet part of Danoph wasn't surprised. Wren's return to the dormitories had been without incident. She was withdrawn and said even less than usual, leaving Tianne to fill the awkward gaps that often littered their conversations. The other students had tended to ignore Wren before her fight with Brunwal anyway, so little had changed there. However, for whatever reason, proximity to danger or notoriety for getting involved, Danoph was receiving more attention from girls.

A disturbance at the main gate drew everyone's attention. A group of older students had returned early from town. Normally they wouldn't return until late into the night and would crawl into their beds, smelling of beer and spicy food. The dishevelled, surly group that walked past looked neither drunk nor in a good mood.

When they saw Danoph's group had a bottle they joined them, adding their own mage lights to the others.

"What happened?" someone asked, as the bottle was passed to an older girl named Tahira.

She took a long pull on the bottle before answering. "The locals in town are all riled up and looking for a fight. It wasn't worth staying."

"They think we're responsible for killing their children," said someone else.

Stories of what was happening to Seekers and children across the west had raced through the Red Tower like wildfire. Being fairly remote, the only news they normally received was weeks or months out of date. Now they received almost daily stories from

visitors, older students visiting town and merchants delivering
supplies. The situation out there was bleak and seemed to be
getting worse for Seekers.

While he remained worried for others it also made Danoph
wonder about his future and that of his fellow students once they
graduated. If no one trusted or wanted a mage, what would they
do? Where would they go?

"Tahira nearly got into a fight with some old hag," said one
of the other students.

"She was blaming the Grey Council. She thinks Balfruss
and the others told the Seekers to attack people. It was a stupid
thing to say." Tahira seemed angry but he thought she was also
afraid. On the surface she looked calm but there was a deep well
of anger inside her that was starting to bubble up. As someone
much closer to graduating, the reality of going out into a world
that was hostile towards mages was difficult to face.

One of the few good things that should have come out of the
war was a healthy respect for Battlemages. After all, if not for
the likes of Balfruss and Eloise, countless people would have
died under the rule of the Mad King and the Warlock. The
turning point of the war came when Balfruss had defeated the
Warlock in battle.

Instead of respecting power, people had become more afraid
of magic after seeing the widespread destruction that a few
mages had wrought. Danoph had thought the monthly visits
from Seekers had helped. It seemed as if they had merely been
masking the underlying fear of magic. Parents were glad to see
their cursed children taken away. Better that than have them
stay and pose a risk to their lives and the entire community.

What had been bubbling under for years had now reached
the surface, painting a bleak future for all the students.

"Will you go back to town again?" asked Vania.

Tahira looked at her for a long time and didn't reply, which was its own answer. The risk was too great. The school was starting to feel more like a prison. On the other hand it was perhaps one of the few remaining places that was still safe for mages, where they would be welcomed without judgement.

Later, when the bottle was empty and people were either going to bed or seeking out more secluded spots, Danoph found himself alone with Tahira. Hers was the only remaining mage light, a swirling globe of blue and white. It flickered, as if there were a host of fireflies trapped inside, desperate to break free. Whenever he tried to create something similar the result was a weak yellow ball that painted everyone in a sickly hue. Hers seemed alive by comparison.

Tahira was lost in thought. Her eyes were far away but when he moved to get up she held out a hand. "Can you stay for a while?"

Danoph nodded and sat down again. "Did something else happen?"

"No," said Tahira staring into the dark. "This is about what happens next."

"I don't understand."

"You need to decide for yourself. Will you be a wolf or a lamb?" Her voice was hushed, as if afraid of waking something lurking in the dark beyond their meagre light. Or perhaps it was something inside she was afraid to awaken. "One day I will be a Battlemage. I'm not going to stay to become a Sorcerer like some of the others. I'm going to go out there and use my magic. But I will not cower, I will not beg and I will not run, and anyone who gets in my way will regret it."

Danoph had to swallow hard before asking his question. The thought of being alone with Tahira in the dark was becoming far less appealing with every heartbeat. "The Grey Council says magic is a gift that must be used wisely. To use it against those without magic goes against one of the founding principles of the Red Tower." Danoph knew he wasn't telling her anything she didn't already know but Tahira didn't argue or chastise him.

"How long has the Red Tower been here?" she asked.

Danoph shrugged. "No one really knows. Centuries, perhaps a thousand years."

"Do you think the original Grey Council were Oracles? Could they have predicted what's happened recently?" she asked.

"I don't know. I don't think so."

"The world is a different place and we must adapt to survive. Magic must adapt as well."

Danoph didn't like the sound of what she was saying but he didn't argue. From her expression it was something she had been wrestling with for some time before coming to this decision. Anything he said now would be meaningless.

"What will you do?" he asked instead.

Tahira's smile was more than a little sad. "Nothing, for now at least. Live my life and play at being a lamb until the day when they come for me."

"And then?"

"Show them my teeth."

The following morning while Danoph and the others were in the practice yard under the watchful gaze of Choss, the sound of a horse's hooves drew his attention. There was a shout at the gate and a rider came pounding through at a gallop. The rider, slumped over the beast's neck, pulled back on the reins before sliding out of the saddle onto the ground.

"Run and fetch Master Yettle," said Choss, grabbing the nearest student. "Take care of the horse," he said to another, who led the sweating animal away towards the stables.

Danoph and the others gathered around the fallen rider who had been propped up into a sitting position by Choss. The middle-aged man was dressed in a familiar black robe with a deep hood and black gloves. There was no sign of his golden mask, but from the blood on his face Danoph guessed it must have come off in a struggle.

"Give us some room. Take a few steps back," said Choss, waving everyone away, and they obliged. A short time later Master Yettle appeared and behind him came all three members of the Grey Council. A space opened up in the crowd as they marched towards the injured Seeker.

As Master Yettle knelt beside the man Garvey and the others looked at the crowd of gathered students. Danoph noted Balfruss and Eloise were looking through the gates but there was nothing to see out there beyond the wall. He sensed a deep pulse from the Source as one or both drew power from it and continued to look into the far distance.

"Killed himself," gasped the injured man, while Yettle cut open the man's robe to inspect his injuries. Danoph saw blood had soaked into his shirt but he couldn't see if the wound was serious.

"You can tell us about it later," said Yettle, moving his hands across the man's body, checking for additional injuries. The Seeker hissed in pain when he touched one of his shoulders. "Dislocated," muttered the healer.

"Can we move him?" asked Eloise, looking at the growing crowd of students.

"Not yet. Let me finish my examination," said Yettle.

The Seeker seemed to be on the verge of unconsciousness but when he saw Balfruss he lurched towards him with grasping hands. "He did it in your name!" he said.

Balfruss knelt down beside the man, taking his bloody hand in both of his. "You're safe now. Try to rest."

"They said he did it for you," said the Seeker. The crowd had fallen silent, soaking up every word. "He killed himself for you."

Balfruss and the other members of the Grey Council exchanged a look. It was clear they would have preferred to have this conversation with the Seeker in private, but it was too late for that now.

"Ask your questions now," said Yettle, drawing power from the Source. "His injuries are severe. I can't risk moving him until he's healed. He'll be unconscious once I'm done."

There was a mild pulse of energy and golden light began to spread across Yettle's outstretched hands, weaving itself together into a complex net.

"What happened?" asked Balfruss.

"A Seeker has destroyed a town in southern Yerskania. He started killing people without provocation and setting buildings on fire. The locals fought back and managed to injure him before he killed himself. Something similar has happened in Shael. A woman killed sixty people before she died."

"Where?" asked Balfruss.

"To the west," said the Seeker, waving his arm vaguely.

"Hold still," hissed Yettle, adjusting the golden weave to concentrate on the Seeker's injured shoulder. There was an audible popping sound as the wrenched joint was put back in place. The Seeker's eyes rolled up in his head and it looked as if he were going to pass out but he shook it off, gritting his teeth.

"Why were you attacked? Who did this?" asked Balfruss.

"The people in town. When they heard the stories they chased me out. There are more stories from everywhere about attacks on Seekers."

"What exactly did the Seekers say before they died?" asked Garvey, fixing the injured man in place with his stare. "Word for word."

"'For Balfruss and the Red Tower.'" The Seeker's body shuddered as Yettle's healing weave settled across his whole body.

"You'll have to speak to him later. If I leave it any longer he could die," said Yettle.

There was nothing more to say. The danger that had seemed so remote was now on their doorstep. But worse than that, Seekers were now starting to fight back and doing so in the name of Balfruss. It seemed unbelievable that anyone who had been at the Red Tower would use their magic against people and yet the stories could not be ignored.

"All right, get back to class. Go on!" said Garvey, shoving people back to create room. He and the other gathered teachers helped the crowd to disperse while Yettle used his magic to carry the injured Seeker to the hospital.

Standing alone in the middle of the crowd, in an oasis of empty space, was Balfruss. Danoph saw many students glance over their shoulder at him, their faces troubled, disbelieving, angry, and, in a few cases, proud. From the little he knew about Balfruss, Danoph didn't believe he would ever have given such an order. The Seekers were using magic to kill and taking his name in vain.

Danoph thought back to his conversation with Tahira the previous night. She had already made her choice about what she would become. Now he wondered if every student would face a similar decision a lot sooner than they realised.

CHAPTER 31

Tammy waved at the Royal Guard as she approached the final gate on her way out of the palace. She pulled it open and gestured for Tammy to pass through straight away.

"See you tomorrow," said Riona. Tammy just grunted.

She'd seen Riona that often in the last few days they were practically best friends. She already knew all about her husband, a glassblower with his own business, and their two children, boys aged four and six. In the few minutes each day, as they'd walked from the outer gate to the Queen's office, Riona talked and Tammy mostly listened.

Once Riona had casually asked about Tammy's family but when she saw that it hit a nerve, she quickly changed the subject. Right now Tammy was desperately trying to focus on dealing with the problems at hand, but the shadow of her past continually lingered at the back of her mind. It was like a sore tooth and every time she touched it the pain flashed through her anew. Burying it and trying to pretend it didn't exist had not worked. It had stopped her moving forward with her life and with Kovac. She hoped finding answers would bring her some peace.

Occasionally she and Riona would compare notes about

training, as Riona was curious about what was required to become a Guardian of the Peace, but mostly she did all the talking. That suited Tammy fine as she could listen with one ear and absorb the information while focusing on one of the many issues she was trying to solve.

Since the Old Man had collapsed in the Queen's office Tammy and the other Guardians had been doing their best to get along without him, but it was becoming more difficult every day. It wasn't just his advice and knowledge they needed, he was also a solid and focused presence that drew everyone together. With everyone feeding him information he could discern patterns in the reports that others missed as they didn't have access to everything. They also didn't have time. Each Guardian had a stack of cases to solve and, while cooperation was appreciated, no one liked having their cases poached or finding out someone was interfering. He held Unity Hall together in a hundred other ways that she was only just beginning to appreciate.

The good news was that the Queen's surgeon had said the Old Man would recover. Unfortunately he'd not been specific about how much time it would take. The bad news was that in the interim he was mostly confined to bed and was under guard to enforce it. If it had been up to the Old Man he would have gone back to work immediately, but the surgeon had said he was suffering from severe exhaustion. He needed bed rest, plenty of hot food and gentle exercise.

That meant Tammy had to act as a go-between and visit him in the palace, armed with a dozen questions from other Guardians about their cases. The surgeon had also left strict instructions that he was not to be bothered for more than a couple of hours a day.

When not carrying answers and suggestions back to Unity Hall, Tammy was digging into what was happening with the Seekers. She had people looking into Torran Habreel and his followers and was due to receive a report when she got back. Just as she'd been heading into the palace she'd been passed a note about an incident with Munroe at Unity Hall. Tammy would have to deal with that as soon as she got back. Hopefully Munroe had managed to get some answers from Grell.

"Busy day?" said a familiar voice as she came around the corner. The frown lifted from her face at the sight of Kovac. He looked tired and dusty from the road, but that didn't stop her pulling him tight against her. He tasted of spicy food from his trip to the north and smelled of horse.

"Very busy."

"Do you have time for a drink?"

"It's going to be a late night," she apologised. "Tomorrow might be better."

Kovac seemed to be weighing something up. In the end he shook his head. "No, you should hear this tonight. It can't wait."

"It sounds serious."

Again he paused and Tammy knew he was holding something back. Part of her guessed what it was about but she was afraid to ask. "I'm staying at the Golden Harp. Come and find me tonight. It doesn't matter what time. We can talk then."

"If it's urgent, tell me now."

"Not here on the street." Normally she was the stubborn one but this time Kovac wasn't budging. She stared at him for a long while, trying to work out what he wasn't saying, weighing up if she really wanted to know. Reading people was part of her job but it was more difficult with him because she was too close and emotionally involved. There was no way to guess if it was good or bad news. Tammy decided to take the plunge.

"Let's go in there," she said, gesturing at the nearest tavern down the street. They walked in silence to a small and expensive place called the Queen's Rest. This close to the palace the prices were exorbitant, the clientele consisted of nobles and rich supplicants and the place was spotless. The owner glanced up from behind the bar, frowning when Kovac came in first, his face changing slightly when he saw Tammy's Guardian uniform.

"Do you have a room we can borrow for a little while?" she asked, ignoring the glances from other patrons. "Somewhere private."

"If you'll follow me," said the owner, sniffing at the dirt on Kovac's boots and the muddy footprints he was leaving on the clean floor. They were led down a short corridor to a private dining room that was elaborately furnished with polished wood on the walls and silver ornaments hanging from the ceiling. Fresh flowers sat in a vase and bright watercolour paintings decorated the walls. Most important of all, it was quiet and private. Tammy shoved some money into the man's hands, thanked him and closed the door in his face.

Kovac took off his sword belt and sat, staring down at his hands as he gathered his thoughts. She'd never seen him so pensive before. Tammy sat down opposite. Normally when they were together she felt as if they were a team. She trusted him with her life, but at this moment it was as if he had become a suspect and she the interrogator. The uniform had never come between them. Until now.

"Start at the beginning," she said, falling back into old habits. Kovac raised an eyebrow and she tried to relax. "I'm sorry. What happened in Zecorria? Talk to me."

"I did as you asked. I kept digging into what happened to your husband. At first no one would talk to me. But after a few drinks, once they realised I wasn't there about the money, people opened up."

Part of her had hoped there wouldn't be anything to find. That the mystery would remain unsolved and nothing would change. For the most, she was content with her life. Her family was well and her son receiving far more than she was capable of giving him. Her only real regret, the only thing that gnawed at her, was not knowing who had murdered her husband. She both loved and hated mysteries.

An unsolved mystery niggled at her like a stone in her shoe. But finding the truth, no matter how ugly, was enormously satisfying. It showed her there was a pattern and a reason for everything if you kept digging for answers. Her sister believed there was a higher power at work. For Tammy it fed into her sense of justice. She didn't believe in waiting for divine intervention to punish the guilty. There was no coincidence or fate, merely patterns waiting to be identified and unravelled.

At the beginning she had tried to find answers about her husband, but the wound had been too raw, her emotions too wild. She'd broken down a few doors and cracked some heads, but no one had been willing to talk. Eventually she'd learned how to live with it, burying it under years of other memories. But somewhere, deep down inside her, it still waited. The grief. Even now, if she dwelled on it for too long it had the power to bring tears to her eyes.

Tammy realised there would be no rest without a resolution. "Tell me what you found."

Kovac nodded. "I will, but tell me something first. Who did you used to work for back in the day?"

"The head of a crime Family. A man named Don Lowell."

"And what did you do for him?"

She'd never volunteered information about this part of her old life and Kovac had never asked. Just as she'd never questioned him about what he'd done before becoming a mercenary. Once he'd mentioned trusting the wrong man, but had never elaborated on it. Some things were better left buried in the past.

"I collected debts for him. Sometimes I fought in the pit fights for money, but mostly because I enjoyed it." The scars on her hands spoke of the punishment she had doled out to her opponents. Some of her nightmares were filled with brutal images of the pain she'd inflicted. At times it was hard for her to recognise who she used to be.

"I found out that your husband worked for Don Lowell as well, but no one would tell me about his job."

"He was good with locks, but mostly he dealt with the money that was collected. Why?"

"That makes sense," said Kovac, before taking a deep breath. "I found out who gave the order to have him killed."

A tense silence filled the room. Thoughts of her old life, before his murder, began to swim to the surface. Days when she'd been a wife and a mother. Someone with family and roots. It was all gone now, like ash on the wind. That was another person and another life. She needed to cut the final thread that was tethering her and move on.

"Tell me," she whispered.

"Are you sure?"

"I need to know, Kovac. I've been carrying this around inside for too long."

"Your husband stole from Doña Jarrow. I couldn't get all the details, but I know that it was a lot of money. He was careful but eventually someone talked and she found out."

"Why now?" asked Tammy. "Why are people willing to talk about it now but they weren't years ago?"

"Because Doña Jarrow is dead and the money is still missing. No one, except your husband, knew where it was buried. He was murdered before being questioned and his accomplices didn't know. There have been rumours, but no one ever found it. Doña Jarrow had people searching for years without success, but now that she's gone it's a free-for-all."

"I never wanted it to be like this," she said, slamming her hands on the table. "To find out who was responsible, only for her to be dead."

Tammy felt no sense of closure, only seething anger that Doña Jarrow would never be brought to justice for his murder. She should have told Kovac to leave it alone. This was worse.

"It wasn't Doña Jarrow." Kovac's voice was little more than a whisper but she heard it above the pounding of her heart. Her fists uncurled and she looked up at him, torn between wanting to know while fighting the urge to run from the room. Unable to speak she gestured for him to continue. "Doña Jarrow wanted your husband's head, but out of decorum she asked Don Lowell first, since Kurne was one of his jackals. Don Lowell gave her permission."

Tammy gripped the edges of the table, suddenly feeling sick and dizzy. It was as if the whole world was shaking with her caught in the middle of a violent storm. Her fingers dug into the underside of the table, her knuckles turning white from the pressure. A wail of grief escaped her lips. The lies and the betrayal burned her. Her eyes were full of stinging tears.

After all these years to find out it was the one person she had trusted from that time. Don Lowell had sworn vehemently to help her find the killer. He had consoled her during the funeral, which he had paid for, and ordered all of his jackals to find those responsible. They were a family and someone had murdered one of their own. He'd offered a huge reward for any scrap of information and had given her time off to investigate any lead that came up. This had gone on for months and every time she seemed to be getting close to the truth it had ended in bitter disappointment.

The normally calm Don Lowell had raged at his people, from the low-ranking Paper jackals right up to his Silver and Gold. He'd cursed them all for their repeated failure. All the while, Tammy had stood by his shoulder, believing he was on her side and that they were a family.

"He swore an oath to my face, by the Blessed Mother and the Maker, that he would find those responsible." She was beginning to feel numb. "All of it meant nothing. It was all just a game to him."

"What will you do?" asked Kovac.

It was too much. She didn't know how she felt, never mind what she would do next. "I don't know. I can't think right now," said Tammy getting up, idly noting the marks her hands had left on the table. "People are waiting for me at Unity Hall. I have reports to deliver and there's so much work to do without the Old Man."

Kovac had come around the table without her noticing and she jumped when he gripped her hands. The physical contact brought her back to the present but her mind was still lurching as if she were drunk. "Whatever time you finish tonight, come and find me."

"I have to get back to work." She didn't want to promise him anything in case she didn't turn up. He seemed to understand and didn't push.

Normally Tammy was in control of her emotions. She could keep them separate until after the event, allowing her to analyse it carefully, but right now she felt muddled. She focused on the task ahead. She had to find out what Munroe had discovered. The work. That was something she could control.

"I'll talk to you later," she said, hurrying out of the door.

By the time she arrived at Unity Hall Tammy felt more in control but all of it was just under the surface. She knew it wouldn't take much for it to boil over. As she came down the corridor towards the Old Man's office she overheard raised voices and an argument.

The new Rummpoe was unsuccessfully trying to deal with three Guardians at once while a fourth sat off to one side, watching it all unfold with an amused expression. The Guardians were all firing questions at Rummpoe, demanding her attention and that she prioritise their request the next time she contacted the Khevassar. As soon as Tammy entered the outer office Rummpoe looked towards her with a pleading expression, desperate to be rescued.

"Quiet!" shouted Tammy, letting off a little of the anger inside. "One at a time."

"Have you just been to see the Old Man?" asked one of the Guardians, a fastidious man called Krolla. He glanced at the notes she was returning and tried to grab them out of her hand but she was too quick. "Is one of those for me? Did he give you any information for me on my case?"

"Rummpoe will go through these notes and pass along the information from the Old Man in due course." Tammy folded her arms and took a deep breath, towering over everyone in the room. "In the meantime, I suggest you try investigating by yourself."

Krolla sneered and opened his mouth to reply, but the words died in his throat when he saw her glare. Instead all that emerged was a sour grunt. The other two Guardians shuffled away with offhand apologies to Rummpoe. Once they were gone Tammy turned towards the fourth Guardian who had been quietly chuckling to himself. Guardian Faulk had been on the job for a long time and Tammy knew him to be an accomplished investigator, despite his left eye staring off in a different direction from his right. His appearance was permanently rumpled and his teeth stained black from chewing tarr.

"Something I can help you with, Guardian Faulk?"

"No, I was just here to drop off a report. Background information about Torran Habreel's former colleagues. I thought you might like to read it." He passed her the report which she flicked through briefly.

"I'll take a look at it soon."

Faulk shrugged. "The information is a couple of years out of date, so it might be worthless, but it's a good start."

"Thank you."

"No problem." He stood up to leave and then stopped, staring at her expectantly.

"Is there something else?" asked Tammy.

"Just one more question," he said, scratching one side of his stubbly face. "Aren't you friends with the mage Munroe?"

"Yes. I was just on my way to speak with her. Why do you ask?"

"Oh, no reason, but you might have trouble talking to her. She's being held in one of the black cells under armed guard. Guardian Yedda is in charge."

Tammy sighed, dreading to think what might have happened to cause Munroe to be locked up. Yedda was an insufferable pedant from a noble house in Yerskania. He thought it entitled him to order around other Guardians as if he was their superior. "Thank you for the warning."

Faulk gave her a little salute as he went out. Tammy dropped off the notes from the Old Man and then went in search of Munroe. The black cells were in the lowest level of Unity Hall and were reserved for the most dangerous and vicious criminals. These were people who were a threat to anyone who came within arm's reach. Such prisoners were housed alone and all questioning was done with a steel gate in between them and the Guardian.

The cells were isolated and access meant going through several locked doors that were guarded at all times. No one was allowed down there without express permission from the Khevassar. She knew the Old Man had not given Yedda permission to house anyone in there and that he must have decided by himself to lock Munroe up in one of the cells.

It took a little persuasion, some bullying and a few hard stares before she finally made it into the cell block. Standing outside Munroe's cell she found Yedda and four armed members of the Watch, all holding loaded crossbows. As Tammy approached she overheard Yedda asking a series of questions that showed his ignorance about the situation.

"Who gave you permission to be down here?" he asked Tammy, somehow managing to look down his nose at her despite being significantly shorter.

"I was about to ask you the same question."

He sniffed and ran a hand through his immaculately coiffed blond hair. "In the absence of the Khevassar, I took it upon myself to act as he would regarding this vicious and dangerous criminal."

Tammy moved closer until she could look through the bars into the cell. Munroe was sitting on a stone shelf with metal shackles around her wrists and ankles. Thick steel chains connected them to iron rings in the walls. "Hello, Munroe."

"Hello, Tammy."

"Been getting into trouble?"

"Oh, you know me," said Munroe, picking at what looked like dried blood on her trousers. There was more of it on her jacket and shirt. She'd scraped her palms clean but Tammy could see blood under her fingernails. "There's always something."

Yedda had been watching them both but now he turned towards Tammy. "Do you know this criminal?"

"She's a friend."

"Well, your 'friend' is a mage and a murderer." The pompous ass probably didn't have any friends, just servants.

"As I've already told you, ten times, the Guardian killed herself." Somehow, despite the situation, Munroe seemed incredibly calm while Yedda was getting more irate.

"That's ridiculous. Guardian Brook would never kill herself."

"What happened?" asked Tammy, directing the question at Munroe.

"That is what I'm trying to establish," shrieked Yedda. "She killed Guardian Brook and a man named Grell."

Tammy ignored him and his tantrum. "Start at the beginning."

"As you suggested, I had a little chat with Grell. I was making some progress when Brook came barging in. She said the Old Man had given her orders to take Grell to the palace for questioning."

"That's a lie. I've been with him today and he never gave that order."

"You gave her access to a suspect?" asked Yedda, his voice turning shrill again.

"How do you think she gained access to an interrogation room in the middle of Unity Hall?" asked Tammy.

"I hadn't really thought about it," admitted Yedda. Tammy rolled her eyes and gestured for Munroe to continue.

"Something was wrong with Brook's story and she started to get twitchy when I questioned her about it. For some reason she didn't want Grell talking to me. It was as if she was afraid of what he might say."

"Why?" asked Tammy, a second ahead of Yedda.

"I think she knew him. Or at least, she had something in common with him. She tried to yank him out of the room just after I got a name." Munroe raised a hand to scratch her face which yanked the chains, startling the armed guards. Two of them raised their crossbows and the others looked at Yedda for guidance.

"Are they really necessary?" asked Tammy, gesturing at the armed members of the Watch.

"You haven't heard what she did," said Yedda. "Tell her."

"When Brook realised I was on to her she panicked. She stabbed Grell and shoved him into me. I heard her calling for help and by then I was covered in his blood." If Tammy hadn't spent some time with Munroe even she would have to admit it sounded implausible. "She sent half a dozen Guardians after me and tried to escape."

"She viciously attacked them!" said Yedda, waving a finger at Munroe. "Two of them were knocked unconscious and the rest have nasty bruises."

"When Brook realised she was trapped, she took her own life rather than be questioned."

Yedda scoffed and shook his head. "Ridiculous. Why would you believe her story?"

Tammy folded her arms and gestured at Munroe. "How, exactly, did you apprehend this dangerous criminal mastermind?"

Yedda pouted and scratched the side of his head. A wave of doubt moved across his features. "Well, a few of us restrained her."

"And this is shortly after she somehow fought her way past a group of Guardians. Is that right?"

"She's a mage, but it didn't matter. We overwhelmed her with our numbers!" Yedda had an answer for everything. It was time to teach him some humility.

"This farce has gone on long enough. Munroe, you're free to go."

"Who put you in charge?" asked Yedda. "I've been a Guardian longer than you. I have seniority."

"That would be true if you'd learned something in those additional years," said Tammy. "The only reason she's in that cell is because she wants to be."

There was a loud clinking sound as all the manacles popped open simultaneously and the chains dropped to the floor. At the same time the cell door opened by itself and Munroe stepped out into the corridor. The four members of the Watch still had their crossbows aimed at her but all of them suddenly found themselves disarmed as their weapons flew out of their hands and dropped to the floor. Yedda gaped in surprise and then yelped as he was lifted off the ground and hung upside down in mid-air.

"You're dismissed," Tammy said to the Watch who all saluted her and quickly scurried away. She turned to Munroe. "Thank you for not doing something drastic. I realise you didn't have to let yourself be taken into custody."

"It was a lot easier at the time. They didn't want to listen and I was covered in blood," admitted Munroe. "Who is Guardian Brook?"

"That's a good question. I'll have someone look into her background, her friends and family. There might be a connection to Grell." Above their heads Yedda started mewling.

"She said something peculiar just before she died," said Munroe, biting her lip.

Tammy put a hand on her arm. "You don't have to tell me."

"I've been going over it for hours and I think it's important. She said 'Forgive me, Mother' then slit her own throat."

"Do you think she meant the Blessed Mother?"

"Maybe," said Munroe, although she didn't sound convinced. Tammy would make sure whoever enquired into Brook's background looked for religious icons or texts at her home. It might give them a few more clues about her final words.

It was only when they reached the end of the corridor that Tammy remembered Yedda. "Will he be up there for long?"

"As long as you want, really."

"Leave him there for a while. He deserves it."

"So what do you want me to do next?" asked Munroe.

"You don't want to rest?"

"No. The sooner we're done, the sooner I can go home. I've been away too long from my husband and son."

Tammy's conversation with Kovac came to the fore again and it took her a while to clear the lump in her throat. She'd been carrying around this pain for too long and without knowing it had been weighing her down. Ever since that night she'd kept people at a distance. It was the only way she knew how to protect herself. Now she finally had the truth.

As a Guardian it would be impossible to convict Don Lowell. She also knew that if she somehow managed to get him into an interrogation room he wouldn't suddenly have a change of heart and confess. Within the confines of the law he would never be brought to justice and punished for his crime. She was powerless to do anything, but she was also much more than a Guardian, or at least she used to be.

Tammy wondered how much of her old self still remained and how far she was willing to go to see that justice was done.

CHAPTER 32

Somewhere in the darkness there was a loud rushing sound and an explosion that shook the world. Brunwal had come for her. He'd been reduced to little more than a blackened skeleton, wrapped in decaying flesh, and yet he was alive, reaching out towards her with clawed hands. He was going to pull her down with him into the earth until she suffocated. She could feel the soil going up her nose, in her ears, filling her mouth and throat. Every breath filled her lungs with more dirt and she was choking for air.

Wren came awake, clawing at her sheets, fighting off the monster lurking in the recesses of her mind. At first she thought it had just been part of her dream, but all around her the other students were waking up. They too were throwing off their sheets and a few even fell out of the top bunks. Something had startled them all awake at exactly the same time.

All of the lights in the dormitory flared to life at once and her thoughts turned to Danoph, afraid that he was having another severe episode. Other than being as sleepy as everyone else he seemed fine but had already started getting dressed, as if he knew something she didn't. Not far away Tianne was sitting on her bed, rubbing her eyes and looking around in confusion.

The noise in the dormitory began to rise as everyone wanted to know what had woken them up and why, but no one had any answers. A few pupils glanced out of the window and reported that it wasn't yet dawn.

The door flew open and Balfruss strode into the long room, a cold wind blowing at his back. Silence fell instantly and all eyes turned towards him. Wren noticed he was dressed for a journey and laden with a heavy pack and a water skin. Most peculiar of all was the wicked-looking axe hanging from his belt, which drew a few stares. Perhaps some of the wild tales about him were true after all.

After hearing so much about him over the years Wren had always been a little intimidated by Balfruss. Over the last few months she had begun to see beyond the myth to the man, but once more here was the figure from legend. Power and confidence radiated from him in such strong waves, she believed they would be safe as long as he was with them. He had changed the course of the war by himself and with it the fate of the world. None of the students would be here now if not for his courage and bravery. Wren felt herself standing taller and saw that he was having the same effect on those around her.

"We have to leave the Red Tower. Tonight." He spoke calmly and firmly, his voice amplified with magic so that it reached every corner of the long room. "Take only what you can carry and nothing else. We will be travelling fast and on foot. Pack comfortable and warm clothing. We have little time to spare."

"Why?" someone asked. "Why do we have to leave?"

Balfruss's gaze drifted across the faces of the students until he found the speaker. "Because this place is no longer safe. We're leaving in an hour and may never return."

"But we didn't do anything," complained one of the younger children.

"I know," said Balfruss, his expression softening. In that moment Wren saw not the figure from legend, only a bluff-faced man being forced to deal with a difficult situation beyond his control. Balfruss seemed more human than Wren ever remembered. She had never questioned that he cared about them, but she'd often wondered what he'd given up to become a teacher and member of the Grey Council. No one really knew where he'd gone after the war or why he suddenly came back a few years later.

"People are afraid of what they don't understand. It has always been this way with mages. Now they think Seekers are responsible for so much death and destruction. Their children are dying and their homes are being destroyed. They believe we did this to them. They're angry and scared and have attacked our people. And now people claiming to be Seekers are taking revenge, some of them doing it in my name." At this Wren saw his hands tighten into fists and some of the steel crept back into his voice. "The danger was always at a distance, but now it's happening here in Shael. So, they are coming, but we will leave and break the cycle of violence. We could fight back and stop them, but that would only cause more harm than good. No more time for questions. We'll speak about this later. For now, pack up your belongings and do it quickly."

He waited long enough to make sure that everyone started to do as he asked before he went back out of the door, leaving it open. Despite the hour no one would be falling asleep again. Fear and adrenaline were flooding Wren's body and she could see others were equally alert and focused on the task at hand.

In the square beyond she could see some of the older students from one of the other dormitories stumbling out, half dressed, shouldering large packs with their belongings. A line of staff were handing out water skins and cloth bags of food for the journey ahead.

Turning back to her own belongings Wren considered what she had acquired since arriving at the school. Apart from borrowing several books from the library and a few curios she'd found on a supervised visit to the town, there was little that was new. Moving quickly she stuffed everything into the bag she'd arrived with and was ready in a few minutes. Others were forced to make difficult choices as they had an abundance of personal belongings.

Danoph had also finished packing and was sitting watching the flurry of activity around him with a modest bag perched on his lap. When their eyes met he simply raised his eyebrows, bemused but seemingly calm about what was happening. Some of the younger students were more emotional, crying and visibly scared about leaving what had been their only home for years.

With a few exceptions, no students had returned to their former homes since coming to the Red Tower. Their relatives didn't want them and their communities wouldn't welcome them back. Each had been exiled and forgotten, as if they had never been born. The school had become their home and the people around them their new family. Now it was all at risk. The ground wasn't shaking but inside Wren felt as if the world could crumble from under her feet at any time.

She was uneasy about this sudden departure, but in some ways it would be a relief. The Red Tower held a lot of bad memories. Since the first day she'd been forced to fight for her place, against Brunwal and then a tide of fear and indifference from the other students. She wondered again what might have happened if Tianne and Danoph had not befriended her.

Tianne seemed to be struggling the most, discarding clothing only to change her mind and stuff it into her growing backpack. Outside in the courtyard Wren could hear teachers urging students to hurry. When the majority of the students had filed out Tianne was still debating over two final items. Rather than be left behind she dropped both pieces of clothing on her bed and shouldered her bag. Wren and Danoph stood waiting for her and Tianne gave them both a grateful smile as they fell in line behind the others.

Wren's breath frosted in the air and she stamped her feet. She was tempted to put on another layer of clothing but knew that once they started walking she would soon warm up. The school grounds were a hive of activity with teachers hurrying to and fro. Members of staff were handing out food and water and a growing crowd of dazed students was milling about in the centre of the courtyard. Despite the early hour it was soon incredibly noisy with people all around her speculating about where they were going and if they would ever return. Wren had never seen all of the students together in one place but she guessed there were about two thousand in total.

She felt a loud and heavy pulse echoing in her mind and conversations around the training grounds began to dry up. A hush fell over the crowd until it enveloped the whole school. Even the youngest pupil, teary-eyed and tired, felt compelled to silence. All eyes turned towards a wagon upon which stood all three members of the Grey Council. Eloise, wrapped up in warm clothing, stood at the front, the other two flanking her on either side. For some reason the sight of them together sent a shiver of fear down Wren's spine.

"There is no time for a debate," said Eloise, her voice carrying to those at the back. She seemed incredibly calm but Wren suspected it was an act. The air was throbbing with tension. No one here was to blame for what was happening, but with no way to vent their frustration Wren could feel the growing anger of those around her. "Time is against us. We will be splitting into three groups and will set off in different directions. In a few hours' time, we'll regroup." Eloise paused and her eyes passed over the crowd. "Think of how far you've come since arriving here. Think of all the obstacles you've faced and overcome. I know some of you are scared, but today is nothing. Just a moment in time that will be forgotten in the years to come. It's not the end. We are leaving the Red Tower behind, but your futures are out there." It wasn't magic, but Wren knew those around her felt reassured, because she felt it too. Grimaces eased and steely determination glinted in the eyes of many. They were all outsiders of a kind who had faced prejudice and fear in the past.

"We will keep you safe," said Eloise, gesturing at herself and the others in the Grey Council. "No harm will come to any of you while you're in our care. It's time."

Teachers moved among the crowd, calling out class names and directing pupils to follow one of them waiting outside the main gates. Other teachers joined each of the three groups, but Wren noticed some were watching from a distance. A few teachers were staying behind with other members of staff. Those without magic were dressed in a mix of armour and each one carried either a sword or a bow over their shoulder. They were trying their best to appear nonchalant about the weapons but she and a few other students noticed. Choss moved among them, dressed in leather armour, steel braces and carrying two short swords on his belt.

"We're in Garvey's group," said Tianne with a grimace. "What are you looking at?"

"They're not coming with us," said Wren, gesturing at the blacksmith Leonie, who stood talking with Choss. The former

Seeker had wasted no time settling in since arriving and had made a name for herself as someone equally adept with magic or a hammer.

"Why not?" asked Tianne.

Wren glanced up at the Red Tower itself. Whenever she looked at it something about the building niggled at the fringes of her mind. Only now it felt different. At first glance she didn't notice what had changed. It was almost as if she wasn't supposed to, but the longer and harder she stared the easier it became. Focusing on it still made her uncomfortable, as if it didn't belong to this world, but now there was a peculiar compulsion to look elsewhere and ignore it.

"They're staying behind to protect the tower," said Wren. She waved a hand at where the door should have been but instead there was only a smooth wall. "There are centuries of discoveries inside. Imagine what would happen if all that knowledge was lost."

"It's not safe," said Danoph, watching those who were staying at the school. Wren didn't know how the teachers and staff had decided who should remain, but she couldn't believe anyone would have volunteered. Choss said something and Leonie laughed, clapping him on the shoulder before wandering off. Wren didn't know if it was customary in Shael to use humour in the face of danger, but even to her ears the laughter had sounded alien and strained.

"There's no time to waste," said Master Jorey, tapping Wren on the shoulder. "You should join the others outside the gates."

"Aren't you coming with us, Master?" asked Tianne.

Master Jorey's smile didn't reach her eyes which made Wren's heart sink. "I'm too old and slow to go running around in the woods. I'll stay here and keep an eye on things."

Wren wanted to say something to Master Jorey. To apologise

for some of the thoughts she'd had and her first impression of the teacher. To impart a small portion of how she respected her and relished attending each of her classes. Custom dictated one thing and her heart another, but even so she couldn't find the words. She didn't know if a hug would be seen as offensive and overly familiar, so she did nothing.

Somehow Master Jorey seemed to know as she touched two fingers to her lips. The others didn't understand but Wren repeated the gesture, tears forming at the corners of her eyes.

"I visited Drassia a few times in my youth," said Master Jorey. "Next time we meet, I'll tell you all about it."

"I would be honoured to hear those stories, Master Jorey," said Wren. Without saying another word she turned away, wiped at her face and joined the others outside the school gates.

The students gathered in their three large groups as the sun started to rise. Once they were all assembled the Grey Council came out of the school last. Each carried a modest pack, plus their own provisions but only Balfruss wore a weapon. It was peculiar to see him carrying the axe and yet she could tell he was familiar with it. Drassi boys practised carrying a sword from an early age, learning how to move and hold it without it being a burden. As Balfruss said his farewells to the others at the gate she saw him carefully hold the axe in place with one hand.

Each of the Grey Council shook hands with Choss who seemed central to the Red Tower's defence. Choss said one last thing to Balfruss who placed a hand over his heart and bowed slightly, making a promise and agreeing to his final request.

After that there were no more words. Each member of the Grey Council moved to the front of their group. Wren tensed as Garvey strode past but he didn't stop or even acknowledge her, for which she was grateful. He seemed intent on where they were going and all of his focus was on the road ahead.

"Stay close and move quietly," shouted Garvey back down the line. "If you must talk, do it in a whisper. Tell one of the teachers if someone falls behind. We'll rest in a few hours."

If anyone had been hoping for words of encouragement they were sorely disappointed. He had no time for hand-holding or weakness. Cruel and sharp as a blade, Garvey seemed to have no tolerance for children, once again making Wren wonder why he had agreed to join the Grey Council and become a teacher.

They set off in a slow shuffle, but soon began to find their own pace and spread out into a long line. The sun came up behind them, slowly warming the land and drying out the muddy track they seemed to be following. So many people created a path that could easily be followed and no amount of magic would be able to hide it. If they put enough distance between them and the Red Tower then perhaps whoever was coming for them wouldn't bother.

After an hour of walking across grassy fields and through small copses, the sun had risen above the horizon. The land was sloping upwards as they moved steadily west, cutting across scrubland and broken rocky ground.

It didn't take long for some of the younger children to start complaining, but those around them did their best to keep their spirits up. A few teachers moved up and down the group to make sure that everyone was coping and drinking plenty of water. They didn't have time to stop for breakfast, so Wren and the others ate some bread and cheese as they walked.

Not once did Garvey come and check on any of the students or alter his pace. He marched ahead of everyone else and expected them to follow without question. Wren was glad they were going to meet up with the others as she would not like to be stuck with him alone.

After a while Wren lost track of time. She knew they had been walking for several hours as people were complaining about being tired and hungry again. Her own feet were a little sore and her calves were aching from going uphill for so long. The teachers were doing their best to relieve any complaints, but it was becoming more challenging with every passing mile. Wren saw a couple of teachers move to the front to speak with Garvey and each time they rejoined the group, ashen-faced or annoyed.

It was only when one of the youngest children collapsed that the group slowly wound to a halt. The message was passed along and everyone gratefully stopped to catch their breath. With obvious reluctance Garvey agreed, allowing them a short break before continuing.

All the teachers had been watching the path behind them but as far as she could tell there were no signs of pursuit. Periodically one of them would fall back and catch up to them later down the track but none showed any signs of alarm. As far as she knew they were alone and yet Garvey would not relent. He wouldn't even sit down and walked among the group, but his eyes remained on the land around them.

"Eat something quickly. We need to get moving again soon," he said.

Everyone was tired, anxious and yet unwilling to disagree with him. If not for the danger that seemed to be following them Wren would have voiced her objection. They could not keep up this pace for long.

Garvey paused in his circuit of the group next to Wren and idly glanced around, before asking "Something you wish to say?" Perhaps she was not as schooled at keeping her emotions off her face as she realised.

Before she had a chance to reply there was a cry of alarm,

followed by a general clamour as people turned to look to the east, back along their path.

There was a light on the horizon, a flickering glow and a huge cloud of smoke. Rising above it she could just see the top of a bloody red needle that managed to cause unease, even at this distance. They all knew what was happening without being told.

The Red Tower was burning.

CHAPTER 33

R ain rattled against the windows of the sitting room in the palace as Tammy waited for the Queen. Normally she visited the Queen in her meeting room where she conducted most of the day's business, but tonight she'd been asked to wait in this snug. Bookshelves filled with works of fiction lined the walls either side of a fireplace. The only furniture in the room was two huge chairs filled with bright cushions. Every day she came hoping that the royal physician would tell her that the Old Man was fit enough to return home and every day she left disappointed.

When the door behind her opened Tammy only glanced over her shoulder, expecting to see the grumpy physician.

"You look like you've seen a ghost," said the Khevassar. "I'm not dead yet."

"No, Sir. Of course not. I just wasn't expecting you. Does this mean—"

"No more sitting around reading for me," said the Old Man, gesturing at the bookshelves with irritation. "They're all fiction. Ridiculous."

As he moved around the room grumbling about being confined Tammy noted his colour was a lot better than she had seen it in the last few months. It looked as if he'd put on a bit of weight and the shadows under his eyes had faded too. He was still an old man, but he no longer looked as if he was at death's door.

"Can you believe it?" he asked. Tammy had only been listening to his complaints with one ear, but she shook her head sympathetically.

"A terrible ordeal, Sir. Are you ready to go?"

"Yes, before that idiot changes his mind again." He gestured for her to follow him and together they walked down the now familiar halls of the palace towards the first of many doors and gates. They were almost out of the main building itself when a voice called out, stopping Tammy in her tracks.

"Guardian Baker?"

She turned on her heel and bowed slightly. Beside her the Old Man bowed as well. "Yes, Majesty?"

Queen Morganse was still at work at this late hour, composing a letter to a scribe who waited with his pen poised above the page. She looked tired but even dressed in a plain blue dress she made it look stylish. "Take care of him. He's not as tough as he thinks."

"I can hear you!" said the Khevassar. "There's nothing wrong with my ears."

"I will, Majesty," said Tammy, ignoring his grumbling. Morganse gave the Old Man a worried look and then turned back to the scribe, her expression turning grave.

They walked in silence for a while before she asked. "What was that about?"

"Hmm?"

"The Queen looked troubled. I've not seen her that worried before."

"She told me earlier this evening. She's signing a national ban on Seekers in Yerskania."

Tammy sucked at her teeth. "Is that wise?"

"I don't know," admitted the Old Man. "But she's trapped. You know what's going on out there. There was already mounting pressure and now there are reports of Seekers killing people in the name of Balfruss. She had little choice."

"Balfruss would never order that." She said it with absolute confidence. "He is not to blame."

"I believe you, but someone is determined to paint the Red Tower and everyone associated with it as killers. It's everyone else you need to convince."

Tammy brooded on it as they walked through the grounds to the final gate. She briefly waved at Riona, but her mind was elsewhere, turning the problem and other things over in her mind.

By the time they made it onto the street the rain had stopped. They'd been walking for a while towards Unity Hall when he tapped her on the arm.

"Slow down a little," said the Old Man, bringing her back to the present. "You walk fast when you're not paying attention."

"I'm sorry, Sir. My mind was elsewhere."

"Let me rest for a minute," he said, gesturing at one of the footbridges crossing the River Kalmei. They paused halfway across and he leaned against the railing, a little out of breath.

"I need to ask you something important, and I want an honest answer." Tammy glanced at the Old Man to make sure he understood the seriousness of what she was saying. "Don't fence words with me. Not about this."

"Ask your question."

"Did you know?" she asked and he raised an eyebrow. "Did you know all this time who killed my husband?"

The Old Man took a deep breath and peered into the rushing water before speaking. "No, I didn't know."

"But it was you who leaked the information to Kovac."

"Like Doña Jarrow I've had people looking into it for a long time. But no one would talk, especially to a Guardian, while she was alive. Even after her death it took a while to find someone because she'd been mixed up in that business with the Flesh Mage." The Khevassar laughed and she had the impression it was at himself. "I used to inspire that kind of fear." He turned away from the water and studied her face. "I just made sure the information found its way to Kovac and he did the rest. I take it you've found out who killed your husband?"

"Yes. But why do this now?"

"Because it was the one thing holding you back." He said it as if it was the most obvious thing in the world about her. As if he could read her as easily as a page in a book.

"From what?"

"Tammy, I'm an old man. I've denied it for a long time and until very recently I've not had any serious health problems. The will is still there, but my body and now even my mind isn't up to the task any more. I can't push myself as hard as I used to." Much to her surprise he tentatively reached out and gently held one of her hands in both of his. The skin on his hands was soft but it also felt thin and brittle. "I don't have any children of my own, but, if I did, I would want a daughter like you."

"I don't understand."

"Very soon, if you want it, you will replace me and become the Khevassar."

Tammy waited for him to say something else but he remained silent, watching her intently. For a moment she was certain she'd misheard him but the look on his face told her everything. Surprise and then shock rolled through her and she swayed on her feet, reaching out to grip the railings with one hand. He still held on to her other hand, anchoring her.

"I don't know what to say."

"You need to understand what I'm offering you." He let go of her hand and part of Tammy felt as if she might drift away into the sky as she had once in a dream. This conversation didn't seem real. "To become what I am you must leave behind everything that you were. There must be no leverage that people can use against you. The mystery surrounding your husband's murder hampered you. It was always there, lurking and weighing you down."

He spoke with such confidence she couldn't understand how he could know so much. Even with his remarkable talent for reading people this bordered on the supernatural.

"Imagine if someone else had found out about it before you. They could have used it to blackmail you. If you take on the office, you will have no name, no past and no family. You must be untouchable by outside forces. You will answer to the Queen, and perhaps, in time, her successor. When you walk into that meeting room and offer Queen Morganse advice, she will listen. You will direct all of the Guardians both here in the city and abroad. It is the greatest challenge you will ever face."

He paused, giving her time to try and process everything. At the far side of the bridge a street seller had a stall with warm pastries stuffed with apple and cinnamon. He wandered over and bought two, handing her one. Tammy ate it slowly, savouring the gooey spicy taste as she thought on what he'd said. When she was done her fingers were covered with crumbs and her mouth tingled from the seasoning.

"What about my family?" she asked. "Would they be safe?"

"Only three people know about them, myself and two other Guardians. If you took the job then you'd have to give them up as well. Your name would be removed from certain documents, as well any references to your past. If you want this, you would have to give up Kovac as well."

Tammy realised that a long time ago someone must have given him the same speech. In recent years they'd become close, but even so she'd not spent much time thinking about who he used to be and what he'd given up for the position. In all the time she'd known him, working for Don Lowell, as a member of the Watch and finally a Guardian, he'd been an untouchable force in the city. The heads of the crime Families didn't respect many of those on the side of law and order, but they all had grudging admiration for the Old Man. He'd outlived and outlasted many of them, faced down countless disasters at home and abroad, and was still here to talk about it. No one had ever been able to corrupt him or use him for their purpose. He was an implacable force for justice and that demanded a level of respect.

"I'm sure you'll understand when I say I know what I'm asking you to give up. Perhaps I'm the only one who can understand. Take some time to think about it, but can I suggest something in the meantime?"

"Sir?"

"Your husband's murder. Settle it, one way or another. Only then will you be able to think about my offer with a clear mind. You know where to find me if you want to talk."

He turned to walk away but she reached and caught his arm, stopping him in his tracks. "That's why you've been sending me abroad all these years. You were training me for this."

The Old Man's smile lit up his whole face. "Every year I send a few Guardians abroad to help all over the world, but most have never left the city, never mind the country. The Khevassar is there to protect Yerskania, but they must also be worldly. You've lived and worked beside so many different people. You're the ideal candidate for the job."

"Just how long have you been preparing for this?" she asked.

"I knew this day would come. I just didn't know when." It

wasn't really an answer but Tammy sensed that was all she'd get from him for the time being. "I told you that one day you would be faced with a difficult choice. So choose, but do so quickly."

He left her standing on the middle of the bridge staring into the water, her thoughts running in many directions. The choice ahead was not one she had ever considered and, now that it was here, she didn't know what to do. Tammy had never been someone to second-guess herself, but now she did.

The challenge ahead seemed impossible and yet the Old Man had done it, becoming a figure almost out of myth in the process. No one knew anything about him and in thirty years' time, if she took on the mantle, would anyone remember her? She would be estranged from her family, but she'd almost done that already, believing them better off without her. If she took on the role of Khevassar it would mean never seeing them ever again and denying all knowledge of them.

The cost of taking on the job was high and she wondered if it would be worth it in the long run.

She had always judged herself by what she accomplished and thought she would be a Guardian for the rest of her life. Now she was being offered an opportunity to do more than she'd ever be able to achieve working alone. It wasn't a question of wanting it, only if she were willing to pay the price.

CHAPTER 34

As the sun rose above the trees Choss closed his eyes and turned towards it, warming the skin on his face and neck. For a little while he was able to forget everything that was about to happen. Forget everyone around him and just soak up the heat like a cat in a pool of sunlight. All too soon thoughts of the present began to intrude and his moment of peace faded.

Standing beside him on the wall was an assortment of teachers and staff. Most of the teachers had gone with the children to protect them, but those who had chosen to stay behind were either too old for such a journey or simply too stubborn.

Although Master Jorey was a grandmother she was fit enough to have travelled with the others but had chosen to remain. When Choss had asked her why, all she'd said was "I don't have the energy to start all over again."

Her family was far away from here, spread out across the west, sailing aboard a fleet of merchant vessels, running a business that she had founded. She'd said coming to the Red Tower was to be her final chapter but Choss suspected she hadn't thought it would end this soon.

Standing to his left was one of the cooks, Mellor, a surprisingly thin man given his profession, with red hair and freckles.

Mellor had no wife or children of his own, but it had been clear since Choss first met him that he cared deeply about the children. The students never saw how much time and thought he put into preparing their meals, but he was usually the first in the kitchen in the mornings and the last to leave at night. Bursting with nervous energy he sampled food all day and never put on any weight. Even now, standing on the wall holding a sword like a butter knife, one of his legs jigged up and down in an endless rhythm.

The rest of those defending the school came from a variety of backgrounds and professions, but only a few had been soldiers or warriors. The rest had no experience of being in a battle. Choss had more knowledge than most, but even he'd never experienced a siege. It didn't really matter. To an outsider approaching the Red Tower all they would see was a lot of defenders manning the top of the wall. It might be enough to make them hesitate.

The people on their way would be a mob, not a formal, disciplined army. And every hour the defenders kept them here, it gave the children that much more time to escape. That was all their defence was designed to do, delay the inevitable. Just one of the teachers could keep a mob at bay with magic by themselves, but they wouldn't do it. It would only scare the mob even more. Make them more terrified of what magic could do and the danger they thought it represented. Fighting fire with fire would make the situation that much worse.

The plan was simple. They would hold the line as long as possible and then Choss and a few others would fall back and run. There were horses already saddled and well provisioned for a journey. Not enough for everyone, but some of the defenders had never intended to leave.

As long as the children were safe that was all that really mattered to him and the others. Samuel was among them, no doubt confused and scared about being without his parents or grandmother, but Choss was confident Munroe would find their son. With a bit of luck he would also be reunited with Samuel in a few days, once he'd led any pursuers on a merry chase around the countryside. The real difficulty would be telling Munroe that her mother had decided to stay behind. Samara had known her illness was fatal before the healers confirmed it. She'd been living on borrowed time and this was her final trip to the Red Tower. At least this way she was able to choose the time and place of her death, on her feet, not lying down in a bed, gasping for air. She came up the ladder to the top of the wall, a bow slung over her shoulder and a bristling quiver on her hip.

"Been a long time since I hunted with one of these," she said. The others shuffled down the wall a bit, giving her enough space to stand beside Choss.

"Well, they're going to be a lot slower than a rabbit or a deer," he said.

"Bigger target, too, which is a good thing with my eyesight."

They'd never exactly been close, and were only related through marriage, but Choss had always admired Samara. It must have been difficult for her, raising a daughter by herself in a city like Perizzi. Despite everything, she had found a way. There had been distance between Munroe and her mother for a long time, but over the last six or seven years the gap had shrunk. Little Sam was the bridge between all of them, and slowly they'd become a family in more than name.

"When we first met, I didn't like you very much," said Samara, squinting at the horizon.

"The feeling was mutual, given the stories I'd heard."

Samara snorted. "I'm sure she spared no details. The past is done and I'm not going to say I'm sorry now. What would be the point?" she asked and he had no answer. "What I'm trying to say is, I'm glad Munroe married you. And not just because you gave me a grandchild. I never imagined that would happen."

It had been a surprise to them at the time. They'd discussed children in the past but Munroe had never shown any real inclination. That had all changed the moment she found out about the pregnancy. Choss had never seen her so excited before and the memory still made him smile.

"Thank you, Samara."

She craned her neck to look him in the face and patted his arm affectionately. "Look after each other, and tell her how proud I am."

Choss had never seen the woman cry and she was not about to start now. The fierceness of her glare told him how much she loved her daughter and what she would do to protect her. She didn't need to say it out loud. "I will tell her."

"Here they come," said someone further down the line.

The mob was bigger than Choss had been expecting. He guessed there were at least two hundred men and women armed with a variety of weapons. There were a lot of bows and a few swords, but most carried crude clubs, hunting spears, wood axes and one or two maces. Greasy black smoke rose into the air above the group from the torches that many were carrying.

Even at this distance Choss thought he recognised a few faces from his regular trips into the nearby town. These people were his neighbours, driven to violence and thirsty for blood.

They were not warriors, but they were compelled by a terrible and familiar rage that Choss could understand. Theirs was misguided and they had been manipulated into thinking the Red Tower responsible, but the time for discussion was over.

"So, what drove them over the edge?" asked Samara, flexing her bow and attaching the string.

"Remember the little village, a day or so to the west?"

"Not very well. I passed through it on the way here, but didn't stop."

"Well, it's not there any more," said Choss. "Someone claiming to be a Seeker torched the fields and all their crops, slaughtered the cattle and then burned down every house. Apparently he did it for Balfruss and the Red Tower."

"Anyone die?"

"About a hundred people. Half the village."

Samara hissed through her teeth. "That would do it."

The first charge when it came was little more than the mob sprinting towards the gate, screaming hatred at the top of their lungs. A few arrows flew towards the defenders but none managed to find a target. They were rushing and angry which made them sloppy. Arrows clattered against the wall or sailed far over their heads.

Leonie, the blacksmith, a short distance down the wall on Choss's left, stood beside Master Jorey.

"If we worked together we could scatter them all," said Leonie.

Master Jorey patted her on the shoulder. "I know, but we can't."

As the mob drew closer they shot a few more arrows and this time some of them could be dangerous. As they'd planned Leonie sent them flying off course with a negligent flick of her hand.

"Return fire," shouted Choss, bellowing at the archers beside him. "Try not to kill anyone," he said to Samara.

"No promises," she said, picking her target. A large man with a stomach that stuck out of the bottom of his shirt was bellowing loudly as he ran. Samara took a deep breath and then released, her arrow lodging in his thigh. With a remarkably high-pitched scream he keeled over and thrashed around on the ground.

"Good shot," said Choss.

Samara shook her head. "I was aiming for his belly."

A dozen or more people in the mob stumbled and fell as arrows caught them, but it didn't stop the charge. Most of the wounds didn't look fatal but one woman went down with an arrow in the head, enraging those around her. The mob rushed forward at a sprint and soon were too close to the wall to use their bows. No one had thought this through as now they were pressed against the wall with no way of getting inside the school. Those opposite the gate tried to heave together to break it open but Choss and others had reinforced it on the inside earlier in the day.

If this had been a normal siege they would have poured oil or alcohol onto those below and set them alight, or crushed them with rocks. At this distance it would also be incredibly easy to kill more of them with arrows. But they wanted to drive the attackers away without too much bloodshed so instead they resorted to pelting them with potatoes which did little more than bruise.

As the cries of pain and alarm mounted the attack faltered and the mob withdrew to a safe distance to tend to the wounded. They left the dead woman where she'd fallen.

Choss glanced at the sky trying to judge how much time had passed since the children had left. It must have been at least four or five hours. He hoped it was enough to keep them safe. The longer they kept the mob here the better off the children would be.

"This is a farce," said Master Stenne, walking along the wall. The sour-faced teacher had surprised everyone by staying behind. She didn't like anyone at the school, including the children, but seemed to hate the mob worse.

"We just need to buy the others some more time."

"I'm very aware of that, thank you, Master Choss," she said, making his name sound like something she'd found stuck to the bottom of her shoe.

With one dead and several wounded, Choss hoped the mob would just give up and go home. The realist in him knew that it wouldn't happen yet. Their blood would have to be spilled to quench the rage coursing through the mob. They believed their friends and neighbours had been murdered and spilling more blood was the only way to balance the tragedy.

A short time later the mob returned and their second attack was more coordinated than the first. Choss watched as arrows were wrapped in scraps of cloth and then set alight. It was just as they had expected. From a distance volley after volley of flaming arrows flew over their heads, landing on rooftops and burying themselves in the ground of the training yard. A few went long, arcing towards the Red Tower itself, but they were immediately extinguished and fell to the ground. The building remained unmarked and undamaged. He didn't know what, if anything, could destroy it.

Arrows thudded into the gates and a few villagers ran forward and placed torches at the bottom of them. It would take a long time for the wood to catch fire, but in the meantime a large cloud of smoke was starting to build up and creep under the gates.

The roof of the stables caught fire but all of the horses had been tethered elsewhere. Choss knew it wouldn't take long for the flames to eat through the roof and for sparks to land amid the hay stored in the loft. After that the smoke and the fire would spread quickly.

"Put out the fires!" he shouted and a couple of mages on the wall turned to deal with them. With a few waves of their hands the smoke dispersed and the flames were smothered. At the same time more arrows rattled against the wall catching a couple of defenders by surprise. With an arrow in his shoulder Mellor stumbled backwards and toppled off the wall before anyone could stop him. Leonie saw him fall but instead of landing below he hung in mid-air a foot off the ground.

"Someone grab him," shouted the smith and a couple of defenders ran down to the courtyard, slowly easing him to the floor. Choss turned back to face the mob just in time to see more flaming arrows soaring towards him. He ducked but Samara ignored them and, leaning forward, shot a woman in the shoulder this time, cackling all the while.

"It seems fair," she said when Choss raised an eyebrow. "They shot one of ours. Isn't that what it says in the Maker's book?"

"I thought it was more about returning an act of kindness."

Samara shrugged. "It's all open to interpretation," she said, taking aim again. One of the villagers squawked and started limping away with an arrow stuck in his arse.

More flaming arrows landed inside the school again and smoke was still drifting in from under the gate.

"Choss, you need to get down here," shouted Master Farshad from below. "You too, Samara."

Choss exchanged a worried look with his mother-in-law and together they hurried down the stairs.

"By the Maker," hissed Samara, running across the courtyard before dropping to her knees. Choss couldn't see what had happened until he drew closer.

"No," he whispered, not really believing what he was seeing. It wasn't possible. And yet he knew what every hair on the boy's head looked like. He didn't need to see his face to know that it was his son.

"What are you doing here?" Samara was asking him as Choss came up behind her. She was shaking and trying her best not to frighten Sam, but he sensed her fear as his eyes filled with tears.

"I snuck away from the others," he said, choking back a sob. "I didn't want to leave without you and Daddy."

Choss didn't know what to do. They had planned for everything, apart from this. His son should have been miles away by now, safely protected by a dozen teachers. Choss was frozen with fear and indecision.

Smoke was starting to build up and people around him were beginning to cough and splutter.

Master Jorey came towards him across the training ground. She glanced at Samara and the boy, shaking her head in disbelief.

"Get him out of here," she said. "We can use the smoke as cover. I think it's time for you and the others to leave."

Leonie and some of their companions came down off the wall and gathered up their nervous horses.

"Keep him safe," said Samara, kissing Sam on both cheeks before lifting him up and passing him to Choss. He held his son in one arm against a hip, keeping one hand free for what came next.

His roan wouldn't stand still but it calmed a little when he laid a hand on its neck. As more grey and black smoke filled the school grounds the others mounted up. Choss held Sam against his chest with one arm, the other on the reins. There were a dozen riders and more than fifty people staying behind to give them a chance.

Master Jorey and Master Stenne stood to either side of the gates. The old sailor spoke a word and, working together, an invisible force struck the gates, blasting them open, spraying the mob with shards of wood and metal. Master Stenne directed the smoke out through the gates, providing them with some cover. Choss spurred his horse forward, urging it to gallop as fast as it could with him bent low over its neck.

*

The riders disappeared into the spreading cloud of grey smoke that was rolling out of the gates across the ground. Jorey could feel Stenne gently nudging the smoke and spreading it across a wide area, giving the riders as much cover as possible. There was a brief thunder of horses' hooves and then a peculiar silence took its place beyond the walls. The school grounds were briefly clear of smoke and with a nonchalant wave of her hand Jorey extinguished any lingering flames on the rooftops. With her Talent she had predicted the day's weather would be clear and sunny. If this was to be her last day she wasn't going to choke to death on smoke and ash. It would be with a weapon in her hand and the sun on her face. It wasn't quite the heroic death at sea she'd expected, but it would have to do.

As the smoke finally edged away from the wall some of the mob saw that the gates were standing open. With a series of ragged cries and a half-hearted cheer, some of the villagers ran towards her and Stenne. The old shrew spat on the ground and stared down the men and women running towards her brandishing weapons. Jorey drew her sabre and rolled her shoulders to loosen them. It had been a long time since she'd fought with a blade.

At the look on Stenne's face several people veered away from her and ran into the school in all directions looking for easier prey. One woman wasn't intimidated by her glare and tried to stab the old teacher with her pitchfork. Stenne snatched it from her hands and slapped the woman across the face hard enough to leave a mark. As she recoiled in horror Stenne said something so vile the woman turned and ran. Jorey couldn't help chuckling at the old woman's mettle.

Even with her weak connection to the Source it would be so easy for any of the mages to defeat the mob and send them away. She could sense it, flickering at the edge of her perception like a candle flame, tempting her to embrace its energy. Taking a deep breath, she tasted the air in her lungs, looked at the sky and ignored the power of her birthright.

Two men came through the gates and angled towards Jorey. To even up the odds a little she drew a dagger from her belt. The bearded man on the left swung his axe as if he was chopping wood, using both hands and all his strength. All Jorey had to do to avoid his attack was to quickly step backwards. Instead his axe whipped past his neighbour's side, catching him on the ribs and leaving a blood trail. The two men stared at each other in horror, giving Jorey ample time to cut them on the back of their hands with her sabre. They dropped their weapons and ran.

Three snarling women carrying pitchforks replaced them. They spread out around Jorey but none of them seemed willing to take the initiative and attack first. All the women were old enough to be her daughters. Jorey felt a pang of sadness that she'd never see her children, or grandchildren, again. Part of her had hoped that, one day, one of her extended family would come to the school and she'd be able to teach them about the joy of magic. Unlike most families, her sons and daughters hoped every child born in the family had the ability. They all knew that one of the reasons the business had been a success for so long was her weather Talent.

The three women were arguing with each other so Jorey made it easy for them. She lunged at one of them and knocked the pitchfork out of the woman's hand with her sabre. As expected one of the others lunged at her. Jorey tried to dance away, but time had made her slower than she realised, and one of the tines bit into her side. As blood began to spread out across her shirt the young woman looked sick.

"Oh no," she said, even putting a hand to her mouth as she began to gag.

"It's their fault, remember?" said the third woman but her two friends had lost heart and one of them lost her breakfast, vomiting onto the ground. Suddenly finding herself alone facing Jorey, the woman spat in disgust and walked away.

For a brief moment Jorey had hope that perhaps the mob would disperse. These were not hardened soldiers. The mere sight of blood, of wounding someone else, was enough to make them physically sick. They were farmers, merchants and traders. They shouldn't be here.

The spark of hope faded as two or three dozen people poured in through the gates screaming at the tops of their lungs. Ignoring the vicious glare one man simply stabbed Stenne in the stomach and moved on, not even waiting for her to fall. Those on the walls turned inwards, firing arrows into the crowd at will, injuring and killing a few, but it wasn't enough to slow their momentum.

They kept coming into the school, desperate to extinguish the rage. Men and women scrambled up the steps towards those on the wall while others used their torches to start new fires, setting buildings alight. Pitched battles were raging all over and now the defenders were easily outnumbered three to one.

As a group of six armed men and women rushed towards her, Jorey caught sight of Stenne on the ground. Blood trickled from the corner of her mouth which still held a bitter twist. Their eyes met across the training ground and although she was too far away to hear the words, Jorey understood the two words that Stenne mouthed.

"Pity them."

Screaming at the top of her lungs, Jorey raised her sword and charged at the enemy.

As he rode into the cloud of smoke something struck Choss on his leg but he kept going, driving his horse forward through the gates. A figure appeared in the gloom, raising a weapon overhead, but he didn't slow and his horse rode the man down. His cry of pain was lost in the fog and more shapes loomed on either side.

Ignoring them all Choss stayed low until he rushed out of the cloud. Quickly orientating himself he turned his horse slightly to the east and kept moving. A quick glance behind showed him the mages had done their job well as most of the school was now concealed in a low cloud of choking smoke. Rising above it, like a bloody splinter, was the tower itself, alien and untouched. Figures stumbled out of the smoke, coughing and spluttering, others vomiting on the ground. A couple of riderless horses shot out of the smoke and Choss hoped that those unseated would still be able to escape on foot.

Someone behind him shouted and, glancing back, he saw a group of men and women giving chase on foot. Choss slowed his horse to a trot, to conserve its energy in case he needed a burst of speed later to escape. After an hour of steadily heading east he felt safe enough to stop and check on Sam. A wave of tiredness swept over Choss, enough to make him sway and almost tumble out of the saddle. The adrenaline from their flight had worn off but it shouldn't have exhausted him this much. Sam had fallen asleep against him and was still dozing. Choss was relieved as it forced him to muffle his alarm when he saw the growing patch of blood on his leg. He'd felt something tug at him as they rode through the smoke and had assumed it was one of the mob trying to pull him from the saddle. Gritting his teeth against the pain he tore off one of his sleeves and tied it around the wound to stem the bleeding.

Choss cocked his head to one side and waited, listening intently for sounds of pursuit. At first there was nothing but then, somewhere in the distance, he caught the sound of several approaching horses and people on foot.

Spurring his horse forward at a walk he carried on east, following the trail he'd used many times. Behind him he heard a cry of surprise from his pursuers. They were louder than before and seemed to be getting closer.

He could try and lead them around in the countryside for a few hours until they became bored, but Choss wasn't sure he could stay conscious that long. His leg was starting to feel numb and blood was seeping through the makeshift bandage. Protecting Sam was the only thing that mattered.

There was only one choice.

A crashing sound and the thud of hooves made him urge his horse into a trot. The riders behind him were clearly wasting no more time by keeping pace with the others on foot.

Knowing how the land twisted about and was riddled with tree roots, Choss kept his horse at a steady pace. His pursuers would gain some ground, but Choss wanted to make sure his horse didn't break a leg. Moving towards the river, he heard the faint trickle of water that soon became a roar as he drew closer to a branch of the River Suzoa.

Staying low to avoid being hit in the face by branches, Choss guided his horse carefully into a gallop, putting some distance between him and the others.

His body was feeling heavier all the time and it was becoming a struggle to stay awake. At some point Sam had woken up but he'd not complained or asked any questions. He merely watched Choss and held on tightly, trusting that everything would be well.

A short time later the river widened into the familiar churning torrent. No one would attempt to swim it, as they would be dashed to death on the rocks or dragged under by the current. It meant he was nearly there.

Choss slowed his horse to a walk and moved away from the main path, following the trail he had made to the cabin.

"Climb down, Sam," he said, helping his son to the ground before trying to dismount. His left leg folded under him and he collapsed face down. The sound of the river was rushing in his ears or perhaps it was just the frantic beating of his heart. He didn't know how much time had passed before he came awake with a growing sense of urgency.

Sam sat nearby, watching him with frightened eyes. Forcing himself onto his hands and knees was a struggle. Standing upright seemed impossible. Leaning heavily on Sam and bracing himself against his horse, Choss shuffled towards the cabin. Behind him he could hear people crashing through the trees. The noises were jumbled and Choss shook his head, trying to get rid of his disorientation.

When they reached the cabin he pushed open the door and glanced inside. "Sam, do you remember my friend Gorraxi?" Sam nodded slowly, trying not to show his fear. "Can you go inside and see if she's in the basement?"

"I don't want to."

"I know, but it's important. I'll be right here," said Choss, leaning against the doorframe. He could hear their pursuers getting closer but was doing his best not to frighten the boy. "All I need you to do is have a quick look downstairs, then come straight back."

"Promise you won't go anywhere?"

"I promise," said Choss, forcing a smile. While Sam went down the stairs he risked a glance back along the path. He couldn't see anyone yet but he knew it wouldn't be long now. In the distance black smoke rose above the trees. The school was still burning.

Master Farshad watched in horror as several people on the training ground were cut down by the rampaging mob. Torches were thrown onto roofs, the stables were already alight again, and now the invaders were scrambling up the stairs to engage with them on the wall. Archers beside him were still picking off individuals but at this distance they barely had to take aim. Unfortunately he knew they would run out of arrows before they ran out of targets. The notion of trying only to wound them was abandoned as members of staff now fought for their lives. The only thing they avoided was using magic, even to save themselves.

Farshad had given up much to teach at the Red Tower but it had been a sacrifice he'd been willing to make. Many thought that, despite the unbearable heat, the desert kingdoms were idyllic, but as someone who'd grown up there he knew that was far from the truth. As a people they were simply better at hiding their problems. In the west he'd found a more temperate climate and a family that went beyond blood ties. And now all of it was at risk, but at least the children were safe. They were the reason he and the others had chosen to stay behind. The children would create a better future, one not dominated by fear of those who were born different. He had to believe it or else his resolve would falter.

Several men and women had made it to the top of the wall in places and they were closing on either side.

"Draw your weapons," shouted Farshad to those around him. Instead of a sword he had chosen a mace, in keeping with his first teachers. It wasn't quite what the Jhanidi used but it would be sufficient.

"You know how to use that thing?" asked Samara holding a dagger in each hand.

"Do you?"

"I cut a few purses in my time," she said with a shrug.

"Purses or throats?" he asked, raising one eyebrow.

"Well, that would be telling," she said. In spite of everything Farshad found himself laughing. He was still chuckling when he smashed the first man on the shoulder with his mace, shattering it. As the man tumbled out of sight off the wall Farshad punched a woman behind him in the face and shattered her right thigh with a wide swing. The woman stumbled to one knee in time for Samara to kick her off the wall.

Seeing two of their number dispatched so quickly the other attackers pulled back slightly.

"Come on then, you ugly bastards," sneered Samara. "What are you waiting for?"

Farshad found himself smiling at her fearless defiance. He knew from Master Yettle that Samara had been living on borrowed time. So whether it happened today or a month from now, lying in her bed, it made little difference to her. Each of them owed a death. Perhaps it was better to go on his feet, staring an enemy in the eye, than to succumb to the ravages of time as it decayed his flesh.

"You heard the lady. We don't have all day," he said.

Howling like a pack of wolves, the mob rushed forward. Farshad charged to meet them, lowering his shoulder at the last second. He knocked one woman off the wall, punched a man in the throat and brought his mace up between the legs of a third. With a pig-like squeal the man collapsed and fell out of sight. Something jabbed him in the stomach but he ignored it and brought his mace down on another man's forearm, shattering the bones. On his left he could hear Samara wheezing as she stabbed and sliced, spraying blood everywhere.

Their brutal assault made those on the wall pull back again. Their rage would only take them so far and now they were not fighting enemies who cowered or held back. They still had homes, lives and families to return to after this. Farshad had nothing.

The cloud of smoke was spreading. A thick patch drifted across the wall making him and everyone else splutter a little. Samara used it as an opportunity to rush forward and he followed, determined to drive the others back. Fighting in near blindness he rhythmically brought down his mace on anything in front, feeling it connect with bone and muscle. His shoulder was burning from the effort and his eyes were stinging but he crept forward, ignoring the growing pain in his side.

Time lost all meaning and he didn't know how long he fought. Muffled screams filled his ears and suddenly he was out the other side of the smoke, his mace coming down on nothing but thin air which sent him off balance.

Farshad stumbled to one knee but when he tried to stand up his legs didn't seem to be working. Looking down he saw something pink and purple poking out from between the folds of his shirt which had turned red.

"That looks nasty," said Samara, limping up beside him. One side of her face was covered with blood and she had an arrow buried in one shoulder. She'd lost her daggers but somehow acquired a hatchet.

"I've had worse," he said, forcing a grin. She offered a hand and, leaning on her, Farshad slowly managed to pull himself upright. It was then that he noticed a trail of bloody footprints behind Samara.

Seeing where he was looking she shrugged. "I'm not done yet."

The wall in front was clear of the enemy apart from several wounded, squirming bodies. Moving slowly, they shuffled past the injured, ignoring their curses although Samara did pause to spit on one woman who'd said something particularly unpleasant.

There were still pockets of fighting here and there across the school, but the fight was nearly done. Everywhere he could see buildings on fire and the roofs of several had already collapsed. Bodies littered the wall and school grounds. Farshad recognised many of them and took a moment to whisper a prayer to guide their souls.

They'd been outnumbered from the start and now the odds had finally turned against them. A group of at least twenty bruised and bloody figures were coming up the stairs towards them.

"I can't say this is how I planned today," said Farshad. The men and women were creeping closer with spears and pitchforks held out in front.

"It could be worse," said Samara.

"How so?" he asked.

She glanced up at the sky and beyond the smoke it was a bright and beautiful day. "It could be raining."

Farshad was still laughing as the mob raced towards them.

Sam came running back up the stairs from the basement shaking his head. "There's no one down there. Just some old smelly fish."

Grimacing against the pain, he used the broom by the door as a crutch and together he and Sam slowly made their way down to the pier.

"Daddy, you're bleeding," said Sam, pointing at his leg.

"I know. Cover your ears," he said when they reached the end of the pier. Taking a deep breath he bellowed as long and as loud as he could for Gorraxi. He didn't know if she was close or beneath the waves beyond his hearing, but he was out of time and out of options. His strength was almost gone. The wound in his leg was more severe than he realised and the world kept turning black for a few seconds at a time. Any moment now those in pursuit would come bursting through the trees and then it would be over.

Again and again he shouted for his friend, a wordless cry composed of his frustration and rage. The well inside ran deep, giving his voice power that carried it across the water, startling birds from the nearby trees. It gave him a burst of energy but it was only temporary. Despite covering his ears, Sam's face was scrunched up in pain from the noise. The shouting from his pursuers had stopped. They'd been scared or intimidated by his cry, but he knew it wouldn't last. They had come this far and would not turn back without finding their prey.

Choss felt his legs begin to tremble and he nearly fell into the water. He managed to correct his balance at the last second but at that moment he knew that he was done. Even his anger would not sustain him this time. It had burned out altogether.

Someone broke through the trees behind him and he heard Sam gasp in surprise. Just before he turned around Choss saw a pocket of bubbles breaking the surface of the river. At first it was only a few but then it became a flurry which slowly made its way against the current towards him and the pier.

"There's nowhere left to run," said a voice behind him. Choss shuffled about on his good leg, leaning heavily on the broom which was about to break under his weight. The rider wasn't familiar but the soot on his clothes confirmed that he'd been among the mob at the Red Tower. Armed with an axe he stood beside the cabin, seemingly happy to wait for the others. Two more riders came through the trees and they quickly dismounted and drew their weapons.

Behind them Choss could hear the crash of people hurrying towards them through the trees. The riders didn't turn but one of the men did call out to his friends to guide them.

Choss stumbled to one knee beside Sam, who had started to

cry again. "I want you to promise to always be a good boy. And I need you to remember something very important. Can you do that?" he asked, waiting for Sam to nod before continuing. "Remember that your mum and I love you more than anything."

Over his shoulder Choss saw nine men and women break through the trees. They were all out of breath and red-faced but each carried a weapon. That made it a dozen people he was facing. Even at his best he couldn't defeat that many by himself.

With the last of his flagging strength Choss forced himself to stand. Stretching to his full height he dropped the broom and cast his weapons aside, waiting with empty hands to see what they would do next. Their anger had kept them going this far, but now that they were facing an unarmed man they hesitated. Killing someone in a fight was one thing. Cutting him down in cold blood was something else entirely.

"Give us the boy," said one of the men, "and you can go free."

"He's a mage. He has to die too!" said someone else.

"He doesn't look a mage," said one of the riders.

A frantic discussion ensued but Choss wasn't listening. The words were all jumbled and he had difficulty following their conversation. Behind him he could hear something moving through the water and feel a huge presence drawing closer.

The argument subsided as the anger drained away from their faces and was replaced with sheer terror. Scooping Sam up in both arms Choss spun around to face the river.

Rising up out of the water was a huge green shape, standing motionless in the middle of the churning river. The water flowed down Gorraxi's body on all sides and she seemed to float upon the surface. From where he was standing Choss could see a massive black shape just beneath the water, but to those further back it would seem like magic.

"I love you," said Choss before throwing Sam with the last

of his remaining strength. The boy sailed through the air, over the water and straight into the arms of the Vorga. Choss fell to his knees, unable to stand and barely clinging to consciousness. He heard screams of terror as many of his pursuers ran away but someone came forward, the wooden boards of the pier creaking beneath their weight.

They were too late. Cradling Sam in both arms against her chest, Gorraxi began to sink beneath the waves. It took only a moment and then she and his son were gone. The water churned unbroken over that spot and there were no ripples or bubbles on the surface to show where she'd been.

Choss was so tired and his body felt so heavy. He could hear voices nearby but they weren't important. All that mattered was that his son was safe and Munroe was far away.

All these years later he could still remember her smile from the first time they'd met. She'd said something in her usual ribald manner which had made him laugh. He normally left being witty to others but his blunt response had surprised Munroe and she'd grinned. A smile touched his face at the memory and then the darkness claimed him.

CHAPTER 35

As Akosh scraped blood off the bottom of her boot on the dead man's back, she found herself missing Habreel.

Without him to coordinate his network of followers it had fallen to her but the transition process was not going smoothly. His lieutenants, six former Guardians from his old days on the job, normally received weekly missives and when one failed to arrive they had assumed the worst. None of them knew where he'd gone or what had happened and they couldn't find him via their contacts. Now it was taking her an awful lot of time, and effort, to persuade them to carry on as normal in his absence and that she was now in charge.

Akosh refused to travel around the west, visiting each of them like a wandering tinker, but had compromised by coming to Perizzi. The six had agreed to meet her in the city and she'd been forced to make the journey.

She'd been here almost a week now and, despite keeping a very low profile, not even once starting a brawl or kicking someone in the face for being ugly, there was an itch between her shoulder blades. The others had sent Vargus to look into the cause of the current issues and she knew he often prowled Perizzi. The sooner she was on the move again the safer it would be.

A couple of her people came into the room, glanced at the corpse and dragged it away without comment. Akosh thought something was stuck to the sole of her left boot and a closer inspection revealed a bloody piece of scalp wedged between the treads. Before she had time to pick it out Dannel came into the room, pausing briefly to stare at the drying blood.

"How many is that?" asked Akosh. She'd lost count and was bored and anxious.

"Four, Mother. But there's just one more to see," he said, stepping over the blood. "The final Guardian has agreed to serve without an audience."

"Some good news at last," said Akosh, scraping her boot on the leg of her chair but it just wouldn't budge. It was worse than getting a seed caught between her teeth.

"I believe a suitable replacement can be found for that one," he said, gesturing where the recently deceased had been.

"Good. Any news about Habreel?" she asked and Dannel's face fell. It was something she asked every day and so far he'd continually let her down. If Dannel hadn't been one of her children he too would have been decorating the bottom of her boots by now.

She wasn't in the mood for another of his apologies and held up a hand before he started. "Just send in the next one."

Normally the private dining room held a large table and several chairs but Akosh had ordered it cleared of all furniture apart from her throne-like seat. She enjoyed being slightly above everyone's eye level when sitting down.

The owner of the Pony and Cart tavern was one of her children and this was the first time Akosh had called on the woman to serve. Rohita's surprise had been familiar but not the indifference that followed. It was as if she'd stopped believing, or perhaps, after so many years with no contact, she'd thought

Akosh a myth. But some faiths had endured for centuries without any direct contact and not even a whisper of a miracle. It made her wonder if Rohita made a monthly donation to the orphanages in the area. It was something she would have to check with her money spider in the city before heading back to the north.

A short time later Dannel came into the room ahead of a tall Yerskani with unkempt blond hair and piercing green eyes. She noticed the stiffness of his back and the way he studied the room, taking in everything from the stain on the floor to the dried lavender in the rafters.

"Mother, may I introduce, Pavel, formerly a Guardian of the Peace," said Dannel, gesturing at the newcomer.

"Charmed I'm sure," said Akosh. The itch between her shoulders was getting worse. She needed to leave the city tonight. "I take it by now you're aware what's happened?"

"You killed Habreel and now you're taking over," said Pavel.

"Not quite," said Akosh, refreshed by his direct approach. "He's still alive, for the time being at least."

"Ah, I assumed that was him," he said gesturing at the congealing blood on the floor.

"No, that was one of your old Guardian colleagues. Negotiations broke down."

"Is the same going to happen to me if I refuse to serve?" asked Pavel.

"That depends on what you want."

"Myself and the others chose to leave the Guardians because the Queen had been led astray by foreign leaders and their wizards," declared Pavel. Akosh knew they'd been dismissed for a range of crimes, but she let it pass. "We believe in this cause and I would rather die than let it be corrupted."

"Don't be so dramatic," said Akosh rolling her eyes. "I don't want you to change what you're doing. I still want you to get rid of all magic. It's evil. It's bad," she said, waving her hands about. "The reason I took over is because Habreel lost his nerve."

"Is this true?" said Pavel, directing his question at Dannel.

Akosh knew they'd previously worked together when Dannel had been a novice Guardian under the tutelage of Habreel.

"He knew sacrifices would be required, but he couldn't stomach what needed to be done," said Dannel, not exactly lying. It was also a polite way of saying they had to kill several hundred children. At least his faith had never wavered, unlike Rohita's which was still bothering her.

"Do I have to decide now?" asked Pavel.

"I haven't travelled all this way to sit around while you make up your mind," snapped Akosh.

"May I at least have a moment to consider? Perhaps a drink?"

"That sounds like a good idea," said Akosh, gesturing for Dannel to fetch them both a drink. She'd resisted so far because the thought of all these tedious meetings would've meant she'd be drunk before the first had finished. At least after this she could relax, perhaps get drunk in a carriage as she headed north.

Pavel took a moment to consider his options while Dannel poured them both wine into crystal glasses that sparkled in the light. While Akosh slurped down her first glass in a few mouthfuls, Pavel merely sipped his pensively.

"What do you want to ask?" said Akosh.

"I don't wish to cause offence," he said, nodding towards Dannel who was standing between them, wine bottle at the ready.

"Right now, I'd rather be offended than bored."

"Would I be expected to convert to your . . . faith?" he asked, choosing his words with care. She had the distinct impression he'd been about to say cult.

Pavel was more astute than the others. Perhaps he would prove to be useful in the future after all. She also noticed him fiddling with something under his shirt. A religious icon perhaps.

"No. You don't need to convert."

"That's a relief. I've seen how they all look at you. It's grotesque," he said. Dannel bristled at the insult and put a hand on his dagger but Akosh found herself smiling at his nerve.

"Anything else?" she asked.

"What would happen if I decided not to work for you?"

"An excellent question," she said, sitting forward and finally just pulling the bit of scalp off the bottom of her boot. "You have a wife and two sons, I believe."

For the first time since entering the room Pavel looked uncomfortable. "Yes, but I don't see them often."

"You left them behind when you set off to pursue your noble cause a few years ago. I'm sure they appreciate the brave sacrifice you made."

"I thought it best not to get them involved," he said.

"Here's the problem," said Akosh, drawing out her words. "You're asking others to sacrifice their children, and yet you've not given up anything for the cause. You've not suffered as they have. That hardly seems fair."

The colour had steadily drained from Pavel's face and now the glass in his hand was shaking, spilling red wine on his white shirt. "What have you done?"

"Me?" said Akosh, pretending to be aghast. "Nothing at all."

He gulped down his wine, then finally managed to ask, "Are they dead?"

"That's the wrong question," said Akosh. "The right question is, are you willing to give up those you love for this cause? I don't need you to believe in me, but do you really believe in it?"

The former Guardian drained his glass and angrily pressed it against Dannel's chest. Juggling it and the half-empty bottle he nearly dropped them both but managed to right himself. While he was doing that, Pavel grabbed the dagger at his belt and pressed it against Dannel's throat. A trickle of blood ran down his neck and he hissed in pain.

"Sacrifice," said Pavel with a wry smile. His whole demeanour shifted and suddenly he wasn't cowering any more. "It's an interesting point. How much are you willing to give up?"

Fearing he was one of her peculiar brethren in disguise Akosh focused on the man but he was merely human. "Who are you really?" she asked with a growing sense of unease.

"Oh, I'm actually Pavel, but, like so many of your followers, I've always been something else as well," he said with a smirk.

"Who do you serve?"

"I'm not allowed to say."

"I could make you," promised Akosh, reaching for one of her many daggers.

"Perhaps, but that won't save him," he said, shifting the dagger against Dannel's throat. "I'm merely here to deliver a message."

Akosh considered her options. She could kill him or make him tell her everything, but whoever he worked for would know that. Whoever it was they'd not come in person, so Pavel probably knew little, only what he had been told ahead of this meeting. It was how she worked with her people to minimise risk.

"Speak," she said.

"My Master knows you don't really care about eliminating magic, merely the opportunities it creates for your people. However, he doubts your commitment. He thinks you've become too sentimental and attached to them," said Pavel, adjusting his dagger and drawing fresh blood from Dannel's neck. "He's asked for a display of your commitment."

Akosh really wanted to stab him in the face. She hated not knowing who he served and hated being manipulated even worse. "What kind of display?"

"Kill this one," he said, nodding towards Dannel.

"I'd gladly give my life for you, Mother."

"No," said Pavel, releasing Dannel and stepping back. "We both know they're stupid enough to kill themselves for you on a whim. You have to do it."

"And what do I get in return?" she asked, stalling for time. Perhaps if she tortured him for long enough he might remember something he'd been made to forget.

"I've been told someone has been sent to find out who is responsible for the war on magic. My Master will keep watch and warn you if they're getting close."

Akosh shook her head. "That's not enough."

"He will also watch the others at the next 'grand meeting'," said Pavel, stressing the last two words, but it was clear from his expression he didn't know what it meant. No human had ever set foot in the banquet hall. "Going forward my Master will discreetly ally himself with you. Experience has taught him that this situation will grow worse before it gets better. He believes you will need each other in the future in order to survive."

"An alliance," pondered Akosh. Such things must have happened in the past but she'd not been aware of any in recent times. Their kind was too selfish, often at odds with each other, and so they focused only on their own survival. In the past Akosh had considered reaching out to others who were worse off than her, but none of them existed any longer. Whoever Pavel served had been at this for a long time. There would be much she could learn from them.

Their one rule, passed down from the Maker, stated that they couldn't interfere with the affairs of mortals and direct events. She'd already broken the rule and besides it didn't mention anything about working together.

"I'm sorry," she said and Pavel misinterpreted her regret. Akosh found herself hesitating as she drew a dagger and realised that he was right. As much as she needed her followers and they sustained her, she'd grown too familiar with several of them. She had feelings of affection for a few. She'd even mourned the loss of two of her children who had killed themselves while disguised as Seekers.

She'd thought of herself as human from time to time and had even considered notions of pretending to be one for a while for the experience. In order to survive she had adapted from her original mould, transforming herself in the process, but now had swung too far in the other direction. They were tools, nothing more, to be used and cast aside.

She wasn't human and needed to stop thinking as one.

The betrayal in Dannel's eyes as she stabbed him in the chest made her stab him another six times. With her hands covered in gore she stepped back and let him drop, adding fresh blood to the old on the floor.

"Is that enough or do you want me to kill some more of my followers?" she asked, feeling lighter than she had in years.

"That is sufficient. I will be in touch," said Pavel, backing out of the room, suddenly in a hurry.

Akosh stared down at the dying form of Dannel and was pleased to note that she didn't really care about him or what she'd done. There was a small nugget of emotion buried somewhere deep inside, but it would fade in time. Perhaps if she killed a few more it would disappear altogether.

CHAPTER 36

"A re you sure you don't want me to come in with you?" asked Kovac.

Part of Tammy wished he hadn't even come this far, but he'd proven to be unusually stubborn of late. "No. It's too risky."

He said nothing but she could tell he was disappointed by her answer. The risk was minimal to him. As a mercenary he could leave the city and never come back. Move to another country or live out the remainder of his days in the desert kingdoms, free from persecution. The long arm of the law would not stretch that far for what they were about to do. Besides, she doubted if the crime would even be reported.

The risk to her was much greater. It had been a long time since she'd been here, but it was possible there were still a few familiar faces. She might be recognised and the repercussions could end both her career and her freedom. She had no illusions about being invulnerable. As a Guardian of the Peace she wouldn't survive long behind bars with so many criminals. The alternative was to run, to live free and be with him, travelling the world together. He didn't want her to be forced to live on the run, but she could see Kovac yearned for her to join him in a life, far away from this city. Instead of acknowledging his pain and desire, she turned away, hardening her heart and burying all her wants.

The leather gloves were old and worn but still fitted her comfortably. They looked ordinary but the steel weights made them dangerous, even lethal if enough force was applied. After tying a scarf across the bottom half of her face Tammy pulled up the hood of her cloak. All her clothes were old, worn and faded. She carried no weapons and the only discernible feature that would make her stand out in someone's mind was her height. There was nothing she could do about that but she was not the only one in the city with Seve blood in her heritage. It wouldn't be much for any witnesses to help identify her.

Beside her Kovac was dressed in a similar fashion. He covered his face as well and pulled up his hood but she could still see his haunted eyes.

"Ready?"

"I'm with you," he said.

She moved out of the alley and walked straight towards the three-storey building at the end of the road. At this hour of the night all the shops on the street were closed and in darkness. The exception was the building she was marching towards which had a light in every window of the first two floors. Two large, armed figures were standing guard outside the front door. She knew they were Wooden jackals, foot soldiers for the owner. They were talking in quiet voices but cut off suddenly as she and Kovac approached. Neither of them drew a weapon but they were alert and both rested a hand on the swords at their waist.

Kovac moved to her right just as they had rehearsed until they each stood face to face with one of the doormen. As one of them opened his mouth to ask their business Tammy hit him in the jaw with a left hook. There was a dull cracking sound as the steel-weighted glove connected and the big man dropped to the ground without a sound. Kovac was having slightly more difficulty with his opponent. The jackal was trying to shout for help while Kovac kept one hand over his mouth and punched him repeatedly in the stomach. Eventually he hit the jackal in the right place and he dropped to his knees, gasping for air. Tammy clubbed him on the side of the head and the man flopped onto his face.

Grabbing one of the men by his ankles she dragged him into the mouth of a nearby alley. Kovac dumped his and then took up their post outside the front door, pulling off his hood and scarf. He stood out in the open, a hand resting on his sword as if expecting and tempting someone to cause trouble. She wanted to say something. To tell him how much he meant to her and how much she appreciated him doing this. Swallowing the lump in her throat she took a deep breath and pushed open the front door.

The interior was more or less as she remembered it. An organised hallway with weapons placed just inside the front door. To her right a winding set of stairs led up to the next floor. To her left were several rooms where the Don's jackals slept, and at the back a small kitchen where they prepared their meals. He liked to have them close and looked after their basic needs, but he didn't want them in his way.

The door was slightly ajar and peering through a narrow gap into the dormitory she saw several men and women asleep. To make sure no one surprised her later, Tammy closed the door and wedged it shut with two heavy barrels. It wouldn't stop them if they were really determined to get through, but it would slow them down for a while.

Creeping up the stairs she paused halfway, listening for more jackals on the floor above. There was a low rumble of conversation and someone laughed in response, but otherwise all was quiet. The next floor contained offices where clerks spent their days sorting debts and making meticulous notes in ledgers. Any money was kept inside a steel cage, inside an impregnable safe that was guarded by two jackals at all times. They were sitting playing dice when Tammy walked up to them, making no attempt to disguise her approach. Expecting someone else, one of the jackals looked up in time for Tammy's fist to collide with her nose. She cried out in pain and fell back, a hand pressed to her face. The other woman started to draw a dagger from her belt but Tammy was quicker, hammering the jackal in the centre of her chest. A right cross sent her spinning off her stool while the woman with the broken nose went for her sword. Tammy's boot caught her on the jaw, snapping her neck to one side, and she slumped to the floor. Both were still breathing but beyond that she didn't know how badly they were injured. It didn't matter. Her luck was holding for now but she knew it couldn't last and that time was against her.

At the top of the next set of stairs was a sturdy door that was always locked. Tammy didn't even try to turn the handle. Instead she pulled a narrow curved piece of metal from her pocket and slowly eased it into the lock. Bracing herself against the door she took a deep breath and then twisted her right hand. The lock crunched, breaking beyond repair, but it sprang open.

Tammy shoved the door wide, grabbed the short sword kept beside it and raced down the corridor to the bedroom at the far end. The rooms on either side were empty and unimportant. Her target would be in bed at this hour.

As she kicked open the bedroom door she expected a crossbow bolt to come flying towards her, but the figure in bed was barely stirring. Checking the room for other people she moved towards the bed and pressed the tip of the sword against Don Lowell's chest.

Seeing him again after so long caused the rage that she'd been holding in check to surge to the surface. All the anguish, all the tears and frustration at not finding her husband's killer over the years flooded her body. Her arms shook from the effort of not pressing the sword down into Don Lowell's body. The Old Man was right. She had been carrying this around for too long. It had been weighing her down for more than a dozen years.

Don Lowell had always played the role of the elder statesman. The old, kindly uncle who cared for his people, but now the façade had become reality. The skin on his face was tight and thin. His hair was all but a memory and it took him a while to wake up and focus on the immediate danger. One of his hands flopped feebly towards the loaded crossbow he kept beside his bed but she idly batted it away.

Slowly his eyes focused on her face and the question formed on his lips. Keeping the sword pressed against his sternum with one hand, Tammy pulled off her hood and scarf.

"Ah" was all he said as recognition dawned in his eyes. She saw some of the familiar intelligence and cunning behind his eyes, but also what she'd been blind to for many years. A total lack of empathy. There was no genuine warmth in his gaze, not even a drop of human kindness. His talk of family and caring for his people was all part of an elaborate act.

"I know everything," she said, trying to keep her voice steady. "I want to hear you admit what you've done."

Don Lowell pursed his lips. "That might take a while."

Tammy leaned against the sword until the point touched his skin and drew blood. Don Lowell hissed in pain and she relented. "Do not play word games with me. For perhaps the only time in your life, I want you to speak plainly and tell the truth."

The wry smile vanished and all of the lies were peeled away.

until she was looking into the face of a remorseless killer. "Yes, I did it. I gave Doña Jarrow permission to kill your husband. Were you expecting an apology? Perhaps you want me to cry a little? Maybe we should hug and cry together?"

Tammy's smile held no warmth and showed far too many teeth. "No, I just wanted to hear you say it. I know that it was all a lie. That you never cared about any of us. We were tools to be used and thrown away the moment we stopped being useful."

"Then why come back here after so long? What do you want?"

Tammy eased back a little on the sword, noticing something she'd previously missed in his eyes. This time her grin was genuine. "It stings. After all this time, it still bothers you. That he stole from her and then lied to your face about it." She laughed, amazed that she wasn't the only one who had been carrying this around for so long. "You had no idea what was going on, right under your nose, and your pride wouldn't allow it."

"That smug little shit was an idiot," snarled Don Lowell, finally showing his true face. It was ugly, bitter and barely human. "He deserved what happened to him for stealing from Doña Jarrow. Who did he think he was?"

"That smug little shit did what you never could. You wouldn't even dare."

Don Lowell sneered. "He only managed it once and still got caught. So don't pretend he was a genius. He just got lucky, that's all."

"Then you have no regrets?"

"None. At all."

Tammy nodded thoughtfully. "That's what I expected you to say."

"So what happens now, Guardian Baker? Are you going to arrest me? We both know I'll not stay behind bars for long. And if, by some miracle from the Maker, you manage to get a witness to come forward for my crimes, I'll be extremely comfortable in prison. I have a lot of friends inside. Whether I'm sleeping in there or out here, nothing would change. My business would continue as normal."

"I know. That's why I'm not here in uniform. That's why no one saw my face and I came alone. I'm here for you."

Don Lowell regarded her with a cool expression. "I've seen many killers over the years, and you don't—" he trailed off, staring at the sword buried in his chest.

Tammy applied more pressure, driving the sword deeper into his torso and then out of his back, pinning him to the bed. The sheets began to pool with blood and his pale face turned white. He tried to speak a few times but only managed to cough up some blood.

Tammy watched him dispassionately as he gasped his final breaths. His breathing slowed and then suddenly stopped, one final, long wheeze hissing from between his dry old lips. She spat on the corpse and walked out of the room.

Kovac jumped when she opened the front door, reaching for his sword, but then relaxed and heaved a sigh of relief. "Done?"

"It's over, and that means it's time for you to leave the city."

"Look me in the eye and tell me that you feel nothing," he said.

"You shouldn't come back here. It won't be safe."

"Tell me that you don't care," said Kovac.

"I can't," she admitted, struggling to stay calm. "You know how I feel, but that's why you have to leave. If you stay, they can hurt me. Please, leave Perizzi and never return."

It hurt. It hurt as much as the pain she'd been carrying around for all these years. Every part of her ached. Her instinct told her to do or say something. Anything. Instead she remained silent and still, trying to fix in her mind every part of him. The

way he moved. The way he smelled. His laugh and every annoy-
ing little habit and joke they'd ever shared. The horror of their
time together in Voechenka and the passion of their long nights
in bed. For now all of the memories of their time together were
fresh, but she knew they would eventually fade.

Tammy turned and walked away, forcing herself to keep
moving. She lost track of time but part of her at least seemed to
know where she was going, as she came back to herself outside
the front doors of Unity Hall.

With a heavy heart she followed familiar corridors until she
reached the Old Man's outer office. Rummpoe was absent and
the room was dark but light filled the Khevassar's office. As ever
he sat behind his desk, writing a report with three oil lanterns
providing enough light to imitate a sunny day.

She went into his office and sat down without being given
permission. He glanced up briefly, finished what he was writing
and then set it aside. Reaching into his drawer he produced
a dusty old yellow bottle of something that was half empty
and two glasses. He splashed a healthy amount into each glass
and passed one across the desk. Tammy downed the spirit and
waited, wanting to feel it burn and match the hurt inside.
Instead she was disappointed that the whisky was remarkably
smooth and rich in flavour.

"I keep this for very special occasions," he said, refilling her
glass. "The bottle must be thirty years old."

"That business with Don Lowell. It's over."

"I thought so," he said, no doubt reading far more from her
body language and expression than she realised. He didn't ask
for any details for which she was grateful.

"I'm ready, but I have one question. What will happen to
my family?"

"They'll never need for money. In fact, just the other day they were contacted by a distant relative, Uncle Jon, who recently retired after being a carpenter for forty years. He wants to live out the remainder of his years close to his family here in Perizzi."

"Is that so?" she said with a faint smile.

"Apparently."

"Why carpentry?" asked Tammy.

"I dabbled in my youth," he said. "Unfortunately Uncle Jon doesn't have any children of his own, so he wants to share his wealth with his remaining family."

"Thank you." It seemed so inadequate a thing to say but he dismissed it with a wave. "Do you actually have any family of your own?" she asked.

The Old Man hesitated before answering. It must have been a long time since anyone had asked him that question. She wondered how often he thought about his old life and who he used to be. "As it happens, no. They all died."

"Do you regret it?" she asked, waving a hand at the office. "Giving it all up for this?"

The Khevassar thought about it for a long time before shaking his head. "Many times over the years I've wondered if I made the right decision. In the bleakest years, when hope and justice seemed laughable concepts, my faith wavered. But the wheel always turns and after forty years in this job, and everything I've accomplished, I don't regret my decision. I've not only been a part of history, I've changed the shape of events, and, in time you will too."

"So what happens now?" she asked, unsure of how to proceed.

"Now, we measure you up for a new uniform, and from tomorrow you will be the Khevassar."

"That's it? There's no ceremony?" asked Tammy.

"No. I become dear old Uncle Jon and you will be the Khevassar. After that every Guardian will follow your orders."

"What will you do?"

"That's a very good question. Right now, I've no idea, but I'm not going anywhere just yet. I'll stick around for a while to help with the transition." The Old Man got up from behind the desk and gestured for her to stand as well. He moved to one side of his chair and waited.

Tammy took the hint and sat down behind her new desk, looking around the office from this side of the table for the first time.

She'd barely leaned back in the chair when they heard the sound of approaching footsteps. A young novice appeared at the door and then paused, glancing between the Old Man and Tammy.

"Report," she said, barking at the young man.

His discipline kicked in and he addressed her. "There's a man at the front gate seeking asylum. He says he has important information to share and asks to speak with you directly."

Tammy glanced at the Old Man and raised an eyebrow. "Does it ever stop?"

"No, not really."

"Did the man give his name?" she said, addressing the novice.

"Torran Habreel."

Tammy took a deep breath. "All right, send him in."

CHAPTER 37

For a brief moment, before she was fully awake, Wren thought she was still in bed in the dormitory at the Red Tower. She stretched and dry leaves rustled all around, dispelling the illusion. Her bed was a patch of dry ground on the forest floor and all around her other students were slowly waking up. The smell of toasting bread tugged at her nose, making her stomach rumble. It had been many hours since she'd last eaten and that was after almost a full day of walking.

Despite Garvey's desire to walk them non-stop until nightfall, probably to death, he'd been forced to relent when students started collapsing from exhaustion. During the afternoon they'd paused several times for a rest but it was never for very long. Her calf muscles ached this morning and the bottom of her thighs from going up and down hills. Digging her thumbs into the muscles she tried to ease away some of the stiffness.

If she'd managed to master any ability at healing she could have instantly removed the pain. Now she wasn't sure if she'd ever have the opportunity to learn how in the future.

Teachers moved around the camp tending to students, helping the youngest with breakfast and generally doing their best to maintain some discipline. So far there had been no real issues

Once they'd seen the Red Tower burning fear had kept them moving, but now it was a new day and the danger seemed far away. If they had not been planning to meet up with the rest of the students, Wren suspected there would've been a lot of complaints. No one wanted to be left alone with Garvey.

He stood on a rise above their camp, looking back along their path through the trees. The Red Tower was no longer visible but he was staring intently. She knew so little about his magical ability or his Talents. Perhaps he had a way of seeing beyond the forest and was watching the path behind for signs of pursuit. Apparently satisfied that they were safe, at least for the time being, he returned to camp in search of breakfast. Everyone gave him a wide berth, even the teachers, who spoke sparingly to him and only when required. Any attempt at conversation was rebuffed with silence or a blunt retort that kept him isolated. Wren wondered what had made him this way and if he had any friends. It seemed unlikely. Perhaps after so much time alone he preferred his own company.

"Pack up. We leave in an hour," announced Garvey. Everyone in camp paused in what they were doing, then started gathering their belongings.

"We can't do this every day," complained Tianne, stuffing her blanket into her bag. "He'll walk us all to death."

"We don't have to," said Danoph. "We should be meeting the others later today."

"What if they don't show up? What if we're stuck with him?" she asked, dropping her voice to a whisper even though Garvey was on the far side of their camp. All three of them turned to stare at him. He'd already packed his belongings and was now waiting for the others as he munched on a piece of toast.

Before the hour was up everyone was ready and all the camp-fires had been doused. There were no words of encouragement.

No praise for doing well to have made it this far. Garvey simply walked out of camp and they all moved to follow. Tianne and a few others glared at his back but that was as far as it went. After all, he was still a member of the Grey Council. Wren couldn't understand what made him more suitable than some of the other teachers she'd met to deserve such an honoured role.

He was incredibly powerful, but if she'd learned anything during her time at the Red Tower it was that strength wasn't everything. Magic could be deployed as a blunt weapon but it could also be used in a complex and subtle fashion. With a slight weave and a weak connection to the Source a mage could heal the body of almost any wound. That seemed the opposite of everything Garvey stood for. She doubted he even understood the meaning of the word subtle. Her growing resentment fuelled her for a while but eventually it too faded.

By midday the pain had returned to Wren's weary legs and when they stopped to eat she flopped down on the ground. Around her there were a lot of tired and worried faces. The students were beginning to realise this was their new life. They would not be going back to classes at the Red Tower, where they were fed three times a day and slept in clean sheets. The novelty of being outdoors was starting to wear off and uncertainty about their future loomed in the minds of them all.

The hardship was getting to some more than others and she heard a few complaining about the conditions. The youngest didn't really understand and, despite reassurance from the teachers, she could see they were scared. When Garvey returned from the edge of their camp with the other two members of the Grey Council beside him there was an audible sigh of relief. Absent smiles returned and the atmosphere changed. Finally, here were two people the students could trust and rely on.

The other students came over the rise behind them and there

were many small reunions as people met up with friends again. Although they had only been apart a few hours there was palpable relief that all three groups had made it this far without being attacked. So far it seemed as if none of the groups had been pursued by those who had attacked the Red Tower. It made Wren wonder what had happened to those who'd been left behind and how many of them had escaped.

Balfruss and Eloise moved about the camp for a while, speaking to individual students, checking in with teachers and sometimes using their magic to heal injuries and ease tired limbs. When Eloise approached her, Wren felt herself involuntarily smiling back and some of the tension eased from her shoulders.

"Gather around," said Eloise, beckoning everyone closer. She and the other Sorcerers stood on a slab of rock so that everyone could see them. Wren felt a brief surge of power as Eloise's voice was amplified so that they could all hear her. "All of you are now facing a difficult decision. The Red Tower is gone, perhaps for ever, but your magic still exists. You still need to be taught how to control it, and if you want, how to use it to help other people."

Behind her Garvey sneered, and Wren saw some of the older students mirror his scorn of that idea.

"There are a few options," said Balfruss, picking up where Eloise had left off. "Each of us has an opinion on what you should do, but we will not decide for you. We will explain the choices and then you will have some time to make up your own minds."

"I have had regular meetings with Jhanidi monks," said Eloise.

"I told you," said Tianne, nudging Wren in the ribs.

"They are warrior mages who live in the desert kingdoms in the far east. They have schools similar to the Red Tower, and if you want to continue with your studies then there is a place among them for each of you. Several teachers and I will also be going, so you will not be alone among strangers. A ship is waiting not far from here to take us east."

"They knew this was going to happen," said Wren, mostly to herself, but Tianne and Danoph overheard her.

"What do you mean?" asked Tianne.

"Why else would they have met with the Jhanidi weeks ago? They knew the Red Tower was at risk. They planned for this day. That's why everyone was so calm yesterday."

"Trouble has been brewing for a while," said Danoph. "The problems with Seekers and the accidental deaths."

She still wasn't convinced. "Maybe, but I think they're hiding something."

"Then what happens?" one of the older girls asked Eloise in a loud voice.

"We hope that by the time you complete your training, the situation here will be different and you can return to the west." Eloise was doing her best not to scare anyone, but neither was she prepared to lie. The situation was dire and it could take years for real change to take effect.

"And if we can't come back?" pressed the girl.

"Mages are highly respected members of society in the desert kingdoms. They can command a high price for their services," said Eloise. That seemed to placate the student for now, but she still looked angry.

"The other choice is to remain," said Balfruss. "Those of you who are old enough can move to another country and live an ordinary life. Become part of a community in a town or village, somewhere that you've never visited before. But it would mean forsaking your magic and never using it ever again."

So far neither choice was particularly appealing to Wren. She wanted to continue with her studies, but she didn't want to live in the desert kingdoms for several years. It felt as if she would just be running away from the problems here in the west. The situation would not resolve itself and more children were being born all the time with the ability to embrace the Source. What would happen to them without the Red Tower? Without the Seekers who would test them and teach them control? Without the Red Tower there would be more accidental deaths, not fewer. Running away from the problem and hoping that it went away made no sense to her.

Equally, the idea of burying her magic and living somewhere quiet to avoid detection was not one she relished. For some students it would be possible to return to their homeland and live in another region away from former friends and family. It would not be possible for her to do the same thing in Drassia. Family ties and communities were much more intertwined, so that meant living in another country in the west.

Moving to Yerskania was a possibility, as it had the most diverse population in the west, but, even so, to give up her magic after only just scratching the surface of what could be done with it felt like a step backwards. It felt like defeat.

"The risks are clear," Balfruss was saying. "You will be alone and without protection. As an outsider it will take you a few years to feel at home, but it is possible, as long as you suppress your magic. I know some of you came to the Red Tower because you didn't have a choice. While you cannot return home, you can have a similar life to the one you had before."

She'd met several students who regarded their magic as a curse. Any hopes and dreams about the future had been shattered the instant their ability had manifested. The Seeker had ripped them away from everyone they knew and loved and they could never go back. Now they were being offered a second chance to have the kind of life they had always dreamed about. For some it would be too good an opportunity to miss and the only thing they had to give up was something they despised.

"There is a third choice," said Garvey, earning scowls from the other members of the Grey Council.

"We've already discussed this," said Balfruss.

"Don't do this, Garvey," protested Eloise but he ignored them both.

"You all deserve better," shouted Garvey, his voice carrying across the camp. "What has happened is not your doing. You should not be punished for it, nor be forced to run and hide in fear."

"Stop," said Eloise.

"Let him speak," said one of the older students, and a few others shouted their agreement.

Garvey was facing Eloise and Balfruss, but they all heard every word. "We promised to be honest with them. They still have to choose for themselves. I'm just presenting them with a third option." It was clear the other members of the Grey Council were not happy, but they didn't try to stop him from speaking again.

"I am not leaving with the others. Nor will I hide my magic. They blame us for what happened, but we all know the truth. So, I am going to fight." Wren had never heard Garvey speak with such passion before, but there was more to it as well, strengthening his voice. As ever he was seething with rage but now he was able to give it a target. "Some countries have banned Seekers, but it is only the beginning. In time they will try to ban all magic. For years they have tried to suppress magic from the world. But children like you are being born every day and I will not abandon them. I will live free and proud of what I am."

She thought Garvey had chosen his words with great care. They felt rehearsed, as if he had been thinking about this moment for a long time. He had not said outright who he would be fighting, but she could guess. Garvey intended to go where he wanted, live as he wanted and if he met those opposed to magic, they would find someone unwilling to be cowed by a mob. They had chosen to leave the Red Tower to avoid making things worse. But here was someone just as angry who would fight back using every magical ability and weapon in his arsenal.

It would be a bloodbath.

"Will you be a wolf or a lamb?" Danoph said, and she raised an eyebrow. "It was something Tahira said to me," he explained.

"You have an hour to make your decision," said Eloise before stepping down.

Everyone was talking at once and all around she overheard a dozen discussions about the choices available to them.

Wren saw the youngest students being manipulated as she overheard teachers telling them about the wonders of the eastern kingdoms. However, she felt that it was the right decision for them. They were not old enough to be by themselves and if they went east at least they would have the opportunity to live without being persecuted. Most were young enough that, in time, they could forget their old lives and perhaps their old families. It was what would happen to everyone else that concerned her.

A group of older students had already made their decision. They were arrayed behind Garvey and a tall girl from Yerskania was already speaking to him.

"Who is that?" asked Wren.

"That's Tahira," said Danoph when he saw where she was pointing.

"I recognise some of the others," said Tianne, who seemed to know the name of every student.

Garvey's speech had been powerful and convincing, but something was still niggling Wren about what was happening. Ignoring tradition and what formality dictated, she approached Garvey, determined to get some real answers.

The Sorcerer looked up as she approached, but he seemed neither pleased nor disappointed. The students behind him misinterpreted her presence, thinking she had decided to join them.

"I haven't made my decision yet," she explained. "I have a question."

Garvey stared at her intently for a long time before speaking. "Ask."

"Did you know this would happen?" she asked.

For a brief moment Wren thought he looked surprised, but it was gone so quickly she couldn't be sure. Instead of answering he seized her by the elbow and dragged her a short distance away from everyone else.

"Let go of me," she said, shaking off his hand.

"Why did you ask that?"

As usual he was answering a question with another question. He always demanded much and gave little in return. Two could play that game. Wren folded her arms and waited. Garvey let out a long, slow breath through his nose and then, much to her surprise, he smiled.

"Yes. We knew this was coming. We've known for almost a year that the Red Tower would fall."

It was the last thing she'd expected him to say. It sounded implausible and yet he was watching her expectantly. As if she already knew the answer to her next question. He folded his arms and waited for her to work it out.

"Danoph. It was Danoph," she whispered and his smile returned. "His dreams of fire."

"Other towns and villages in Shael were burned during the war, but not his. The Morrin in charge was more inventive. It was possible they were dreams of his people's suffering elsewhere, but when we questioned him it became clear it was something else. It took us months to piece together, because he could remember so little after each dream. When he mentioned the tower burning we finally knew."

"He's an Oracle."

Garvey shrugged. "Of a sort. He sees different possibilities and, as recent events unfolded, we knew that his dream would come true. We tried so hard to avoid this happening," he said, gesturing at all of the students camped in the woods. There seemed to be genuine compassion and warmth in his eyes. It was so alien it unsettled her. She'd never seen him like this before. "When the time is right, you should tell him about his Talent."

Wren was still struggling to come to terms with the revelation. "You've known all this time."

"We have and we desperately tried to stop it happening, but our efforts were in vain."

"Then why not stay and fight?" asked Wren.

"You know why."

"It would only make it worse," she said.

If they stayed at the Red Tower and fought back, it would only add fuel to the fire. People hated magic and were afraid of those who wielded it. One mage could hold off a mob, perhaps even an army. A whole school full of mages must be a terrifying idea for most people.

"You were the last student admitted to the school," he said. "Anyone found since then was sent east to the desert kingdoms, together with any Seekers who wanted to leave."

"There's more you're not telling me," she said.

"Of course."

"How can you expect me to trust you?" asked Wren. She needed him to give her something more. A reason to believe anything he'd told her was the truth.

"I do not require your trust, only your obedience. Isn't that what's expected of you, Drassi girl?" asked Garvey.

Wren felt as if she'd been slapped across the face. She staggered back a little in shock. The others weren't close enough to have overheard, but they all saw her distress. He knew exactly what to say to hurt her the most. The others wouldn't understand. In their countries gender did not follow the same tightly prescribed role. Their societies were not as rigidly controlled. Respect for one's elders had been part of her daily life and had been instilled in her since birth. It was her duty to seek out their counsel and learn from them.

But every time she had gone to Garvey for help it had left her feeling more confused and the situation was made worse. He knew enough about her and Drassi society to wound her with his words and yet all his advice had been vague or unhelpful. He must have known how it would affect her. For all his faults she could see that he was an intelligent man. So why did he work so hard to hurt her?

A horrible and unsettling thought surfaced. It didn't seem possible. It was cold and cruel and manipulative. And yet she had heard all those words applied to him many times in the past. To even consider such an idea was unworthy but it rang true when she thought about him.

"You did this to me on purpose," she said, uncertain of how to proceed.

"Did what to you?" he asked, raising one eyebrow.

"For months you've been planning the evacuation of the school. So you must have thought about what came next." Wren said it as a statement, but she still wasn't sure it was true. When he said nothing she continued, feeling her way forward as if finding her way in the dark. "You knew how I would react every time I came to you for help. You've been manipulating me since the day I arrived. You want me to defy you."

But it wasn't just her. He had been manipulating them all. To keep himself apart. To make sure that he was seen as an angry and defiant presence at odds with everyone, even the other members of the Grey Council. He'd done it to be respected but also feared by the students. On her first day Tianne had said he was a bastard. Even the other teachers found it difficult to speak with him and yet he was a member of the Grey Council.

When she'd been convalescing in the hospital Balfruss had said there was nothing more important to the Grey Council than the students. Garvey had agreed and said everything they did was for them. She began to wonder how much of him was real and how much a façade.

Wren came back to the present when she felt someone's hand on her shoulder. She looked up at Garvey whose kind eyes were watching her internal struggle with sympathy. Gone was the cruel and angry man that she knew. In front of her stood someone she'd never met before. It was him and yet she felt as if he were a complete stranger.

Everything she knew about him, from the moment they'd first met, had been a lie.

"You've been manipulating everyone. Do the others even know?" she whispered, glancing at the teachers in the camp. "Why did you do this to me?"

"Oh, child, we all have our roles to play, and you must play yours." He squeezed her shoulder once and then stepped back. The warmth faded from his eyes and the cold Sorcerer returned, full of rage and hatred. The mask was so perfect he had become the other man again. He stalked away through the camp and people were quick to move aside, giving him a wide berth.

"What did he say?" asked Tianne, as she and Danoph approached. "Are you all right?"

Wren couldn't answer them. She didn't know how to explain what had just happened or if they would even believe her. As far as they knew Garvey was nothing more than a cold and cruel man. She was still trying to process it when she remembered something he'd said. He'd mentioned her role. Did that mean he was still manipulating her? What was she supposed to do?

A short time later they were all called together to announce their decision. The three members of the Grey Council stood in separate areas of the camp. Those who wanted to continue with their studies in the desert kingdoms were told to stand beside Eloise. Those who wanted new lives without magic to stand with Balfruss and those who chose to fight to stand with Garvey.

As Wren had expected the majority stood with Eloise. About thirty of the older students moved to stand with Balfruss. He would remain behind to help them find communities where they could resettle and live in peace without their magic. More surprising were the twenty or so students who were grouped around Garvey. But not everyone had yet to decide. Thirty students, including Wren and her two friends, stood apart from all the others.

"You must decide now," said Eloise.

"I will not run," said Wren. "Nor will I fight against those without magic," she said glancing at Garvey.

"Then you must give up your magic," said Balfruss.

"I will not." Wren didn't care if this was what Garvey wanted her to do or not. She could only do what was in her heart.

"Then where will you go? What will you do?" asked Eloise.

Wren shook her head. "I don't know, but running and hiding will not fix this."

"Even though you will be alone?" said Balfruss.

"If they find out you're a mage, it could mean your head," said Garvey.

"I will go my own way," said Wren.

She could tell they wanted to argue further, to try and convince her, but they had made a promise in front of everyone and now had to honour it.

"So be it," said Balfruss.

Wren turned towards her friends and the others stood beside her. "What will you do?"

"I'd like to come with you," said Tianne.

"My path lies with you," said Danoph and Wren wondered if he had already seen this moment played out in a dream. The others in the group also chose to follow her, even though she made it clear she didn't know where she was going.

All too soon it was time to say goodbye. Wren stood apart watching as students and teachers shook hands, hugged and cried against one another. It was likely some of them would never see each other again. No one came to see her off and yet a group of students stood with her. She didn't think they would remain with her for long. They were simply torn between three difficult decisions and would soon drift away from her company. At least her two friends remained. Wren didn't want to think about how she would have felt if either of them had decided to leave.

Wren glanced at the sky and chose a direction at random. They would head north for now.

Balfruss gave the others a final wave goodbye and then led his group away to the west. Garvey set off south with his fighters and Eloise went east towards the river and the waiting ship.

Together with her friends at her side, Wren turned north and started walking with no plan and no destination in mind. But the decision had been hers, not because she was required to make it. She was choosing her own path because she felt that it was the right decision for her.

Whatever happened, good or bad, it was hers, and although she was scared about what lay ahead, for the first time in her life she was free.

ACKNOWLEDGEMENTS

With thanks to Juliet and Nathalie from CaskieMushens for their incredibly hard work.

I would also like to thank the team at Orbit for giving me another chance to tell stories in the same world.

extras

www.orbitbooks.net

about the author

Stephen Aryan was born in 1977 and was raised and educated in Whitley Bay, Tyne and Wear. After graduating from Loughborough University he started working in marketing, and for some reason he hasn't stopped. A keen podcaster, lapsed gamer and budding archer, when not extolling the virtues of *Babylon 5*, he can be found drinking real ale and reading comics.

He lives in the West Midlands with his partner and two cats. You can find him on Twitter at @SteveAryan or visit his website at www.stephen-aryan.com.

Find out more about Stephen Aryan and other Orbit authors by registering for the free monthly newsletter at www.orbitbooks.net.

if you enjoyed
MAGEBORN

look out for

SNAKEWOOD

by

Adrian Selby

Once they were a band of mercenaries who shook the pillars of the world through their cunning, their closely guarded alchemical brews and stone cold steel. Whoever met their price won.

Now, their glory days behind them and their genius leader in hiding, the warriors known as the "Twenty" are being hunted down and eliminated one by one.

A lifetime of enemies has its own price.

Chapter 1

Gant

My name's Gant and I'm sorry for my poor writing. I was a mercenary soldier who never took to it till Kailen taught us. It's for him and all the boys that I wanted to put this down, a telling of what become of Kailen's Twenty.

Seems right to begin it the day me and Shale got sold out, at the heart of the summer just gone, down in the Red Hills Confederacy.

It was the day I began dying.

It was a job with a crew to ambush a supply caravan. It went badly for us and I took an arrow, the poison from which will shortly kill me.

I woke up sodden with dew and rain like the boys, soaked all over from the trees above us, but my mouth was dusty like sand. Rivers couldn't wet it. The compound I use to ease my bones leeches my spit. I speak soft.

I could hardly crack a whistle at the boys wrapped like a nest of slugs in their oilskins against the winds of the plains these woods were edged against. I'm old. I just kicked them up before getting my bow out of the sack I put it in to keep rain off the string. It was a beauty what I called Juletta and I had her for most of my life.

The boys were slow to get going, blowing and fussing as the freezing air got to work in that bit of dawn. They were quiet, and grim like ghosts in this light, pairing up to strap their leathers and get the swords pasted with poison.

I patted heads and squeezed shoulders and give words as I moved through the crew so they knew I was about and watching. I knew enough of their language that I could give them encouragement like I was one of them, something else Kailen give me to help me bond with a crew.

"Paste it thick," I said as they put on the mittens and rubbed their blades with the soaked rags from the pot Remy had opened.

I looked around the boys I'd shared skins and pipes with under the moon those last few weeks. Good crew.

There was Remy, looking up at me from his mixing, face all scarred like a milky walnut and speaking lispy from razor fights and rackets he ran with before joining up for a pardon. He had a poison of his own he made, less refined than my own mix, less quick, more agony.

Yasthin was crouched next to him. He was still having to shake the cramp off his leg that took a mace a month before. Saved his money for his brother, told me he was investing it. The boys said his brother gambled it and laughed him up.

Dolly was next to Yasthin, chewing some bacon rinds. Told me how her da chased her soak of a mother through the streets, had done since she was young. Kids followed her da too, singing with him but staying clear of his knives. She joined so's she could help her da keep her younger brother.

All of them got sorrows that led them to the likes of me and a fat purse for a crossroads job, which I mean to say is a do-or-die.

Soon enough they're lined up and waiting for the Honour, Kailen's Honour, the best fightbrew Kigan ever mixed, so, the best fightbrew ever mixed, even all these years later. The boys had been talking up this brew since I took command, makes you feel like you could punch holes in mountains when you've risen on it.

Yasthin was first in line for a measure. I had to stand on my toes to pour it in, lots of the boys taller than me. Then a kiss. The lips are the raw end of your terror and love. No steel can toughen lips, they betray more than the eyes when you're looking for intent and the kiss is for telling them there's always some way to die.

Little Booey was the tenth and last of the crew to get the measure. I took a slug myself and Rirgwil fixed my leathers. I waited for our teeth to chatter like aristos, then went over the plan again.

"In the trees north, beyond those fields, is Trukhar's supply caravan," I said. "Find it, kill who you can but burn the wagons, supplies, an' then go for the craftsmen. Shale's leadin' his crew in from east an' we got them pincered when we meet, red bands left arm so as you know. It's a do-or-die purse, you're there 'til the job is done or you're dead anyway."

It was getting real for them now I could see. A couple were starting shakes with their first full measure of the brew, despite all the prep the previous few days.

"I taught you how to focus what's happening to you boys. This brew has won wars an' it'll deliver this purse if you can keep tight. Now move out."

No more words, it was hand signs now to the forest.

Jonah front, Yasthin, Booey and Henny with me. Remy group northeast at treeline

We ran through the silver grass, chests shuddering with the crackle of our blood as the brew stretched our veins and filled our bones with iron and fire. The song of the earth was filling my ears.

Ahead of us was the wall of trees and within, the camp of the Blackhands. Remy's boys split from us and moved away.

Slow I signed.

Juletta was warm in my hands, the arrow in my fingers humming to fly. Then, the brew fierce in my eyes, I saw it, the red glow of a pipe some seventy yards ahead at the treeline.

Two men. On mark

I moved forward to take the shot and stepped into a nest of eggs. The bird, a big grey weger, screeched at me and flapped madly into the air inches from my face, its cry filling the sky. One of the boys shouted out, in his prime on the brew, and the two men saw us. We were dead. My boys' arrows followed mine, the two men were hit, only half a pip of a horn escaping for warning, but it was surely enough.

Run

I had killed us all. We went in anyway, that was the purse, and these boys primed like this weren't leaving without bloodshed.

As we hit the trees we spread out.

Enemy left signed Jonah.

Three were nearing through the trunks, draining their own brew as they come to from some half-eyed slumber. They were a clear shot so I led again, arrows hitting and a muffled crack of bones. All down.

In my brewed-up ears I could hear then the crack of

bowstrings pulling at some way off, but it was all around us. The whistle of arrows proved us flanked as we dropped to the ground.

The boys opened up, moving as we practised, aiming to surprise any flanks and split them off so a group of us could move in directly to the caravan. It was shooting practice for Trukhar's soldiers.

I never saw Henny or Jonah again, just heard some laughing and screaming and the sound of blades at work before it died off.

I stayed put, watching for the enemy's movements. I was in the outroots of a tree, unspotted. You feel eyes on you with this brew. Then I saw two scouts moving right, following Booey and Datschke's run.

I took a sporebag and popped it on the end of an arrow. I stood up and sent it at the ground ahead of them.

From my belt I got me some white oak sap which I took for my eyes to see safe in the spore cloud. I put on a mask covered with the same stuff for breathing.

The spores were quick to get in them and they wheezed and clutched their throats as I finished them off.

I was hoping I could have saved my boys but I needed to be in some guts and get the job done with Shale's crew.

Horns were going up now, so the fighting was on. I saw a few coming at me from the trees ahead. I got behind a trunk but I knew I was spotted. They slowed up and the hemp creaked as they drew for shots. There were four of them, from their breathing, and I could hear their commander whispering for a flanking.

I opened up a satchel of ricepaper bags, each with quicklime and oiled feathers. I needed smoke. I doused a few bags with my flask and threw them out.

"Masks!" came the shout. As the paper soaked, the lime caught and the feathers put out a fierce smoke.

My eyes were still smeared good. I took a couple more arrowbags out, but these were agave powders for blistering the eyes and skin.

Two shots to tree trunks spread the powders in the air around their position and I moved out from the tree to them as they screeched and staggered about blind. The Honour give me the senses enough to read where they were without my eyes, better to shut them with smoke and powders in the air, and their brews weren't the Honour's equal. They moved like they were running through honey and were easy to pick off.

It was then I took the arrow that'll do for me. I'd got maybe fifty yards further on when I heard the bow draw, but with the noise ahead I couldn't place it that fraction quicker to save myself. The arrow went in at my hip, into my guts. Something's gave in there, and the poison's gone right in, black mustard oil for sure from the vapours burning in my nose, probably some of their venom too.

I was on my knees trying to grab the arrow when I saw them approach, two of them. The one who killed me was dropping his bow and they both closed with the hate of their own fightbrew, their eyes crimson, skin an angry red and all the noisies.

They think I'm done. They're fucking right, to a point. In my belt was the treated guaia bark for the mix they were known to use. No time to rip out the arrow and push the bark in.

They moved in together, one in front, the other flanking. One's a heavy in his mail coat and broadsword, a boy's weapon in a forest, too big. Older one had leathers and a long knife.

Him first. My sight was going, the world going flat like a drawing, so I had to get rid of the wiser one while I could still see him, while I still had the Honour's edge.

Knife in hand I lunged sudden, the leap bigger than they reckoned. The older one reacted, a sidestep. The slash I made wasn't for hitting him though. It flicked out a spray of paste from the blade and sure enough some bit of it caught him in the face. I spun about, brought my blade up and parried the boy's desperate swing as he closed behind me, the blow forcing me down as it hit my knife, sending a smack through my guts as the arrow broke in me. He took sight of his mate holding his smoking face, scratching at his cheeks and bleeding. He glanced at the brown treacle running over my blade and legged it. He had the spunk to know he was beaten. I put the knife in the old man's throat to quiet my noisies, the blood's smell as sweet as fresh bread to me.

I picked up my Juletta and moved on. The trees were filling with Blackhands now. I didn't have the time to be taking off my wamba and sorting myself out a cure for the arrow, much less tugging at it now it was into me. I cussed at myself, for this was likely where I was going to die if I didn't get something to fix me. I was slowing up. I took a hit of the Honour to keep me fresh. It was going to make a fierce claim on the other side, but I would gladly take that if I could get some treatment.

Finally I reached the caravan; smoke from the blazing wagons and stores filled the trees ahead. The grain carts were burning so Shale, again, delivered the purse.

Then I come across Dolly, slumped against the roots of a tree. Four arrows were thrusting proud from her belly. She saw me and her eyes widened and she smiled.

"Gant, you're not done . . . Oh," she said, seeing the arrow in me. I might have been swaying, she certainly didn't look right, faded somewhat, like she was becoming a ghost before me.

"Have you a flask, Gant, some more of the Honour?"

Her hands were full of earth, grabbing at it, having their final fling.

"I'm out, Dolly," I said. "I'm done too. I'm sorry for how it all ended."

She blinked, grief pinching her up.

"It can't be over already. I'm twenty summers, Gant, this was goin' to be the big purse."

A moment then I couldn't fill with any words.

"Tell my father, Gant, say . . . "

I was raising my bow. I did my best to clean an arrow on my leggings. She was watching me as I did it, knowing.

"Tell him I love him, Gant, tell him I got the Honour, and give him my purse and my brother a kiss."

"I will."

As I drew it she looked above me, seeing something I knew I wouldn't see, leagues away, some answers to her questions in her eyes thrilling her. I let fly, fell to my knees and sicked up.

Where was Shale?

My mouth was too dry to speak or shout for him, but I needed him. My eyes, the lids of them, were peeling back so's they would burn in the sun. I put my hands to my face. It was only visions, but my chest was heavy, like somebody sat on it and others were piling on. Looking through my hands as I held them up, it was like there were just bones there, flesh thin like the fins of a fish. My breathing rattled and I reached to my throat to try to open it up more.

"Gant!"

So much blood on him. He kneeled next to me. He's got grey eyes, no colour. Enemy to him is just so much warm meat to be put still. He don't much smile unless he's drunk. He mostly never drinks. He sniffed about me and at my wound, to get a reading of what was in it, then forced the arrow out with a knife and filled the hole with guaia bark while kneeling on my shoulder to keep me still. He was barking at some boys as he stuffed some rugara leaves, sap and all, into my mouth, holding my nose shut, drowning me. Fuck! My brains were buzzing sore like a hive was in them. Some frothing liquid filled up my chest and I was bucking about for breath. He poured from a flask over my hip and the skin frosted over with an agony of burning. Then he took out some jumpcrick's legbones and held them against the hole, snap snap, a flash of blue flame and everything fell away high.

There was a choking, but it didn't feel like me no longer. It felt like the man I was before I died.